CHANGING TODAY'S WORLD

DAYS IN THE LIFE OF YAROSLAV KANDYBAVYCH MELNYKENKO

CARL DOUGLASS

NEUROSURGEON TURNED AUTHOR
WRITES WITH GRIPPING REALISM

PUBLICATION
CONSULTANTS
We Believe In The Power Of Authors

8370 Eleusis Drive, Anchorage, Alaska 99502-4630
books@publicationconsultants.com—www.publicationconsultants.com

ISBN Number: 978-1-63747-407-5
eBook ISBN Number: 978-1-63747-408-2

Library of Congress Number: 2024940080

Manufactured in the United States of America

DEDICATION

To the Ukrainian heroes who gave their all for the cause of their country and its fight against the barbarians at its gates. I salute those who struggled to preserve an island of democracy in the shadow of the old USSR and its present dictator. The book is also dedicated to the proposition that those Ukrainians are the last great hope against the dictator's desire to launch the Third World War with all its unthinkable catastrophes.

Disclaimer

Changing Today's World is a book of fiction. The characters, events, and story described, are the product of the author's imagination. The place, Ukraine, and several of its cities and locales exist, of course, but all else about them is fabricated to fit the story and its fictional characters and events. There is no intention to suggest that these events ever took place in those cities, mountains, and battlefields. In fact, public news broadcasts have told the grim stories well and showed that such events, as the author describes are largely at odds with reality. I suppose one could look upon this book of fiction as wishful thinking about what might have been.

Contents

Contents

Contents

PROLOGUE

Occupied Popasnaya, Luhansk Oblast, Ukraine

November 21, 2024

The moon hung high in the ink-black starless sky, casting a dim glow over the desolate landscape of Donblast, a war-torn region within the eastern borders of Ukraine. The air was heavy with tension, as if the very earth held its breath in anticipation of the imminent operation. It was treacherous mine-strewn terrain. Their State Emergency Service unmarked olive drab Antonov An-178 medium troop transport plane landed in Dnipro on the Ukraine side without being detected among the heavy military traffic. The first barrier—the Dnipro River—was crossed without incident. The Ukrainian SBU intelligence service's intel had been accurate; no ships or patrol boats passed by during the brief period defined by the SBU agents on the ground. A tense group of eleven Ukrainian soldier-spies made it into the Russian and collaborator-controlled region free of contact with the enemy and without loss. The young agent who was responsible for the mission–Yaroslav Kandybavych Melnykenko—had prepared himself for an existentially crucial mission that could change the course of his nation and its arch enemy.

The team observed absolute radio and conversational silence from that point forward. It was all tap shoulders, point, and sign language, to achieve understanding and compliance of Yaroslav's orders. Every man wore thermal imagers, as used by the army's R-18 drones, to detect the infrared radiation given off by warm objects and display them using bright colors. R-18 is a Ukrainian unmanned combat aerial vehicle designed to attack enemy targets with ammunition, developed by the Ukrainian organization Aerorozvidka.

The first military night-vision systems—from the second world war—used infrared searchlights whose sweep could be seen only by special detectors. These worked well unless the enemy had infrared sensors, in which case the user stood out like a beacon. Modern armies have two types of night-vision gear that avoid this problem: thermal imagers and photomultipliers.

The team's secret newest thermal imaging devices also included photomultipliers to turn light into electrical signals, in effect amplifying what little light was available. These turned the world an eerie monochrome green. The night vision goggles were the kind gift of their favorite uncle in the west, affectionately known as "Uncle Sugar" by the agents and military rank and file, as were their weapons, ammunition, and combat protective camouflage gear. The enhanced vision gave them a huge tactical advantage.

The highly trained and ultra-fit team members marched double-time over the pock-marked landscape 52 miles to Pavlograd in central east Ukraine. During the 2022 Russian invasion of Ukraine, Pavlograd—an important railway transportation hub—was subjected to a missile strike which destroyed the Pavlograd-2 train station in the city, and the tiny airport was obliterated. On March 22–a year later—some semblance of a utilitarian airport had been reconstructed. Humble though the short runway airport was, Melnykenko and his team boarded Ukraine's defense ministry Il-76 transport plane painted with Luhansk flags for the clandestine flight to the outskirts of Popasnayayaya, 316 miles to the east.

Protracted battles had taken place throughout the ten years of the Donbas conflict, with clashes between Ukrainian and Separatist forces being frequent every year, prior to the full-scale invasion by Russia in early 2022. The Battle of Popasnayayaya was a military engagement during the Eastern Ukraine campaign as part of the Battle of the Donbas which began on March 3, 2022, and ended on May 7, 2022. In August, a video and photos of the head and hands of a Ukrainian prisoner of war stuck on poles appeared. The video showed the mutilated body of the captured soldier with his head stuck on a wooden pole and his hands on metal spikes on either side of it, in front of the garden of a house in occupied Popasnayayaya.

A war correspondent from a Russian media outlet reported in *Telegram* newspaper that the Wagner PMC [Private Military Company] base was set up in a five-story residential building that had apparently been abandoned at Myronivska Street, 12. That had sparked the emergency clandestine mission to kill or capture Lt. Col. Dmitriy Utkinov ("Wagner"), Yevgeny, Wagner commanders, Col. Konstantin Pikalov, and Col. Andrei Troshev. The Wagner Group is a private paramilitary organization run by an ally of Russian dictator Vladimir Rasputinov. The group had tens of thousands of fighters and has operated in Syria and in various African countries as a violent kleptocracy.

Melnykenko paused the headlong rush to the putative Wagner Headquarters building to remind his men, "Time is critical. If we have figured out where Pikalov, Troshev, and General Mizin-tsev are hiding out; so, will the army. We can expect a missile attack any hour."

The unit had to rely on a local unknown to them to guide them through the enemy territory city as quickly and as safely as possible. It was going to be light soon, and they had to be set up for their attack in their hiding place before they were discovered. The soonest the attack could commence was when darkness fell on the 24th. Every detail of the mission depended on that critical detail. Yaroslav also knew from his own experience that no plan ever went off without a hitch, and he dreaded the possibility of an almost inevitable Murphy's Law complication coming his way.

CHAPTER 1

Leningrad/St. Petersburg, Russia, 1989

The SBU'S principle quarry was 62-year-old General Mikhial Viktorovich Mizin-tsev, Russian oligarch, PMC Wagner Group founder, owner, and on-the-ground strategical and tactical battle commanding general. The sadistic Wagner group was better militarily than President Rasputinov's legal Russian military; but, of late, short of ammunition and materiel owing to a heated discord between Mizin-tsev and the heads of defense and the military of the Russian Federal Republic, a regularly recurring feud.

Mikhial was born and reared in Leningrad in the Soviet Union on June 1, 1961, to Violetta Tarasovna. His father—who died early–and stepfather, were of Jewish descent; so, his mother supported him and his sick grandmother by working at a local hospital. During his school years, Mizin-tsev, aspired to be a professional cross-country skier. He was trained by his stepfather Viktoro Zhehov–who was an instructor in the sport–and attended a prestigious athletics boarding school from which he graduated in 1977. However, his career in sport was ultimately unsuccessful. He had a difficult childhood, spending time in a children's home and then in a juvenile detention center. He had been caught torturing puppies for pleasure.

In November, 1979, 18-year-old Viktorovich Mizin-tsev was caught stealing and given a suspended sentence, his first as an adult. Two years later, in 1981, he was again caught stealing, and sentenced to twelve years imprisonment for robbery, fraud, and involving teenagers in crime. He and several accomplices were convicted of robbing apartments in upscale neighborhoods. He was pardoned in 1988 and was released in 1990. In total, he had spent nine years in detention. After his release from prison in 1990, Mizin-tsev began selling hot dogs alongside his mother and stepfather at the Apraksin Dvor open-air market in Leningrad. Soon, by his own statement: "the rubles were piling up faster than my mother could count them."

He worked as a cook and then opened his own restaurant in St. Petersburg. From 1991-1997 and into the early 2000s, Mikhail–by then an astute and brash businessman–became a 15% stakeholder and manager of Contrast, which was the first grocery store chain in Saint Petersburg. He also came to own a number of restaurants and catering companies, including Concord Catering, which won billions of dollars in government contracts. Like other aspiring Russian oligarchs, Mikhail had cultivated tight bonds with the *Bratva* [The Russian mafia (Russian: *máfiya*) otherwise referred to as *Bratva*—brotherhood, or "thieves in law]; and through the Thieves in Law, he gained access to governmental bureaucrats who were excited by the profitable dark side of capitalism, especially in the historical capital city, Kiev. Another Medieval Latin name for Rus› was Ruthenia after one of its capital cities in what is now Ukraine [also calling themselves the "Rus: and claimed origination from Medieval Ruthenia.

He followed the entrepreneurial spirit of the times and founded or became more heavily involved in the grocery store business. After Mikhail became the manager of Contrast, he began to win government contracts to feed school children. He was generally a fine cook, and especially known as a baker. He became the owner of a number of restaurants and catering companies–including Concord Catering–which won billions of dollars in government contracts.

It was during that time that he met and became a close associate with a former KGB officer who was the Mayor of St. Petersburg at the time, Vladimir Rasputinov. That association persisted and increased. He was seen in newspaper reports touring his Concord Catering factory in 2010. His guests were Presidential envoy to the Northwestern Federal District Ilya Klebanov, Chief Sanitary Inspector Gennady Onishchenko, Leningrad Region Governor Valery Serdyukov, and then Prime Minister Vladimir Rasputinov.

CHAPTER 2

Kviv, Ukraine

January, 2005

Ivan Hennadiyovych Bakanov was born in 1975 in Kryvyi Rih, [aka Krivoy Rog] an iron producing industrial city in Dnipropetrovsk Oblast, Ukraine near the Dnipro River which later fell under constant bombardment by Russian invaders. It so happens that, he was a childhood friend of Volodymyr Zelensky. The two studied together and later worked over different projects, most importantly, Kvartal 95 Studio.

Ivan graduated from the Kyiv National Economic University in 1997 and the Academy of Labor, Social Relations and Tourism in 2006, with a specialty in "Court, advocacy and prosecution". In the early 2000s, Bakanov was an entrepreneur in the field of hydroelectric power plants. For several years, Bakanov controlled 7 hydroelectric power stations. Two of the largest–Boguslavskaya HPP and Dybinetskaya HPP–were located in the Kyiv region That gave him frequent and close association with his old friend Volodymyr and advancements in the Kvartal 95 troupe and Kvartal 95 Studio. Bakanov was part of Volodymyr Zelensky's team during 2019 presidential campaign, among other things. He was the leader of the Servant of the People party from 2017 to 2019.

He was a vigorous, handsome, and effective man, who became an admired Ukrainian politician and remained publicly and privately a loyal supporter of Zelenskyy, who became president in 2019. Bakanov became head of the Security Service of Ukraine the same year.

Yaroslav Kandybavych Melnykenko was born August 14, 1995, coincidentally in Kryvyi Rih like his future mentor and commander. His uncreative father gave him the three most common names in Ukraine (to match his unpresupposing surname with the most common given name and patronymic). He was four-years-old when his parents, two older brothers, and younger sister, were killed in a mortar attack by Donblast Separatists. He survived because he was having an overnight stay with his aunt and uncle in the suburbs. All records of his birth, ancestry, and parental associations, were lost in the conflagration.

His aunt and uncle did not go untouched by the unprovoked attack on their city. Uncle Dmytro lost his business, his fleet of trucks, and his will to live. His aunt Hanna was overwhelmed by the disaster and by her responsibilities to care for young Yaroslav and her own four children. She committed suicide the next month. Ivan Bakanov and his wife, Oksana Lazarenko, became foster parents for the boy by their own choice. Yaroslav and the Bakanov's son Artur became inseparable brothers and friends.

Yaroslav very early on demonstrated multiple important aptitudes. He and Artur excelled in grade school, but Yaroslav became a sports star in every sport he tried. He was bright, fast, and tough. Artur was also intelligent but not inclined toward body contact sports, nor was he especially ambitious. He went on to study engineering and succeeded very well in the growing Ukraine economy.

Ivan Bakanov took close note of Yaroslav's abilities and had the boy evaluated by the local recruiting office of the SBU, which was vocal about the coming need for special agents to counteract the increasing menace of the Separatists and their Russian big brothers. Ivan was friendly with the local agents, and Oksana became a popular hostess for all SBU affairs. It was evident that young Yaroslav was taking after his athletic and fit adoptive father. In fact, no one remembered his different parentage, especially the Jewish genealogy. Ivan was—in fact—rapidly becoming a valued clandestine agent of the security service, and his godfather Col. Davyd Oleksyovych Kravchenko, a ranking SBU tactical officer, took special notice of the precocious boy.

Ivan had an unusual interest in wrestling and excelled against all comers. Kravchenko talked Ivan into enrolling Yaroslav in the security service's private academy. The boy was young–arguably too young–to be enrolled; but he was much bigger than the other boys and girls who were being recruited. He was also growing at an unusual rate. Ukraine had been befriended by Israel, which was one of the few genuine friends the newly hatched democracy had. They sent IDF krav maga instructors and Mossad agents to teach the youths their best self-defense and combat techniques. Kravchenko was a rough-hewn man who spared none of his recruits the pitfalls of such hard work. Yaroslav had two broken arms, a broken nose, and a mid-shaft tib-fib fracture, during his first three years working with the hard-nosed practitioners of the brutal arts.

Kravchenko and Ivan were both impressed with Yaroslav's stoicism in the face of pain and by his quick healing qualities. By the time, the boy was fourteen, he had mastered the rigors of Krav maga, Brazilian Jiu Jitsu, combat boxing, wrestling, and was being taught the finer techniques of unarmed combat, including how to kill people. No one pretended that Yaroslav Melnykenko was being groomed for anything else but to fight for his country behind the scenes.

Yaroslav was a man by the age of sixteen; and his father, Ivan, and godfather Davyd, decided it was time for the indefatigable boy to be introduced into the real world of spy work: sink or swim. His first assignment was fairly straight forward.

President Volodymyr Zelenskyy had two opportunities to prove himself to the aspiring agent Yaroslav. The first time came about when SBU analysts discovered corruption within the ranks not unlike what went on under former President Viktor F. Yanukovych who was convicted of treason by inviting Russia to invade Ukraine and reverse a pro-Western revolution that ousted him from power.

The evidence was clear that in some regions of Ukraine—esp. Donetsk–the SBU teamed up with local criminals taking part in *prykhvatizatsiya* [privatization of state property] ignoring their sworn operational objectives and resulting in major fraud and theft from hard working Ukrainian cities and a sky-rocketing level of local violence. A local citizen-Yuriy Shevchenko–was arrested by SBU agents, interrogated, and brutally tortured, for three days. He refused to confess to trumped up murder charges and died in SBU custody. Later, agents from the Kyiv office found damning evidence that the real killer was Anatoly Onoprienko. He was arrested the next year, and the criminals among the local SBU unit went on as if nothing had happened.

Three agents of the Kyiv office went to Donetsk to arrest the corrupt locals three months before Yaroslav was assigned to a second unit. The first three men were never heard from again. When the six-man arresting unit arrived in Donetsk, they found an out-of-the-way hotel and began debating over a dinner of *Zelenyj Borshch, Guliash*–the Ukrainian version of Hungarian goulash, a meat and vegetable stew seasoned with paprika and other spices, *pampushky*, and hard rye bread. The insipid fare was washed down with copious amounts of Opillya Korifey beer; the water was not fit to drink. The chief agent for the raid suggested—as he always did—a surprise no-knock center raid with lots of noise and gunfire. Who cared if there were casualties among the crooks? There was nearly complete unanimity with Sgt. Zapliuisvchka. [Cossack lit. "dip-spit the candle"].

It was probably the amount of beer that loosened Yaroslav's tongue. Otherwise, no fresh-faced boy who had not shaved would have dreamt of criticizing his sergeant. It was not done, especially in front of other officers.

"Sergeant, it seems to me that we stand to get several of us hurt if we do that. Why not slip in the back door and get the drop on them? That way, few of us are likely to get wounded, and there will be more of them to rat on the rest of the dirty agents here in Donetsk."

He said it matter-of-factly and in a calm deliberate voice.

He might as well have given the sign of the fig to the sergeant. The man erupted in righteous anger and swung a ham-fisted punch at the younger, but larger man. In their after-action report, none of the other officers could say exactly what young Yaroslav did. But the result was that the seasoned old sergeant was laid out on the floor unconscious where he stayed for half an hour. The other ten men were so impressed that none of them hinted anything but "self-defense, and a very good job of it" to their questioners.

The raid itself was an anti-climax after that impromptu display of martial art. They sneaked through the back door of the house the crooked SBU agents had taken over. The Kyiv agents pointed twelve ugly looking AKs, lighter and newer PKMs, and slightly battered Italian MG-42/59 and German MG-3s, and the single different gun—the preference of Yaroslav Melnykenko—a standard Israeli uzi submachine gun. It was over almost without speaking. It was not up to the arresting officers to explain the charges against the Donetsk officials. They were just there to secure the suspects and to take them back to Kviv.

One of the criminals–a coarse thuggish looking man–who looked like he had muscles on top of his muscles, did not like the look of the youngest arresting officer.

"What chu lookin' at, brat? You the big man now... standin' there with that toy gun? Not man enough to take me without all these dozen guys? Think you would have me if you didn't have that pea shooter? Huh?"

"Time to go," Yaroslav said.

"I can take you with one hand tied behind my back."

"No. Put your hands behind your back while I put the zip-tie cuffs on you. I don't want to have any trouble with you."

"Oh, mister big man. I am so scared. Lookit me tremble all over."

He demonstrated.

"Hands behind your back."

There was a kind of finality in Yaroslav's voice that annoyed the older man.

Suddenly, Big Man whirled to face Yaroslav and simultaneously pulled a large serrated knife from his inside coat pocket. The razor-sharp edge glistened in the light of the table lamp.

He swung the long blade in a semi-circle intent upon decapitating the boy.

That was a mistake.

In less than a second and a half, Yaroslav ducked under the hissing blade aimed at his vulnerable throat, dealt a left-hand karate chop to the bend in his opponent's right arm snapping it sharply, whipping his own arm over and around the man's right arm and bending it forward with a rewarding crack. Yaroslav used his keen sense of kinetic motion and position to keep the failed SBU officer in an awkward motion toward the man's left and down. He kicked his opponent's legs out from under him and pirouetted to his own right to put the big man into uncontrolled Ferris wheel flight and onto his back landing on Yaroslav's bent knee from six feet in the air. Three sounds resulted: a high-pitched crack as the man's shoulder dislocated, his humeral head split in half, and a spiral fracture reverberated down the large arm bone's shaft; a loud, dull thud as two thoracolumbar vertebral bodies underwent compression fractures; and a burst of exhalation that sounded like a minor explosion as Big Man's lungs deflated on the hard concrete floor. There was a brief futile scream, then silence, as the man lost consciousness.

There followed an almost reverential moment of silence among the arresting officers and their arrestees. Any thought of further resistance evaporated.

CHAPTER 3

Kviv, Ukraine

Late January, 2005

President Viktor Hryhorii–Ukrainian president at the time–was notable for his pro-Russian policy, building of a kleptocratic regime, and tightening of the screws on freedom of speech and peaceful protests. Consequently, parliament passed laws benefiting certain oligarchs as a common practice. This created a vicious circle of oligarchy while money siphoned from the Ukrainian economy was laundered through Western financial systems.

The next president—the one under whom Yaroslav did his training and early work for the Security Service–made waves. He had the audacity to propose reform as more than just a catch phrase during the election cycle. He worked to get something down about it for the first time in decades and became very unpopular in his country and even among the profiting Western countries. Most commentators described him as a fawning commie.

But his appointee as the new head of the security service, Adolf Chebotarov, took the new president at his word. He began—without announcement or fanfare—to launch a quiet crackdown on the criminal oligarchs. He fired every officer of Department "K" [The bureau specifically designated to fight corruption and organized crime] and quickly replaced them with unknowns—i.e. junior officers who had not yet been contaminated. The new head was a woman named Olena Yuriivna Matveyeva who was a tough as any man in the Security Service, and the stern daughter of ranking priest of the Kyivan Metropolitanate of the Ukrainian Orthodox Church which made her an austere moralist and the perfect person for the position.

Olena Yuriivna appreciated young Yaroslav for several of his attributes: he was too young to have been much contaminated; his teachers were purist Ukrainian Russian haters; and he personally showed real promise. Under Director Matveyeva's guidance, Yaroslav was appointed an officer in Department K with his first assignment to matriculate in the National Academy of the Security Service of the Ukraine. Per her instructions, Yaroslav studied part time, and served on active duty part time. As he saw it, his life was split into three halves: one half student, a second half soldier police agent; and the third half, an advanced martial arts student with a minor in small weapons defense, and handgun and long rifle competitor.

Olena Yuriivna met some resistance when she gave Yaroslav his arduous assignments—not from him, but from the more senior officers. His godfather, Ivan Hennadiyovych Bakanov assured Olena that the boy could do it all and do it well; and that was good enough for her. She kept tabs on his progress.

Yaroslav was assigned to Kuzma Mykolavich Stefanenko, considered to be most intelligent and best teacher in the new officer corps. He was flexible in his thinking, rigid in his moral opinions, and an old-school stiff-collar military enforcer when it came to rules—for himself, his officers, and the identified perpetrators. Kuzma and Yaroslav soon became more than fellow officers; they became friends on a first-name basis. Yaroslav went on three missions with his new leader in rapid succession—all before the younger of the two was 17.

In the second week on the Department K service, Kuzma's unit traveled separately–dressed in mufti and keeping a low profile. They met in a rundown motel behind the Bucha Glassworks [Kirov Street] in Bucha City on the outskirts of Bucha Raion. The analytics division had identified a scheduled meeting to be held in the Hotel Gostynnyi Dvir located on Yasnopolyanskaya Street 9a. It was near perfect for oligarch Dmytro Ponomarenko's purposes, but even better for the arrest team.

The hotel was 16 miles from the accommodation, while Kiev Train Station and Saint Sophia Cathedral were 16 miles northwest away on good roads. The nearest airport was Igor Sikorsky Kyiv International Airport, 17 miles from Hotel Gostynnyi Dvir. St. Cyril's Monastery—14 miles away—was to cater lunch. The hotel bar was restocked with Russian vodkas for the special meeting. The hotel featured family rooms, and reservations for Ponomarenko and his personal entourage were in place. The entire Hotel Gostynnyi Dvir dining room was blocked off beginning the next day at eleven to accommodate Ponomarenko's luncheon and business meeting for his prospective clients from Rostov-on-don, Russia.

The Gostynnyi Dyir did not pay its wait staff particularly well, and several were amenable to learning how to place bugs for the benefit of the security service. Jinyi Mp3 spy magnetic hidden voice activated mini auditory recorders supplied by the US CIA, produced clear, and fully audible, recordings usable in any court. There were six devices placed around the dining room, under tables and chairs. The recordings were damning because every man and woman in the room was certain that he or she was among friends and candid conversation was the order of the day among those friends. Much of what they had to say related to their ongoing criminal enterprise and their consuming greed.

The parasitic figures who helped gut Ukraine over the previous few decades–often acting as foot-soldiers for the Kremlin–were publicly now extremely interested in upholding Ukrainian democracy and Ukrainian sovereignty publicly; but in the trusted quiet of the hotel's dining room, it was all about money—the money that came from the Kremlin to further its aims versus those of the Ukrainian people, their people, and their government.

As soon as Kapitan Kuzma Mykolavich Stefanenko heard the incriminating recording, he dispatched his squad to arrest the oligarch and also any Ukrainian citizens present. The shock was total as Yaroslav and eleven other officers and noncoms marched double time into the hotel dining room.

Yaroslav made the announcement in both Ukrainian and Russian, "Every person line up facing the east wall. Place all bags, cases, and any other containers, on the floor in front of you. Take out your identification cards and hold them in your hands with your hands fully extended over your head. Do not talk. Do not ask questions. Anyone who attempts to leave will be shot. I will not repeat the orders. Move now!"

There was a rapid fire clatter of chairs, tables, and hurrying footsteps toward the east wall. No one spoke; but if looks could kill, there would have been multiple fatal casualties. Yaroslav and two sergeants stepped up to Dmytro Ponomarenko and relieved him of his identification cards and documents.

"Young man, do you have any idea who I am?" Ponomarenko snarled with the quiet patrician hauteur of his oligarch class which always produced cowering compliance.

Except this time.

Yaroslav said, "I do. Thank you for confirming your identity. Place your hands behind your back. Do not move otherwise."

Staff sergeant Rokosylana Mykolaivna Udovychenko applied the handcuffs on the oligarch a bit too tightly under the watchful eye of Yaroslav who suppressed a slight smile. Ponomarenko flashed a special devil's gritted teeth look at the young man and marched away to the troop transport headed for Kyiv. Five other Ukrainians joined him, and seven Russians—including four oligarchs from Rasputinov's inner circle—were bum-rushed to a waiting plane which lacked seats. They were delivered without their identifications, pass-ports, or other papers. When the Kremlin complained later, Kapitan Stefanenko accepted full responsibility for the bureaucratic oversight. He was deeply remorseful.

Various Ukraine regions, 2004-2005:

During the rest of 2005—despite his youth–Yaroslav became the second in command to Kuzma Mykolavich Stefanenko; he turned eighteen; and the head of SBU, Olena Yuriivna, promised the young sergeant a unit command if he passed his next test as well as he had done during his four other assignments over the year. He and Kuzma had tracked down, cornered, and captured, four oligarchs: US sanctioned Moldovan politician and oligarch, Vladimir Plahotniuc for treason; Llan Shor, leader of the pro-Russian Sor Party–a network orchestrated by Moscow in a bid to destabilize the country through demonstrations after Yaroslav managed to infiltrate the group which was being trained by people traveling from Russia and financed by the Şor Party. In April, Shor was convicted of fraud and sentenced to 15 years in prison.

He was aided to escape prison by Sor Party agents and attempted to flee to Israel. Kuzma and Yaroslav got wind of the plans and additionally, that Ukraine's Vice President, Marina Tauber was part of the plot. Both of them were arrested at the airport trying to leave the country for Israel following investigations into the Şor Party finances by the SBU team.

The other two corrupt politicians and oligarchs were Moldovan Dumitru Gutu; Moldovans—unlike other former Russian satellite countries–no longer followed a patronymic system; and Sergey Vladimirovich Cherkasov.

An investigation linked six Russian diplomats with twenty-eight Russian citizens holding temporary visas for Montenegro and two local citizens in a spy investigation. The diplomats were expelled because they had immunity. The Russian citizens—who were long-term secret agents–were later banned from Montenegro and the two locals–one an ex-diplomat–were executed after conviction for charges of illegal weapons trafficking, organizing a criminal organization, and espionage. And there was the infamous Sergey Vladimirovich Cherkasov.

He had a long and successful history as a deep cover Soviet then Russian federation spy. The break for the SBU came when a Dutch intelligence agency publicly identified "Victor Muller" as the long-sought Sergey Cherkasov who was operating under NOC [under Nonofficial Cover]. In late April, the US arrested and deported 10 Russian operatives as part of a spy swap with Moscow–one of whom went under the name of Victor Muller–had graduated from Harvard's John F. Kennedy School of Government 10 years before and had been living in Cambridge with his wife and two children. He was able to escape to Ukraine before he could be indicted.

Cherkasov then similarly built an alternate identity over the course of years he lived in the Carpathian Mountains of Ukraine. The Dutch intelligence agency published a crude "legend" that it believed was probably written by Cherkasov in mid-2005, laying out his false history as a Brazilian man born in Rio de Janeiro in 1989. He detailed this fake family history through multiple generations, offering a myriad of small personal idiosyncrasies: a hatred for fish, a beloved aunt, and a crush on a geography teacher.

In 2004, Cherkasov began attending college at Trinity College Dublin, studying political science and graduating in 2005. The same year, he traveled to the United States to obtain his master's degree through the SAIS [Serving and Accrediting Independent Schools]. The revelation of Cherkasov's true identity roiled faculty at SAIS. But to former intelligence officials, Cherkasov fits a well-known pattern: Russia—among other foreign powers—seeks to place bright young intelligence operatives in American academic institutions to help build their deep cover identities. Cherkasov was a spy operating under an identity not apparently linked to the Russian government in any way. All he had to do was little more than simply to establish legitimacy as a student.Enter your email to sign up for CNN's "What Matters" Newsletter.

Like other Russian illegals, Cherkasov went through a long process of credentialing himself in order to establish credibility as a US graduate student. Cherkasov appears to have carried out his mission successfully. He attended Johns Hopkins' School of Advanced International Studies. He denied being able to speak Russian. Former professors and classmates spoke to US security agencies on the condition of anonymity out of fear of retaliation from the Russian security services.

While the Western security services were dithering about what to do, Cherkasov dropped out of sight. He reappeared in Ukraine, under the name of Nikos Bogonikolos, a Greek citizen. He claimed to be the founder of a satellite technology company Aratos Group in the Netherlands. The SBU looked into the character who seemed to have appeared in Ukraine with no history. Bogonikolos was arrested on May 9, 2023, charged with providing Russia with ultramodern technology in breach of US sanctions, including semiconductors used in cryptology and nuclear testing.

Head of SBU, Olena Yuriivna, sicced Kuzma and Yaroslav on "Nikos"; and in less than three months, their unit had unraveled the entire tangled web of intrigue and espionage that Cherkasov had woven over decades as an insider spy. Besides giving the Russian military and FSB [Federal Security Service of the Russian Federation] ultramodern technology in breach of US sanctions–including semiconductors used in cryptology and nuclear testing–he was carrying top-secret Ukrainian information related to the criminal cases of several oligarchs facing the International Criminal Court. He was trapped by Yaroslav's team in an alley in Lviv while on his way to his phony workplace and was arrested without resistance.

The United States Department of State asked Ukraine to transfer him to the US once he completed his prison term in Kyiv. Ukraine agreed. The SBU figured he would be somewhere between 112 and 116 when he became eligible for trial in the US. The Office of the Director of National Intelligence declined to comment on the case.

CHAPTER 4

Minsk City Hall, Belarus

September 5, 2014

A t 1000 on the bright September morning, the bodyguards and translators from the countries involved arrived in limousines at the front entrance to the Minsk City Hall and were swiftly escorted inside the heavily guarded edifice. The Minsk City Hall is a symbol of the city's enduring government. It appeared in the city in connection with the acquisition of Magdeburg Law in Minsk including the fifteen largest cities in the Grand Duchy of Lithuania. The first mention of a stone building of the Minsk City Hall was in 1583. Over time, it was rebuilt many times and changed its appearance every time.

In the 19th century, it was the court, the police guardhouse, archive, and the City Theater Hall. Times and laws changed, as well as the status of the city and country changed; it became the North-Western province of the Russian Empire. In the autocratic Tzarist regime, it was not ideologically correct to leave the City Hall as a reminder of its former Magdeburg liberties and freedom. Emperor Nicholas I himself issued a decree to demolish Minsk City Hall under the formal pretext that it spoiled the overall appearance of the city.

The building was razed to the ground in 1857; building materials were used to cover roadways, to construct small architectural forms of the city; and metal structures were used to cast signs on citizens' houses. As a result of archaeological excavations, remains of the foundation of the building were found in the 20th century, and cultural strata from the surrounding areas gave historians materials for a complete picture of the life of the earlier times.

Reconstruction of the Minsk City Hall first began again in 1980. During part of that time, various archaeological research projects were carried out. Many historical docu-ments, graphic and pictorial images, were analyzed in order to rebuild with authenticity. It took fifteen years to prepare a draft restoration work. The project was successful despite its complexity. The restored Minsk city hall was inaugurated on November 4, 2004.

The layout was in the spirit of the Northern Renaissance—a rectangle as at the base with the tower visually increasing the height of the build-ing. The tower was set with a bell and a clock. There is the Museum of Minsk city under the roof of the City Hall, there is a hall for forums, meetings, and VIP-persons, on the first floor. That is where the meetings and formal signing took place.

All participants—including guards and staff—were in full diplomatic formal dress. Young Yaroslav Kandybavych Melnykenko was wearing a full dress uniform for the first time in his life. In fact, he rarely wore a uniform. He was angry—as were almost all the guards—and it would not take much to ignite a serious and overdue fight. Most of the arguments and details had been finalized the previous day; little was left but the formalities. The meeting was called to order.

A large Belarusian emblem hung from the curtain lengths overhead. It is shaped like the border contour of the republic placed in the rays of the rising sun and the star over it framed by ears of wheat, clover, and flax. The wreath of the flowers with wheat was wrapped up three times with a red and green ribbon. The sign of the country name was placed in the center.

Belarussian honor guard soldiers planted the coat of arms and the horizontally striped red-green national flag with a vertical stripe of red and white at the hoist in the center behind the signatories. Other guard units planted the blue and yellow flag of Ukraine; red, white, and blue, Russian and rebel flags on the left and right of the Belarus banner; and the self-proclaimed DPR [Donetsk People's Republic]—black, blue, and red–and LPR [Luhansk People's Republic]—light blue, dark blue, and red–which were accepted by the separatists and the Russian Federation but never recognized by the international diplomatic community.

A specially vetted Belarus marching band played the anthem/hymn of Belarus—*My Bedlarusy* or *We, as Belarusians.*

All stood for the anthem; then the entirety of the treaty was read aloud in Russian, Ukrainian, French, and English. The Minsk Protocol was drafted throughout 2014 by the Trilateral Contact Group on Ukraine, consisting of Ukraine, Russia, and the OSCE [Organization for Security and Co-operation in Europe] with mediation by the leaders of France and Germany in what they termed the Normandy Format. The discussions produced a treaty of sorts which the Russian presidential spokesman described as "Ukraine's neutrality in the style of Sweden or Austria... which could be considered a settlement." The protocols— flawed as they ended up—were a dubious attempt to stop the war the Russians had been waging against their neighbor for many weeks.

The signatories were a Swiss diplomat, an OSCE representative, a former president of Ukraine, the Ukrainian official representative, the Russian representative, and the leaders of the self-proclaimed DPR and LPR without giving recognition of their status as governmental entities. The "Great Powers"—France and Germany—had assisted in the negotiations and final preparations for the treaty document. The United States was represented at arms-length by vice-president Biden.

The agreement quickly broke down after both sides violated the terms; and subsequent attempts at improving the "Minsk Treaty" failed owing to the intransigence of both parties to the conflict. By January, 2015, the Minsk Protocol ceasefire had completely collapsed. The United States elected to conduct lukewarm diplomatic efforts including insipid sanctions against Vladimir Rasputinov and his Russian aggressors.

At the start of January, 2015, the separatist forces of the DPR [Donetsk People's Republic] and LPR [Luhansk People's Republic] began a new offensive on Ukrainian-controlled areas, resulting in the complete collapse of the Minsk Protocol ceasefire. After heavy fighting, DPR forces captured the symbolically important Donetsk International Airport on January 21–the last part of the city of Donetsk that had been under Ukrainian control. Following this victory, separatist forces pressed their offensive on the important railway and road junction of Debaltseve in late January. Yaroslav—now in command of his own SBU unit—was reassigned to fight in the war directly, leaving the arrests of corrupt oligarchs to others. Kuzma Stefanenko was promoted to deputy director of the SBU and headed up all anticorruption activities.

The renewed heavy fighting caused significant concern in the international community. French president François Hollande and German chancellor Angela Merkel put forth a new peace plan on February 7. The Franco-German plan, drawn up after talks with Ukrainian president Petro Poroshenko and Russian president Vladimir Rasputinov, was seen as a revival of the Minsk Protocol. President Hollande said that the plan was the last chance for resolution of the conflict. The plan was put forth in response to American president Barack Obama's proposal to send armaments to the Ukrainian government, something that Chancellor Merkel said would only result in a worsening of the crisis.

President Hollande said that the plan was the last chance for resolution of the conflict.

A summit to discuss the implementation of the Franco-German diplomatic plan was scheduled for February 11 at the Independence Palace in Minsk, which was attended by Russian president Vladimir Rasputinov, Ukrainian president Petro Poroshenko, German chancellor Angela Merkel, French president François Hollande, DPR leader Alexander Zakharchenko, and LPR leader Igor Plotnitsky.

Negotiations went on overnight for sixteen hours and were intense and difficult. The following day, it was announced that the parties to the conflict had agreed to a new package of peacemaking measures, called Minsk II. Some of the measures agreed to were: an unconditional ceasefire from February 15, withdrawal of heavy weapons from the front line, release of prisoners of war, and constitutional reform in Ukraine. It was, instead, the beginning of the Russo-Ukraine war in earnest.

CHAPTER 5

Chernivtsi, Ukrainian Carpathian Mountains, Saturday
January 14, 2016

T he main claim to fame for Chernivtsi [located in the historic region of Bukovina–currently shared between Romania and Ukraine] was its internationalism. Chernivtsi is in the southwest of Ukraine, in the eastern Carpathians, on the border between the Carpathians and the East European Plain]. Its greatest strategic value in the early 2000s, was its close proximity its lose proximity to Romania to the south, Moldova to the southwest, and Poland on the west, which provided an escape route for corrupt Russian and Ukrainian oligarchs fleeing from Ukraine and other former USSR satellite countries to the financial havens of the European Union. It is one of the most multinational cities in Ukraine. Chernivtsi serves as the administrative center for the Chernivtsi *Raion*, the Chernivtsi urban *hromada*, and the *oblast* itself.

It is located in the Carpathian Mountains, a long unbroken stretch of harsh mountain country which has long been a safe harbor for bandits of all stripes. The Ukrainian Carpathians are a section of the Eastern Carpathians, within the borders of modern Ukraine. They are located in the southwestern corner of Western Ukraine, within administrative territories of four Ukrainian regions [oblasts], covering northeastern part of Zakarpattia Oblast, southwestern part of Lviv Oblast, southern half of Ivano-Frankivsk Oblast and western half of Chernivtsi Oblast. The area is vast, largely primitive, and sparsely popular-ted. What more could an out-of-favor oligarch want?

In October, 2002, a man known to Norwegian *Politi-og lensmann-setaten* [the Norwegian national civilian police agency] as José Assis Sousa, was arrested above the arctic circle in the Scandinavian country. There, he posed as a Brazilian oil entrepreneur, who had spent time at the University of Calgary, Canada. He was an intern at UiT [The Arctic University, Norway] and was prominently involved with the Center for Peace Studies. University officials suspected him because of his Russian accent, checked out his credentials from Canada and found that he had never been in the country. The UiT adminis-trators then asked for an investigation by NSM [Nasjonal *sikkerhetsmyndighet*–the National Security Authority (Direktoriat)], a Norwegian security agency which is responsible for preventive national security. NSM identified the bogus student as Russian national Mikhail Valerievich Vinogradov, believed to be a Colonel in the GRU.

When apprehended, Vingradov was en route across the arctic region between Norway and Russia, which consists of a 121 mile land border between Sør-Varanger, Norway, and Pechengsky District, Russia. It further consists of a border between the two countries' exclusive economic zones in the Barents Sea and the Arctic Ocean.

There is only a single border crossing–located at Storskog in Norway–and Vingradov was zeroed in on making it there before he was discovered by the NSM or border police. The Norwegian side is patrolled by the Garrison of Sør-Varanger. Radio communication is faster than any dogsled team, and border police were waiting for him when he and his dogs reached the crossing. He was charged with gathering intelligence linked to state secrets and escorted back to Oslo to await trial.

While being escorted from Oslo District Prison on Akebergveien 9, to *Oslo tingrett* [Oslo District Court] at the intersection of Bryunsveien and Hamangskogen Streets three days later, an incident occurred which was never fully understood or explained. Vingradov was in an unmarked black Chevrolet Suburban SUV driven by two trusted prison guards with an NSM agent minding the shackled prisoner in the back seat, when a dump truck hit them broadside as they were passing through the Evjetunnelen. There were surprisingly few witnesses, none of whom saw anything of use to law enforcement. The truck and SUV blocked all lanes of traffic in the direction of the courthouse, causing a traffic snarl and a five-hour delay before traffic could resume.

At the scene of the accident, Oslo police found that all occupants of the SUV and the truck were missing; the vehicle had been scrubbed clean of all fingerprints; and no evidence was found to aid the investigators in their search for the escaped Russian spy. It was not until early January, 2016 when SBU agents–acting on a call from a phone booth in mid-town Chernivtsi, Ukraine—that Vingradov was seen purchasing a bus ticket for a destination in Poland and for another destination in Bucharest. Chernivtsi has access to the M19 highway, which is part of the European route E85, which links it to Bucharest (south) and Ternopil and Lutsk (north); so, it was possible that he could be about to leave the country for almost anywhere in Europe. He was using the alias, Heinz Müller, German exporter of pencils made in Frankfurt.

The caller was never identified, but the information was good. The local SBU agents traced the man to a nearby hotel—the AllureInn Hotel and Spa on Tsentralna Ploshcha 6, which was a mere 2,300 feet from the center of Chernivtsi and its main bus station. His departure date for his bus escape to Poland was January 14, two days hence. Yaroslav pointed out to Kuzma, that it was highly probable that Vingradov was planning to take advantage of the chaos, confusion, and traffic snarls, which always took place on the Saturday of the annual *Krasna Malanka* [Gregorian calendar New Year's Eve celebration] with its bizarre pagan show with strong men carrying 66 pound straw bears on their shoulders for two days, gypsies, and evil spirits, in Chernivtsa. The Malanka starts wandering across the village casting out evil spirits from the evening of January 13. It takes the whole night and the following day to visit every single house.

A large-scale international Malanka celebration—now known as MalankaFest in Ukraine takes place at Chernivtsi Philharmonic Square and features the participants from the neighboring countries, as well as other regions of Ukraine. But unlike Krasna Malanka elsewhere, MalankaFest in Chernivtsi features many more elements of pop culture, including riotous street shenanigans by youths, almost mandatory drunkenness, illicit drug use gone rampant, and girls locked in their homes by careful fathers.

The SBU unit assumed its places throughout the crowded hallways, stairwells, lounges, and restaurants, of the hotel taking furtive glances at the photographs of their quarry, Heinz Müller/aka Mikhail Valerievich Vinogradov. Three agents walked the beat from the hotel to the bus station to be able to take down Vingradov if he got past the majority of the agents in the hotel proper. The wait was nerve wracking.

Yaroslav had developed a cynical view of the world by that time, having seen a great many twists and turns during his formative years as an arresting agent. He was on the lookout for anything unusual from his perch on a soft armchair on the mezzanine. He had a commanding view of the entry way, the stairs and hallways, and the large mezzanine Ballroom, without making himself obvious by moving about and craning his neck to see all around him.

He was the first to spy the unusual: a bent over little old peasant lady making her limping way out of the elevator and onto the mezzanine's parquet floor. She might as well have had green hair and an iridescent red dress. Besides, she was wearing a ragged wool head scarf which was none too clean and a vivid red and yellow paisley—obviously Russian–pashmina to cover her lower face. It was not doing its job well, because the face had a beard which became evident every now and again.

Yaroslav put down his newspaper, stood up and stretched, then casually walked in the direction taken by the poorly dressed peasant lady. He was behind her by two stair steps halfway down the curving staircase.

He whispered into his coms: "Am on the south stairs following the package; at least I am pretty sure."

He saw four other agents get up from the places where they were seated and begin to walk nonchalantly toward the bottom of the stairs. Kuzma moved a bit more quickly until he was a couple of stairsteps behind Yaroslav.

The peasant lady took a couple of furtive looks around before stepping out onto the entryway floor. Yaroslav took note of a waiting taxicab in front of the hotel's revolving doors. She stepped carefully onto the black and white tile square floor and began to walk more purposefully toward the cab.

"Now!" whispered Yaroslav.

Six big, strong, young, men closed in around the peasant lady. She instantly became aware of her predicament, threw off her headscarf and pashmina, and began to run toward the revolving door. The disguised man was hampered by his skirts, and it was evident that he was not experienced in how to navigate in them. He took a humiliating face plant five feet from the doors which caused an uproar of laughter from all the drunks in the lobby.

Yaroslav and Kuzma reached her/him before he could get back to his feet. Kuzma nodded to Yaroslav: "You do the honors, young sergeant. This is the final touch on your application to be the next leader of the unit."

Yaroslav assumed a serious demeanor, leaned over, and extended his hand to the fugitive to help him to his feet, smiled and said, "GRU Colonel Mikhail Valerievich Vinogradov, I presume."

Vinogradov looked as if he might cry.

CHAPTER 6

DPR [Donetsk People's Republic]

September 1, 2016

Before 2005, Donetsk was a middling industrial city in eastern Ukraine located on the Kalmius River in Donetsk Oblast. It was largest city of the larger economic and cultural Donets Basin [*Donbas region*]. To rid it of the Russian names of the city and its environs, it was renamed Donetsk in 1961. The city today remains a center for coal mining and for the steel industry. After shedding the Russified nature and control of the area, Donetsk experienced a period in the 1990s which was most difficult for ordinary citizens because it became a center of gang wars for control over industrial enterprises,

To complicate matters in the 1990s and the 2000s, hundreds were killed in coal mine collapses in Donetsk and the region, including the 2007 Zasyadko mine disaster, 2008 Ukraine coal mine collapse, and the 2015 Zasyadko mine disaster. Ukraine has had many mining accidents since the collapse of the Soviet Union in 1991, with one reason cited as the linking of miners' pay to production, which is an incentive to ignore safety procedures that slow production.

Donetsk received worldwide criticism for the strong mafia [*rússkaya máfiya– Bratva* (brotherhood), a collective of various organized crime elements originating in the former Soviet Union. The initialism

OPG is Organized Criminal (*Prestupnaya* in Russian) Group, used to refer to any of the Russian mafia groups, sometimes modified with a specific name, e.g. Orekhovskaya OPG] in connection with its growing Ukrainian oligarchy, and for an increasing poverty rate. Some analysts warned that the city could share Detroit's gloomy fate, due to its failure to combat crime and poverty.

On April 7, 2014, pro-Russian activists seized control of Donetsk OSA [Oblast State Administration], declared the "Donetsk People's Republic", and asked for formal Russian intervention, which was quick in coming, since Russia had been ready for years. On May 11, 2014, a referendum of sorts on self-rule was held in Donetsk. The head of the self-proclaimed Donetsk People's Republic election commission said that almost 90 percent of those who voted in the Donetsk Region endorsed political independence from Kyiv. Many throughout the rest of Ukraine and the world outside the country do not recognize the referendum. The EU and US stated flatly that the polls were illegal.

Heavy shelling by the Ukrainian Army and paramilitary units began almost immediately and caused civilian fatalities in Donetsk. Both warring factions used unguided Grad missiles in populated areas, which Western countries declared was a violation of international humanitarian laws and constitute a war crime. It also called on the insurgents to avoid their deployment in densely populated areas.

No one listened; and Yaroslav Melnykenko–now a *Starshyi leitenant* [senior lieutenant, comparable to a US army first lieutenant]–was in the thick of the fight, having been seconded to GUR MO [the main directorate of intelligence of the Ministry of Defense of Ukraine]. The agency was established from the existing intelligence assets of the Kyiv , Odesa, and Carpathian, military districts of the Soviet GRU.

Yaroslav's last assignment before the actual war started, was in the Carpathian military district. Before the Russian invasion of Ukraine, the only field reconnaissance unit was a special unit subordinated to the Directorate's 4th Special Intelligence Service. Yaroslav became an early member of that seasoned unit.

Ukraine did not need more artillery or infantrymen in the early days and weeks; it needed good behind-the-lines intelligence, tanks, and airpower, in that order. The main orders for Yaroslav's unit were to obtain information about Russian artillery and infantry placements and to launch surprise commando attacks from behind the Russian encampments.

Donetsk lies in the steppe landscape, surrounded by scattered woodland, hills, spoil tips [piles built of accumulated spoil, the overburden or other waste rock removed during coal and ore mining, typically composed of shale], rivers and lakes. The northern outskirts are mainly used for agriculture. A wide belt of farmlands surrounds the city. Although the bombing and artillery forays caused extensive damage in the city proper, the location of the Russian troops and their artillery launching sits were in those woodland hills hidden by the natural forest growth.

As early as April 9, the Directorate's 4th Special Intelligence Service field reconnaissance unit had set up clandestine camps behind Russian emplacement their scouts—including Yaroslav—had identified. By the 10th, plans were finalized for the first four attacks on the main artillery sites. The sites were selected in a random pattern to confuse the enemy and to cause alarm among the raw troops fresh from Russian prisons for duty. Some of those troops had not yet even been given rifles.

Yaroslav was ordered to hit the largest artillery launch site and its huge ammunition dump. It was located in the center of three tall spoil tips [piles built of accumulated spoiled waste material removed during mining, not including actual mine slag] arranged such that they could not be detected from the front, and all movement took place from the rear. The exit opening was twenty feet from a particularly dense birch, maple, and hornbeam, woods. Yaroslav and his eleven men crept stealthily and slowly among the trees and brambles in radio and voice silence. Yaroslav and his sergeants directed soldiers into positions across from the rear opening of the large artillery site and were in place before midnight.

Although since late April, the US State Department had sold artillery ammunition to Ukraine, the new and better munitions had not filtered down as far as the 4th Special Intelligence unit; so, they were armed with Soviet artillery left over from the Cold War era. The weary Ukrainians carried in "nonstandard ammunition" that can be fired from Ukrainian weapons such as 122mm, 152mm artillery shells, 120mm mortar rounds, and other small weapons. Slogging through the difficult wooded terrain was arduous and vexing. But—by the time they were ready for their attack—the unit had AGM-114 Hellfire Land-based man-portable semi-active laser homing anti-materiel missiles, 2S22 Bohdana, CAESAR, Archer Artillery System, 152mm SpGH DANA, 155 mm SpGH Zuzana wheeled self-propelled artillery howitzers, and 82 mm and 120 mm Soviet manufacture mortars. Yaroslav counted on the precious high-caliber shoulder-mounted weapons he had managed to procure: reloadable rocket RPG-7 launcher, shoulder-fired reload-portable recoilless rifle, and two Carl Gustaf 8.4 cm recoilless rifles.

His men were well trained and ready. Discipline in the Russian camp was lax; men were smoking, drinking beer and vodka, laughing, and talking. There were women present in a non-military capacity—to distract the men's attention, as the Ukrainian unit saw it. Yaroslav and his two chief *starshina* senior sergeants carefully plotted the position of every heavy Russian weapon, ammo dump, and the current concentration of tents.

In order to minimize noise, Yaroslav and one senior sergeant headed in different directions to convey the order of battle and its start time: 0130. The men all synchronized their watches and waited in the humid night air for the minutes and seconds to crawl by.

Yaroslav counted down: "ten, nine, eight, seven, six, five, four, three, two, one."

"Fire," he whispered into his coms.

Every weapon manned by every man answered his order. Rockets, grenades, artillery shells, and a mad minute of rifle fire, suddenly ripped open the sleeping night. The ammo dumps erupted like 2-ton bombs had landed in three separate positions. The camp became an inferno with tents, HQ buildings, tanks, troop carriers, and screaming men, being immolated. No one in the camp had the faintest idea where the attack had come from, and their return fire was so off course that hundreds of bullets were fired skyward, and more Russians died from friendly fire than Ukrainians ensconced in the bush behind their camp by 10:01.

A second Russian gun emplacement location met the same fate within minutes of the first. Both Ukraine units beat hasty retreats back away from the holocausts they had caused; and, in the confusion of the wounding, the flames, and the fog of war, no Ukrainian soldier was even wounded. It was a good start for a battle plan and an indicator of the value of the hard-nosed training, the Ukrainians had undergone in their preparations.

CHAPTER 7

Along the Kalmius River linking the Sea of Azov from the city of Donetsk DPR

September 22, 2016

The Sea of Azov lies 60 miles south of Donetsk and is both a major supply site for the city and a popular recreational area for its populace. The Kalmius River flows through Donetsk Oblast, Ukraine. Its source is in the Ukrainian city of Yasynuvata, and its mouth is in Mariupol. The Kalmius flows into the Sea of Azov near the Azovstal steel manufacturing complex in Mariupol. Both of those cities were under heavy Russian artillery barrages as Yaroslav and his unit set up a sabotage camp on its banks, two days after the first attack in the rear areas of Donetsk. The Kalmius is a fairly large river, located mainly on the plains. The average distance to the bottom is about six feet, but there are also deeper places. A large water artery that passes through several settlements and plays an important role in their economic life.

Given the nature of the river and the general antipathy for the Russian invaders by the Ukrainian people they held in thrall, the sabotage unit had several advantages. The river was shallow and many small to medium boats traversed in both directions. One more or less would not be noticed. The river and the haphazard structures along its lengthy serpentine route allowed for a gratifying number of safe havens and escape avenues. Many individuals among the populace were known for their willingness to assist the Ukrainian side, helping Yaroslav and his unit's clandestine activities to remain obscured.

There were three targets from among the many Russian invader strongholds: in Donetsk City, on the headwaters of the Kalmius River—a location which became progressively more important and more Russified after the collapse of the Soviet Union in 1991–pro-Russian protesters had occupied the Donetsk RSA [Regional State Administration] building [first two floors] in March. That was the principal objective for the saboteurs. By April 14, the Russophiles had taken control of government buildings in many other cities within the oblast, including Sloviansk, Mariupol, Horlivka, Kramatorsk, Yenakiive, Makiivka, Druzhkivka, and Zhdanivka.

In the Donetsk RSA, the militants also took over the municipal administration building unopposed two days later and the offices of the regional state television network the following day. Immediately after barging into the CEO's office, the Russophiles and Wagner Group senior officers assumed full control of the broadcasting center and began to transmit Russian television channels. Disrupting function by Russians in those two Donetsk buildings constituted the second and third primary targets.

Each target required different MOs of attack; so, Yaroslav divided his forces into three specialty units consisting of six men/women each. Women were particularly sought after by the SBU because they could take advantage of the general Russian disdain for women. They could flirt, entice, or sneak by the sentries, without detection because the young Russians did not consider women a threat–a discrimination ingrained in generations of boys and girls in the mother country–which would prove to be a serious tactical error when it came to espionage and war.

Ivan was assigned to lead his three men, three women, unit's sabotage on the RSA building; Davyd was to attack the municipal administration building—the most dangerous assignment—with his four men and two women. Grygoriy and his two men, three women unit was to render the television station completely inoperative for months to come.

For maintenance of security, Yaroslav huddled with Ivan first.

"The SBU theater group has provided us with appropriate outfits; so, you can blend in with the Russia lovers. Speak only Russia; everyone you meet in or around the building will be avoiding Ukrainian. The safe house with all the gear and weaponry is on this street address in Makiivka near the Donetsk Sergei Prokofiev International Airport. Memorize the street address and tear it to pieces and flush it before you leave here today."

Ivan nodded his understanding and assent.

"This is your objective in the RSA building."

He showed Ivan three photos taken secretly by SBU spies over the previous two weeks. The pictures detailed the first two floors as completely as it was possible to do.

"See the officer's toilet in the back of the room on the second floor by the space heater?"

"Yes, sir."

It is seldom used because there are few actual Russians in the building and still fewer officers. Russian officers are and arrogant bunch; they won't sit on the same toilet of a guy who was a peasant farmer a couple of weeks ago and disdains people who are former Ukrainians. Be careful with this set of thermite explosives. Put them in the toilet tank; set the timer; and get your tails out of there. You will have about five minutes. Try not to run. The thermite should destroy the second floor and the one above it and the one below it with an intense heat fire. The Donetsk SR records should be destroyed, and a lot of the traitorous collaborators incinerated. That should set the system back for a long time; and that is a good thing which makes this an important mission."

"We won't fail you, Yaroslav, or the country... no matter what."

"Get started with your setup. I will send a signal when all three setups are ready. We want to see simultaneous effects, ones that will ensure that we were here; and there was nothing they could do about it. Have Dayvd come in when you leave me."

Ivan gave Dayvd a nod, and he went into Yaroslav's impromptu office in the laundry room.

"Yes, sir," Dayvd said.

"Thanks for coming in and for your service, Dayvd. You are going to take on the Municipal Office Building, and it has high security. We have a mole in there who has left you an opening on the fourth floor. You will have a bunch of stuff to haul in, because we intend to remove the whole place and everyone in it from the Russian sphere. We wish them all the best when they get to hell," Yaroslav said with a grim face.

Dayvd was not much of a talker. He nodded.

"I want Olena Yuriivna and Eva Matveyevna to set up the explosives and for you, Leonid, Oleksiy, and Vasyl, to protect them and their setups with your very lives if it comes to it. Are you willing to take that on, Dayvd."

"Yes, sir," Dayvd replied without hesitation.

His willingness to take risks was the reason he was among Yaroslav's saboteurs, and why he had been given the heaviest and best weapons to do his job.

"Send in Grygoriy as soon as you get back to the room."

"So, Grygoriy, you ready for tomorrow?"

"Yes, sir, we are."

"Let's go over it on last time. You have the busiest mission, and the best people for it, Grygoriy. You are going to have to finalize and orchestrate the protest at the TV station as a diversion, and somehow get some bombs planted outside and on every floor of the building. You are going to have to kill as many of the traitors as you can find and get yourselves out of there and back to safety. That is your first priority… no dead heroes. Understand?"

"I do. It has been drummed into my head for five years that the agents are the most important assets and are more important than the missions themselves; so, we can live to fight another day."

"And no one who knows anyone assigned to you to be any part cowardice, my friend. But, no unnecessary chances."

"I understand the difference, Boss."

"You're a good man, Grygoriy."

"Where do you figure in all of this, Boss? I remind you about the 'no dead heroes' policy."

"I will be busy planting a pig on the Russkies and their toadies. I leave tonight—a long way to go and several cities to visit. But, I will be back with you and your agents tomorrow morning when we make our hellfire gift to our "dear friends.""

CHAPTER 8

Brief visits to Sloviansk, Mariupol, Horlivka, Kramatorsk, Yenakiieve, Makiivka, Druzhkivka, Druzhkivka, and Zhdanivka, in Donetsk Oblast

September 22-23, 2016

Yaroslav took three of his most trusted and effective agents on his whirlwind tour of the several targeted cities outside Donetsk proper. He could count on them to carry on with the least supervision and with the best people skills. He and his cohorts were going to have to ensure readiness of multiple "spontaneous" protests in the adjacent cities currently under Russian control. The men were Mykola, Volodymyr, Petro, and Pavlo. They were to function mainly as muscle and intimidation to show that the message and arrangements explained by the women agents—Rokosylana, Bipa, and Zoryana—were to be taken seriously. They had the imprimaturs of the highest ranking SBU and army brass in writing. He was going to arrange diversions for the drone bombings which were going to pepper the local Donetsk SR official buildings with a veritable firestorm of small bombs—a message to both the Russians and their lackeys.

He took his right arm in the unit–Irina Andrukhovych–who was a tough, seasoned, delicate looking, blond girl, whose looks belied her tough inner core and her deep—almost core—hatred of anything, any-one, and everything, Russian, stemming from the wanton rape and mur-ders of her family members four years earlier. Irina was the best pistol shot, best martial artist, and coldest killer in the squad, bar none. She had a peasant's look and a scholar's polymath brain. She would have his back.

They were closest to Mariupol; so, the two SBU agents went there first. Irina met with a contingent of loyal Ukrainian women at a pre-ar-ranged site—the Horosho Guest Villa on Flotskaya Street Brigantina, room 274. It was located in the rear of the main row of small villas and permitted entrance of personnel and vehicles in the alley behind the main thoroughfare Flotskaya Street. The determined, grim-faced women—looking older than their years—entered at different times and from different directions.

Irina wasted no time.

"Comrades, this is the outline of tomorrow's protest march against the Russian Federation Embassy. I will call Comrade Brushenka with the exact time, but please have all your people ready in hiding to pour out onto Brudzinski Street in front of the Russian consulate. I ask you now: how many of you are ready to face the Russian thugs when they come at you tomorrow?"

Put that way, the women faltered and stammered but all raised their hands in compliance and developed a new facial hardness that said more than words about their determination to stand up to the Russian threat.

Yaroslav had his own trial to contend with. He met the committee in charge of recruiting fighters against the phony Russian Donbass states, the Donetsk and Luhansk RSs. The chair of the committee raised a seri-ous question which might well determine the outcome of the planned firm stand against the Russian barbarians at the gates.

"Captain Yaroslav, I have but one question: when is the Ukraine government going to finance our militia, give us modern weapons, and guarantee aid when... not if... we engage the Russian army because we foolishly challenged the Kremlin to its face?"

"I give my personal guarantee that I will be here and that my SBU unit will come with me. The head of the SBU, Lt. Gen. Olena Yuriivna, solemnly promised to back any promise I make to any Ukrainian fighting unit. She has the arms of the Ukrainian oligarchs twisted. They either obey the law, contribute to the military, and pay their taxes, or they go to prison. I for one believe her. It is time to fight or at least get ready to do so. Which man here has the courage to stand up for his country and his family and pack a rifle? Raise your hands."

Every man in the room stood up, raised both hands, and shouted "Hooah!" copying the Americans with whom many had trained.

One recent American trainee shouted another Americanism, "It's time to fish or cut bait."

This experience was largely duplicated in every city Yaroslav and Irina entered that day and night. The people were ready to speak out and to shoulder a rifle. Yaroslav called acting SBU leader Yuriivna.

"Is this a secure line?" Yuriivna asked with her smoker's husky grumble.

"Yes, and it is urgent. I cannot talk long. My ID number is 2111VKM2017."

"Oh, Yaroslav, what's the problem?"

He quickly explained the needs of the local militia for military materiel very quickly for the imminent battle with the Russian backed Donetsk forces. She replied in the affirmative.

"It's a good place to start the action, Yaroslav. Are you ready?"

"Yes, General, my people are ready but few in number. The militia members are untested but seem to be fairly well organized and are tough. Anything they lack in experience will be made up by their courage and their unanimous hatred of all things Russian. We will fight as a guerilla action unit."

"Good plan, Yaroslav. I will send a plane load of weapons from Kyiv tonight. Pick it up at exactly 0200 at the secondary domestic airport. Do you know the place?"

"Yes."

"God speed then, young man. Remember to avoid becoming a hero."

"Understood."

The shipment was too crucial to entrust to anyone else; so, Yaroslav himself led the unit and their three trucks to the Zoryana Domestic Airport. It was 0130; they were half an hour early which gave them time to position the trucks and the dozens of battery-lit ground lights to guide the air force planes safely along the base leg to the unloading area. He positioned a dozen men along the flight lane to turn on each light individually when he got his first indication that the transports were coming in. The sentries silently roved the unit's perimeter to assure that no Russians or Russian collaborators were nearby.

One young Wagner Group private—fresh out of prison in Russia's central Mari El Republic—was on watch for the unimportant airport's security. He was bored, and he chanced to take a drag on his CJSC Donskoy Tabak—a Russian cigarette made located in Rostov-on-Don, Russia and moved across the porous border—a 500 mile trip on good highways–almost completely at will.

That was a fatal rookie mistake. He was silently taken out by one of the SBU sentries with a garrot.

The planes came in groups of five and obviously had been scraped up for the mission on an urgent—rather haphazard—basis: 5 1989 Tupolev Tu-204 medium-range narrow-body jet airliners, 5 Beriev Be-12 *Chayka* [Seagull], Soviet era turboprop-powered amphibious air-craft designed in the 1950s for anti-submarine and maritime patrol duties, 5 Mil Mi-26 Soviet/Russian heavy transport helicopters recently captured on the ground by SBU clandestine operatives, and 5 Mriya transports–the world's largest aircraft—all showing battle scars from the first days of the war. Every one of them had been packed with useful war materiel and fuel from the decks to the ceilings of their fuselages. There were no passengers.

The planes were all flying dirty—extendable surfaces [flaps down and landing gear out]—to be able to approach at high speed and land quickly without incident on the soft and short landing strip. The high groundspeed was noisy and created its own windstorm. All of that cre-ated tension for the pilots and crews, the SBU agents, and the volunteers signed on to transfer the military equipment before being discovered by their vicious enemies who did not understand anything about "rules of war" or the Geneva Convention.

Men and mules raced to move guns, ammo boxes, uniforms, gre-nades, and larger items as fast as possible in a controlled chaos. At his back, Yaroslav could always hear enemy engines closing in on them, even though there were none anywhere near at that time. They were busy hunting down SBU and Ukrainian infantry men elsewhere to kill, torture, and intimidate.

It took two full long hours to move everything to a makeshift improvised fleet of transport vehicles including a variety ranging from sports cars and donkey carts to milk trucks and 16-wheeler tractor-trailers. It did not look like a well-planned and orderly military transport mission; it was not one; but it had to serve as a temporary substitute, sufficient for the time being.

The planes were ready for a short fast takeoff as soon as the last box of grenades was carried out of the cargo area. They narrowly missed the entrance of the Donetsk militia.

As the last donkey cart disappeared into the to the verdant forests over the Donets Ridge along the course of the Donets river in the approaching pre-dawn, Yaroslav could hear the heavy rumble of Soviet trucks moving ponderously onto the grassy airfield of the Zoryana Domestic Airport. It seemed to him that he held his breath until they reached their dropoff depot for the new equipment deep in the Carpathian Mountains.

CHAPTER 9

Hot engagement: Chernivtsi, Ukrainian Carpathian Mountains

September 26, 2016

Yaroslav spent a feverish day and a half obtaining the plane load of armaments at the airfield in middle of the night and training the militia in their use for the rest of the day. His SBU unit barely had time to organize the local citizens to throw up makeshift Parisian type barricades of the 1500s and 1800s along the narrow city streets of Chernivtsi and to hide themselves in reasonably secure firing positions before the Russian army led Donetsk "volunteers" invaded the city in force. So much for this being a local Ukraine uprising.

Under Yaroslav's direction, a feverish effort led to the construction of street barri-cades which were little more than a tangle of old furniture, dilapidated cars and trucks, bedsteads, whiskey barrels, and truckloads of debris trucked back into the city from the junk yards and trash piles. Yaroslav and his men and the city volunteers knew the barri-cades were no match for the Russian tanks, but no one seemed particularly distressed.

WWI and WW II sappers, and local construction companies, lent their muscle, time, energy, and equipment, to dig trenches, hidden fox holes, and large excavations covered with sheeting and layers of trash that turned Chernivtsi into a down-at-the-heels appearing decrepit old city suffering from a particularly failing economy. It was altogether similar to how Chernivtsi had looked after the Axis forces evacuated the bombed-out wreckage of their city in 1945. Bad memories to be erased drove the townspeople to a fever pitch to create a Potemkin Village in reverse for the benefit of the expected invaders.

It was a cloudy day with dark clouds obscuring the sunset and hastening the onset of darkness. The Donetsk SR mercenaries and their Russian regular army partners began moving down the approaches to the city from the Carpathian Mountains. The city itself lies almost 820 feet below sea level, and the Russians had the advantage of coming in from the heights. Long columns of MSV 113 FSV Russian armored troop carriers and WW II T-24 tanks, old Soviet/Ukrainian tanks, truck pulled howitzers, and converted ZSU SPAAG 1945 anti-aircraft gun carriers to machine guns mounted in the backs of the vintage Soviet vehicles, approached the center of the city, finding the periphery devoid of people.

A month previously, Russia's armed forces had around 3,800 armored vehicles stored at its Vagzhanovo depot in Russia's Siberian republic of Buryatia and had taken about 40% of them out of mothballs in a frantic hurry. Behind the armor marched two-thousand Russian and Donetsk SR troops, the latter in an assortment of uniforms and other clothing and carrying an even more haphazard collection of weapons—some not even guns.

The first armored troop carriers entered the main square before the tromping jack boots of the fighters began to be audible and to strike terror into the minds of the towns-people whose last experience with war had been seventy years previously. Yaroslav and his SBU agents were nowhere to be seen. Nor were any fighters visible anywhere, just worried and frightened older people standing around in disconsolate capitulation. None of them had any kind of weapon.

Mark Dmitriyovich Bezrodny, newly appointed *Generál-mayór/* Major General of the Donbas *Gruppa Vagnera/*PMC Wagner Group–a Russian state-funded private military company was in battlefield command on that dangerous day by virtue of his ascendancy to be head of the recently refurbished Donetsk National Guard. Bezrodny was facing a test of his loyalty to the Russian State and to self-appointed Colonel General Anatolievich Baranov—who was in all aspects of the Russian war with Ukraine, the commander, presently from Moscow—personally, as well as regarding his military capability. He smiled at his 2nd in Command, Polkóvnik/Colonel Maksim Mikhailovich Gavrilenkov whom he trusted as much as Baranov trusted him. This was their chance for rapid advancement, and both men were well-aware of that fact.

"Maksim, let's make a show of it. Bring up the marching band, the drum corps, and the cavalry to march in head of the armor with the infantry bringing up the rear. Do not fire unless provoked; you be the judge of that and include disloyal utterances and gestures, any show of a firearm, or military uniform, or anyone who fails to obey an order with the necessary speed."

"Yes, Comrade General. This dumpy little mountain town will be a part of the Donetsk SR by midday or my name is not Maksim."

He gave his commander a particularly stiff and formal salute and ordered his vehicle driver to move to the front of the assembled Donetsk militia. He barked orders to his adjunct to make all haste to get the band and drum corps to the front and ready to play with full gusto and to send the commander of the cavalry to him for orders.

The unit was not as polished and efficient as Polkóvnik Mikhailovich might have hoped for; so, the assembling took an awkward forty-five minutes and did not form up neatly. The fact that there was a diversity of uniforms did not help, either; but that was not Maksim's fault. Bezrodny could surely be expected to show a little leniency, this being the militia's first time to fight together. What they lacked in décor, he was confident they would make for in courage and their love of fighting.

Colonel of Cavalry Ivan Verenich had been difficult to locate; so, he was half an hour late in presenting himself and his loosely organized cavalrymen and their horses which did not form up at all well, having had no training in the refinements of military formation.

"Glad you could make it, Colonel," Maksim said sarcastically. "Better never than late, as we always say."

Chapter 9: Hot engagement: Chernivtsi, Ukrainian Carpathian Mountains

"My apologies, Senior Colonel, but you are well aware that this is very short notice. Let my men get a battle under their belts, and I assure you that they will become a sharp unit the Russian army can be proud of."

"Better hope so, for both our sakes, Ivan. We are under scrutiny as you well know. Let's move the units out."

Col. Gavrilenkov issued the orders, and the mercenary militia moved forward with something short of precision and the level of speed he would have liked to have seen.

Yaroslav had chosen a mountainside hideaway with an excellent view of the entire town. He had a map on his lap which showed the location of every squad he had placed. He was pleased that he could not see a single one of his soldiers and kept telling himself that it was not because they had all deserted.

He sent out a general order over his coms:

"Two clicks if you are ready and in place. Respond in order of your assigned numbers."

A series of double clicks came in at ten second intervals in good order. They were ready.

"Good work. Keep full silence. The Russians and their stooges are beginning to move at long last. Let them get into position before launching your attacks."

He hoped for one further thing: that the Russians would choose to begin firing on some feeble pretext which would allow him and his men the moral high ground. Whether or not they did fire first, he had to give the order to any position when the Donetsks made themselves into an inviting target. He was not there in Chernivtsi to make friends with Germans, nor was he overly concerned about his reputation for keeping to the moral high ground. This was war.

The Wagner Group began to pick up speed and to be something of a semblance of an orderly military marching unit. There were itchy trigger fingers all around, but no one had made the first hostile move yet.

The Wagner Group band was playing *The State Anthem of the Russian Federa-tion* which uses the same melody as the *State Anthem of the Soviet Union*. It was intended to grate on the sensibilities of the Ukrainian population of the city of Chernivtsi which was being invaded, and it did. An old soldier in his WW II uniform displayed something he had learned from the yanks. Without giving a moment of thought, he flipped the bird at the nearest sentry guarding the orchestra.

That sentry reacted automatically and fired a full magazine of his Ak-47 into the assembled crowd of old people and children.

Yaroslav immediately gave the order to position one to "Fire at will!"

It was as if seed pods of soldiers suddenly hatched from the fertile earth. Rifles bristled, grenades flew from seemingly everywhere, and men and women took the one knee firing position behind any possible personal physical barrier. A-K 47 soprano/staccato fire came from behind the Drama Theater and the Organic and Chamber Music Hall; shotguns belched 00 rounds at nearby Russians and Separatists from the cover of basement stairwells; bazooka fire and antitank rounds flew at their targets from the puppet-theater, the Museum of Local Lore, and the Museum of Fine Arts.

The Separatists—facing their first experience in combat—began to break ranks and to run toward anything that resembled cover from the deadly crossfire. Some made it to the Star Alley in Teatralna Square and were cut down like so much ripe wheat by automatic rifle bullets. Unlikely looking Byzantine era buildings became traps for fleeing hysterical weekend warriors who threw down their guns, brooms, rakes; and some unarmed men and women simply fell to the ground, put their cupped hands over their ears and waited for death.

Seasoned Russian sergeants shot many deserters in the back for lack of better targets among the populace of the city. Junior Russian officers deserted by knocking cavalry-men from their horses and escaping by going up the roadway from which they had so recently entered in pomp and ceremony to the arrogant sound of drums. A major shot to death a private from the army news corps who was dutifully filming the debacle. It was a bloodbath and a humiliating debacle.

Over the noise and fog of war that had descended upon the city, Yaroslav yelled over his coms for his intelligence officers to get control of the friendlies and to push them into the roiling cauldron of a city to finish the job in a way that would be an unforgettable message to the haughty Russians all the way back to Moscow and St. Petersburg. Once ignited, the SBU troops, the old WWI and II soldiers, women who had been raped, even children who had seen their parents murdered, took up any weapon they could find—including Russian arms lying around on the ground useless to their owners, and set about to complete the victory and to ensure a lasting message of revenge.

Wagner Group soldiers abandoned the scene in all haste and headed back deep into the Donbas to regroup and to wait for another day to bring the Ukrainians to heel.

CHAPTER 10

Mariupol, Ukraine

September 28, 2016

T he military unit that attacked Mariupol two days later consisted of a larger percentage of real soldiers, about half of whom had seen previous combat. A third were hardened criminals released from Russian prisons with the promise of pardons if they performed well in combat. Most of them are well armed. The rest were nothing more than conscripts who had been prevented from fleeing from the Donblast and from Russia proper. Their rifles had never been out of the wooden crates. No one seemed to know where the ammunition was stored or which bullet was to be used in which rifle. They were largely farm boys, spoiled university students, and *krutoy chuvaks* [cool dudes snatched away from Moscow night clubs, university dorms and dance halls, and street protests]. Unlike their "comrades-in-arms", the convicts and few real soldiers, the *krutoy chuvaks* scarcely knew which part of a gun to point at an opponent and nothing about how to insert ammunition.

The attack came as no surprise to Yaroslav and his intelligence unit. Russians traveling in Soviet military transports; soldiers marching goose step for mile after exhausting mile; medium range artillery—some from as far back as pre WWII 37 mm anti-tank guns M1930 (1-K), others as new and modern as Skoda 220 mm siege howitzers but none as modern as 152 mm howitzers, RPGs, or missiles. Apparently, the Mother Country was saving those and other more modern armaments for its own forces and for a later date. The government and military of the Russian Federation was all but certain that its surrogates in the newly hatched Russian republics could handle the problem with only a little help from the *Rodin* [Motherland].

As they had done in the Second World War, the army—little changed from three-quarters of a century before—marched with no attempt to conceal its movements and with a decided effort to make as much noise as possible—in order to strike fear into any watching enemies. It worked. The patriotic Ukrainians were almost paralyzed by fear. Too many of them remembered the Red Army Bolsheviks invading their country in December, 1918, the Nazi Wehrmacht stream into their country on June 22, 1941, and then the Soviets again in 1944. No one watching the Russian military march through Ukrainian territory as if it were their own, dared hope. Vladimir Rasputinov's invasion and annexation of the Crimean Peninsula in March, 2014 with hardly a mention by the world powers or even the government of Ukraine, had rested a chill on the entire population of Ukraine.

Yaroslav and his brotherhood of spies watched as the Russian battle force inched slowly toward Mariupol with both military and civilian trucks hauling men, ammunition shells, and missiles toward the seaside launching platforms on the loading docks.

Michail said, "Yaroslav, they are slowing down. Looks like they are stalling. Want to attack?"

"Yes, but wait until they are more bogged down. Then, let's do a set of lightening strikes on every third or fourth vehicle; so, they have to stall to get the injured vehicle going again or dragged out of the way."

The two leaders and their unit of handpicked commando subordinates watched with educated eyes as the Russian advance ground to a halt, motors expending scarce fuel as they idled. It became apparent that Russian planning was bad, and her execution was worse. The efforts of the Separatist lackies were worse still. The roads were muddy and rutted, and the large trucks and heavy tanks and artillery were grinding the wet gravel and dirt into a deep, slick, quagmire.

Several of the big military grade trucks were being sidelined because their tires had flattened and made going in any direction very difficult, even hazardous. A flat on one side had led to two of the trucks tipping over in the direction of the flat.

Yaroslav said to Mikhail, "think about modern warfare and its soldiers, trucks, tanks, and artillery—all heavy and difficult to move about from one place to another. The most important of these is something on which they all rely: the humble truck. Armies need trucks to transport their soldiers to the front lines, to supply those tanks with shells, and to deliver those missiles. In short, any army that neglects its trucks does so at its peril.

"Russians have never learned how to take care of the details. They have a seemingly inexhaustible and cheap supply of manpower that they have always considered to be expendable. That slovenly way of thinking about the war machine is what we are looking at right now. Our photographs of damaged Russian trucks show tell-tale signs of Moscow's logistical struggles, and failures. They tell us that Russia's efforts are undermined by its reliance on conscripts—often forced–widespread corruption and use of civilian vehicles, and the relatively huge distances involved in resupplying its forces. And that is not even to give credit to us. Everyone in the Ukraine resistance forces is highly-motivated and tactically adept.

"Look, my friend, everything an army needs to do its thing comes by use of a truck." He took his eyes away from his binoculars and pointed. "I have been checking the huge pile of photos since we first started fighting the Russkies. I have checked out every clue available about to how our war is going. I am convinced that the real weapon isn't the tank, it's the shell the tank fires, and that shell travels by a truck. Food, fuel, medical supplies, and even the soldiers themselves, depend on logistical supply lines heavily reliant on trucks.

"Look closely and you will easily see the problem of that supply line."

His index finger pointed at a Russian military truck with the letter 'Z', a symbol of its invasion of Ukraine which was broken down in the middle of the military column. Men were working frantically to remove the large rear tire. Even at some distance away, the two intelligence officers could see that the tire was battered and torn. A group of eight or ten soldiers were heaving and straining to lift the rear end of the heavy truck.

"See that. They don't have a jack."

Mikhail said, laughing, "For the want of a nail, the shoe was lost…"

And Yaroslav went on, "For the want of the shoe, the horse was lost…"

Three vehicles behind the one with the flat tire, they could see tire damage in three wheels on a multimillion-dollar mobile missile truck–a Pantsir S1.

"I'm telling you, Mikhail, that is the canary in the coal mine for Russia's logistical efforts. He paused to wipe the dust off his binocular lenses. "For such an expensive piece of equipment, you would expect its maintenance to be first-rate. Yet here it sits, blocking traffic like four of five other trucks up and down the line, its tires already crumbling just a few weeks into the war. I'm telling you, the Big Bear is mired in what I would call, 'a failure mode'."

Mikhail finished Yaroslav's thought, "If trucks are not moved frequently the rubber in their tires becomes brittle and the tire walls become vulnerable to cracks and tears. When tires are run with low inflation to cope with the sort of muddy conditions we're facing in the Ukrainian spring, they break down after something like 100 miles of travel."

"The condition of the Pantsir S1 is a revealing mistake—part of the 'failure mode'. I have heard Russian bosses, even Rasputinov, talking about their strategy of attrition… I remember a famous quote by the US General Omar Bradley, 'Amateurs talk strategy, professionals talk logistics.'"

Mikhail raised one questioning eyebrow.

"Yeah, Major, I agree. It is time to make use of the logistical error we see going on before our very eyes. Get the men and equipment ready. I'll scout out a safe route down to their column. It'll be dark pretty soon. We'll get set up before dusk and launch our countermeasures before full darkness."

Sometimes walking; sometimes duck walking; and sometimes crawling; the well-trained young men of Yaroslav's command silently inched their way down the sides of the ravine until they were able to set up by each of six large expensive vehicles—tanks, personnel carriers, pick-ups, and ammo trucks. Yaroslav tested his coms. A clear response came back from each position along the line.

"On my zero count, blow them to hell," Lt. Col. Yaroslav (a temporary rank pending parliamentary vote awarded Yaroslav as a battle promotion by his very pleased colonel) said. The only sounds other than his men's own breathing were that of metal-on-metal clanging as repairs moved along slowly in the dimming light.

"Three... Two... One... Fire." Yaroslav said into his shoulder mic as a stage whisper.

For the better part of a mile, five explosions, brilliant white fires, and the terrible screaming of the wounded men opened up the night. Up and down the Russian line, all was chaos and confusion.

Without further orders, every man and every piece of equipment disappeared from the positions along the roadside. It took half an hour for the unit to regroup.

"All accounted for. No casualties. Head out for the first dock in Mariupol port. Follow me. Every now and again touch the shoulder of the man ahead of you. Mute mics, no smoking, no talking. Secure metal parts; so, there is no clanking to give us away. Let's go."

Yaroslav and Mikhail led the way along a sheep trail putting distance between the unit and the Russian column at the rate of three miles per hour, even in the dark.

CHAPTER 11

Mariupol, Ukraine, early morning
September 29, 2016

Yaroslav and his intelligence team considered Mariupol to be a major strategic city—the largest on the Sea of Azov–and therefore a target for Russian forces to expend considerable manpower, lives, and treasure, to overtake it. It was the largest city in the Ukrainian-controlled portion of Donetsk Oblast and was also one of the largest Russian-speaking cities in all of Ukraine, making it all the more desirable for the Russian federation to annex.

Rasputinov used the old Hitlerian-type excuse that it was actually a Russian city which should revert back to the Rodina. Mariupol was a major industrial hub, home of the Illich and Azovstal Iron and Steel Works. Control of its port on the western shore of the Sea of Azov was vital to the economy of Ukraine. For Russia, it would allow a land route to Occupied Crimea and allow passage by Russian marine traffic. Capturing the city gave Russia full control over the Sea of Azov. The Ukrainian SBU agents were certain that Mariupol would be far harder to protect than any other city in Ukraine they had worked in up to that time.

In part—due to the Ukrainian unit's efforts—the Russian and DPR [Donetsk Peoples Republic] armed forces column marching toward

Mariupol was delayed, probably for weeks until spring breakup cleared and drier weather hardened up the roads. The intelligence team had one fairly major ally in the city, one with a major drawback. Prior to invasion by Russian forces, the city was defended by the Ukrainian Ground Forces, the Ukrainian Naval Infantry, the Territorial Defense Forces of Ukraine, and irregular forces the National Guard of Ukraine–primarily the Azov Regiment. One of the most instrumental groups for defense of Mariupol was the Azov Battalion, a Ukrainian volunteer militia, controversial for its openly ultra-nationalist, NeoNazi, and Nazi, members. By October, Azov was integrated into the National Guard of Ukraine, with Mariupol as its headquarters.

The city was largely and traditionally Russophone, while ethnically the population is divided about evenly between Russians and Ukrainians. Since one of Vladimir Rasputinov's stated goals for the invasion was the "denazification" of Ukraine, Mariupol represented an important ideological and symbolical target for the Russian forces. Yaroslav fretted about how much of an ally the Azov Battalion was, and whether it may even be another extremist enemy to cope with.

He remembered the old Russian proverb *Кто ложится спать с собаками, встаёт с блохами.* [He who sleeps with dogs, wakes up with fleas]. That certainly seemed to be one of the major outcomes that would occur with any kind of partnership.

The long straggling column moved with glacial celerity from the DPR toward Mariupol. No Russian heavy armor or artillery presented itself in the south of the Donetsk Oblast, or on the coast of Sea of Azov for three weeks giving the citizens of Mariupol enough time to set up perimeter defenses, to bring in large supplies of food, water, fuel, guns, and ammunition.

Every building of any consequence had a protective shield of men and women ready to fight to the death for their city, for their country, and for their hard-won democracy. Morale was high. By a mayoral decree, 100,000 noncombatant citizens fled out of the city to the countryside and to distant cities; some leaving Ukraine forever. There was scarcely a woman or a child left to be seen in the city.

With a figurative finger on its pulse, the city waited for the Beast to arrive in force. Before the attack, Mariupol was the country's 10th largest city, with a population of more than 430,000. It was a bustling modern metropolis filled with arts and culture. Mariupol was a center for industry, hence a prime target for the Russians and their surrogates, the DPR. It was a handsome metropolis and a vibrant center of higher education and business.

Its downside came from the pollution generated by the factories. During the mid-twenties, pollutant concentrations from the state's industrial activity regularly exceeded maximum pollution limits: 1.3 times for ammonia; 1.3 times for phenol; and 2.0 times for formal-de-hyde. Wind intensity and the city's geographical flatness offer some relief from the accum-ulation of long-standing pollutants, somewhat easing the problem. But, gaining control of pollution remained a major problem for the city and its government.

Yaroslav and his men returned to the city to report to the mayor and local military authorities about the progress being made by the extremely long centipede of avaricious and violent attackers. They met in the club house of Park Veselka situated among sets of playground swings on the lovely tree-lined residential area. They had travelled freely to the easy-to-find address, Peremohy Avenue, 58.

The wives of the city government men had prepared an elaborate lunch featuring their best efforts to create a festive atmosphere amidst the gathering gloom. Despite the anxiety surrounding the impending fight, their traditional dishes had undergone a complex and time-con-suming heating process; first fried or boiled, and then stewed or baked—the most distinctive feature of Ukrainian cuisine. The assembled officials and guests avoided talk of war, tactics, the brutish enemy, and how to keep themselves and their children alive, during the meal.

The national dish of Ukraine is red *borscht* [many varieties of beet soup], and the small park building was crowded with half a dozen boiling cauldrons and pots of cold borscht which was the favorite taste of day, both for its culinary value and its symbolism of a persevering Ukraine. Other wives had created *varenyky* [boiled dumplings similar to *pierogi*], *holubtsi* [cabbage roll], and ancient peasant dishes based on plentiful grain resources such as rye, as well as staple vegetables including potato, cabbages, mushrooms and beetroots. Ukrainian dishes incorporate both traditional Slavic techniques. It was the best meal the intelligence unit had enjoyed in months.

Yaroslav was touched by the island of civility and decency in the sea of gathering horror; but time was short; and he and his men had to push the civilians to hurry the meal; so, they could convey their message and instructions.

"The Cabinet of Ministers of Ukraine and the SBU have instructed us to tell you about the need for specific and urgent planning for your city. Our unit has been studying the approaching column of militants along highway 14 from the east for weeks. The weather is letting up, and they are beginning to make better progress. It will take them two or three weeks to gather in the outskirts of the city and to set up their plans for the attack in force. First, they will create a perimeter blockade to try and starve you out, then, they will begin an artillery fusillade, as Russian militaries always do.

"Our instructions, therefore, are that you move with all haste. First, evacuate all women, children, and the aged, away from Mariupol on west 14, north 20, and northwest through Azov toward Volodarskoye. They must begin today, and they can only take what they can carry. People are more important than things. Remove all city records and treasures to hiding places beyond the city.

"Muster all the men over the age of 14 and set them up as the last ditches of defense around important buildings and defensive positions. Arm them as best you can and have them bring their own guns and ammunition as much as possible. We will help you with that, but our time is short. We must get back to the column and do as much damage as possible as they move toward Mariupol.

"Gather every weapon of offense and defense available to you and bring them to these five locations which we think will be the primary targets of the invaders. In addition, collect and hide out of sight as much water and food as you can possibly find in the next couple of weeks. Start food rationing now.

"Keep all doctors and nurses in the city; defend the hospitals at all cost; gather and protect medical supplies. You are going to need every bit of them.

"And, here is the worst order: check your records and divide the population into those who are pro-Ukraine and those who are pro-Russia or separation. Clear out several large apartment buildings and move the anti-Ukraine people into them. Use force if necessary. If anyone presents active resistance, presume they are combatants and shoot them. You won't have time to lock them up and feed them. Allow any of them who want to go east to do so. They are of no use to the city and may be of considerable threat.

"Any questions?"

The listening men were solemn faced and tight lipped to the point of taciturnity. There was sadness at the realization that the young man's orders were the only way to survival. They were going to have to do things that a day ago would have been unthinkable, even Nazi-like. For the first time, the men had to come face-to-face with the reality that shortly they were going to enter a primeval world of kill-or-be-killed. Obedience had to be full and earnest. The young man's requirements were existential for the Mariupolians. No one needed to ask a question; they knew what they had to do.

CHAPTER 12

Mariupol, Ukraine

October 22, 2016

The ugly centipede of men, dray horses and mules, and towed instruments of mass destruction, made better time on the drying road. Highway 14 was at long last living up to its name. The cumbersome column made only about two-three miles per day during break-up; but now, they were weaving along at ten-fifteen miles a day—decidedly less than swift; but it was progress at last, for the determined Red Army and the militias of the DPR. During the slow-forward moving time, they were hindered further by having to extract food and other supplies from a determined local populace to resist. They had to murder peasants and their families and to dispose of the corpses to avoid bad public relations videos getting out to the watching public. It was time consuming. They were creating a minor scorched earth corridor along the highway as they moved forward. Videos were getting out about that, but this was war after all and could not be helped.

The men in the column were forbidden to talk about the worst source of delay in their progress—that of sabotage and frightening lethal attacks by partisans. Those saboteurs/assassins were led by Lt. Col. Yaroslav Kandybavych Melnykenko and his now 42-man commando unit, the best equipped in the Ukrainian ground forces. They were terrorists in the most literal sense of the word. Their almost daily sporadic attacks on the line truly struck terror into the minds and hearts of the marching would-be conquering heroes.

Yaroslav had studied the US Phoenix Program extensively and employed many of those hunter/killers' practice. Here and there along the way, they hung crucified corpses, put mutilated bodies in what were interpreted as Satanic ritual tableaus by the superstitious young peasants, farmers, factory workers, and freed convicts. The most effective of those tactics was to drain the blood from a dead Russian and hang the bodies along the tree-lined route. None of the DPR/regular Russian soldiers was objective enough to believe the officers' explanation that those bodies were not the victims of vampires, one of the great bugaboos of Russia.

When the centipede reached the halfway point in its journey to Mariupol and was well west in the oblast, Yaroslav and his marauders set to work on the actual performance of war–at least clandestine war. Here a bomb, there an ambush of a straggling unit, then a solitary surprise killing or two with no attempt to take or hold ground, and disappear into the night like so much smoke. The evidence of their success was in the temporary forward pauses by entire miles of the long centipede of Russian invaders.

By October 22, the vanguard of VSRF [armed forces of the Russian federation] brigade troops made its stand in the Donetsk Oblast and aimed all guns at the heart and port of the Mariupol. Serious damage was done over the next three days to the Azovstal steel plant, the Donetsk Regional Drama Theater, a few blocks north of the Sea of Azov in the city's center with its striking red roof, to houses along Peace Avenue, and residential buildings on the corner of Shevchenko Boulevard and Kuprina Street. Budivel'nykiv Avenue in central Mariupol.

The Kyivstar Building was on Russian General Sorbon Khayyomnovitch Dzhuraev [a rising star from Tajikistan]'s key target list. The building on Budivel'nykiv Avenue in central Mariupol was not particularly imposing. The seven-story gray sided office structure–a mobile and internet service provider–stood between a Greek cultural center to the left and a nightclub with a bowling alley to the right. Its most prominent feature was a large white and orange Kyivstar logo above the entrance—a typical corporate facade. Although unimposing, it was one of the most important buildings in southeast Ukraine. Physically, it was almost completely destroyed in the initial bombardment and entirely destroyed in its function.

Yaroslav, his SBU fighters, and Mayor Oleksander Mykytavitch Domitrovich and his partisans, had not been sitting idly by as the massively destructive barbarians broke through the gates of the city.

As they watched the Kyivstar Building crumble, Mayor Domitrovich asked Yaroslav, "Is it time to unleash the partisans… before there is no more Mariupol left, my friend?"

"It is. Their anger will drive them on, and that is exactly what we need. Give the signal, Oleksander."

Both men radio contacted their lieutenants and separated from each other to start the counteroffensive. To the astonishment of Russian General Dzhuraev and DPR Lt. Col. Tkachenko, and the unfeigned horror of their exhausted men, a vast horde of warriors seemingly rose from the ground, climbed out of the windows of buildings, dropped from trees, and came flocking out of tunnels. On close inspection, some of those new warriors were armed only with farm implements and household tools. All the invaders saw was the enemy warriors of Armageddon.

CHAPTER 13

Mariupol, Ukraine

October 22, 2016, midafternoon

The Russian and DPR vanguard attackers were surrounded and cut off from the rest of the centipede of invaders behind them within minutes of the appearance of the Mariupol defender hordes. The noise was deafening and paralyzing. Russian artillery, rockets, and missiles, stopped firing. DPR units began to break up and run. Russian officers shot many of the deserters in the back, screaming *"Трус! Трус!"* [= *Trus*! *Trus*!, Eng. Coward! Coward!] But when their front lines began to crumble, many of those officers commandeered troop carriers and Mercedes Benz automobiles they had appropriated during the centipede's crawl toward its victim Mariupol. They also deserted.

Mayor Domitrovich led his partisans from the front, zig-zagging, ducking, and taking cover, but all the while pulling his enraged fellow citizens ever closer to the now frightened and largely leaderless military unit which was rapidly turning into a mob. And the mob was beginning to disintegrate.

Yaroslav and his commandoes took every advantage afforded by the chaos and developing panic. His snipers were taking out the officers and senior noncoms right and left; booby traps caught stragglers running into the inner-city streets; and groups who began to see a pathway out of the now impenetrable city were met by previously hidden machine gunners and riflemen. Sometimes, the lot of others was even worse; they encountered women armed with crude, cruel weapons, and pent up rage. In forensics, there is a finding in murder cases that includes excessive, rapidly administrated, and horrifying quality wounding even to hardened medical examiners. The city streets became littered with corpses that scarcely looked human. And the red-eyed, screaming mothers, daughters, sisters, aunts, and grandmothers, presented a Stygian scene that unhinged even the best of soldiers.

The Russo-Donetsk force of disciplined attackers became an unnerved and frenzied pack of terrified men with no military discipline left. They ran pall mall from the city leaving behind all the sophisticated weaponry, their own small arms, swords, uniforms, and dignity. The shortest route away from Mariupol was back the way they had entered the unfortunate city—along Highway 14 headed east toward the Russian border. Their progress was far faster than their rate of passage west had been. They had a further incentive of significance: Enraged citizens led by Oleksander Mykytavitch and a loosely disorganized—but equally determined and effective band of women.

The hindermost of the Russo-Donetsk force withered away from the shelling of the SBU commandoes and Mayor Domitrovich's partially trained and inspired masculine citizens and wanton hacking and clubbing of the women. Thus spurred on, the previously ponderous and slow moving attack centipede began to involute and disintegrate upon itself more and more rapidly. Russians and Donetsks began trampling their fellows in their haste to escape. When the local Mariupol citizens began to run out of breath about two miles east of town, they found it unnecessary to continue the chase. The panic and chaos had taken full control.

The well-planned siege attack and destruction of Mariupol became—for the Russian army and the Donetsk puppets—a defeat that was expunged from all written works and forbidden to be mentioned on news media in the Rodina. Something near normal settled back onto Mariupol with time. Mayor Oleksander Mykytavitch Domitrovich was re-elected to his office by a nearly unanimous vote in the next election. Lt. Col. Yaroslav Kandybavych Melnykenko and the SBU commando force was in northern Donbass by then.

CHAPTER 14

Ukrainian positions at
Troitske and Luhanske, Donbass

February 22, 2018

Pro-Russian forces launched attacks on 20 occasions during Thursday, February 22, 2018—some in each of the illegally annexed regions: Donetsk, Kherson, Luhansk, and Zaporizhzhia. The majority were in the Luhansk region. Ukrainian forces responded 17 times. Col. Yaroslav's SBU unit accounted for 12 of that total and was acknowledged grudgingly by both sides to have been responsible for the lions' share of the damage inflicted against the DPR or DNR, and LPR or LNR, [collectively the Donbass]. That was despite Yaroslav's emphatic effort for his unit and himself to remain anonymous and in the shadows.

Most incidents took place within the area of Svitlodarsk dam, part of the northern front; and that is where Yaroslav maintained his main base—a highly mobile one. The dam region received intense fire from infantry weapons, 82 mm mortars and 120 mm mortars. Pro-Russian armored vehicles engaged Ukrainian redoubts around the dam. The final hours of the Svitlodarsk dam battles were fought by entrenched pro-Russian forces trying to fend off a very determined guerrilla group. The attacks were sporadic, impossible to predict or contain; and then the guerrillas evaporated into the fog, gloom of dusk, and acrid smoke, of the battle.

Even with the sporadic successes by his SBU unit, Yaroslav could see that he and the pro-Russians were settling into a sort of escalating stalemate, which reminded him of his studies of the American experience in fighting the elusive North Vietnamese almost half a century earlier.

He consulted with his second-in-command, *Bunchuzhnyi* [company first sergeant] Rokosylana Mykolaivna Udovychenko. "We're not getting much done sitting around in the trenches, Rokosylana Mykolaivna. The regular army is designed and prepared for that. We need to keep moving. I want your suggestions."

She responded in her usual well-thought-out laconic fashion, "Yaroslav, what if we took time to study out a way to attack the Kerch Straits Bridge. That would get their attention."

"Wouldn't it though?" he laughed. "And it is just so audacious that we might be able to pull it off. You're so smart, I should recommend you to lead your own unit; but I am selfish; and I am not going to do that. I need you too much."

"Ah, Boss...," she blushed.

"I mean it. In fact, why don't you work up a plan; and let's see what the logistics will be."

While the rest of Yaroslav's unit settled into the World War I unproductive trench warfare—complete with invasions of mice and rats in such numbers that the unit's several cats were overwhelmed—occasionally sneaking out to inflict a bit of damage on the enemy and to counter such attacks against their side.

Rokosylana was nothing if not dogged. She learned everything there was to know about the bridge. The Crimean Bridge [romanized: *Krymskiy most/ krimskʲije most,* or Kerch Strait Bridge or Kerch Bridge], was a double structure, parallel bridge–one for a modern paved four-lane highway and one for a double-track railway. It spans the Kerch Strait between the Taman Peninsula of Krasnodar Krai in Russia and the Kerch Peninsula of Crimea. It was built by the Russian Federation after the illegal annexation of Crimea in 2014. The bridge cost $3.7 billion USD and is twelve miles long, making it the longest bridge in

Europe. Needless to say, its security measures were easily the equivalent of the US Fort Knox.

The bridge is a pivotal symbol of Russia's annexation of Crimea, and by association something of a legitimization of Vladimir Rasputinov's war perpetrated against Ukraine and its people. Rasputinov describes it as a "strictly civilian thoroughfare for light traffic", with is another lie. In fact, it is a major military conduit between Crimea and the Russian territory.

Rokosylana Mykolaivna had no trouble finding useful data on their potential target. Construction began in spring, 1944 shortly after the liberation of Crimea from the Nazis by the Red Army. Materials left from an unbuilt bridge of the occupying German forces were used by the Soviets in the construction of their bridge. While construction was still incomplete in December, the winds and ice of a particularly cruel winter halted construction. By that time only part of the protective stark-waters were completed; and in February, 1945, ice again severely damaged the bridge, destroying the bridge pillars. For a long period thereafter, the injury was considered to be fatal. In March, 1945, ice destroyed 46 pillars and 53 spans. 1016 pillars out of 2357 were severely damaged. Attempts to weaken the ice by artillery and ground-based ice blasting were ineffective, and aerial bombing of ice was impossible due to very bad weather. Icebreakers were also unable to reach the bridge.

The records of the construction engineers revealed that the bridge used piles up to 98 feet long; the bridge was 2.8 miles long and 9.8 feet wide; it had 111 ninety foot-long ordinary spans, two movable 89 foot-long spans and two movable 180 foot-long spans. The movable spans were of a swing bridge design, rotating horizontally over two adjacent navigable shipping lanes in the strait.

The bridge idea hibernated for decades; it did not become a reality or even go beyond proposals. But finally, in February and March 2014, Russia annexed Crimea amidst international dismay and a universal failure to recognize the annexation. Rasputinov thumbed his nose at the rest of the world and decided to build twin permanent road and rail bridges across the Kerch Strait for his own purposes.

From still extant engineering data regarding the bridge, Rokosylana and her handful of cohorts now assigned to the project learned that the most senior and most serious bridge engineers harbored doubts about the potential for longevity for the Kersh Bridge. The main reason was haste and compromise—a holdover from the Soviet era. There was a lack of effective protection of the bridge, resulting largely from a wrong decision to allocate protective measures to a second stage of construction. Another issue was the problem for the Soviets having to use inferior leftover Nazi materials which compounded the haste.

Other design and construction errors included inconsistency between small-span design and ice regime in that area of the strait; construction of the bridge with incomplete engineering inquiry–wavering on the needed ice protection measures–and lack of technical, material, and work-force supply, of the construction. Much of this stemmed from hurried approach to the project, and little knowledge of that went beyond the politburo and Rasputinov's office.

Following the demands of the dictator of Russia, the opening date was pushed up for heavy road transport to early 2018, and for passenger trains at the end of 2019. For all intents and purposes, the construction was completed and sitting idly by for a year. Rokosylana was given permission to interview a POW who had worked on the "Crimean Bridge" as it was called then. She learned that the spans were too long; savings on material had guaranteed that the middle would sag inevitably given all the geological and technical circumstances of its construction.

He said, "Apart from the sheer scale of the project, there is the tricky geology of the region as well as severe climate factors—especially pack ice–to consider. Kerch Strait sits on a tectonic fault, and there are multiple challenges of the strait's bedrock being covered by a 130+ foot layer of silt, and the presence of 70+ mud volcanoes in the area. These conditions mean that the bridge would require 7,000 piles to support it. They had to be driven nearly 200 feet beneath the water surface. Some of the piles needed to be placed at an angle to make the structure more stable during expected earthquakes. None of these safeguards had been implemented in haste to complete the project by Comrade Rasputinov's deadline.

Multiple communiques obtained by SBU showed that Russian officials were complaining that Ukrainian ships were maneuvering dangerously, requiring the strait to be temporarily closed for security reasons, and that they had worries that the bridge would not stand against another harsh winter with ponderous icebergs bearing against the bridge at speed; or against a well-placed bomb.

Rokosylana Mykolaivna presented her report to Yaroslav and the rest of the SBU commando unit after a full month of preparation.

"Boss, my fellow Ukrainian soldiers, here my conclusions: 1. The Kerch Bridge is a crucial military objective. Its destruction will set back Russian invasion plans by years. 2. The bridge has many flaws that can play into our plans. 3. The middle, sagging, portion is most vulnerable and most inviting for attack. 4. It will require serious logistical planning, the necessity to obtain explosives, transports, and other things we do not have from the cousins in North America. It is difficult, but it is doable.

"The costs may be great, but the rewards are almost beyond calculation: 1. Rasputinov gets a black eye from the actual destruction, but also from the repercussions that his security was not good enough, and his illegal bridge was built no better that similar Soviet projects, i.e. it could not withstand an attack by foot soldiers and some dynamite. 2. The actual injury to his war planning and to the ongoing fighting— despite the Minsk Agreement—will be huge and will take funds not readily available to him. 3. He will lose face among his gang members, among other dictators around the world, and from the civilized world. They will laugh at him.

"Boss?"

"Lets get on with it," he said.

CHAPTER 15

Chushka Spit of the Krasnodar Krai linking the Kerch Peninsula of Crimea

October 13, 2018

The Chushka Spit is a sandy spit in the northern part of the Strait of Kerch which extends from Cape Achilleion to the south-west in the direction of the Black Sea for eleven miles. Geographically, it is something of a rest between two seas. By military fiat, the Spit belongs administratively to Temryuksky District, Krasnodar Krai, Russia. Historically it was known as Circassia. It forms the northern shore of Taman Bay. The krai's Taman Peninsula is situated between the Sea of Azov in the north and the Black Sea in the south. In the west, the Kerch Strait separates the krai from the contested Crimean Peninsula. It has many long branches extending to the south and was formerly joined to the Kerch Peninsula by the 1944 Kerch railway bridge.

The main harbor on the spit is Port Kavkaz. It is also the terminal of the Kerch Strait ferry line connecting the Taman Peninsula with the Crimea from the period when the bridge was under construction. and 9969 ships passed via the Kerch Strait in 2013, 2014, and 2015, respectively. An important ferry line connects Port Kavkaz [Krasnodarsky Krai] and Port Krym [Russian occupied Republic of Crimea].

Winter extends from mid-October to late March in the Spit, and the winter is arctic and unpredictable. Some years, the straits fill with ice blocks so deep and extensive that no icebreaker can penetrate them. The wind howls down through the Strait—often at gale force—and always with a severe wind chill index. The cold is so intense that it tends to make the steel brittle, and that is aggravated by the spring freeze and thaw cycle.

It was the ideal time for Yaroslav and his commandoes to attack the bridge, unless one factors in the human condition and comfort. The first partly wooden railway bridge over the Kerch Strait was built in autumn, 1944, just after the liberation of Crimea by the Soviet Army; but already in February, 1945,—three months after opening—it was destroyed by moving ice and then demounted. Strong northeast wind pushed ice to the Kerch Strait in 2-3 foot piles and on February 18, 1945, 32 bridge piers that had no ice guards were destroyed which were necessary to avoid rough consequences of complex meteorological conditions. Sometimes, bidirectional currents—often well pronounced, and with high velocity—were observed by meterologists.

Juxtaposition of climatic events: Every year, the Azov Sea gets covered with ice, completely or partially. Small depth and heat content of the freezing sea determine the dependence of its icing regime on air temperature and, consequently, winter severity. Over nearly 120 years of observation, the duration of periods with severe, moderate, and mild, winters has varied considerably.

Every year the Azov Sea becomes fully or partially covered by ice during the cold season. In severe winters, ice is often carried to the Kerch Strait and even the Black Sea. Ice formation and drift features on the way from the Azov Sea moves through the Kerch Strait—sometimes at speed—as well as ice interaction with the piers of the main and technological bridges under construction. It was found that—even under strong northeast winds—ice can pass neither through the piers, nor via the widest shipway with any ease. It is hard to discern the impacts of the two bridges of floating ice. Both Russian and Ukrainian hydrologists and engineers realized that—when the construction is complete and the technological bridge is gone—the main bridge will strongly affect ice conditions in the Kerch Strait. Another characteristic is that ice lasts shortly; it can appear and melt a few times during one season.

It was into this fluid, dangerous, and uncomfortable, place and time, that Rokosylana Mykolaivna brought together the best demolition team in the world. In addition to the doggedly determined SBU commandoes, there were six US Navy Seabees commanded by Captain Henry Clifton, XO Commander Martin Blacksmith, and Command Master Chief, Donald Spark, of Amphibious Construction Battalion 2, approved by the President of the United States and by the commander of Expeditionary Strike Group 2 Amphibious Construction Battalion. The Atlantic unit is one of two such "Seabee" battalions in the Navy and is based at Joint Expeditionary Base Little Creek, in Virginia Beach, Virginia. They were responsible for all naval combat construction for the Atlantic. Their fellow sailors and marines affectionately referred to them as "dirt sailors."

Seabees are organized into battalions and essentially function as the Navy's combat engineers; assisting with ship-to-shore operations, reinforcing positions, and providing other logistical support involved in frontline and support operations, including handling bulk fuel and water needs, as well as salvage and sabotage.

The SEALS were shipped in to the agreed landing site on Chushka Spit via two submarines—USS *Hyman G. Rickover* (SSN-709) and the USS *Seawolf* (SSN-1), both nuclear-powered. In addition to the SEALS, per se, the US contingent included Navy divers—service personnel including a restricted fleet line [Engineering Duty] officer, civil engineer corps [CEC] officer, Medical Corps officer, and an enlisted [ND or HM rating] all of whom were qualified in underwater diving and salvage. Some of the mission areas of the Navy divers included: marine salvage, harbor clearance, underwater ship husbandry and repair, submarine rescue, saturation diving, experimental diving, underwater construction and welding, as well as serving as technical experts to the Navy SEALs, Marine Corps, and Navy EOD diving commands.

All of them were experts at all phases of underwater warfare, including the very fit looking young doctor.

They had all graduated from the Navy's Tektite program funded by NASA. The Tektite project was a product of the Cold War. It caused the US Navy to realize the need for a permanent Underwater Construction capability that led to the formation the Seabee Underwater Construction Teams. For this mission, William Carl Radders Chief Machinist mate, and Darnell Howard Braklin, Master Chief Boatswains Mate, were in overall command.

Ukraine's elite 73rd Naval Special Purpose Center sailed in from the Black Sea two days earlier under cover of the inky black starless night on Project 58181/58503 Centaur-LK class small armored assault craft designed for carrying patrol service on rivers and coastal maritime areas, and delivery and landing of marines. The divers covertly set about to survey the coastal zone, looking for anti-submarine and anti-landing mines. After establishing a safe passage, they gave running and updating signals to the boats of the main group and the commandoes ashore.

The 73rd Naval Special Purpose Center is the special forces unit of the Naval Infantry (marines). Often referred to as Spetsnaz, they are broadly equivalent of the US Navy SEALs or British SBS. The SBU commandoes, SEALS, and Ukraine 73rd, low crawled ashore lugging their gear and were guided by Rokosylana and Yaroslav to their inelegant staging area behind the village trash dump, which smelled of a thousand years of collected organic matter.

That night, huddled in their low huts, the leaders hashed over final details using digital infrared lights to enable visibility. Considerable preparation time and schooling had gone on before, and this final conclave was for polish of fine points. As diverse as the group was, camaraderie was strong, and cooperation complete. They all recognized that no heroes were needed nor credit to be expected. The mission was too important for any of that.

Somewhere out in the Black Sea, the bulk of the Ukrainian navy floated in reserve. The naval forces consisted of five components: surface forces, submarine forces, naval aviation, coastal rocket-artillery, and naval infantry. In 2022, the Ukrainian navy had 15,000 personnel, including 6,000 naval infantry. In October, 2020, Ukraine and the United Kingdom signed a memorandum in which the UK government pledged to provide a 10-year loan of $1.6 billion for the re-equipment of the Ukrainian Navy. Most recently, an agreement had been reached for two *Sandown*-class minehunters to be transferred to the Ukrainian Navy upon decommissioning from the Royal Navy. The officers and men were anxious to please.

CHAPTER 16

Chushka Spit of the Krasnodar Krai linking the Kerch Peninsula of Crimea

October 14, 2018, 0 dark thirty

Yaroslav and six of his commandoes left Chushka Spit at midnight to prepare for their part in the upcoming mission. The rest of the men moved about in what looked like a silent controlled frenzy of activity. The plan for the mission was complicated, dependent on precise timing, and multi-pronged. Not the least of the issues was escaping. They had to do the deed, pack up and/or destroy the gear, and board submarines within minutes of the planned explosions. The diversions before and after the explosions had to cause enough general chaos to draw the ferocious attention of the Russians elsewhere for just long enough for the submarines to disappear.

Rokosylana Mykolaivna had spent a week fraternizing with the overworked, neglected, and generally dissatisfied, women of the poor little village which was nothing more than an inconspicuous and unsuitable corner of the land in the Kerch Strait. She learned of their disillusionment with Russia, the seemingly never-ending conflict with Ukraine, and their lazy Slavic husbands who had long since given up the struggle to make a decent life for their families. There was a nearly unanimous sense of ennui among the women, and Rokosylana was sure that they would not be in any hurry to report the presence of foreigners in their village. That would surely bode ill for them.

The villagers scarcely talked to one another out of suspicion. For such a small town, it had an incredible and nearly impossible degree of diversity—both of ethnicity and alliances. There was a fairly even division among Armenians, Ukrainians, Tatars, Caucasus Greeks, Georgians, Gypsies, Azerbaijanis, Turks, Circassians, Belarusians, Germans, and Assyrians. Conversation among the women was a Tower of Babal nearly incomprehensible polyglot. 88% of the people were Russians, and despite their numerical superiority, they were mistrusted and shunned.

Rokosylana put out the message that the mayor was throwing a party that night—plenty of meat loaf with vegetables and *Chushka burek*—a welcome relief from the polluted fish they caught in the strait–washed down with cheap Polish *Luksusowa*–a Polish potato vodka distilled 10 times from corn in a column still and blended with water, Ukrainian Goodoff vodka, probably better for removing stubborn paint from a wall than for human consumption, and barrels and barrels of *Baltika Zhigulevskoe Firmennoe*. It has a low 4.5% alcohol by volume, a golden appearance, and a foamy white head that fades away within a blink of an eye; but it leaves some lacing behind. The value—from Rokosylana's perspective–is that its consumers cannot seem to get enough. Her little party started just after darkness settled in and lasted three hours until the last adult had blacked out for the night.

The hastily put together—thanks to the Seabees—mission preparation platform became a buzz of controlled and coordinated activity. Boats, bombs, rifles, submersibles, deep diving gear, and boxes of ammunition, were laid out for ready acquisition when needed. The United States NEDU or NAVXDIVINGU–Navy Experimental Diving Unit–the primary source of diving and hyperbaric operational guidance for the US Navy. It is located within the Naval Support Activity Panama City in Panama City Beach, Bay County, Florida.] The men lined up in their Martian-like assortment of necessary costuming. They were ready two hours before take-off time which depended on precise signals from Yaroslav on the bridge, and Darnell Howard Braklin, Master Chief

Boatswains Mate and senior diver from his vantage point in the depths of the Kerch Strait, directly under the sagging mid-section of the bridge.

Communication was made to the two American and two British fighter pilots waiting in Odesa in their F/A-18E/F Super Hornets and Eurofighter Typhoons, respectively. Given the coordinates and timing, all four seasoned pilots toggled back "Ready, Wilco, Good hunting, brothers!"

Their combined weaponry was most impressive: GBU-28 is a 5,000-pound bomb with roughly four times the penetrating power of the 2,000-pound GBU-31v3 previously supplied to the Israeli Air Force. The attack force comprised four planes that established a "race track" pattern over the target at altitudes around 20,000 feet. The lead plane was to run in and release one or two bombs, then turn through a semi-circle and fly around the "race track" while the Weapon System Officer guided the weapons to impact. At intervals, the remaining planes in the force followed the initial attacker, each flying the same track.

When the lead aircraft completed its trip around the "race track", it delivered a second attack, and the process was repeated until every plane had expended its ordnance or the structure was destroyed. The two planes in the lead flight each carried two 2,000-pound Electro-Optical Guided Bombs (EOGBs), and each of the rest carried two 2,000-pound laser-guided bombs (LGBs).

The problem was hitting it at a weak part, a point where the weapon would cause structural damage and drop a span 2,000-pound bombs in its anti-bridge operations, though it used many different types. These included the GBU-24 with a hardened bomb body, the GBU-10, and the GBU-15.

With help from their crews, the four deep divers were silently towed out to a point less than ten yards from the center of the bridge and gradually lowered into the frigid depths of the black river. On land, Dr. CDR Ryan Nielson and his crew had their aid station complete with hyperbaric chamber set up and ready to go.

SEALs, SBUs, excess Seabees, and Ukraine 73rd naval soldiers, patrolled the village, the spit, and the associated waterways including the rivers, Taman and Azov Bays, communicating frequently. Before the witching hour struck, all was calm, secure, and quiet, except for the annoying post inebriation snoring in the village. There were already several hundred ships of varying size waiting their turn to pass under the Kerch Bridge. The saboteurs mixed with them. Heavily armed rubber pontoon boats spread out among the waiting ships. They held British SBS. SBU commandoes, SEALS, and Ukraine 73rd Naval soldiers and were on watchful edge to protect deep water divers with their large stores of high explosives destined for the bridge pilings on the floor of the strait.

The combat swimmers were driving underwater vehicles, maneuvering them ever closer to the middle span of the bridge. The divers were wearing breathing apparatus and deepwater insulated wet suits while submerged. Most of the SDVs allowed the divers to be inside. The Ukrainian Navy seconded a force of similarly trained divers to take part in the hazardous top-secret mission. The navy jets in Odesa went to full alert.

Rokosylana Mykolaivna and two other SBU agents quietly directed traffic and reexplained mission requirements as necessary. It would not do to have a loud head-on collision in the dark or to have a fighting unit moving north instead of south toward the sounds of the guns.

Yaroslav and his six commandoes made good use of their time in Krasnodar Krai. The Ukrainian SBU had a deep agent who was ideal for the job at hand. Yaroslav knew his dossier by heart, and still had misgivings about using him. Borys Petrovych Stefaniuk was perfect for the plan, but Yaroslav felt more than a twinge of guilt about enlisting him. Borys was 84 years old, wrinkled, bent, and had gnarled hands. His skin was blotched and all the elastin and superficial fat of youth had disappeared. The man was thin, skeletally thin; but he carried himself with pride and with an aura of inner strength of a man who knew he could get the job done.

Borys was a true Ukrainian, and a patriot true to his heritage. He had resisted the onslaught of the Bolsheviks and survived the starving time of the dirty thirties. He had served Ukraine as a partisan against the invading Nazis. And he had gone into hiding as a saboteur when the communists came back. He hated the communists and Rasputinov's pseudoKGB with an equal degree of venom. He would have volunteered for Yaroslav's mission even if the deciding factor had not been foisted upon him. He was a life-long three-pack a day smoker and now was cursed with severe COPD. The coup de grace for him was learning that he also had cancer of the lung—both lungs—and he could not expect to survive more than three or four more weeks.

Borys had served the intelligence services of his native country his entire adult life, and for most of his childhood and adolescence. Knowing his condition, he volunteered for any suicide mission the SBU might need him for. Yaroslav had the perfect mission for the courageous Ukrainian patriot, but the humanity within him balked.

"Young Yaroslav, I am pleased that you came to see me and to know that there are still Ukraine patriots working to save our country from Stalin's lackey. Someone from the underground let me know you would be contacting me. It must be important if a high young officer such as yourself should come in person. What do you need?", Borys asked in his usual direct way.

"Borys, I am part of a mission to strike a serious blow to the Russkies, one that might please you."

"Any blow against those criminals is a good thing."

"I hope you realize that what I am about to tell you is top secret."

"Certainly."

"We have a complicated plan to blow the Kerch Bridge in half while a convoy of Russian soldiers is crossing the mid-point. We intend to strike from the bridge itself, from the air, and from the sea floor."

"I think 'complicated plan' puts it lightly. I assume all parts are compartmentalized—need to know—so, I won't ask questions, except what am I expected to do."

"Nothing much, my friend, just drive a truck."

"A very heavy truck, I'm guessing"

"Um hmmh."

"Why me?"

"You are an experienced driver, a known fighter, and a patriot. We need all of that."

"You know I have advanced stage lung cancer and I am little more than one of the walking dead. I'm not up to much."

"The country is asking for all you have, my friend, Borys."

Borys scratched his head.

"A suicide mission."

"I'm afraid so. And Borys, I will be with you most of the way."

"No suicide for you, young Yaroslav. If that's the plan, I won't do it. You remind me too much of my handsome grandson and all his friends."

"No fear there, Borys, I have more missions to accomplish before my end. Here is the plan as it affects you. Do you agree to your part?"

"Glad to. Better than wasting away in some Russian cow shed they'll provide for such as me."

CHAPTER 17

On the Kersh Strait Bridge
October 16, 2018, approaching noon

Borys Petrovych Stefaniuk had experience with the Russian Ka-mAZ-5350, a modern Russian tactical truck. This one was supplied by the local partisans. It was a 6X6 variant of the KamAZ Mustang series of trucks so popular throughout the Russian military. This newer series was more rugged and militarized than the previous KamAZ lineup. The most important thing from Yaroslav's viewpoint was that the chassis allowed for a wide variety of body configurations and included cargo, shelter, tanker. and various weapon systems. Borys's new truck allowed for 7 to 12 tons of cargo along with 30 to 40 troops. For Borys and Yaroslav's mission, every cubic foot of space other than for the driver and passenger seats was crammed with high explosives, detonators, and the electronics to set them off.

The intricately wired high explosives in the bed of the truck included: thermobaric weapons which suck in oxygen from the surrounding air to generate a high-temperature explosion. They typically produce a blast wave that lasts significantly longer than that of a conventional explosive and are capable of vaporizing human bodies and massive destruction of concrete buildings; GBU-57A/B MOP [Massive Ordnance Penetrator] a precision-guided, 30,000-pound "bunker buster" bomb used by the United States Air Force. This is substantially larger than the deepest-penetrating bunker busters previously available, the 5,000-pound stock of high explosives—a supply of which were place on the truck–GBU-28 and GBU-37 bombs. They can be detonated in place with the proper electronics; conventional incendiary bombs of two main types. The burning material of the intensive type is thermite, a mixture of aluminum powder and iron oxide that burns at a very high temperature. It is capable of melting heavy metal such as bridge girders and railroad tracks.

The SEALS, SBS, Ukraine 73rd naval soldiers, and US deep divers, carried large, touchy, quantities of smaller explosives, strategically placed within the structure, used to catalyze the collapse. Nitroglycerin, dynamite, and other explosives—even 200 fifty pound bags of ammonium nitrate fertilizer [It was good enough for Timothy McVee], were intended for use to shatter reinforced concrete supports. The sea soldiers planted a twenty-girder span of such explosives giving the uprights the look of being infested with hordes of monster barnacles. Every man and woman in the water knew that it would not be any kind of cakewalk. Iran was a world leader in the new technology of Ultra High Performance Concrete, or UHPC.

Emblematic of the commitment of the United States to Ukraine's freedom and sovereignty, the Pentagon had sent its best weapons for the day's important purpose. General-purpose bombs have a thin steel casing filled with explosives; the bunker buster had a narrower profile, with a thicker casing and less explosives. This design concentrates all the weight on a smaller area, making it an ice pick rather than a hammer; so, the bomb can smash through concrete or burrow through earth to strike deeply-buried targets.

The lead plane was equipped with a single new GBU-72 "Advanced 5K Penetrator" bomb encased in Eglin Steel. That specialty metal is a low-carbon, low-nickel, steel with traces of tungsten, chromium, manganese, silicon, and other elements, each contributing a desirable property to the whole. Eglin Steel is the gold standard for bunker-busting munitions, although it is in competition with even newer USAF-96 steel, which boasts similar performance but is easier to produce and work with.

At 10:22, all units—sea, land, and air—were in ready position. All they had to do was to wait for the final signal from Yaroslav.

CHAPTER 18

On the Kerch Strait Bridge

October 16, 2018, noon

Yaroslav and Borys wedged their ponderously heavy KamAZ-5350 into the miles long column of Russian Red Star Kalun 6X6 armored vehicles, armored personnel carriers, KamAZ Mustangs and KamAZ 6560 cab-over forward- 8X8 truck, 6×6 missile launch vehicles, GAZ Tigr armored troop transports, Ural 4320 multi-purpose 6×6 trucks, artillery towers, T-9OA main battle tanks, Sprut SDMI light tanks, and mortar, howitzer, and missile and towing vehicles. In the controlled chaos of the bridge opening for traffic, one vehicle more or less was not noted.

It was 08:41 when they finally touched the bridge highway. Little girls in fluffy red Russian dresses handed out small bunches of posies to every driver, which slowed the pace significantly. The rumble and roar of engines, traffic directing bullhorns, and the friendly profane smack talk bespoke camaraderie among the military drivers and guards. A mile or so behind the military column a rag-tag stream of vehicles shuffled along intent on doing their day's trade, business, or farmwork. Yaroslav looked at his watch more often than necessary out of time-stress anxiety; but he did not need to: they were right on schedule.

As soon as Yaroslav and Borys arrived in Krasnodar Krai, and especially when they pulled their KamAZ onto the bridge highway, they became acutely aware that they were in Russia's A2/AD zone around Crimea–a multi-layered and multi-level system of defense to counter military encroaches from the air, sea–both surface and underwater–as well as land. The A2/AD zone was designed to prevent foreign military forces from entering the area and to protect the Russian military bases there. They were also charged with security at the oil refineries in Krasnodar and Tuapse and a chemical complex at Belorechensk. It was cumbersome and impressive. Yaroslav did not underestimate it in the least. They were halted and their papers examined every mile or so; but they had made it thus far without being hassled.

The unseen activity underwater at the base of the bridge and the concomitant work of the mid-levels of the bridge piles and connection points with the joined spans, was a whir of dedicated activity, comparable to an everyday New York Sandhog project. The deep cold water muffled the sounds—and there was considerable noise—the Seabees and engineers took great pains to minimize light flashes from arch welding and cutting. Several powerful swimmers maneuvered along the attack lines to monitor the welder-divers' helmets, diving knives [needed for cutting into project material, wedging open a door, or to free themselves from an entanglement; and umbilical cord where gas is pumped from the diver to and from the surface. Boats had to be positioned over the sites where bubbling surfaced. The guardian angel also had to be mindful of the harnesses, to keep the diver buoyant and in one place while doing his or her work.

Specially qualified Gas Panel and Compressor teams monitored gas gauges and kept a steady life sustaining supply of air coming to the divers below. They were using a low-pressure gas system because of its low maintenance and virtually unlimited air supply.

For all the encumbrances and inconveniences of working under water, the highly skilled and driven underwater divers and Seabees were making rapid progress. At 10:54, the team leader informed Yaroslav and the other officers that they were ready. One wag appended a note that read: "SEABEES CAN DO".

At the hastily improvised airfield, pilots and ground crew were into their second pre-flight check, including the positioning of bombs, missiles, and ammunition.

"Enough," said Major Gwendolyn Proctor, the pilot of the first plane and designated leader of the air strike. It was 11:00. All participants synchronized their watches for the final time.

Yaroslav pointed out to Borys the upper part of a bridge consisting of a structural system in the form of beams, girders, arches, gleaming white suspension cables, and trusses collectively called the superstructure.

"That's the mid-point of the entire bridge..."

"And our objective," Borys finished his sentence. "How much longer until you think we get there, Yaroslav?"

"At the rate we're going, my guess would be half an hour to forty-five minutes."

"That will cut it close, won't it, Colonel?"

"I think we'll make it on time if we don't run into some sort of delay."

"Like stopping for guards or wrecks; stuff like that."

"Yeah, like that."

It was 11:22 by their watches. Yaroslav began to sweat a little.

Shortly thereafter, the pace of the traffic flow began to pick up measurably. Borys pointed out the reason. A large GAZ Tigr armored troop transport had two flat tires and was being towed to the right side of the deck. Things improved considerably after that. They passed the first welded joints of the suspension cables on the east end of the center girders. They were no more than fifty yards from the center of the Kerch Bridge, and it was only 11:36.

They were moving fairly quickly to the middle spot on the roadway deck and could see across to the center of the railway.

Yaroslav said to Borys, "See where those two beams come together. We have to park the KamAZ-5350 right in the middle of the road, but we can't come to a full stop until exactly noon. Check your watch and give me readings every five minutes."

Yaroslav began to weave and to start and slow down irregularly as if something was wrong with the truck. He exaggerated the impression to be sure he captured the attention of the other drivers and the sentries with their automatic submachine guns.

"11:51," Borys said.

Yaroslav slid to a stop and paused for a minute or two.

"11:56, Colonel."

"I'll pull up another ten feet and stop dead. Come around and take my place in the driver's seat. At exactly 12:00, flip the switches. Goodbye my friend."

He got out of the driver's seat and quickly walked to the hood and lifted it up. He poured a cupful of ground white candle wax into an empty coke can, added a mix of sulfur, sugar, phosphorus [KNO_3], a handful of ground match heads, and gun powder, then pushed a sturdy wick into the powder mix and sealed in under the loosely fastened radiator cap.

It was 11:59 exactly. He lit the fuzz, and a burst of thick acrid smoke belched out of the radiator in an excellent simulation of an engine fire.

Hardly anyone had noticed what was happening, presuming this was just another of the interminable delays, and the KamAZ would be hauled to the side.

Yaroslav ran in an out of the line of vehicles until he had a clear line of sight back toward the Krasnodar Krai side; then he started the sprint of his life. 12:00 chimed in his mind. He did not even glance back. The noise from the blast was as if a dozen bombs had gone off two feet behind him. The compression force of the explosion nearly knocked him off his feet, but he was able to right himself and to benefit from the surge at his back.

He was in good company. Men and women were leaping from their vehicles, military and civilians, and joined the pall mall rush to safety on the Krasnodar Krai side. The noise was nearly deafening: a screaming human cacophony, the shrieking and cracking of parts of the crumbling bridge, a series of vehicle explosions as the train of fuel trucks were hit by shrapnel and burning debris. Yaroslav was confident that there would never be any forensic evidence of where the explosion started, who set it off, and who would have to pay the price.

Meanwhile, sixty feet below the surface of the Strait, finishing touches were being applied to the pillars, girders, abutments, and electrical facilities. Deep diving climbers put the last limpet bomb on the last of the doomed arches. SeaBee Captain Henry Clifton—who had overall command of the underwater operation—left off his final task of cutting through a central girder, checked his watch and saw that he had a little less than three minutes before blast. He clicked his coms twice, a message for all under his command, that it was time to disappear. He got single clicks back from every man and woman. And gave his final order:

"Leave."

No one from the surface saw any of the activity below, but it was a near traffic jam of swimmers, HOVS [human-occupied vehicle] and unscrewed craft, ROVs [remotely operated vehicles], Unmanned Underwater Vehicle (MUUV) program and towed underwater equipment streaking—each in his/her designated sea lane—a few inches above the soft silted bottom of the strait, headed in the direction of Taman Bay and relative safety.

Capt. Clifton was a very powerful swimmer and had assigned himself the final and arduous task of dragging the 250 foot long heavily insulated electric cord and its battery-attached detonator. He checked the time: 11:55—five seconds before ignition. He swam as fast as his weary legs and fins could go, and then pressed the red button. It was 12:00. He heard the immense blast only dully since he was so deep and so far east. His great hope was all his sons and daughters made it out—they were his family, his only family.

Major Gwendolyn Proctor, sat in the cockpit of her F-18 and watched the middle section of the Kerch Bridge through her binoculars with fascination. It was 11:35. The area of the center piers appeared to be getting more and more crowded. Traffic was grinding to a snail's pace, and guard units were gathering to keep it moving. She gave the thumb's up to the other three pilots and heard their jet engines rumble into action.

She and the other pilots waited impatiently until 11:52, then she put her left arm out of the cockpit and gave the agreed upon round-and-round arm signal to "take off, and follow me." The engine noise of the four jets was thunderous even beyond that coming from the bridge traffic. All eyes stopped to look at the source of the jet noise and stared in awe as the sleek unmarked planes roared down the make-shift runway and swooped in two different directions toward the center of the bridge. Alarm sirens began to wail; a few wasted antiaircraft shots were fired, and all attention riveted on the incoming planes. Four Iranian Shahed drones rose into the sky and were promptly shot down by the incoming allied jets. The last drone exploded over the bridge a fraction of a second before noon.

The jets swooped in and dropped precision guided missiles at the dead center of the bridge and at the same second Borys's KamAZ erupted into a mushroom shaped cloud which later reporters called a nuclear strike. Half a second after that, the bridge below the deck disappeared in a dense cloud of powdered concrete dust and huge fragments of the bridge which were hurtled three hundred feet in the air. The worst was yet to come for the truckers hopelessly stranded on the deck. Those immense boulders crashed down on the vehicles and their passengers for a mile in each direction.

Maj. Proctor's airwing swept out and away from the bridge, then executed a spectacular acute turn on the Crimean side. On the way back, they swung low to annihilate deployments of Russian Armed Forces' air defense systems near the Kerch Bridge entrance on the Crimean side. The installations had been an attempt by the occupiers to defend against Ukrainian cruise missiles. One site included a Pantsir S1/2 anti-aircraft missile and gun system along with an S-400 launcher, while the other was comprised of three S-400 launchers. This information has already been relayed to the Ukrainian Defense Forces by Yaroslav's unit.

Then, they roared low over the bridge two by two and strafed an additional mile of the span at both ends of the Kerch Bridge before streaking off and away toward unoccupied Ukraine.

CHAPTER 19

Northeastern Ukraine

2018 to February 22, 2022

The day following the bridge explosion, every man, woman, and child in Chushka village was arrested, and their village was made into a prison camp, one whose draconian security measures and policies would put a German stalag or Russian Siberian camp on a near charitable resort status in comparison. Over two weeks, every imaginable humiliation, deprivation, and torture, known to the long and monstrous history of the imperial, USSR, and modern Russian history, was inflicted by the outraged Russians.

The unfortunate citizenry paid a dreadful price for the accident of their having lived in a place where an egregious military mission had been carried out with great success. Those poor people were made to atone and suffer for the humiliation and loss suffered by the invading Russians, whether they were guilty or not. In the end of the awful "interview" period, none of the citizens of Chushka village had eaten a single bite of food, drank more than one cup of fetid water every other day, had escaped rape, had all their limbs intact, or could see. Of the 384 citizens originally in the village, only six 9 millimeter bullets were required for the final extermination.

The villagers were good stoical Russians. They knew how to suffer. Their tormenters did not gain a scintilla of useful evidence from the village, in large part, because they had no information to convey. Most of the overt killings were from foramen magnum gunshot wounds from the new Udav pistol [whose magazine holds 18 9x21mm rounds] which is similar to the American .40 S&W cartridge. The bodies were bulldozed into a deep pit where the village—such as it was—once stood. They were sprayed with napalm, set afire, then buried under four feet of polluted soil. In the years to come, new people commented on how good that soil was in comparison to the top-soil surrounding it.

There was no proper cemetery near the village as such, but behind the trash dump stood two simple white wooden Russian Orthodox crosses with diagonal foot bars. The Russians were not interested and left them unmolested. A survivor later related to Ukraine authorities that they were for the two heroes of the Kerch Bridge explosion: Borys Petrovych Stefaniuk, who drove the truck, and American SeaBee Captain Henry Clifton, who was in overall command of the underwater segment of the mission but could not swim fast enough or far away enough to save himself from a Russian depth charge. Both men gave the last great measure of devotion to freedom, and the markers failed to designate their final resting place, nor will those markers long persist.

The Americans, British, and partisan groups left the scene promptly and without fanfare. There were official top secret records kept, but they would not see the light of day for another thirty years, if then. There were heroes aplenty, and they will go unrecognized. Yaroslav Kandybavych Melnykenko and his SBU unit left for a new assignment in Kyiv to protect the new and promising candidate for president, Volodymyr Zelenskyy, a television comedy show actor and producer. The head of the SBU, Lt. Gen. Olena Yuriivna, personally requested that the elite unit protect this particular politician because—unlike most of those in recent history—he seemed to be personally honest and determined to stamp out the corruption by oligarchs that threatened the security of Ukraine.

Yaroslav announced the orders to his men with something less than overt enthusiasm, "Think of it as a bit of R&R. We'll have regular people food, sleep in a bed—if you can remember what that was like–and wear civilian clothes, including shoes that fit both feet."

Everyone laughed. They knew it would be short term, and they also knew that the Russian Bear was still at the gates. It was not over yet; not by a long shot.

Presidential meeting regarding the ongoing war with Russia and Donbas; May 27, 2019; in the Office of the President of Ukraine [unofficially "Bankova" in reference to the street it is located on]:

Officials present: President Volodymyr Zelenskyy, who took the oath of office on May 20, 2019; Prime Minister Denys Shmyhal; Verkhovna Rada representing parliament; the entire Cabinet of Ministers; Prosecutor General of Ukraine; one-half of the members of the Council of the National Bank of Ukraine; The High Command of the Armed Forces of Ukraine and main military formations; one-third of the Constitutional Court of Ukraine; Presidential first aide, and Presidential press secretary. [Note–The Government of Ukraine utilizes a semi-presidential system in which the roles of the head of state and head of government are separate, thus the president of Ukraine is not the nation's head of government.]

Single item on the agenda; The War in Donbas:

Mr. Zelenskyy: During my recent call with the President of Russia, we had a meeting of the minds. I am confident the Russian president is sincere about his expressed wish to avoid any armed or diplomatic conflict. In my campaign, I vowed to make peace with Russia and end the war in the Donbas; and at this point, I intend to honor that vow.

Mr. Shmyhal: Has there been any change in Rasputinov's belligerence that leads you to believe that he is sincere or that he will keep his promise to allow our sovereignty this time when he has never done so before? Let me point out that he violated the Minsk Agreement and Minsk II almost before the ink was dry on the documents.

Admiral Yuriy Ivanovych Ilyin, Chief of the General Staff: Respectfully, Mr. President, without exception, Rasputinov has it clear that leaving Ukraine intact will require us to give over all the Donbas to him and to allow it to become Russian territory. In addition, he demands that we forswear our desire to join NATO forever, and that we strike a new treaty of friendship and trade exclusivity with the Russian Federation. Are you willing to accept such a price? Are we to become lackeys of the Russians again as we were under Stalin and to do so without a fight or a whimper?

Mr. Zelenskyy: What is the alternative, Admiral? A war we cannot win? Eradication of any and all of our Ukrainian values, language, history, heritage, and national character?

Adm. Ilyn: Again, with respect, that is exactly what will happen if we appease Rasputinov and give in to his confiscatory demands. He is waving a club at our country and at you, Sir. If we give him an inch of our territory or one written line of capitulation, he will never stop. All Ukraine will be his.

Head of SBU, Olena Yuriivna: Gentlemen, may I point out factual information bearing on the subject. First, we have a source in the politburo in Moscow who reports that there is a working paper signed by Rasputinov for the Russian people and all its resources be dedicated to the extermination of Ukraine as a bastion of NATO power and that preparations to do so–including invasion–be commenced forthwith. Second, we have warehouses full of videos of recruitment from prisoners, boys on the street, and of the unemployed, for military duty and training for duty in a "Great Patriotic Struggle to reclaim our Russian land now illegally occupied by the Nazis". Third, we have a copy of a contract between the Federation Army and the Wagner Militia to augment the troop size in the event of need in any upcoming conflict with Ukraine— in other words, a license for them to steal in the name of the Rodina.

Mr. Zelenskyy: I have a face-to-face conference with President Rasputinov later this year. I will bear in mind everything you have told us today. I ask something of you. Since this Russian threat looms ever more seriously, we need to do several things immediately: One—our diplomatic service, banking concerns, health services, etc. must all set to work to warn our like-minded diplomatic neighbors of the crisis. Two—our military must contact their counterparts throughout the free world of our need for men, money, and materiel, to carry on a long war against Russia if diplomacy fails. Three—Ukraine opened 18 diplomatic missions in 1992, and 15 more in 1993, almost all of which—excepting Russia—operate on friendly terms with us. We must have a diplomatic blitz to gain their support. Four—Prime Minister Shmyhal, Minister of Foreign Affairs Vadym Prystaiko, and I, will make it our sacred mission to meet multiple times with the leaders of the free world, including UN officers, diplomatic, military, business, and religious, authorities. Five— SBU officers will also run a blitz campaign to inform and seek help from their counterparts among the world's intelligence services (with some exceptions, of course). Thank you for your input. Now, let's get to work. Gen. Yuriivna, please bring your senior staff and meet with me in my office right after this meeting is adjourned.

Presidential meeting regarding the rumors of all-out war with Russia and Ukraine; May 27, 2019; Oval Office:

Officers Present: POTUS, VPOTUS, Secretaries of Defense, State, Treasury, and HS, entire JCOS, Heads of all fifteen intelligence services, DNI presiding, Speaker of the House, and Senate Majority Leader.

Agenda: 1. Border security, 2. Budget, 3. Missile production in DPRK, 4. Dealing with the hostile press and fake news, 5. Conflict in Ukraine. Time allotted for each topic—40 minutes for 1.; 22 minutes for 2.; four minutes for 3.; five minutes for 4.; 2 minutes for 5. Break for lunch in the Rose Garden immediately after the meeting. Opportunity to meet the President of Hungary, Viktor Orban (2 hours)

POTUS: The nagging problem of Ukraine's never-ending demand for money to prop up their corrupt and failing government and military run by criminal oligarchs has come up again, this time with so-called "intelligence briefings" about a Russian plot for war, the thousandth request for admission to NATO, and for a state visit from their president Zelski complete with speeches to both houses of Congress. I will dispense with this matter first and simplest; no, no, and no. No more of our hard-working tax payer money wasted on Middle-eastern diplomacy which goes no place, does nothing for us, and has no future. I could stop Mr. Rasputinov's planning in a day with a single phone call. Him and me have a great working relationship. We can transact a deal that will take care of all of that.

The remainder of the commentary was directed at the main measures of the agenda. POTUS gave directions, and the assembled authorities unanimously concurred. Minor corrections to the notes were made; Zelski was corrected to Zelenskyy, and Middle-east was changed to Balkans. The lunch was a resounding success and widely televised and commented upon most favorably by all but the "Fake News" press.

Presidential planning meeting May 29, 2019; the Grand Kremlin Palace, official working residence of the president of Russia

Officers Present: President Vladimir Rasputinov; Prime Minister Ivan Petrovsky Zevar; Ranking Deputy Prime Ministers–Feliks Nikolayev-ich Mishustin [First Deputy Prime Minister], and Mikhial Grigorenko [Chief of the Government Staff], Alexandre Gromov Michael Grigor-ovich Pestotnik]; Chairman of the Federation Council of the Federal Assembly of the Russian Federation [Speaker, presiding officer of the Upper house of the Russian parliament], Anton Karamosov; Chief of Staff of the Presidential Executive Office, Vaino Belousov; Federal ministers–Viktoria Kurenkov [Finance]; Alexander Abramchenko [Minister of Civil Defense, Emergencies, and Disaster Relief], Minister of Justice Konstantin Chuychenko; Igor Sergeyev Marshal of the Russian Federation; Army General Valery Gerasimov Chief of the General Staff ; Ganady Alexeiov Chekunkov Admiral of the Fleet; and Patriarch Kirill of Moscow and all Rus'[secular name Vladimir Mikhailovich Gundyayev] head of the Russian Orthodox Church.

Agenda: Special Military Operation

President Rasputinov: It is clear to anyone who is not a moron or a traitor that Ukraine is part of Russia, and it exists illegally as if it were a separate and sovereign state. It is not an independent nation; it is not even a country. All good Russians hold that truth in their hearts.

We often say that Mother Russia goes back a thousand years. That is not strictly true. The great Russian city of Kyiv is the mother city of all Russia, and it was established 1,200 years ago when Moscow was still a forest. Ukraine was part of the Soviet Union, before unilaterally and illegally declaring itself an independent country in December, 1991. That was an act by the Nazis who had gained power, and the entity has maintained its faux independence ever since. Kyiv, ostensibly the Ukrainian capital cannot remain so. It is simply not possible that the "mother of Russian cities," be located outside its own... my own... Russia must reclaim Ukraine from the Nazis in order to reestablish her rightful place on the world stage as a great power that has existed for millennia.

It has always been my firm opinion that Ukrainians and Russians are the same people, and that they are part of the Slavic Brotherhood of Russia, Belarus, and Ukraine. During my administration, we shall restore that fact for all the world to face; and we shall erase the stain of democracy from a nation that has never been and never will be less than part of Russia and under its rule.

Belarus is already a Russian partner state rendering a military invasion of it pointless and unnecessary. Ukraine—on the other hand–has fallen deeper and deeper into folly by increasingly aligning itself with the decadent West in recent years. I tell you this: Ukraine has been important to the Russian political soul for decades, even centuries, and will again assume its rightful place as part of all the Russias. Also, not to be overlooked, Ukraine's territory has aided Mother Russia's economic strength throughout its long history, including supplying much of the Russian Empire's, and the USSR's coal, steel, and iron.

Our Donbas region—falsely claimed to be part of the so-called nation of Ukraine—has been an invaluable part of Russia since at least the 19th century. Russia might not have been such a great power at the end of the 19th and into the early years of the 20th century without Donbas, and that region will again take its rightful place alongside other Russian republics, krais, and oblasts.

I will be perfectly clear. Russia has a right to rule Ukraine. Russians and Ukrainians are one nation, one language, one people. They were illegitimately and artificially separated when the Soviet Union collapsed, and I place full blame on the West for trying to pull Ukraine out of Russia's natural orbit and friendship. Mark my words, NATO's expansion beyond its borders into eastern Europe is forcing my powerful Russian hand.

NATO doesn't simply expand, but countries apply to join, usually motivated by a perceived outside threat, military or financial. In eastern Europe, the leaders and their people falsely claim that the threat comes from Russia. Just last February, Lithuania's prime minister, Ingrida Šimonytė, reported that her country joined NATO because of me, of all people. That is the level of propaganda against Russia that we have to endure.

When our patriotic troops entered Ukraine to protect our beleaguered countrymen in Luhansk, and Donetsk, NATO's wicked ties with Ukraine deepened after the Treaty of Minsk in 2014. Estonia, Latvia, and Lithuania, joined NATO after 2004. Then, recently Finland joined the unholy alliance. Only Russia's vigorous demands kept NATO from actually putting additional troops in the region in order to prevent the illegal addition of those countries created this military force on Russia's doorstep. We have had no alternative other than to push back.

Every Russian knows that Nazis continue to run Ukraine; so, Russia must intervene to stop them. I tell you this, Comrades, our Russia is being forced to intervene more frequently and more powerfully. We can produce ample evidence that there are those who identify with Nazi ideology in Ukraine, just as there are Western Nazis infiltrating Russian and even American politics. I repeat, also Nazis in Russian politics. Of course, there are Nazis in American politics. We must be the power that stands against the abomination that invites the spread of Nazism. We must do it now, and we must do it here. Nazism is Russia-phobia to us. The Ukrainians demonstrate that they are Nazis because they're anti-Russian, a situation we can no longer tolerate on our border.

I am under no public pressure to invade Ukraine at this time; I take credit that my reasoning and understanding of the Ukraine/anti-Russia/

Nazi sympathism. I am the long great leader who sees the great power struggle and understands it personally in his heart. It will be my lasting legacy to bring Ukraine into obedience with the Russian world and sphere of interest. I shall not fail to bring back order to Russia by removing the runt state of Ukraine back into the warm arms of Mother Russa. I look to the day when Vladimir Rasputinov's name will be revered in our history books alongside Lenin, Stalin, Vladimir the Great, (my namesake), Peter the Great, Catherine the Great. That is one of the motivations to attack when we are ready.

Am I going to be a footnote in Russian history or are they going to write books about me like they do Peter the Great, Catherine the Great, Stalin? What have the great Tzars done? They have expanded Russian territory. It shall be written that Rasputinov is known as a great historic leader restoring the rightfully Russian lands back to the homeland where they belong. I will do so by the time I am 70 and not like the doddering old fools of the West who cannot even manage to walk without a cane or a wheelchair.

It is time posthumous that we move on Ukraine for several reasons: 1. The arrival of Zelenskyy in 2019 who is an actor, a comedian, and is now the court jester. He has not got the brain capacity to crack a joke or make a man laugh, let alone, move the weak-minded populace into good government. Together, the cabinet, plus the brain power combined in the military, does not match up to a baby Chimpanzee. 2. They do not have the men, training, the food stocks, the guns, ammunition, or armored vehicles, to stand against us for a week. I think it can be done with our older stock-pile from the fifties Cold War! 3. Until late 2014, I believed that—at best—this Zelenskyy was basically harmless, and I could manipulate him in a way best for his country. He seemed to be rather pro-Russian. After all, his first language is Russian. But then, the clown decided on a course of fighting what he called "corruption". He falsely accused one of our most important real pro-Russians, Viktor Medvedchuk, and drove him from Ukraine. Zelenskyy has to go. And now is the time. In coming conferences, we will outline concrete plans as they evolve, and you will live to see us make Russia great again.

You may ask, why have I not acted before? I point out the obvious to you, my loyal Russian compatriots. Part of the reason was that a populist American president was elected. That man was a true leader with a vision. He was very friendly toward me, and also publicly criticized NATO showing his superior intelligence. I thought the NATO alliance would likely shatter from within. But the corrupt Americans stole the office from my good friend and falsely elected a fool who was a much stronger proponent of NATO.

I argue that Ukraine has become a vassal of the West and that—therefore—it is pointless for Russia to attempt to hold a dialogue with the Ukrainian authorities, who are weak, ignorant, and unreliable. Therefore, now is the time to prepare our attack. Zelenskyy has a low approval rating, and some squabbling among Ukraine's elite strongly suggests that those ununited so called Ukrainian wisemen are not likely to unite under Zelenskyy against me.

The "Big Brother" of the West is in chaos; witness the clown show withdrawal from Afghanistan. There are new leaders of Germany and the UK, and pressure for France's president all points to the fact that there is no capable Western leadership. They will not actively oppose any Russian movements to restore Ukraine to its rightful role as a dutiful and loyal Russian. When we launch our Special Military Operation as a great bear charging, we will invade Ukraine and take Kyiv in a matter of mere days.

CHAPTER 20

Kharkiv, Northeastern Ukraine, at the confluence of the Uda, Lopan, and Kharkiv, rivers, twenty-five miles from the Russian border

February 22, 2022

Fighting in Eastern Ukraine reached a haphazard stalemate with either side gaining or losing territory and population without any real change in strategic position. That bode ill for Ukraine because it was becoming a war of attrition which Ukraine was bound to lose in the long run. Russia knew that and apparently locked into a medium expensive hold-out-at-any-cost policy.

There had been a massive Russian military build-up near the Ukraine border in March and April 2021, and again in both Russia and Belarus from October 2021 onward. Members of the Russian government—especially its greatest spokesman, the Dictator, repeatedly denied having plans to invade or attack Ukraine. Any citizen in the nominally Ukrainian city could tell that a full-scale invasion by a mighty land army was imminent. Ukrainian spies–like Yaroslav Kandybavych Melnykenko–were actively setting in motion counter-invasion measures. None of the Ukrainian political or military authorities or their counterparts in America had any misinterpretations of the intentions of the Barbarians at their gates. By that day, there were no Pollyannas left among the hopefuls of the Western world.

Russia began a slow evacuation of its embassy staff at Kyiv in January 2022. The motives for the evacuation were—at the time—unknown and subjected to multiple speculations. By mid-January, an intelligence assessment produced by the Ukrainian Ministry of Defense estimated that Russia was in its final stages of completing a military buildup at the Russo-Ukrainian border, amassing 127,000 troops in the region. Among the troops, 106,000 were land forces, with the remainder comprising naval and air forces.

In addition, 35,000 Russian-backed separatist forces and another 3,000 Russian forces were reported to be present in rebel-held eastern Ukraine. The assessment estimated that Russia had deployed 36 SRBM [Iskander short-range ballistic missile systems] near the border, many stationed within striking distance of Kyiv. The close proximity of the huge Russian military force felt as if individual Russian soldiers would be able to throw rocks at Ukrainians across the border. In mid-January, six Russian troop carrier landing ships were redirected from their home ports to the Port of Tartus. The Turkish government prevented them from transiting the Bosporus.

On January 20, Russia announced plans to hold major naval drills in the month to come that would involve all of its naval fleets: 140 vessels, 60 planes, 1,000 units of military hardware, and 10,000 soldiers, deploying in the Mediterranean, the northeast Atlantic Ocean off Ireland, the Pacific, the North Sea and the Sea of Okhotsk. On February 5, 2022, US officials reported that Russia had assembled 83 battalion tactical groups, estimated to be 70 percent of its combat capabilities. On February 11, the US President issued a public warning to Americans to leave Ukraine as soon as possible. On February 21, 2022—following the recognition of the Donetsk and Luhansk republics—Rasputinov ordered additional Russian troops into Donbas, in what Russia called a "peacekeeping mission." The clouds of war were rapidly closing in.

0400 Moscow time on February 24, 2022: Rasputinov announced that [maintain spaces Between words] Russia was initiating a "special military operation" in the Donbas region, and launched a full-scale invasion into Ukraine. Ukraine and the rest of the Western world recognized that Dictator Rasputinov was attempting to restore the Russian Empire/ Soviet Union. Shortly after, reports of large explosions came from multiple cities in central and eastern Ukraine, including Kyiv and Kharkiv. The US timidly announced that it would not send its combat troops into Ukraine to intervene militarily due to fears that it might offend Rasputinov and could provoke full-scale war between the United States and Russia.

The naysayers who predicted a quick capitulation and oblivion of Ukraine were proved wrong. Russia was unable to eliminate the Ukrainian government following the failure of the Kyiv offensive and experiencing major setbacks as a result of the 2022 Kharkiv and Kherson counteroffensives.

Yaroslav and his commandoes had been certain that Russia was planning an attack for the previous six months. He and his SBU superiors, especially the Head of SBU, General Olena Yuriivna, began planning specific missions designed to produce doubt as to the "weakness and ignorance" of the smaller country by Rasputinov. Yuriivna ordered her spies to attend the The Rosoboronexport State Corporation to begin preparation for an important and timely strike, given the obvious and threatening military build-up on Ukraine's eastern border.

The SBU disguise department supplied the team with authentic FSB [Federal Security Service] uniforms and rank insignia for three *polkovniks* [colonels] and three *leytenants*. From war captures, they procured three large 1976 Ural-4320 general purpose off-road 6×6 vehicles, produced at the Ural Automotive Plant in Maiass, Russia, and captured during a flash raid on a Russian supply column along the Lopan River the previous year. Perfectly fitting Kirza combat boots made of thick and strong materials–nailed on kobra leather shafts and rubber soles were removed after a battle from men who would no longer need them. Wearing them made the pseudo-FSB officers appear to be of some importance in Rasputinov's military apparatus.

After painting large Zs on the front, back, and sides, of the 4320s, SBU command sent the empty carriers toward Moscow to Stromynka Street,

Moscow, headquarters of Rosoboronexport State Corporation to await the annual major sale. It was announced that the sale was going to be attended by an extra three *polkovniks* and three *leytenants* authorized to purchase an unlimited supply of armaments. They had the papers to prove their identifications as purchase and transport authorities. The large Zs on the trucks had become a militarist symbol in Russian propaganda and is used by Russian civilians and soldiers to indicate support for the invasion. Russian senior officers encouraged the placement of the large, white, and clearly visible "Zs" on Russian vehicles to identify them clearly for the soldiers on their side—to avoid collateral damage. Unfortunately for the Russians, the purpose backfired. The big "Z" clearly identified targets for the Ukrainians and resulted in a loss of a great many trucks and tanks.

Yaroslav, and four other commandoes: Rokosylana Mykolaivna, Fedir Blyznyuk, Boryslav Vovk, and Vasyl Haranchak—were all selected for their ability to pass as Russian military. All were native fluent in Russian, fairly light in complexion, and relatively tall—officer material. They flew first class from Warsaw, Poland to Sheremetyevo Alexander S. Pushkin International Airport in Moscow. Their luggage was passed through without inspection since they were active-duty military.

That was a good thing given the fact that each of them had a duffel bag and a sturdy hard side roll-on suitcase containing hundreds of millions worth of rubles and gold [at 91.24 RUB/USD, or 1.00 RUB/410. 55 UAH (Ukrainian Hryvnias)], dozens of handguns, grenades, boxes of ammunition, det. fuses and cord, mines, and series electric blasting circuits for mines, and ANFO–an explosive material consisting of ammonium nitrate and fuel oil. They planned to obtain more ammonium nitrate fertilizer and Russian fuel oil from their deeply embedded secret Moscow supplier of PJSC Lukoil Oil Company [LUKOIL] after leaving Sheremetyevo.

The SBU sabotage unit moved quickly out of the airport traveling in separate vehicles including cars, trucks, and buses. They met the rest of the squad and their three large 1976 Ural-4320 general purpose off-road 6×6 vehicles, at a coffee house just outside the airport on Mezhdunarodnoye Highway 3 in Khimk suburb. The CoffeeMania shop was crowded with people not paying attention to each other.

The parking lot was empty on the southeast corner, and the three big Urals were parked in different locations in the corner to avoid calling attention to themselves. Yaroslav and his officers—who had come in by plane from Poland—exited their separate cars, trucks, and buses, and walked the half mile across the asphalt parking lot to the rendezvous point.

It was bitterly cold and windy, which served Yaroslav's purposes of concealment well. Everyone in and around the CoffeeMania shop was bundled up in heavy Moscow winter clothing—down jacket or other warm filling material inside heavy leather or stylish synthetics– everyone was wearing a fur lined hood to keep their heads warm. For Yaroslav, hooded and masked meant anonymity. The fashion conscious and winter-wise Muscovites were wearing a pair of touch screen gloves and an additional pair of thick mittens over the top. Like the rest of the CoffeeMania customers, the SBU team all wore warm scarves wrapped around their necks and faces to shield their faces from the wind and to hide them from face-recognition CCP, traditional Russian *ushanka* fur caps with the ear flaps. including face masks to allow warming of the freezing air a bit before inhaling.

The SBU unit members looked similarly fashion conscious, if a bit more seedy. They wore Valenki traditional Russian winter felt boots, arctic wool boots, or well broken in heavy leather combat boots. In short, it would have been as difficult to recognize the SBU members out of the crowd as it would be to know a particular mummy out of a collection of wrapped dead people in the *Qarafat al-Kubra* [City of the Dead, southern Cairo cemetery].

The team met, drank a few 15 ounce cans of welcome hot canned "Energy of the Day" coffee with Chicory & Ginseng , reconnoitered, and went over their plans for the fortieth time. The first crucial move was to buy Russian made arms and explosives with rubles confiscated from Russian/Separatist units captured over the past four years—amounting to a small fortune.

Yaroslav decided to take the bold approach and to drive his trucks into the loading zone of 27 Stromynka Street, Moscow City Center, headquarters of Rosoboronexport State Corporation built in 1998. [Rostec, for short.] Most Russians and foreigners prefer that to the

Corporation's full name in the English language: State Corporation for the Promotion of the Development, Manufacture, and Export, of High Tech Products]. They drove carefully, obeying all speed limit postings for the 2.5 miles from the Kremlin through the Basmanny District traveling northeast on Stromynka Street to the Rusakovskaya Embankment. From there they could see the blocky Khruschev type building teeming with trucks, tanks, and armaments, of all kinds. Yaroslav turned left, then left again on a small delivery road south of the main building.

Rokosylana Mykolaivna, Fedir Blyznyuk, Boryslav Vovk, Vasyl Haranchak and Yaroslav Kandybavych parked in the buyers' lot and stepped out of their trucks projecting an all-business and all-Rasputinov military demeanor. Yaroslav entered the main building and walked directly up to the reception desk.

"Col. Dimitri Ivanovich Strabinski to see Colonel Pavlovsky," he said and looked at the girl with his steely serious eyes.

"Oh, yes, Colonel. Col. Pavlovsky is waiting upstairs on the second floor for you. Will you need an escort, Sir?"

"No," Yaroslav said brusquely, made an about face, and strode purposefully to the stairs.

He found Col. Strabinski's office "Procurement Office for the Army" and knocked firmly three times on the heavy door.

"Come in," a pleasant woman's voice said. "Col. Strabinski, I presume?"

"Correct."

"Follow me, Col. Pavlovsky will see you now. Thank you for being punctual."

The two colonels shook hands, shared cups of thick black Russian coffee brought in by the receptionist along with some delicious savory *pirozhki* fresh from the oven and got down to business.

"I envy you your opportunity to go to the front for our glorious country and our leader. But, we all do as we are ordered, right?"

"Indeed, we do. And it is an honor and a privilege."

"Have you the requisition papers, all properly signed and with the seal of the Kremlin, Col. Strabinski?"

"Certainly. Here," and he handed Col. Pavlovsky his folder of official papers.

If he had been a praying man, Yaroslav might have taken advantage of any help proffered at that moment. In the circumstance, he just held his breath.

Col. Pavlovsky perused the faux documents with a careful eye, then smiled, and affixed his stamp of approval.

"I will inform the loading staff to get the items ready. Just before loading, please pay 2nd Lieutenant Cermovna in rubles, and our business is concluded."

"Thank you, Sir," Yaroslav said and gave a crisp friendly salute.

He retraced his steps back to the parking area and ordered the SBU unit to drive to the large item loading dock. It was the most efficient operation he had ever seen. He gave Lt. Cermovna the sealed container of rubles. She unlocked it, counted it using a handheld tally counter, nodded her approval, and left the dock with the money in hand.

The stevedores, low-ranking enlisted men and women, along with their officers, mounted their forklifts and manned the overhead cranes. In less than an hour, the hefty load of explosives and sabotage equipment were aboard the trucks and the entrances into them locked securely.

To show that they were regular Russian army men and women, Yaroslav had the trucks stop at the Doner Kebab Restaurant on Stromynka Street where they loaded up victuals for the journey to Kharkiv.

The SBU unit set out in a convoy for Kharkiv–a 463-mile trip taking nine hours. They were favored with light traffic. Most of the time, they were among similar convoys headed for the battle front. They arrived at their safe house at 21:40 Kharkiv time, allowing them plenty of time to move their explosives to their targets and to make two reconnoiters over the selected escape route. They were a full day ahead of schedule.

CHAPTER 21

Kharkiv, Northeastern Ukraine, at the confluence of the Uda, Lopan, and Kharkiv, Rivers, twenty-five miles from the Russian border

February 23, 2022, 04:00

The safe house was a rustic dacha on the west bank of the gently meandering Lopan River in the exurbs of Kharkiv. It had originally been free land allotted by the tsar to his nobles. The space was large with two hectares being actively used for growing vegetables. There were neat, well-weeded rows of green vegetables and herbs: potato, cucumber, zucchini, pumpkin, tomato, carrot, red bell peppers [capsicum], beet-root, cabbage, cauliflower, radish, turnip, onion, garlic, dill, parsley, rhubarb, and sorrel.

Further afield there were neat orchards of the most common dacha fruits in cool temperate regions of Russia: apple, blackcurrant, redcurrant, gooseberry, raspberry, and strawberry, apple, blackcurrant, redcurrant, gooseberry, a few sometimes sour, downy, sweetberries, cherry rose hips, plum, pear, sea-buckthorn, black chokeberry, serviceberry.

On otherwise unused plots of ground, there were crops of papaver, earth apple [a species of perennial daisy traditionally grown in the northern and central Andes from Colombia to northern Argentina. It is known for its crisp, sweet-tasting, tuberous roots, similar to jicama and horseradish. For the autumn harvest there were cellars and dugouts for storage. In autumn, the grown potatoes and other crops were gathered and transported to the city where they are stored in cellars and dugouts.

The scenery was very comfortably rural with extensive pasture-land dotted with copses of trees, ponds, and the rare faraway farmhouse. It would have been an idyllic place for a vacation or even a honeymoon, especially since it was going to be a sunny day with a cloudless sky above. However, this day held no vacation, honeymoon, or sightseeing. Instead, the day began at 04:00; and it was frigid outside and in the trucks.

All four trucks loaded with the latest and greatest sabotage materiel and the best of Ukrainian operatives traveled in four directions. Yaroslav and Vasyl left for Moscow; Rokosylana, Fedir, and Boryslav made the short trip into Kharkiv. Their single-minded purpose was to sew fear and destruction among the invading Russians and their Separatist vassals: fear that the enemy they had come to dominate with ease, was not so docile, weak, or afraid, as they had been assured they were, and destructive enough to give them a harbinger of what was to come for the ill-trained, ill-equipped, ill-fed, generally low morale, Russian boys who had been essentially kidnapped to come to Ukraine to kill people they knew nothing about and about whom they could care less.

Rokosylana Mykolaivna, Fedir Blyznyuk, and Boryslav Vovk, had a fairly simple, well drilled mission. They were to wreak havoc on three site categories that would be meaningful to the Russian boys and their commanders in Ukraine's second largest city and the closest major city [25 miles] to the Russo-Ukraine border. First, they planted explosive charges with timers on grand bronze statues of Lenin, Stalin, Khrushchev, and Pushkin. Then, they rushed to The Alexander Pushkin Street, named for Russia's most celebrated 19th-century poet whose cult was seen by most Ukrainians as "cultural imperialism". There they set three grenades to destroy the statue of Lenin. Fedir waited behind on Freedom Square until the much-publicized pro-Russian demonstration was to take place. He hurled three grenades in rapid succession into the milling crowd, then evaporated into the smoke and chaos to regain his fellows.

On the day of the attack, Kharkiv authorities renamed the street and the nearby subway station after Ukrainian philosopher and educator Hrigory Skovoroda, a direct and intended slap in the face of the Russians and their sympathizers.

While Fedir caused measurable destruction on Freedom Square, Rokosylana and Boryslav made a series of 440 yard dashes around the banking center of the city. They methodically planted high explosive thermite bombs with timers on selected buildings which largely served Russian speaking and preferring clientele. When they were satisfied that the explosions were set to occur with the push of a mobile telephone key at their discretion, they stealthily moved on to Russian Central Bank [CBR], Sberbank [SBER], PrivatBank on Peremohy prospekt 64, VTB [VTBR], Gazprombank [GAZP], Promsvyaz-bank, Russian Agricultural Bank, and the Bottom Line.

The four commandoes met up with each other as first light began to appear in the east. Together they broke the front door lock to the old Russian Orthodox Dormition Cathedral, and rushed in carrying arm loads of TNT, dynamite [an explosive usually made of nitroglycerin, sorbents—such as powdered shells or clay—and stabilizers. In this case SBU chemists provided a dynamite substitute, formulated without nitroglycerin containing: 75% RDX, 15% TNT, 5% SAE 10 motor oil, and 5% cornstarch. It is much safer to store and handle for longer periods than Nobel's dynamite. Military dynamite substitutes much more stable chemicals for nitroglycerin. The scientists had fiddled with the separate ingredients to make the mixture less unstable, safer, and to pack a bigger punch per milli3380gram], and eight 50 pound bags of ammonium nitrate fertilizer.

They worked up a sweat since it was not only a big job, but one that had to be done faster than they were moving. Dawn was opening up the city, and the sun would peak over the horizon any minute. The critical goal of their hurried efforts was to place explosive materials in critical structural connections to allow gravity to bring it down—in effect to implode it, rather than explode it.

"Done," Rokosylana said, and each team member paused for a few seconds to review what they had done in detail.

They each gave the rest a head nod, and without saying anything more, all of them except Fedir made their way out the rear exit of the venerable old church. They ran along the shady side of buildings, through dark alleys, and into parts of town still sleeping. When they were about a mile from the Dormition, Rokosylana raised her hand, and they all stopped for a brief rest, chests heaving.

They found their trucks, and each drove toward the relative safety of the house on the bank of the Lopan River. Before they left the dense urban section of Kharkiv, an immense deep thunder of an explosion polluted the sky behind them. In each of their minds' eyes, they imagined the end of the magnificent landmark of Russian heritage go down. The remarkable example of the best of Ukrainian baroque construction was constructed in 1657, had survived in a series of three destructive iterations as the pride of Russia. Now, it became nothing more than one church spire surrounded by pulverized rock rubble. As a stroke of irony,–on the third day of the Russian invasion–the invaders misfired a missile which took out the spire and finished the life of the Dormition Cathedral.

Fedir's next and final assignment of the day was to start a fire at FSB Headquarters. The task was almost risk free. It was still dark; citizens were hunkered down in their homes after announcements about the impending Russian invasion; and the building itself was largely evacuated by order of Rasputinov in anticipation of the soon-to-occur invasion. the Ninth Directorate of the Department of Operational Information housed in the building was represented by a staff of only five most valuable employees whose final effort in Ukraine was to destroy all significant Russian documents lest partisans find a treasure trove of secrets and learn that Rasputinov had been planning his heinous unprovoked war for ten years.

They were too busy shredding and burning to see a lone man in a Russian army winter uniform creep around the foundation of the old structure. He set small thermite bombs all along the base and connected them with detonating cord and fuses. The first explosion in the SBU's day of destruction was the commencement of a deafening explosion and a group of fairly large fires that become a conflagration and consumed the building and four out or the five occupants doing their work. The fifth was killed with a single bullet to the head fired by the first Ukrainian patriot named Fedir Blyznyuk in the Russo-Ukrainian [Rasputinov's] war of 2022.

The following morning, February 24, 2022, at 04:00, Rasputinov commenced his attack on innocent Ukraine. Painful histories remained visible in the buildings dotting Kharkiv's streets, from aristocratic manors to Stalinist neoclassical structures to cathedrals, monuments to poets, and modern-era cultural centers. 4,500 residential buildings were destroyed and 1,600 damaged by Russian attack. These included schools, nurseries, hospitals, and clinics, senior assisted living centers, and residential apartments. Few actual military targets were destroyed in the first onslaught. Russian troops poured across the border early that morning with residents reporting loud explosions, apparently caused by artillery shells or missiles landing on the outskirts of town, and the screams of the dead and dying.

The number of dead and wounded could not be counted under the rubble. Authorities closely monitored the situation, and investigations were set underway to determine if any or all these attacks constitute war crimes.

As Russian bombardments increased in intensity, Kharkiv became a sign of the next—even bloodier—stage in the war after Russia's hopes for a swift victory were dashed. Kharkiv remained a major target of Russia's invading forces because it has a special place in the Kremlin's and Vladimir Vladimirovich Rasputinov's distorted version of history, which portrays it as the place that demonstrates the folly of Ukraine trying to live apart from Russia. Closer to Russia than any other large Ukrainian city, Kharkiv has long loomed large in President Vladimir V. Rasputinov's view that Ukraine is no more than an appendage of Russia unjustly snatched away by the machinations of foreigners and misguided Ukrainian nationalists.

CHAPTER 22

Rostov-on-Don, Southern Federal District of Russia, 20 miles northeast of the Sea of Azov, 670 miles south of Moscow

February 24, 2022, 17:30

General Olena Yuriivna of the SBU sent Yuri Syrskyi and Anatoli Moisiuk to Rostov-on-Don as the Russian forces began to gather along the Ukrainian border. Their purpose was to enlist cooperation with the anti-Russian underground to mount a response to the inevitable Russian invasion. Yaroslav Melnykenko and his unit were told to meet the other agents as soon as they completed their sabotage in Kharkiv.

The meeting took place at 10:00 at the Port of Rostov-on-Don on February 24, after news of the beginning of the invasion reached them. Yaroslav and his commandoes met with Yuri and Anatoli from the SBU and two unnamed young men who were verified to belong to the anti-Nazi Rasputinov government partisan movement known as Black Bridge. Yaroslav was impressed by the careful planning, access to materiel, and professionalism of the young freedom fighters.

"Let me call you Ivan and Igor, just so I don't have to say 'hey you' or point at one of you when I need to speak directly. Our intelligence superiors have verified your authenticity, and our unit here on the ground has agreed to work with you at this important time. We have access to funding and to weapons and explosives that may be somewhat difficult for you to obtain. You have manpower and precise knowledge of the cities and most useful targets. I propose a joint venture this one time to see how well things can work, and if later missions should be shared. Sound all right with you, Ivan and Igor?"

"Da, da," the one called Igor replied. They were all speaking Russian with a hint of the southern dialect, which tended to put them at ease with each other.

The six men drew up formal plans including addresses and notes on how to get to the targets, how many men or women would need to be involved in each separate attack, and included information on safe escape routes.

They separated and began setting up the attacks while the city was in a frenzy of excitement over the immense attacks on Ukraine obviously about to take place so nearby. No one paid any attention to a few more angry men milling about; they fit into the crowds comfortably.

Yaroslav contacted Gen. Yuriivna by sat phone and arranged for six R-18 unmanned drones to be flown into a mountain glen as a start for the earliest hostilities by his unit. His commandoes were to be responsible for attacks on the port and the shipyard; the Black Bridge partisans accepted responsibility for attacks on a center for helicopter and farm machinery manufacturing, the Center-Invest bank—the largest in the Rostov region, and selected railway facilities.

Yaroslav and Yuri obtained mechanics' uniforms for the *Natsionalnaya Sluzhba Pau Remontou Vertoletov* [National Helicopter Repair Service], commandeered a company repair truck, and went about setting up their sabotage operations as if in a regular workaday set of problems. Limpet mines were fastened to the hulls of three large Russian oil transporters— one in the mouth of each water exit-way from the harbor. Thermite explosives were placed in the dry shrubbery around the port authority annex, the customs offices, and harbor police station.

Chapter 22: Rostov-on-Don, Southern Federal District of Russia…

The final choice was the helicopter hangars of the VSRF Coast Guard Rescue Service. That was the assignment of Rokosylana Mykolaivna, Fedir Blyznyuk, Boryslav Vovk, and Vasyl Haranchak, who joined Yaroslav and Yuri in the middle of the night. It was a dicey thing. Rokosylana and her team were working in broad daylight among enthusiastic Russian infantrymen and coast guard sailors who were frantically trying to get their part of the invasion into some sort of orderly arrangement in order to escape the wrath of the overzealous officers looking to enhance their careers in this once-in-a-lifetime-opportunity. That element of chaos and greedy ambition made many officers and enlisted blind to the obvious that was going on around them.

A harried secretary walked up behind Rokosylana as she was twisting a blue wire and a yellow wire together inside an olive drab colored box about the size of a cigar box.

"What are you doing, Lieutenant?" the girl asked Rokosylana.

"Repairing the security system for the hangar. This is part of the security of the Rodina, and you will forget that you will ever laid eyes on it… understand Ms…?"

The secretary backpedaled away in an almost comical fashion. The word "security" was to be avoided in any conversation her entire life, her FSB officer father had warned her; and she was not a stupid girl.

There was something of a repeat of that scene involving Fedir Blyznyuk who was wearing the insignias of an FSB lieutenant colonel. He was bent over a telephone connector box being linked to det cord. Fedir was the coolest and calmest of the SBU agents—with the possible exception of Yaroslav—and he waited to complete the connection of the two disparate sized electric wires before slowly standing up to face the questioner who was wearing a nearly new uniform of the Naval Forces of the Border Troops of the Russian Federation and wearing the brightly polished insignia of a *Matros* [Seaman], the lowest rank among the enlisted.

"I am doing the work assigned me by the FSB and the *Sluzhba Beregovoy Ochrany Rossia* [Russian Coast Guard], young man. What is it you are supposed to be doing, young man… young Seaman?"

The young man snapped to attention, "Loading barges to further the great effort of our Supreme Leader, President Rasputinov, Sir."

"Do you recognize my rank, Son?" Fedir asked in a gentle friendly voice.

"A… a…a, I am not sure, Sir. I enlisted only last week. Could you tell me, please?"

"I am a lieutenant colonel of the border marines. I am in charge of security here. You wouldn't wish to be questioned by me, would you, Son?"

"Oh, no, Sir. My captain will be wondering where I am. It is probably best for me to return to my work detail… Of course, with your permission, Sir."

His voice trembled a little.

"Don't let me keep you, Seaman. You are dismissed. Be proud of your work and do the best for your captain and for the Rodina."

"Certainly, Sir. I am proud to serve. I hope to be an important officer like you one day. May our important work succeed."

"Indeed. Carry on Seaman. You wear the uniform well."

The boy moved away and back to his duty post with alacrity.

Fedir hoped the boy had not noticed the sweat beginning to gather on his forehead.

The SBU team synchronized the timers on their explosive setups and left the port separately. Vasyl Haranchak drew the short straw and remained behind to make the detonations. He secluded himself in an alcove formed in the brick perimeter wall used to deposit trash. He had seven hours to wait.

Vasyl was tense; not because of the stress and worry over being caught, but because of the importance of his assignment. He simply could not fail. Rostov's favorable geographical position at trading crossroads promoted economic development. The Don River is a major shipping lane connecting southwestern Russia with the north. Rostov-on-Don is a trading port for Russian, Italian, Greek, and Turkish, merchants selling wool, wheat, and oil. It is also an important river port for passengers. The Rostov-on-Don agricultural region produces one-third of Russia"s vegetable oil from sunflowers.

The most difficult target to attack was the FSB building used by the FSB [Russia's Federal Security Service] in the southern end of Rostov-on-Don. Yaroslav and two of his commandoes, along with Yuri and

Anatoli from the SBU, and two Black Ridge partisans, took that assignment. The demands of the invasion attack in chief required almost every person on active duty or employed by the Russian government to be on the wharfs and docks of the harbor to push the invasion forward without mishap or wrong turn. The FSB border patrol building had been temporarily evacuated and its doors locked. In the rush to leave for the port, someone neglected to lock the rear service entrance, making the sabotage team's work easier and quieter.

The Black Ridge partisans had had ample opportunity of reconnoiter the building's perimeter and even had several chances to find a bogus way to check out the interior. As a result, they had drawn up a structural engineering map of the supports of the building and of the parts of the interior lined with fine and flammable wood. It took the team less than an hour to set the charges and to dump dozens of gallons of petrol around and upon the wood lined areas. Now, all that was left was to strike the match.

Another unit made up completely of Black Ridge saboteurs, had studied the huge Gazprom Neft refinery–third largest oil producer in Russia–for two years and had succeeded in infiltrating several members into the operations and repair departments. The refinery–oil arm of Russian gas giant Gazprom–was a local economic mainstay; the company's proven reserves totaled 1.2 billion tons of oil equivalent, and its reserve replacement ratio was more than 286%.

30% of its residents worked at the production field which supplied 40% of Moscow's gasoline needs and 50% of diesel fuel, and was also the main supplier of fuel for the capital's airports. The company and the plant were of such importance that in February, 2022, Russian Prime Minister Mikhail Mishustin signed an order giving Gazprom Neft the right to form its own private army.

The sabotage preparations outside and inside the sprawling plant took nearly two hours of running work by two dozen partisans. All was in readiness at 01:45.

At 02:30, explosions and fireballs erupted in the skies over and the ground of Moscow and Rostov-on-Don in several clearcut locations. At that disturbing moment flames erupted from the largest oil refinery in Russia's capital. Moments later, a large fire could be seen raging over multiple buildings, triggering an alarm. Residents of the districts of Kapotnya, Maryino and Brateevo reported explosions, flames leaping into the sky and a prolonged glow in the sky at around 02.30 and dock workers and area residents of the Port of Rostov, made similar frightening reports.

Pro-Kremlin news outlet *Shot* reported the fire at the refinery, complete with videos and still photographs. Telegram channel *Ostorozhno Moskva* also shared evidence of the incident at Gazprom Neft refinery, but said it was due to planned work at the plant, and added: "An oil refinery torch frightened residents of south-east Moscow." *Pravda* and RTTV—aka *Russia Today* and *Rossiya Segodnya*—contributed, "The glow was visible at night in different areas of the southeast of the capital. A column of fire rose from the chimney of the Kapotnya refinery; residents mistook the outbreak for a fire. The flare was explained by planned work at the plant."

Presuming that—as usual—the government outlets had been censored the news and sought to learn what really happened from secret connections to Western outlets as always.

Western news outlets reported that Vladimir Rasputinov's nuclear bombers–NATO reporting name: "Bears"– flew over north of Britain in the Norwegian Sea that day enroute to Ukraine. Footage from the Russian defense ministry showed Tupolev Tu-95s [large, four-engine turboprop-powered strategic and nuclear bomber and missile platform] overflying Moscow and Rostov-on-Don "during war game drills", according to the Kremlin. NATO air forces monitored the flights which lasted five hours. The videos of the event were shown throughout Europe on multiple TV outlets, excepting Russian.

Earlier on the same day, four Russian and foreign students–aged between 17 and 18–were arrested in the city of Ufa, the capital and largest city of the Republic of Bashkortostan in western Russia. An RBC Ufa source in law enforcement said that the students set fire to a switching station and signaling control equipment. The media indicated that first there was a major explosion, and then the fire spread to the warehouse.

The incident came amid regular Ukrainian kamikaze drone strikes on Russia along with sabotage attacks linked to the war on energy and transport infrastructure.

The government instituted a search by professional inspectors for involvement of Ukrainian drones as being the culprits. The government added a note to the RBC Ufa article, "All the Ukrainian drone inspectors died as a result of the incident." Apparently, not those involved in the railway sabotage. Russian government official communications are sometimes difficult to understand almost as if government officials seek to hide such incidents, concealing how far Ukraine can reach in Russia.

CHAPTER 23

In the trenches between Sverdlovsk to Dovzansky, Ukraine and Gukova to Novoshakhtinsk, Russia

May 17, 2023

On May 13, 2023, the Russian-appointed governor of Sevastopol claimed that Sevastopol Shipyard, belonging to Sevmorzavod, was struck by a Ukrainian "missile attack" at 02:00, causing a large fire. He was relieved of his command before noon. Around the Western world, that act of state sponsored clandestine war heralded the long-awaited Ukrainian "Spring offensive". In rapid succession the Ukraine army, aided by generous increases in monetary and materiel aid from most of the nations of the Western world moved through the mud and flooding of the Ukraine Spring breakup to neutralize the Russian occupied cities of Eastern Ukraine: Novosvitlivka, Izvaryne, Krasnodon, and Rovensky, in rapid succession. They appeared to be on an unstoppable offensive, and the war would be shortened considerably by their successes.

Neither Ukraine nor any Western donor had factored in the considerable power of Russia's dominance of the skies over Ukraine presently held in reserve. President Rasputinov, however, recognized his advantage from the beginning; and now, he ramped up the air war with a complete enthusiasm. He had been saving his more modern and competitive planes and ordnance until he could be sure what the United States was willing to commit. It became apparent that the American president and his military underlings were so strongly adverse to the possibility of provoking Russia into a hot war instead of the cold one they had, that there was no way they would allow American boots on the ground or F-18s, and F-35s in the sky to thwart the Russian successes. During the late afternoon of May 14, Rasputinov pursued his advantage with a vengeance.

Yaroslav, Boryslav, and Rokosylana, had left their cozy positions in the trench midway between Sverdlovsk to Dovzansky, which was the oldest, best made, and least attacked, of the entire trench system. The trench was stretched out along the banks of the Southern railroad. It was a lazy, sunny, afternoon; and the three were fighting the need for an afternoon nap.

It was Rokosylana's turn on the high-powered Arctic P9 Military Telescope-4K 10-300X40mm, waterproof Super Telephoto Zoom Monocular Telescope, High Power Scope Night Vision with smart-phone holder. Its interferometer arrays provided the highest resolving power, because resolution is proportional to the array size rather than the aperture of the individual telescopes. The theoretical limit of useful magnification for a telescope is 50 or 60 times the telescope's aperture in inches, or two times the aperture in millimeters. So, for a 60mm refractor, the maximum useful power is 120x (i.e., 120 times the magnification of the naked eye). The beautiful instrument Rokosylana cuddled in her grip was double that with perfect clarity. She took care of the scope with all the love and attention she might have for a newborn baby.

She went from drowsy and inattentive to electrically wide awake and aware of very tiny image, sound, and movement, around her and out in the sky. She wasted less than a second to confirm what she was seeing. There were several dozen Russian Su-57s beginning to darken the sky between Dovzansky, Ukraine and Novoshakhtinsk, Russia.

Rokosylana shouted to Yaroslav, "Russian bomber squadron headed toward us. Hurry up and check it out through the scope! We have to report to all bases. Hurry, man!"

Yaroslav woke up with a start and catapulted himself to where Rokosylana was sitting. He looked through the Arctic P-9 scope and confirmed her observation.

He went to his coms and sent out a top-secret coded message, which, translated, read, "20+ Su-57s enroute to Ukraine border, coordinates attached. No mistake," and affixed his code numbers.

Within two minutes, Yaroslav, Rokosylana, and Boryslav, watched spell bound as the trench south of the railroad emptied of combatants, and they were transported by any and all available vehicles to the bomb shelters north of them. The three SBU agents quickly threw on ghillie suits and hunkered down to watch the coming melee.

The Russian fighter jets had escaped radar detection until they were within ten miles of the border. Upon detection, the pastureland north of the railroad suddenly bristled with what looked at first like cemetery stakes pushing out of the ground. Ack-ack gun barrels appeared from hidey-holes all along the nearly fifty mile stretch of trenches.

The Sukhoi-57's design emphasizes frontal stealth, with RCS-reducing features most apparent in the forward hemisphere; the shaping of the aft fuselage is less optimized for radar stealth compared to American stealth designs such as the F-22 and F-35, likely related to cost reduction. The Su-57 is a twin-engine stealth multirole fighter aircraft and is the first aircraft in Russian military service designed with stealth technology. It was intended to be the basis for a family of stealth combat aircraft. Due to a lack of funds after the dissolution of the Soviet Union, the development program was repeatedly delayed and the first flight of the MiG 1.44/1.42 prototypes did not appear until 2000, nine years behind schedule.

Owing to the high costs, the MFI and LFI projects were eventually cancelled while the Russian Ministry of Defense began work on a new next-generation fighter program incorporating cost reductions that reduced stealth capacity. Further cost-saving measures included an intended size between that of the Su-27 and the MiG-29 and normal takeoff weight considerably smaller than the MiG MFI's and the Su-47's 26.8 tons. The modern and deadly squadron was a far cry from a few weeks before when Russian pilots in Ukraine had to use civilian GPS units taped to the dashboards to navigate.

The Sukhoi-57s dropped down from 20,000 feet to 200 feet altitude, divided into two attacking flanks, and strafed the trenches from east to west and west to east, at Mach 1.3 [870 mph] leaving a streak of flame from their 1 × 30 mm Gryazev-Shipunov GSh-30-1 autocannons and a follow-up scream of their 2 × Saturn AL-41-f1 afterburn-ing tur-bofan [two each] engines that could be seen from a distant satellite.

The Russian flight commander, Capt. Irina Bogdan, reported back to her base–5th Aerospace Defense brigade, Petrovskoe, Moscow Oblast. When the first reports of the triumphant air attack came into President Rasputinov's office, Capt. Bogdan was recommended for a badge of merit for her heroism. The following day, when intelligence reports told of the fact that not a single Ukrainian person had been killed or wounded, the unfortunate air force captain was reported by *Pravda* to have "died of a massive stroke".

Presidential meeting regarding the use of air power in the war between Russia and Ukraine; May 18, 2023; White House Situation Room:

Officers Present: POTUS, VPOTUS, NSA [National Security Advisor], Secretaries of Defense, State, Treasury, and HS, entire JCOS, Heads of all fifteen intelligence services, DNI, Speaker of the House, and Senate Majority Leader.

POTUS: I have only been in office for my second term for a few months. This air raid disaster is the fault of the previous administration. I want that to be entered into the record. I have always recommended the use of US air force patrols and fighters for the war in Ukraine that the previous president got us into. I have always said that we had to have our F-35s flying over Ukraine and taking control of the skies.

NSA: But, Mr. President, some of us are confused about your orders. We have been forbidden to put American boots on the ground or American planes in the Ukrainian skies. Are you articulating a new order for us to send F-16s, F-18s, and F-35s to the front, Sir?"

POTUS: Moron. Are you also demented? Or deaf? You just heard me. I have always been in favor of winning that war.

NSA: But, Sir, what about antagonizing President Rasputinov and widening the war?"

POTUS: Fool! You are fired. Is that clear enough?

NSA: Crystal.

POTUS: Then leave. As of now, I assume the position of NSA. General Hoyt, you and your staff are hereby ordered to send as many planes of as many different types as needed to win this silly little war today.

CJCS: The DOD does not have funding. That will have to come from Congress.

POTUS: I am surrounded by morons. Don't you think I know that? Was that intended as an insult?

CJCS: Certainly not, Sir. Just a matter of protocol and simple necessity.

POTUS: I will have that taken care of before the end of the workday today. You are now all dismissed. Get back to work.

Presidential meeting May 18, 2023; the Grand Kremlin Palace, official working residence of the president of Russia

Officers Present: President, Prime Minister, Ranking Deputy Prime Ministers, Chairman of the Federation Council of the Federal Assembly of the Russian Federation [Speaker, presiding officer of the Upper house of the Russian parliament], Chief of Staff of the Presidential Executive Office, Federal ministers–[Finance], [Minister of Civil Defense, Emergencies, and Disaster Relief], Minister of Justice, Marshal of the Russian Federation, Chief of the General Staff of the Fleet, and Patriarch of Moscow and all Rus', head of the Russian Orthodox Church.

Agenda: Special Military Operation, Stealth planes and additional air support.

President: Our first Su-57 sortie for the special military operation was not quite as successful as we had hoped owing to the personal failure of its leader, Captain Bogdan, who was relieved of her command this morning. Our best intelligence indicates that it was not on account of mechanical failure, poor planning, or communications errors. Fortunately, every pilot and plane returned to the Rodina intact and ready to fight another day.

All of you are hereby ordered to continue this meeting to come up with a new and flawless plan of attack by the end of the day before the

Americans and my friend, the president, feel duty bound to send in their own planes and escalate the conflict. Marshal of the Russian Federation, I order you to take full charge. Make it a certainty that we act before the Americans can muddle through their impossibly complicated procedures to get planes in the air. I will call their president and reason with him. I have some confidence that I will be able to convince him of the folly of engaging our air force.

Marshal of the Russian Federation: I commend that ruling, Sir. We have serious limits in our modern air force and even more serious lack of funding ever since the collapse of the glorious Soviet Union.

President: We will not speak of such things in public, is that understood by everyone here?

The voting was unanimous.

CHAPTER 24

A New Battle for Kyiv

July 30, 2024

The United States Congress continued to dither about funding for Ukraine, no longer about how much, but whether to do so at all. It was the silly season in America and sillier than usual. The divisions in the country were drawn more sharply than ever before with far rightists against far leftists, Republicans v. Democrats, democrats (true liberals) v. the populist dictator base (hard right evangelicals), young v. seniors, blue collar v. white collar educated, rural v. urban, and secessionists v. unionists. Progress in sending enough F-22s and F-35s to Ukraine was being lost in the commotion. Above all–it was an election year–and nothing really mattered to lawmakers as much as getting re-elected once again.

The president continued to cast blame on the previous administration. The previous administration was now the not-so-loyal opposition. President Zelenskyy and a delegation of Ukrainian parliamentary and military officers were on a state visit, which had become basically an old fashion barn-storming Harry Trumanesque affair. Zelenskyy had given up on Congress and its political machinations. He was taking the Ukraine survival cause to the American Public to see if he could have more success with the sensible citizens of the fifty states. As a reward for his stellar–if largely secret–service and his movie star good looks, Yaroslav Kanybavych Melnykenko accompanied the president wherever he went as his chief of security, and—on the QT—a secret military advisor.

The American president was beset on all sides with recommendations and demands regarding what to do or not to do about Ukraine. He personally feared the big bear, Rasputinov and his irrationality, and he was afraid that he would lose the looming presidential election if he continued to appear to be weak in his confrontation with Rasputinov. He was also concerned deeply about his private business dealings with the mercurial Russian dictator; he stood to lose hundreds of millions. He and Zelenskyy arranged for a top-secret meeting at Camp David with their top military advisors to come up with a solution before it was too late.

The president welcomed Zelenskyy and his entourage fulsomely, and Zelenskyy responded with bear hugs all around.

"Mr. President," Zelenskyy said, "I can see your dilemma clearly. Nothing can happen until after the elections. From our viewpoint, it will no longer matter by then. I am not a defeatist, but we Ukrainians will be defeated in the next few months and will be resorting to guerilla warfare to keep the idea of Ukraine alive by November 20.

"I have a suggestion, one which would require you to go against the government that is opposed to anything you do. The Congress is so nearly evenly divided, that neither you nor Congress is going to be able to break the logjam before it is too late."

"What can we do, then, Mr. President?"

"You see the young man behind me, Sir?"

"The sturdy looking blond man?"

"Yes, him. He has been directly involved in our war against the Russians since 2014. The number of people who know that could be counted on the fingers of your two hands, and he likes to keep it that way. So do I. He is effective, and I can officially count him as head of a Ukrainian committee negotiation with your intelligence services to tap into their resources—including funds expropriated from Russian oligarchs, from frozen fortunes held by the treasury as part of the sanctions against the Russians, North Koreans, Iranians, and deposits in foreign countries, like the Caymans and Vanuatu held as evidence by the US government in legal cases against gang lords, drug lords, the mafia, and the like. Some for decades. Our intelligence is certain that the cumulative amount of money is more than sufficient to get an adequate supply of fighter jets and bombers to us in time and in sufficient numbers to stave off the current drive by the Russians. We think this is a do-or-die moment."

"What is your man's name, if I may ask?"

"Yaroslav Kanybavych Melnykenko. That is a top-secret piece of information, Mr. President. I ask that you not share it with anyone."

"Before I decide on anything rash in the way of clandestine operations, I want to meet the man, and so will my intelligence chiefs. We will have to trust one another to the enth degree, if we are going to have any hope of success."

Yaroslav and Rokosylana were beckoned forward to meet the US President. Their assuredness and physical presence captured his favor immediately. His brief communication with them was the clincher.

The president asked, "May I call you, Yaroslav?"

"That is my name, Sir, but it would probably be better to refer to me by my code name: "Common Man", and with this fine soldier as "*Vovchytsia*" which means "she-wolf" in Ukrainian.

"Of course. Have you ever met our intelligence officers, especially any of the heads of service?"

"No, Sir, but Vovchytsia and I are looking forward to the opportunity. Frankly, Sir, time is wasting; and we believe your decision should be made now; and let us get moving with the intelligence chiefs and their contacts before day's end."

"And with their sources of money, *tse ne tak*? [Ukrainian for "not so?"]

Yaroslav and President Zelenskyy both laughed.

Yaroslav replied, "of course. We have made good use of your funding thus far, I hope you agree. We will not let you down, this time, either. With your planes, we can stop the big bear of Russia from destroying our democracy."

"And then, will you be coming to me or my successor for approval to put American soldiers on the ground to fight with you?"

"Fair question, Sir. You and I both know that a number of your fine SEALs and Green Berets have worked with me and my SBU unit on several occasions. Other than that, we cannot foresee American troops fighting directly in Ukraine against the Russians. That would be more dangerous than helpful in the long run, because we would then likely see the beginning of World War III, and—in the end—mutually assured mass destruction—of the people of the earth."

"You are wise beyond your years, young man. I am going to put my trust and that of the American people in you to get this job done. Don't let me or your president Zelenskyy down."

"I won't, Sir. You can count on Ukraine, and you can count on me."

CHAPTER 25

A New Battle for Kyiv

July 30, 2024, 21:00

T he ODNI [Office of the Director of National Intelligence] summoned all seventeen heads of US IC [Intelligence Community] agencies and their deputies to a top-secret meeting at Camp Peary, Virginia that afternoon at the behest of the president. Even the president was not to know the decision or any operational plans.

The US intelligence community is composed of 17 distinct organizations that operate under different levels of secrecy and oversight. These organizations include two independent agencies, the Office of the Director of National Intelligence and the Central Intelligence Agency, and 15 other agencies under the Department of Defense or other departments. The intelligence community employs hundreds of thousands of people, both in government and in private companies, working on counterterrorism, homeland security, and intelligence. The total budget for American intelligence is unknown, but it is at least the equal of the GDP of the majority of the nations of the world. The DNI addressed the assembled spies.

"President Zelenskyy, ladies and gentlemen, this has been a most interesting and complicated day. We have spent nine hours researching the possibilities, evaluating the risks, and—not least—searching out sources of funding which are not only sufficient for the matter at hand, but also ones that can remain unnoticed and as top-secrets for longer than most of us will live.

"I am pleased to inform you of two important things: first, we have enough money for completion of the mission, and for expediting it; second, we have the full cooperation and permission from the President of the United States and certain members of the Congress, the judiciary, and treasury, to use the funds as needed. I cannot emphasize more, that this is a mission based on mutual trust. Any leak or sale of information will be considered treason, but also such a breach of trust, that our two nations, NATO, and the European allies, will never trust us fully again.

"I will not say that again. Police yourselves, and keep your lips zipped. I have passed out copies of the sources of funding, and a rough outline of our plan of action. None of those papers is to leave this room or to be copied in any fashion. In brief, you will see that we have sources of funds ready today to begin the transport of twenty-two F-35s, thirty F-22s, fifteen F-18s, and sixty F-16s. President Zelenskyy and his code-only intelligence agents, Common Man and Vovchytsia, will handle all details of actions and expenses outside the US, and the ODNI will manage everything that begins or ends in the United States.

"One more thing before I take questions. You have the top-secret names for the Ukrainian intelligence agents involved. Their code names are never to be used outside the circle of men and women assembled here today. The code for ODNI is Ozymandias. No laughing permitted about the serious choice."

Everyone in the conference room laughed.

The selected Treasury Department employee–a septuagenarian of considerable renown, and a face known to the public—asked, "Who obtains and how is the money to be transferred and accounted for?"

"You, Sir, will be in charge of that. Remember, this is an urgent situation; and you are to use your highly vaunted intelligence to work ways out. I have counted on you before and expect to do so this time as well."

The Army deputy chief of staff for intelligence—a lieutenant general–asked, "What is the arrangement for policing the operation? This much money could be tempting; there could also be a Aldrich Ames or John Anthony Walker, Jr. or two lurking about."

"The DDCIA has accepted that assignment. As you all know, he is eminently qualified."

"And if we have questions as we go along?" the Assistant Director of the CGCIS [Coast Guard Intelligence] asked.

"The importance of the mission is so great, and the need so urgent, that I have instructed my office to get hold of me as quickly as humanly possible day or night for any serious or time-sensitive questions. Just call the ODNI and give the code name "Oxymandias". You will get an answer. Your agency protects the Coast Guard from foreign agents who might attempt to penetrate their ranks or compromise their operations, and I expect every other agency to do their uttermost to accomplish such security missions as well. Do not feel as if you need to stand on protocol; get the job done, however difficult or odious it may be. Get forgiveness afterwards.

"That reminds me of a story told by Seneca. He made reference to the Second Punic war Rome fought with Hannibal and Carthage. Hannibal ordered a military mission to sneak up behind the Romans by crossing the Alps in winter. He had a huge number of elephants brought along to carry the heavy loads up the steep and treacherous trails of the Alpine barrier to attacks against Rome. Elephants fell; men died of the cold and hunger; and Hannibal's generals finally joined together to convince him that it was impossible to cross the Alps by elephant or any other way during a winter such as this one.

"His reply showed the steel of his spine, "*Aut inveniam viam aut faciam*", he said [I shall find a way or make one.] He went on to defeat the Romans at the Battle of Zama. So, I say to you, find a way, make one, or get help from any or all of us, your brothers in arms."

Knowing the two great advantages the Russian Federation held over Ukraine and the West—especially America—Rasputinov launched a second front in his war with a new Battle of Kyiv, a Russian air dog fight against Americans on August 24, 2024 at 11:00, notably Ukraine Independence Day from the USSR in 1991. Rasputinov's advantages—as he saw them—were that the US president was a coward, afraid to take on the vaunted Russian Sukhoi-57s, or to provoke the leader of all the Russias by introducing aerial warfare which could lead to Rasputinov's ace-up-his-sleeve, thermonuclear war.

A sortie of twelve Su-57s and eighteen Su-24s, a supersonic jet that could be used in all weather conditions—streaked across the Russo-Ukraine eastern border. The Su-57 has a twin-engine, variable-sweep wing design as well as a twin-seat arrangement—with seats side by side—for two pilots. Bringing up the rear—coming in from the north out of Belarus—were 16 MiG-29s, originally developed in the late 70s, and introduced in 1982 as a counterpoint to America's F-16s.

Rasputinov and his generals, including the dictatorial leader of the Wagner Mercenary Group, Col. Gen. Mikhail Oleksandrovich Mizin-tsev; Commander-in-Chief of the General Staff of the Russian Federation, Army General Oleshchuk Razvozhaev; Defense Minister, Lieutenant General Mykola Oleksiy Neizhpapa; Commander of the Air Force, General Igor Kolokoltsev; Commander of the Ground Forces, Lieutenant General Anatoliy Pavliuk; Director of Procurement, Col. Gen. Denis Barhylevych; Commander of the National Guard; General Valery Nikolay Bogdanovskyvich, Commander of the 11th Separate Airborne Assault Brigade; Oligarchs Grigorie Serhiy Nayev and Radion Tymoshenko; and an even dozen spectacularly beautiful young Russian actresses, ballerinas, and sporting stars, gathered with the Great Leader Rasputinov in the General Staff Building located in Moscow on Znamenka Street 14/1 in the Arbat District.

They were each part of the "in-group" of Vladimir Rasputinov, some in commanding positions, some ex-officio members of the behind-the-scenes government [the *eminence grises*], others heavy donors to Rasputinov's occasional political campaigns, and still others were window dressing +. There was a jovial celebratory mood as they turned their attention to the two 75-inch television screens on either side of the room.

Rasputinov himself, introduced what was about to be seen in full color and real time.

"You, my friends, are here to witness history; namely, the end of the 'special military operation' in Ukraine. Watch closely as our horde of

Su-57s, Su-24s, and other equally superior Russian fighter jets annihilate Kyiv as we serve as observers. Does everyone have a flute of champagne ready for the cheering when we see the end of the insurrection by the Ukrainians?"

The screens opened with a rapidly passing ground scape over pastureland, then destroyed cities, then the majestic Carpathian Mountains, and finally the very familiar approaches to the exurbs of the Ukrainian capital city, at supersonic speed. Staccato streaks of machine gun fire and occasional rocket launch now signaled the opening of hostilities.

The Polish Air Force Commander, Lt. Gen. Kacper Gasiorowski; NATO Commander, General Sir Percy Whitcomb-Leigh; the Commander of the United States Air Force, Gen. David H. Brown; and the Commander of the Ukraine Air force, sat on the edge of their chairs in the command center of the Rzeszów NATO airbase in Poland, 20 miles from the Ukraine western border watching the same video footage as Vladimir Rasputinov and his inner circle. When the first Su-57s appeared on screen, and it was firmly established that their trajectory was vectored toward Kyiv, Ukraine, every man's head nodded; then the Commander-in-Chief of the Armed Forces of Ukraine, Gen. Ruslan Zaluzhnyi, raised his right hand and brought it down sharply by his side without saying as word.

Below—on the tarmac—the idling engines of thirty US Air Force F-35 fighters, twenty-five F-16s, and five Boeing B-52 Stratofortress bombers—rated the best of the best in the world—roared into full throttle and began an orderly, but extremely rapid transit down the four selected runways and into the skies on GPS coordinates for Kyiv. The bombers were on a different and less rapid course. Their GPS coordinates were fixed on Rostov-On-Don Russia.

All pilots and crews were highly experienced aviators who had— the week before—completed an especially rigorous training program in Florida on how to use F-35s and F-16s in coordinated dog fight air battles. Each man and woman in the training program had had to complete the Top Dog training requirements in the William Tell contest. The contest is a biennial aerial gunnery competition with fighter aircraft held at Tyndall Air Force Base in Florida by the USAF [United States Air Force] in every even-numbered year. In the competition, teams representing the various major commands of the USAF and other competing countries take part in live-fire exercises for air-to-air dog fight and missile engagements.

The winner is rated as "Top Gun", and every Ukrainian had to achieve a rating within a very few points of the Top Gun. Having done so, they were considered to be ready for any battle situation.

When President Rasputinov and his guests at Znamenka Street saw the departure of the United States fighters and bombers from Poland on their TV screens, they were too shocked to speak; they sat with their mouths agape.

CHAPTER 26

A New Day for Kyiv

July 30, 2024, 22:20

The Russian frigate *Admiral Makarov* in the Black Sea was involved in late morning Zircon 3M22 Hypersonic Missile attack on Kyiv. A second missile was fired from the *Admiral Gorshkov* frigate in the White Sea. A Zircon missile can reach eight times the speed of sound—upwards of 7,000 mph–has a range of 625 miles, and can carry a 660-pound warhead. A Zircon fired from a ship or submarine docked in the only known base in southern Russia's Astrakhan Oblast, or from the Russian naval base in Novorossiysk, could hit London in five minutes. Added to the fact of its speed, the Russian Zircon hypersonic missile has stealth features. The Patriot missile defense proved to be inadequate—too slow. However, both Zircons missed their targets and created huge craters in open pasture land owned by farmers, Viktor Myrhorodskyy and Maksym Khorenko.

The missiles fired during the July 30 attack included short-range ballistic missiles as the primary weapon, but also included medium-range ballistic missiles, cruise missiles, surface-to-air missiles, and various sea-launched missiles. Ukraine's military shot down more than three-quarters of the incoming missiles including several cruise missiles during the attack but made no mention of intercepting a Zircon.

The secret ad hoc border crossing on the A4 highway into Ukraine's western Lviv region regularly supplied Ukraine from its NATO neighbor. On July 26, more than 30 Russian cruise missiles targeted the sprawling Ukraine side storage and supply-chain facility that is less than 15 miles from the closest border point. Poland is a key location for routing Western military aid to Ukraine.

The Ukrainian air armada had only a relatively few miles to go and therefore reached Kyiv before the Russian fleet of Su-57s, but the appearance on the horizon of the Russian supersonic jets was daunting. Ukraine's air defenses had proved relatively effective over the previous year, often intercepting up to three-quarters of the missiles fired at its territory. But in recent months, Russia had been launching increasingly complex barrages of different missiles and drones in an attempt to saturate and penetrate these defenses.

In the previous week, a Russian long-distance attack included 64 Russian cruise missiles, ballistic missiles, and drones, which killed five people in a village and took out the hospital and a pre-school. The Russian fleet of Su-57s was daunting, but that pessimism was countered in a dramatic fashion by the surprise appearance of America's dogfighting champion, the F-22 Raptor–the acrobatic prize fighter Lockheed Martin F-22 and the impressive and highly vaunted F-35s.

The Russian pilots had express orders not to allow any Su-57s to hit the ground; and if F-22s or 35s were seen, to retreat because the Russian Air Force senior officers were fully aware that the Sukoi were no match for either stealth fighter in a dog fight. The command was given brusquely, and the large Russian force made a sudden and intense about face and flew back to their bases in Western Russia. The Ukrainian Air Force recalled the B-52 Stratofortress bombers before they reached their targets in Rostov-on-Don.

On the return flight, two Su-57s went down, one from a surface to air missile, and the other from antiaircraft fire. The Ukrainians and Americans were jubilant at the opportunity to investigate the Su-57s and learn the Russian's top secrets. Taken together, there was enough left intact in the wreckage to keep investigators on a steep learning curve for months. The capture of the planes had the opposite effect in Russia.

Rasputinov went ballistic and had the lead pilot of the squadron executed; the cost of the downed planes resulted in a full stop of any more planned supersonic attacks. The cost of production was too high to allow any of them to be destroyed; they had to be conserved for international sales, which lined Rasputinov's personal coffers greatly, and that overrode any combat value. High costs limited production, profits, and supply of scarce materiel, for the complex aerial machines. Rasputinov backed away from the risks of loss posed by using his precious planes and nest egg for his project in Ukraine and because Russia was obviously experiencing problems with its Kalibr cruise missiles after successful strikes by Ukrainian forces in Crimea.

Furthermore—by the end of August–Russian forces were running low on air-launched cruise missiles because Russia had to preserve that inventory as part of its declining stocks of precision guided munitions for a possible time when they were losing serious ground. An additional major benefit for the Ukraine cause was that no longer did the American president or NATO shrink from creating a no-fly zone, probably the single most important development in the conflict thus far. There was no longer a good reason to ignore President Zelenskyy's pleas or to limit the contribu-tion of USAF F-35A Lightning II Joint Strike Fighters to the war effort based on the erroneous fear that it would trigger a wider war with Rasputinov.

Rasputinov–ever the profit-driven huckster—announced to the world that Russia's sophisticated Su-57 Felon jets had been "brilliant" for Moscow's war effort in Ukraine, despite Western propaganda over just how often the aircraft had actually been deployed over the war-torn country. If an Su-57 jet were to be shot down in Ukraine, he knew, it would prove that the plane is not truly a top-tier fighter, killing any hope of it selling around the world. Therefore, he omitted any information about war casualties for his planes or that they added to the financial drain of the Ukraine war and Russia's limited manufacturing capabilities. The Russian dictator continued to insist that the Su-57 "represents the best of Russian aviation and exceeds the capabilities of fourth-generation fighter jets such as the F-15 and F-16." He omitted that it is no match for the F-22 or F-35.

The UK's MOD [Ministry of Defense] reported its intelligence that although it was highly likely Su-57 aircraft had been operating over Ukraine, the missions were probably actually completed in what was currently Russian territory. The MOD suggested the Kremlin had a strong "risk-averse" policy to their prized aircraft, fearing "the compromise of sensitive technology," without revealing that information had already flown the coop.

From their forensic dissection of the downed Su-57s, the Americans, NATO, and Ukraine, learned that Russia's Su-57 is the least stealthy of the 5th generation entrants and unanimously agreed that in a dog fight with the American fighters, the Su-57 would be taken out very quickly. However, they were also confident that such a dog fight was unlikely to occur unless World War III were to break out.

With Kyiv apparently able to defend itself for the time being in this long and frustrating war, Yaroslav and Rokosylana worked on a long-term plan to turn the tide. It was detailed and logical, given the current circumstances and expectations for the future. They presented their plan to the Head of SBU, General Olena Yuriivna who quickly got the general staff to review it. The costs and risks were minimal in comparison to the losses being sustained in the trench warfare situation in Donbas; it could be done largely in secret; and—best of all—it contained highly desirable plausible deniability. After two weeks of tweaking the plan, it was approved.

CHAPTER 27

Along the Donbas Front

October 21, 2024

Yaroslav and Rokosylana lived a vagabond existence traversing the ever shifting battle zones in the Donbas Region after leaving Kyiv. The stalemated trench warfare era of the war had shifted significantly since the end of July that year, 17 months into Rasputinov's War. The change was more of a see-saw with territory changing hands and control frequently. It was very difficult for soldiers on both sides, particularly for the Russian conscripts. Even by that late stage in the war, many Russians–like those Americans dragooned from prisons or kidnapping akin to the impressment of sailors into the British navy almost 300 years before—were being kidnapped off Moscow's streets. More than 75% of wounded Russian boys were left to die in the field, abandoned by their leaders and their country.

The SBU commandoes were involved in a series of bomb attacks on trains. Their first—and most successful–caper was the derailing of a fuel train passing over a rail bridge on the Baikal-Amur Mainline in the Russian Far East [Vladivostok] during the first week in August. They assisted partisans in an attack on a Russian military refueling station in Melitopol just north of the Sea of Azov. The fuel tanks, railroad tracks, and support buildings, were blown up; and several soldiers and railway workers were killed. Best of all, six carloads of military equipment were damaged beyond repair. They were behind an attack on an interrogation building in Krasnodar, Russia and were able to free twenty-three much abused former POWs.

Yaroslav, Rokosylana, Boryslav, Fedir, and Vasyl, were instrumental in enabling Ukraine forces to down 18 out of 25 Shahed-136/131 drones and one X-59 missile intended for Bila Tserkya. They also trucked in domestically made electromagnetic warfare systems equipment from Lviv to protect soldiers from radar-guided weapons and drones.

Vasyl became the commandoes'—and by extension—the army's, premier drone specialist. In early September, drone video showed a targeted strike blowing up three antennas on the roof of an apartment block. Vasyl—acting as drone commander—destroyed a Russian Pole-21 electronic warfare system on the eastern front near Donetsk.

The five main SBU operatives were the first to recognize that Ukraine was going to have to enter an Electronic Warfare game of cat and mouse if their country was ever going to break free of their recurring unproductive stalemate with the enemy. With the aid of Russian support and forces, separatists in eastern Ukraine conducted combined arms operations and was highly proficient at enabling integration, particularly information operations (IO), electronic warfare (EW), and unmanned aerial systems (UAS).

They teamed up with Pavlo Fedorov–the drone commander of the Ukraine 59th Motorized Brigade–and dedicated themselves to catch up and then surpass Russia in electronic warfare, thereby achieving a meaningful change.

Pavlo said, "Look, we have to destroy these EW systems of the Russians or lose. It is as simple as that. Successfully destroying these systems is critical if Ukraine is to liberate more territory. Liberate enough territory before next winter sets in, and we win the war. Fail to do that, and the war drags on long enough for us to die of attrition."

The Pole-21 system--designed to jam GPS signals to protect Russian assets from incoming drones or missiles–is one important feature of Moscow's growing electronic arsenal. Pavlo and the SBU commandoes stopped shooting at people and began in earnest to execute strikes against Pole-21 systems which proved to be very successful.

Pavlo made an elementary observation that proved to be both simple and effective.

"Right now," he said, "the best hope we have is that videos we've made go viral. Most of our Ukrainian troops are on social media—even in the field–so, any viral footage like we've made could act like a photographic handbook. They can identify Russian antennas on the battlefield or be on the lookout for otherwise inconspicuous mechanical stuff on trucks, tanks, or planes. That we can have a huge source of targets to direct our own EW [electronic warfare] at."

The six of them began to compile an actual handbook for the Ukrainian troops to let them be aware of the new and important change warfare was taking and how important it was to keep up. They explained the fundamentals: Electromagnetic warfare or electronic warfare involves the use of the electromagnetic spectrum or directed energy to control the spectrum, attack an enemy, or impede enemy operations. The Russians started doing it the day they first invaded Ukraine. The purpose of electromagnetic warfare is to deny the Russkies the advantage of—and ensure friendly Ukrainians, Americans, and other friendlies, unimpeded access to the EM spectrum we use.

Pavlo again made his point, now as instruction, not to sell his ideas.

"Electromagnetic warfare can be applied from air, sea, land, or space by crewed and uncrewed systems, and can target communication, radar, or other military and civilian assets. An electronic attack is offensive use of EM energy–electronic defense and electronic surveillance. Activities used in EW include electro-optical; infrared and radio frequency countermeasures; EM compatibility and deception; radio and radar jamming and deception.

We have to know electronic counter-countermeasures/anti-jamming; electronic masking; probing; reconnaissance; intelligence; electronic security; EW reprogramming; emission control; spectrum management; and wartime reserve modes. We can't afford to be ignorant of all this technology, otherwise Russia will have us for lunch."

They spelled out every term, made a simplified description for how all of it worked, included videos and still photographs—everything the otherwise uninformed troops needed to use EW to Ukraine's advantage. They first had to recognize how behind the curve they were, then to convince the officers and higher command, and to get everyone to admit that not only did they live in an electromagnetic environment, but it amounted to a chink in Ukraine's armor, especially since they received so much of the armor from NATO. Russia's electronic arsenal was rapidly growing, and they had to do some quick catching up.

Next, they had to recognize two fundamental problems regarding EW that the Russians were using against them: Russian jammers had turned the technological advantage of Ukraine's Western/NATO-provided arsenal of "smart"-guided–weapons into a vulnerability. Precision-guided missiles and guided multiple launch rocket systems–such as HIMARS– are by their nature, more vulnerable to electronic warfare than unguided weapons because they rely on GPS to hit their targets.

Unguided weapons, common in the Soviet-era stockpiles of both Russia and Ukraine, pre-2022, do not; and Ukraine had to recognize that the older weaponry could be both useful or a detriment in the new environment. Useful, because EW had no power over them; a detriment, because the EW weapons were so much more sophisticated that sometimes they might as well be throwing rocks as using the old ways.

Pavlo and the SBU commandoes began—on their own initiative– to teach classes. They learned as they taught such things as jamming, as spoofing GPS [a technique which effectively tricks an enemy drone or missile into thinking it's some-where else] which also disrupts radar, radio and even cell phone communications, are all part of the Kremlin's playbook and needed to be incorporated into Ukraine's and fast. Experts and Ukrainian officials agreed openly that Russia had now fully integrated electronic warfare with its troops. Ukraine could no longer be cavalier about the need for education and to weed out the men and boys, women and girls, without adequate backgrounds or the intelligence to learn quickly.

Russia was now fully invested in trench electronic warfare. The tactical level of the Russian troops was saturated with the equipment; and even with equipment losses, Moscow still maintained significant electronic warfare superiority, the Ukrainian armed forces command-er-in-theater told his troops.

"Take for example," he said, singling out American-made Excalibur shells. "They are now losing their capability because the GPS target-ing system is very sensitive to the influence of enemy electronic warfare, and the impact of Russian jamming has been observed in certain United States-provided systems, including HIMARS rocket launchers. The sys-tems are not altogether ineffective, but our own technology is being used against us increasingly."

Ukraine had been able to increase domestic drone production a hun-dredfold during that year, and that was something that transformed the battlefield. But Yaroslav was watching Rasputinov's War against Ukraine make an early transition from drone army to electronic army. Ukraine's minister of digital transformation, Anitoli Myrhorodskyy, now hoped to repeat that success with electronic warfare–not least because drones are so often the victims of EW.

Although, at heart, the young soldier/spy was a boots-on-the-ground, hunter/killer soldier, he recognized that electronic warfare capabilities and tactics had to be integrated into conventional force operations. Somebody–probably the top brass–was going to be needed to think about the next technological stage in the war. Yaroslav could envision the problems in dealing with drones v. EW, and he did not want to be involved.

The thorny problem they all faced was oversaturating the battlefield with EW, but Ukraine instead needed to design EW systems that can be controlled remotely, so they target only enemy equipment. Otherwise, there was a real risk that electronic warfare systems could work against the army using them, resulting in downing their own drones—essen-tially electronic fratricide.

He concluded that it was not going to be him. Yaroslav Kandybavych Melnykenko needed to get away from the machines and science and back to what he did best—find and take out enemies the old-fashion way. He was proud of his country and his army. They were gradually succeeding. Kyiv was rushing to destroy Moscow's technology on the battlefield–a sign of how important it may be for the future of the war. That side of the military was making progress predominantly through electronic jammers that throw-off GPS guided targeting systems, causing rockets to miss their targets. Fascinating–and a good thing–but he was looking elsewhere to contribute and to make his mark.

He and his SBU commando team applied to SBU Chief General Olena Yuriivna for permission to move on to the plan they had agreed upon together in Kyiv. She recognized that the EW aspect of war was moving beyond the restlessness of Yaroslav's youth, and she granted his request.

The unit was transferred to Zaporizhzhia Oblast, southeast Ukraine, to be part of the Battle of the Donbas in the east which began on March 3, 2024, and continued sporadically to the present day. In August, a video and photos of the head and hands of a Ukrain-ian prisoner of war stuck on poles appeared. The video showed the mutilated body of the captured soldier with his head stuck on a wooden pole and his hands on metal spikes on either side of it, in front of the garden of a house in the occupied region.

A war correspondent from a Russian media outlet reported in *Telegram* newspaper that the Wagner PMC [Private Military Company] base was set up in a five-story residential building that had apparently been abandoned at Myronivska Street, 12. That had sparked the emergency clandestine mission to kill or capture Lt. Col. Dmitriy Utkinov ("Wagner"), Yevgeny, Col. Konstantin Pikalov, Col. Andrei Troshev, and Col. Gen. Mikhail Mizin-tsev, Wagner commanders. The Wagner Group is a private paramilitary organization run by an ally of Russian dictator Vladimir Rasputinov. The group has tens of thousands of fighters and has operated in Syria and in various African countries as a violent kleptocracy. It was Yaroslav and his commandoes' big chance to make a real difference.

CHAPTER 28

Zaporizhzhia, Zaporizhzhia Oblast, southeast Ukraine, on the banks of the Dnieper River

November 14, 2024

The search for the Wagner Group hierarchy began in earnest as soon as the team arrived in Zaporizhzhia, following leads from dissidents among the Wagner mercenaries, Ukrainian sympathizer patriots, well-meaning frightened common people, spreaders of disinformation, and other spies. Zaporizhzhia was considered to be pacified and largely back under Ukrainian governmental control and therefore safe. That only applied to the hours of daylight. After dark, all bets were off throughout the oblast and on both sides of the Dnipro River.

The Dnipro splits the city in two; between them is Khortytsia Island. The name "*Zaporizhzhia*" refers to the position of the city: "beyond the rapids", ie. downstream or south of the Dnipro Rapids. These were previously an impediment to navigation and the site of important portages. In 1932, the rapids were flooded to become part of the reservoir of the Dnipro Hydroelectric Station. During periods of relative peace, the city is an important industrial center. Steel, aluminum, aircraft engines, automobiles, substation transformers, and other heavy industrial goods, are produced in the region, making it generally successful economically and desirable for the Ukraine or Russia to own or control. The population is ±700,000 depending on the status of the war since 2014.

The city has a long history of military violence, beginning well before Rasputinov's "special military operation". Zaporizhzhia was founded in 1770, when the Aleksandrovskaya Fortress was built as a part of the Dnipro Defense Line, to protect the southern territories of the Russian Empire from Crimean Tatar invasions. During the Russian Civil War, Zaporizhzhia saw fierce fighting between the Red Army and the White armies of Denikin and Wrangel, Petliura's Ukrainian People's Army of the Ukrainian People's Republic, and German-Austrian troops. The opposing armies used the strategically important Kichkas Bridge to transfer troops, ammunition, and medical supplies.

After the outbreak of the War between the USSR and Nazi Germany in June, 1941, the Soviet government began evacuating Zaporizhzhia's industries to Siberia; and the Soviet security forces began shooting political prisoners in the city. In August, 1941, elements of the German 1st *Panzergruppe* reached the outskirts of Zaporizhzhia on the right bank and seized the island of Khortytsia.

The Red Army blew a 394 foot × 33 foot hole in the Dnipro hydroelectric dam on August 18, 1941, producing a flood wave that swept from Zaporizhzhia to Nikopol. The flood killed local residents and soldiers from both armies. Historians estimated a death toll between 20,000 and 100,000. Despite reinforcements, Zaporizhzhia was taken on October, 1941. The German occupation lasted two years; during which the Germans shot more than 35,000 people, and sent 58,000 people to Germany as forced laborers.

The Germans reformed Army Group South put its headquarters in Zaporizhzhia in 1943. In August, 1943, the Germans built the Panther-Wotan defense line along the Dnipro from Kyiv to Crimea. The Soviet Southwestern Front attacked Zaporizhzhia on October 10, 1943. The defenders repelled these attacks, but the Red Army launched a surprise night attack on October 13, which succeeded in reclaiming most parts of the city.

During 2014, there were Euromaidan regional state administration occupations, protests against President Viktor Yanukovych in the city with violent occupations of government buildings; and there were clashes between Ukrainian and pro-Russian activists in April, 2014. Russian forces were engaged in ongoing attacks on Zaporizhzhia since the beginning of the 2022 Russian invasion of Ukraine. On February 27, Russian forces began shelling the city. On March 3, Russian forces approached the Zaporizhzhia Nuclear Power Plant, raising concerns about a potential nuclear meltdown. Russian military forces fired missiles on Zaporizhzhia, endangering the plant in mid-May.

On September 30, hours before Russia formally annexed Southern and Eastern Ukraine, the Russian Armed Forces launched S-300 missiles at a civilian convoy in Zaporizhzhia, killing at least 30 people. On October 9, Russian forces launched rockets at residential buildings, killing 17 people.

Yaroslav and his team had two basic issues to contend with: to avoid entanglement with the ongoing conflicts in the Donbas region, and to complete their assigned mission of finding and either capturing or killing the ranking officers of the Wagner PMC who had control of nearly three-quarters of the Russian fighting force in the Separatist areas. For three months after arriving in Zaporizhzhia, the SBU commandoes created a hunting grid that stretched from Donestk in the northwest to Novoazovsk in the southeast where all reports indicated the Wagner PMC was operating. The problem was to find an encampment or city headquarters where the leaders remained for at least a few days at a time.

The area selected for the grid was huge and necessitated that Yaroslav's group split up into pairs, cultivate locals, move about efficiently in decidedly unfriendly territory, and to do so without arousing attention or exposing themselves. It was also crucial that the several units communicate well with each other and centrally with Yaroslav. He and Rokosylana naturally assumed leadership, and that status was neither disputed nor begrudged because of their native abilities and better training and experience. They worked separately for the first month, both investigating the area south of Zaporizhzhia and along the coast of the Taganrog Gulf of the Sea of Azov where the most recent Wagner v. Ukraine Army battles had been fought.

Yaroslav received intel from the intelligence officers of the regular army that the Wagner chieftains were hiding out somewhere along the smaller rivers passing through the city to enter the Dnipro: Sukha, Mokra Moskovka, Kushuhum, and Verkhnia Khortytsia Rivers. One night during their search, Yaroslav and Rokosylana had to hide among the trees on a ravine along the Verkhina Khortytsia River to avoid Separatist patrols.

It was a very cold dry night with two inches of frozen crunchy snow on the ground. Rokosylana was not feeling well, mostly due to the unrelenting march required to search and to avoid capture. Her teeth began to chatter, and she had hard shaking chills. The sun had just gone down behind the horizon, and the temperature dropped nearly ten degrees Fahrenheit. She was stoical as usual, but Yaroslav was concerned about her, recognizing the hypothermia setting in.

He spread their tarp in the seclusion of a lush Sogdian Ash forest under the branches of two exceptionally large trees whose branches curved toward the ground because of their great weight. With dusk came a cold northern wind and a light dusting of Graupel pellet-like snow which added to the discomfort. [also called soft hail, corn snow, or snow pellets, which is precipitation forming when supercooled water droplets in air are collected and freeze on falling snowflakes, forming 0.10-0.20 inch balls of crisp, opaque rime.]

Rokosylana looked to be increasingly ill, and Yaroslav was now worried. He emptied both of their backpacks and put every coat on his ailing partner and friend and covered her with all their blankets. It was still not enough. Her level of consciousness was waning. His people had lived in the wintry Carpathian Mountains and had learned how to adapt, even to emergencies. He considered this situation to be an emergency. He stripped off his clothing down to his skivvies and slipped under the pile of clothing and blankets to share his warmth with her. She warmed up some, but still needed more heat. He elected to forego any element of modesty or parlor room propriety and stripped her of her clothes. He wrapped his body around hers and drew all the covers over them.

The snow changed to a heavy wet blanket; and—in so doing—warmed up to 32° F., a livable temperature. Rokosylana's skin became

157

warm again, and she snuggled close to his life-giving warm body and went to sleep. Once he was convinced that her breathing was normal and indicated deep, healthy, sleep; Yaroslav, too, fell into a deep and dreamless sleep. By first light, they were covered with a smooth six-inch blanket of snow, which effectively acted like a Quincy hut as developed by Canadian Algonquin indigenous people. It also served as nearly perfect camouflage.

When it appeared safe to Yaroslav to do so, he heated up a steaming pot of tea and required Rokosylana to down three cups. She put out her palms to indicate that any more would induce vomiting and that she was better. For the first time, she became fully aware of the couples' state of complete undress, and she blushed and began to laugh.

"Uh, Yaroslav, did I put up resistance?"

He blushed at that.

"Rokosylana... it wasn't like that... I mean... we didn't... I wouldn't..." he stammered.

She laughed and treated him to a warm smile of gratitude.

"I know you wouldn't, my dearest friend. I trust you completely. I know you saved my life, and I will never forget it."

She now had a mischievous smile, "and I have to admit that the experience was not half bad."

Yaroslav turned beat red, knowing that she could read his mind. He had been damping down his feelings for her for two years, and now the secret seemed to be out.

"Rokosylana, this is probably not the time to say such a thing, but I care greatly for you. Besides that, you are the most beautiful woman I have ever seen."

It was her turn to undergo a scarlet metamorphosis, evidence that she was definitely feeling better and pretty much back to her old, hearty, and vigorous, self. Yaroslav began to wonder if this was a good thing or if it was going to complicate matters. He decided that he did not care. He was glad his feelings had been spoken out loud and had not been received negatively.

They did not speak of it again as they walked along the mountain trail back to the sandy beach of the river. There were no boot tracks in fresh snow and no sight or sounds of Separatist patrols. It was slow going because the ground surface was cut by *blaka* [large ravines] and tangled forests with copious amounts of deadfall]. When they returned to their apartment in the city, they gave the rest of the commando team their report, omitting a few details. Before bedtime, and after a belly warming goat stew, Rokosylana gave Yaroslav's calloused hard hand a squeeze, one that expressed everything without giving away anything to the others.

CHAPTER 29

Occupied Makariv/Makarov, Bucha Raion, Kyiv Oblast, Eastern Ukraine, on the banks of the Dnipro River

November 26, 2024

An urgent message came from SBU Headquarters, 32–35, Volodymyrska Street, Kyiv, to the commandoes' impromptu headquarters in Zaporizhzhia, that Lt. Col. Dmitriy Utkinov Yevgeny Col. Konstantin Pikalov, Col. Andrei Troshev, and Col. Gen. Mikhail Mizin-tsev—the Wagner PMC commanders—had been seen and videotaped by Ukraine Army Intelligence services in the small town of Makarov, in Kyiv Oblast. The evidence was attached to the top-secret message and was indisputable. The unit pulled up stakes from Zaporizhzhia and was transported by a Ukrainian Air Force Ilyushin Il-76 transport plane to Kyiv.

They were under the protection of the Alpha unit, Spetsnaz Force of the Security Service of Ukraine, 35th Aviation Group, a multi-role rapid reaction formation. The plane had nine crew members and 40 troops on board. The skies were clear of clouds, Russian airplanes, drones, missiles, and artillery shells—which the flight crew considered a promising harbinger of things to come for the SBU unit.

The majority of the SBU commandoes boarded two Canadian armored Roshel Senators—a wheeled military car based on a Ford

F-550 chassis. As an APC, it was desi-gned to protect against small arms fire. It was more effective as a highly versati-le SWAT platform, for peacekeeping and law enforcement activities; but in Ukraine it was modified to be useful as a light duty APC [armored personnel carrier] and IMV [infantry mobility vehicle]. They had two pickup trucks for their gear—a Toyota Hilux and a Mitsubishi L200–and a jeep for Yaroslav and Rokosylana to use for reconnoitering and which they drove rapidly over the recently repaired highway for the rural enclave west of Kyiv, Makarov.

As they entered the small city, the commandoes were struck by two things. First, there were almost no people in the streets, military or otherwise. Secondly–at first glance–the Ukrainian government's report that its forces had pushed Russians out of this town seemed true; armed Ukrainian soldiers stood guard at a checkpoint at the entrance seemingly in full control. The stripes of golden yellow and azure blue Ukrainian flag fluttered from what was left of the city administration building. Media around the world reported the news as the latest indication that Ukrainian forces were waging skillful counterattacks and defeating the Russians in vital locations.

A closer inspection was not quite so sanguine. Significant destruc-tion was present in the larger city, Makarov, and in Makariv, a Ukrainian village 30 miles west of Kyiv. If it was a victory at all, it was a hollow one. In the village major damage to apartment complexes, schools, and a medical facility was woefully evident. One stark image was a large hole in the northern wall of an apartment building. Many of the buildings in the photos have sustained damage on their northern facades, evidence that points to military strikes that hit them were Russian. Several hun-dred feet east of that apartment building, a kindergarten also sustained significant damage. There were still dried pools of blood in and around the school belying the "victory".

The battle had taken place recently enough that smoke could be observed still billowing up from the building; the roof had completely caved in and the windows had all been blown out. This, despite the Russian Ministry of Defense repeatedly claiming that they are not tar-geting civilians.

At another apartment building just west of the school, the roof and a number of upper floor residences were destroyed; and the infrastructure supports appeared to be of dubious value for sustenance for the building.

An old man with one leg, leaning on a gnarled wood cane, confirmed the obvious: the battle was over; the Russians had moved on; and there were only a handful of Makarov citizens left in the city. And, no, he had not seen the infamous Wagner chieftain. He had been hiding in an out-house during the battle.

The SBU unit moved on to Makariv, a small and apparently empty village. There, the Russians had retreated more recently. Just south of the school, the Adonis-Makariv Medical and Diagnostic Center was still on fire. The street in front of it was littered with debris and the windows have been blown out of the center—the debris in front of it is all that remains of the north-facing front facade of the building. Immediately west of the school and medical center, near the center of Makariv, a massive crater was observed in the road. The medical center was evident in the background on fire. Next to that crater, a residential building with a grocery store on the ground floor had been hit and destroyed.

In the center of town—a cultural center that had also housed government and police offices—had been struck by a high explosive weapon. A portion of the building was dest-royed and a structure on the roof appeared to have been clipped off by some sort of munition. "Glory to Ukraine! Glory to the heroes" was written on a large tattered sign in the front of the building. South of central Makariv, a preschool also sustained significant damage. The windows had been blown out and portions of the roof appeared to be damaged. Littered about were remnants of children's backpacks, library books, coats, and here and there, little boys' and girls' shoes.

A hollow faced old woman, her face, hands, and clothing coated with soot and con-crete dust, responded meekly to Rokosylana's kindness. Rokosyolana showed Lt. Col. Dmitriy Utkinov Yevgeny's, Col. Konstantin Pikalov's, Col. Andrei Troshev's, and Col. Gen. Mikhail Mizin-tsev's photos to her.

"I do remember that awful bad man, Dear. I was hiding in my basement and looking out. They didn't know I was there. There were three of them. They were wearing Russia army uniforms, but sort of different. They all had arm patches that said "*Щагнер ПМЦ*" [Wagner PMC] and lots of gold metal things; they were high officers, I think."

"By any chance, did you overhear them say anything about where they were going next?"

"I did. It was Izium in Kharkiv Oblast. I wish we had one of those telephone things; so, I could call up someone there and warn them. Poor things."

"Thank you, Dear," Rokosylana said.

She gave the lady a box of canned vegetables, bottled peaches, two loaves of good bread, several bottles of real Morshynska water, and a large Ukrainian summer sausage. The woman wept.

Rokosylana reported what she had learned, and the commando force quickly boarded the two Roshel Senators and the jeep and headed southwest in a two-hour race to Izium.

CHAPTER 30

Izium/Izyum, Administrative center of Izium Raion, Kharkiv Oblast, Eastern Ukraine

November 26, 2024, early evening

The situation in Izium was extremely dangerous when the SBU commandoes arrived. Because of the danger and ongoing violence, it seemed likely that at least one—and perhaps all of the Wagner leadership, Lt. Col. Dmitriy Utkinov Yevgeny, Col. Konstantin Pikalov, Col. Andrei Troshev, and Col. Gen. Mikhail Mizin-tsev—would be headquartered here. Part of that reasoning came from the fact that the commandoes and their informants saw and reported only Wagner troops in Izium Raion—no regular Russian army soldiers.

Yaroslav's first order of priority was to establish a secure and secret site to be a temporary headquarters of sorts. Izium is located at the foot of Kremenets Mountain, on the right bank of the Donets river. The commandoes agreed to locate on top of the mountain despite its inconvenience and the strain of climbing the steep sides whenever they needed to meet with each other or get to safety. They considered the area to be safe since the Russians had destroyed most of the buildings and monuments there during their previous attack—the original Battle of Izium—in 2022. Historically, there were several ancient Polovtsian/Cuman stone statues known as "stone *babas*", dating from the 9th-13th centuries. The statues were heavily damaged in 2022, with one being completely destroyed. There was nothing left for the marauders to destroy, and no people living there to kill.

Once they had created a well-hidden and somewhat fortified safe house/head-quarters, the team split up again into pairs and set off separately to find the Wagner headquarters. Yaroslav and Rokosylana formed one pair—to no surprise for the rest—and more than a few good-natured smirks and raises of eyebrows about the big secret that was apparent to them all. Rokosylana erased all doubt by affectionately taking Yaroslav's hand as they set off down the mountain side.

Izium is 75 miles southeast of the administrative center of the oblast, Kharkiv. Once the factories of Izium produced optical equipment, mechanical components, concrete products, building materials, and foodstuffs and had large industries for railroad repair and brewing. Its importance as a rail hub made it an important target for the invading Russian military. It held economic significance for centuries due to its position as a transportation link between Kharkiv and the Donbas region to the southeast. The city was recaptured by Ukrainian forces in a 2022 Kharkiv counteroffensive and lost again during the recent past four months of 2024. Removal of The ruins from the 2022 Battle of Izium had barely gotten tunderway, and the 45,000 people of the city were beginning to return, when the Wagner Group returned to rape, pillage, plunder, and destroy, the unfortunate city.

Yaroslav and Rokosylana made their way gingerly through the rubble strewn streets and open spaces, ever wary of the possibility of stepping on a land mine—planted by the hundreds of thousands by both Russian and Ukraine armies. Russia had begun trying to take Izium in March, 2022, at the beginning the Battle of Izium. When the Wagner PMCs returned in 2024, their mercenary forces used a large airborne munition on a civilian apartment building in Izium, killing at least 44 civilians in what Human Rights Watch called one of the deadliest attacks on civilians during the war. The rear portions of the apartment building were relatively intact; and—according to SBU assets left in the city— the Wagner chiefs were using the empty rooms as their headquarters to conduct the remaining plan to destroy Izium completely and forever. It was a major engineering deconstruction project.

The going was difficult: the commandoes had to avoid the ongoing fighting and to overcome their natural desire to destroy units and equipment of the Wagner mercenaries; and they had to rely on an old map to find Vulytsia Khlibosavodska and the remains of the partially destroyed apartment building. It took 18 hours to locate the building—which, in the end, was not so difficult—since in the distance they sighted a lone building surrounded by an assortment of obvious and well-marked Wagner vehicles teeming with security guards. Wagner's mercenaries displayed an entire zoo of various military equipment.

There was no doubt about the presence of the Wagner mercenaries as opposed to regular Russian professional military. They liked to advertise and were insistent upon making their brand known. In addition to the omnipresent "Z" on vehicles, Yaroslav and Rokosylana easily made out the Wagnerites' signature armored vehicle– the Ural Chekan, It is a sort of "reincarnation" of a Soviet BTR-152 armored personnel carrier—a telling piece of military hardware that erased any doubt that they were looking at Wagnerites was a jury-rigged hybrid vehicle made of BMP-2 chassis with an additional ZU-23-2 anti-aircraft gun sitting on a lowboy truck and another hybrid of a BMP-2 armored vehicle with a ZU-23-2 AA gun. BMP-97 Vystrel T-90M Proryv on a lowboy.

The makeshift changed vehicles were presumably taken from storage T-80BV along with tactical "Z" markings and Kontakt-1 reactive armor, and even something similar to a T-72B3 with a slat armor cage on top as a stationary firing point. The menagerie of weaponry included a T-80BV tank; two T-72B3s with grill cages; several unknown vehicles on KamAZ chasses; a S-60 anti-aircraft gun; and half a dozen UAZ vans. It was obvious that they chose their equipment in such a way that made them obviously different from Rasputinov's armed forces. That narcissistic choice helped Yaroslav and Rokosylana be certain that they were in the right place.

Now, their questions were, "Is this the right time? i.e., are the senior officers present? and can they be dealt with?"

The first tactical question was how to find them without it being a suicide mission; and the second was, what could they do once they set eyes on the monsters? As the two spies reconnoitered the old building, they found that the Russian missile attack had destroyed all but the front entryway as a portal of entry or exit. The second question—how to get them—had an obvious answer. They could not do it in daylight. A night approach would have to do. They found a miserable hidey-hole created by blasted blocks of concrete which had formed a three-sided box with a partial lid over it. Together they moved a fairly large flat slab of concrete to serve as a temporary fourth side, but small enough to permit egress when they needed to.

It was cold, but not unbearable. Rokosylana offered a mischievous suggestion.

"Yaroslav, do you think it would be a good idea for us to strip down again to share warmth?"

She asked it with a calculated look of contrived innocence.

He laughed, "Great idea, my dear fellow officer, but just perhaps suicidal, do you think?

"Oh," she said... "I didn't think of that... had other things on my mind."

He gave her a facetious wave of his index finger as if scolding a naughty child, and they shared one of those understanding moments reserved for dedicated couples.

And they took a nap holding hands.

Rokosylana took the first watch once they agreed that the darkness was thick enough to keep them invisible. She put on her $3,000 AN/PVS-7B NVG Government Issue NSN MFG ID Night Vision Goggles and found a vantage point where she had a full view of the still intact front door. For five hours she sat motionless except for shivering and observed a change of shift with six burly noncoms minding security each shift. It looked to her as if it was going to be simple suicide to attempt entry to the building.

At 22:00, she watched the night watch come on duty. To her surprise and contentment, that shift consisted of only two men. They could only be in two places at once, at most; and it did not appear that they were going to leave each others' presence. Furthermore, she could see the lights still on in the twelfth story room, that she presumed had to be the workspace for the officers to do their planning. She hurriedly made her way back the hidey-hole to tell Yaroslav her findings and her plan.

"We can kill the two sentries and head upstairs to find the bosses," she said with assurance.

Yaroslav paused to think before responding.

"To much risk of noise or of someone stumbling over the bodies. What do you think about finding a broken-out window and sneak up to the lighted office?"

The way he phrased the sentence touched her sensitivities; he was showing her respect and consideration which was not required. He was the senior officer, after all. Because it was framed as a question, she had a chance to agree gracefully without losing face. More than ever the beautiful and talented young woman was sure that this was the man she wanted to spend her life with.

"Smarty-pants," she said and playfully stuck out her tongue at him.

He laughed, and nothing more needed to be said.

Yaroslav donned his own pair of night vision goggles, and together they set out to find a quiet entry way into the apartment building and one that would also provide an escape route. It was not hard. All they had to do is to follow trails of broken glass until they found a big hole. It took less than half an hour.

Once inside, they thanked the gods of night vision goggles and were able to progress quietly through the building and up the stairways, stepping over broken glass and other impedimenta, aided by their gift from the gods. They counted the floors as they went up until they reached the twelfth. Yaroslav carefully pushed the door open, gun ready. Rokosylana kept her hand on his shoulder to ensure that neither of them disappeared into the gloom or made a loud noise.

A slit of light came out from under a doorway halfway along the corridor and was the only light in the building that was as black as a mineshaft. They paused at the door, listened intently for two full minutes, and heard nothing. The lock on the door had an old time keyhole which did not have a skeleton key in it to block vision. Each of them took a turn to squint through the opening which had a narrow angle of view. No one was seen in that angle.

Yaroslav opened his narrow brief case and took out a laser scope and camera especially designed to enable spies [American spies] to see almost an entire room. Peeking through a keyhole had become even more useful. An imaging technique that measures the path of a laser to build up a three-dimensional picture could now let spies map an entire room through a tiny hole.

In 2012, researchers had invented a laser to see around corners. The system worked by firing short laser pulses at a nearby wall, bouncing light around a corner to a hidden object, which then bounced some of it back to a camera next to the laser. The camera only measured light arriving during a very short window of time and changing the gap between the laser pulse and this interval allowed the viewer to measure light that had traveled different distances, building up a 3D image of a room and hidden objects.

There was nothing to see, not even furniture. Rokosylana softly pushed the door open, and the two spies entered the room. A ten-second perusal convinced them that they had been on a goose chase; so, they retreated back the way they came in. Since they were already wide awake, they made a forced march back to the base of Kremenets Mountain where they dug shallow foxholes to spend the rest of the night.

The other pairs of commandoes turned up considerable information from the local residents who had been hiding from the Russian invaders. Several of the residents graphically reported being imprisoned and tortured by Russian soldiers during the occupation. Three weeks previously—according to several observers–two Russian soldiers were killed and 28 others hospitalized after Ukrainian civilians handed out poisoned cakes to Russian soldiers of the Russian 3rd Motor Rifle Division. Several people described the scene during the frantic Russian retreat. The Russian soldiers completely gutted the Lyceum No. 2 school which they had used as a base looting everything of remotely possible value, including water heaters and small sinks from each classroom.

In response, the director of the school was one of the residents of Izium accused of collaborating with Russia, and was scheduled to be put on trial later in Kharkiv by Ukraine after the end of occupation. The survivors reported a second case, that of Andrii Bohomaz. Bohomaz is a

Ukrainian civilian who was shot by Russian Armed Forces in Izium, in the Kharkiv in June during the Russian invasion of Ukraine. Bohomaz and his wife Valeria Ponomarova accidentally drove into Russian occupied territory. Their vehicle and Bohomaz were struck by gunfire, before Ponomarova was led to safety by a Ukrainian military drone. Russian forces assumed Bohomaz to be dead, but he awakened the next day and walked to safety. Ukrainian police were pursuing a Russian commander for attempted murder.

A policewoman reported to Boryslav Vovk that after Ukrainian troops secured the liberated city, local police officers found mass graves of 440 bodies in Izium. According to other city officials–by the end of the occupation–more than 80% of the city's infrastructure was destroyed; about 70% of multi-story buildings were destroyed. City administration officers estimated to Vasyl Haranchak that about 1,000 people lost their lives under the Russian occupation.

The rest of the teams also failed to find the Wagner bosses anyplace in Izium, but Boryslav Vovk, and Vasyl Haranchak did learn that the advance unit of the PCM had pulled out the previous day and were headed south. An eavesdropper told them that they had overheard a couple of conscriptees griping about being forced to go to Piski, a god-forsaken little burg somewhere all the way back down toward the Sea of Azov.

That was a long way, and Yaroslav and the others expected a stiff fight most of the way.

CHAPTER 31

Ghost Villages-Sulyhivka, Virnopillia, and Kamianka, Eastern Ukraine

November 30, 2024

The SBU commandoes left the eastern Ukrainian city of Izium and turned west onto rougher pot-holed and scarred dirt roads where dead trees, twisted broken power lines, and carcasses of burned and bombed vehicles gave way to a string of shattered villages. The ruined enclaves were once the backbone of Ukraine's agricultural eastern steppe but were reduced to ruin as the war passed over them like a flood tide. The hapless villages were recaptured by Ukraine's army; but even then, the villages of Sulyhivka, Virnopillia, and Kamianka, were at risk of being lost–not to artillery or pitched battles, but to overgrown weeds, wildflowers, and minefields. The minefields alone made it impossible to farm and hazardous to walk about in grassy areas of the villages. They were one more kind of casualty in a war that had claimed many.

The few residents who returned home after the Russians retreated were struggling to live. They had waited 10 months–in vain–for electricity to be restored, for their fields to be cleared of explosives, and for neighbors to come back to restore some semblance of community. The

Ukrainian government's attempt to formalize some type of reconstruction effort had changed little.

The first battle torn village in the line was Sulyhivka, population two at the time. They met one of the two people—70-year-old Victor Kalyberda—who was clearing a small patch of weeds next to his nearly destroyed home. His intent was to create a small vegetable garden, but he was risking his life in beginning the task since he could not be sure whether or not there were hidden mines.

A second man was taken with interest in seeing a rare visitor and came to enter the conversation. He was Anatolii Solovei, 52. Before the war Sulyhivka was a two-street village of around 50 people, and the two men were little more than acquaintances. Mr. Kalyberda had been a tractor driver. Mr. Solovei had been a well-to-do landowner who grew wheat, corn and barley–staples of Sulyhivka's harvest.

Russia's invasion forced both men to flee, along with the rest of the residents. Mr. Solovei placed one of his brand-new tractors along a secluded embankment with hopes that it would survive Russian occupation. When he returned after the liberation from Russian occupation, he found it so burned that it was scarcely recognized as a tractor. A cordial relationship was inevitable in a two-person cipher of a town. Both men's houses were sheared apart by artillery. Hope for the future was not so inevitable.

Ukrainian troops liberated Sulyhivka in September. The two men returned shortly afterward. Mr. Kalyberda took up residence in a neighbor's summer kitchen. On the other side of the village, Mr. Solovei returned home, erecting a community-donated foam plastic shelter among the ruins of his house. The two men were currently Sulyhivka's only permanent residents. There was no electricity or gas.

"I got used to surviving on my own," Mr. Kalyberda said. "Everything is needed, because there is nothing left."

He got most of his food from volunteers and water from the village well which was of dubious quality.

At least once a day, he walked to see Mr. Solovei, past the war's detritus of armored vehicles, pick-up trucks, cars, and destroyed farm equipment–all blasted open and ruined. The overgrown cemetery where both men's families are buried was now littered with small land mines that can blow a person's foot in half. Visiting the gravesites is out of the question.

Recently, Mr. Kalyberda helped move some surviving farm equipment for Mr. Solovei, who planed to start cultivating his fields after clearing the explosives himself when he can get himself going again.

Often, the two men sat and drink tea or coffee, saying little.

Rokosylana asked them, "What do you talk about, gentlemen?"

"What's there to talk about?" Mr. Solovei asked.

Maybe it was the terrain or Russia's stalled tactics, but after passing through Sulyhivka, the frontline froze a few miles to the west two springs ago, near where it was 80 years earlier, when Hitler's army advanced toward Moscow.

The second village—Virnopillia—with 120 was a bit larger. The first building–more accurately, skeleton of a building–was the village school. The commandoes took a rest break and walked through the gutted edifice. An abandoned book was the only article left. It lay in the corridor of the destroyed school that had once been the only source of education for Virnopillia. The view through the hole in a wall which had once been a window in what once had been a classroom window, revealed a wrecked tree and automobile standing in a minefield.

Virnopillia is roughly five miles west of Sulyhivka. Nina Shoigu–the self-appointed village elder–was toiling to keep her community from disappearing. Nina was sitting in the dusty secretary's office of Virnopillia's partially destroyed community center. It was cold, and she wore an old army jacket and a tattered shawl. A plastic sheet covered the smashed windows. In front of her was a collection of printed checklists that she would use to record her village's first wartime damage claims. It would prove to be the first of many futile submissions. Since the 1990s, Ms. Shoigu had been the head of Virnopillia, which had a prewar population of 654 but now had roughly 120 residents. Her authority was diminished under laws passed by the Ukrainian government in 2020 and again under martial law after the invasion.

Ms. Shoigu has taken it upon herself to do what she could with the few resources afforded to Virnopillia. She also acted as a go-between for her neighbors and the complicated bureaucracy involved in trying to procure damage payments. That was about the extent of the city services still available.

"There are a lot of unclear questions about how to do it," she said. whose village elder has been mostly absent. Only recently had volunteers appeared there to discuss potential damage claims. Russian troops never managed to occupy Virnopillia–though much of it was destroyed by shelling–just as it had been in World War II. It took three decades for the village to recover from that war."

The chief complaint of Virnopillia's residents was that there is no electricity. Its return has been slowed by the arduous process of clearing explosives next to power lines. Rumors vary on when it will be restored– as is the case in most of the villages nearby–ranging from "this fall" to "after the war ends."

Undeterred, the determined survivor climbed into an aging gray sedan with her papers and a measuring tape. She was ready for a long day of putting a price tag on the destruction of her lifelong home, refusing to surrender.

Despite being recaptured by Ukraine's military in the fall, Virnopillia is one of the villages at risk of being lost to the eternal weeds and brambles present before the village was even conceived of.

The last ghost town in the string–the small village of Kamianka, which lies between Izyum and Sloviansk, nine miles northeast of Virnopillia, and only one of a very many in the oblast—was Kamianka. The patient and war-weary commandoes listened to the few survivors tell the stories of their lives. Fewer than half a dozen people stayed behind in shell-raked Kamianka during its Russian occupation. One of them was Vasyl. He lost his leg to a small land mine after the Russians fled, but his injury had done little to assuage his neighbors' suspicions about his pro-Russian leanings.

"He was an elder with the Russians," said Svitlana Pinchuk, whose house was destroyed by an airstrike. "Now he walks around, and no one is going to prosecute him. He cooked moonshine for the Russians, they lived with him."

She was consumed with her neighbor's betrayals. The Russians occupied the village–with a prewar population of more than 1,000 people–for half a year, leaving the 'Z' symbol of their invasion on homes and vehicles. With approximately 80+ current residents, Kamianka is reckoning with the same problems as Virnopillia and Sulyhivka: no electricity, land mines everywhere, and a national government that they believe had forgotten them.

Before the war, the residents of Kamianka had a vibrant social life, celebrating holidays and spending time together as a community. But with rumors of Vasyl's coziness with the Russians circulating among returning residents, the small community had only made some headway toward returning to its prewar cohesiveness.

Ms. Pinchuk claimed that Vasyl had taken parts from her family's tractors during the occupation.

"Maybe he did it because of the instinct of self-preservation," she suggested, but her claim could not be verified.

Rokosylana asked, "Can you learn to forgive him?"

Ms. Pinchuk shook her head. She would not, could not, forgive him. She and her husband had planned to pass their property down to their son.

"Now, most was destroyed and some items that remained were stolen by Vasyl," she said.

Kamianka was once a beautiful bucolic place—population 1,000—in a lush green valley bisected by a lazy river. After the Russian occupation, its landscape was truly apocalyptic, and the architecture was unrecognizable. There was not a single house left standing in the entire village. Every habitation had been completely destroyed. Empty ammunition boxes, destroyed civilian cars with the insignia "Z" used by Russian troops, and the remnants of the desecrated library of the village of Kamianka, testified to the decimation of the once thriving little town. The only recent piece of construction in the entire village was a roadside memorial at the site where a Ukrainian soldier died the previous year while fighting Russian forces on the outskirts of Kamianka.

Orders came down from SBU General Olena Yuriivna for Yaroslav's unit to depart forthwith to a destination in Donetsk Oblast called Pisky. Reliable sources had sighted the Wagner PCM brass in Donetsk launching artillery barrages at the tiny village which was barely holding on.

CHAPTER 32

Rush through Kharkiv Oblast to Donetsk City-Donetsk Oblast, the unofficial capital and largest city of the larger economic and cultural Donets Basin/Donbas region, and the besieged Village of Pisky

December 2-15, 2024

A s the team drew nearer to Donetsk and Pisky Village, the distant and constant sound of artillery was audible, like an unmoving summer thunderstorm. The unwelcome sounds grew ever louder the closer they came. Gen. Yuriivna sent an iPhone digital photograph of Col. Konstantin Pikalov–one of the primary Wagner PMC leaders—standing on the Donetsk side of the razor wire barrier with Pisky. The photo was time stamped December 2, 2024 13:26:48, less than an hour previously. It was proof positive that their quarries—at least one of them—were near. Adrenaline, blood pressure, and heart rates, all went into the stratosphere among the SBU commandoes. The chase was on.

Pisky changed hands several times during the earliest phase of the Russia-Ukraine war back in 2014 and 2015, but the Ukrainians ultimately prevailed. Even after Russia occupied Donetsk City, a battalion of the Ukrainian navy's 56th Motorized Brigade dug in, hung on, ...

and waited. Now the Russians were trying, again, to take Pisky. A fresh Russian assault in recent days has turned the village into "Hell," according to Ukrainian President Volodymyr Zelensky.

Gen. Yuriivna at SBU and Lt. Gen. Irkady Memlov sent a joint message to the president: "The Russians have an overwhelming firepower advantage in Pisky, like they do across eastern Ukraine. We must have more artillery, more rockets, and more close air support. The invaders also have more troops in the area. All we can do is to fight on and try to hold on. We cannot completely break the Russian army's advantage in artillery and manpower."

In his top-secret, eyes-only, directive to Gen. Yuriivna, Zelensky conceded.

Then, he pointed out, "But fortifications count for a lot. The 56th Motorized Brigade's trenches and earthworks are visible in commercial satellite imagery, crisscrossing Pisky's abandoned and ruined buildings. We are faced with well-armed attackers; but we have well entrenched defenders–the basic ingredients for a grueling, bloody battle. General Yuriivna, we are left with having to depend on your SBU commando force, even if it becomes a suicide mission. The general staff and I are desperate to have Yaroslav and his raiders pull a rabbit out of a hat. Our very existence depends on it."

A first-hand account of the fighting–by a Ukrainian soldier–circulated on social media. "This is a meat grinder, where the battalion simply holds back the onslaught with their bodies."

That was the grim situation that faced young Yaroslav Kandybavych Melnykenko, his beloved Rokosylana, and his entire team of commandoes, as they passed through the east perimeter of Pisky to join the struggle. They were very much aware that it was not their role to fight to the death along with their comrades in the regular army. They had to find a way to cut off the head of the snake, and hope that the body would die. That appeared to be the only way to level the fighting theater in favor of Ukraine.

Yaroslav had a little too much of an education—a classical education—at least, to be comfortable in any aspect of the old Greek allegory. His nerve wracked mind brought up another piece of mythology that he kept to himself: the Lernaen Hydra was a Greek monster that had many heads and each time a head was cut off, two would grow in its place. The Greeks generally believed that the Hydra had eight mortal heads and one immortal one. That great head could not be harmed by any weapon. In addition, there were siblings of the Lernaean Hydra. She was the daughter of the monsters Typhon and Ekhdna and had the body of a huge hairless dog.

Yaroslav was neither religious nor otherwise superstitious. He did not believe in luck, charms, crosses, symbols, or fables. He did, however, recognize the wisdom of the Greek allegory. He either had to kill or capture the three heads of Wagner PMC or stand by and watch in horror as the Russian juggernaut swept through his country and turned it into a slave state or an unpopulated grain field to enrich Russia.

The village of Pisky lies mere yards from Russian lines just outside Donetsk, an industrial city of one million that–since 2014–has been under the control of pro-Russian separatists. The punishment its defenders were enduring endless artillery barrages–upwards of 300 152-millimeter shells falling in short order. Worse, the Ukrainian battalion's several hundreds of soldiers lacked any means of effectively shooting back at the big guns. Their heaviest weaponry had been reduced to a pair of mortars—completely unsuited for artillery-on-artillery counterbattery. The soldiers and SBU agents recognized that without a counter-battery fight, the new Battle of Pisky was going to turn into the senseless meat grinder, where an insane amount of Ukrainian infantry will be ground up in a day.

Yaroslav and Rokosylana took their turn on the front line by the razor wire fence. Russian troops broke through the Ukrainian lines. The Ukrainian battalion sent in its reserves. The reserve marched to the position, closed the breakthrough; and, after five minutes, only one of the 15 Ukrainian battalion people remained alive. Little Pisky Village had become a meatgrinder for two armies.

Ukraine in recent months had acquired hundreds of modern artillery systems from its foreign allies, including 18 of Germany's best PzH-2000 tracked howitzers and—perhaps most consequently—16 American High-Mobility Artillery Rocket Systems. However, the fact was that none of those systems was helping to defend Pisky or was in line to do so. Ukrainian commanders were prioritizing deep strikes against Russian supply dumps and bridges in Russian rear areas—especially in southern Ukraine. It is not so much that the Ukrainian army does not have artillery; it is that Ukrainian commanders were using their artillery at the places of their choosing. And Pisky Village was not one of them.

Rokosylana took a piece of shrapnel in her upper arm and had to be moved back from the front. That experience convinced Yaroslav that time was quickly running out.

After two deafening, mind numbing weeks of artillery barrages, the officer in command of the reserves pointed out to Yaroslav that the artillery barrages of any sort were declining in frequency, length of time, and ferocity. He had been taking a tally each day's numbers of Russian shells coming the way of the village. There was a clearcut diminution in the fusillades.

"It can only mean that the Russkies are running short of ammunition from the home covern and unable to keep up the intensity they need here to drive us out. Maybe, it is time for the brass to send us a battalion and make an attack, what do you think?"

Yaroslav said, "I think your assessment is probably right, but another battalion here will just invite more Russians to come. Rasputinov cannot allow his Separatist enclaves to fail. I think there is another way; but, my friend, I cannot share it with you. Forgive me, it is above both our pay grades."

Yaroslav had been given carte blanche to execute his orders to take out the heads of Wagner PMC. He rushed to collect his comrades in the SBU unit and held an impromptu pre-battle meeting.

"We have some idea where the Wagnerites are holed up, and we have Donetsk uniforms we can use. At dark, we go through the wire and into the hornet's nest. We absolutely must try. However, I want each of you to form up a straight line in front of me."

He waited until the line was straight and silent.

"Now, I want any one of you who does not want to go in with me to step forward, make a right face, and walk away to join the regular forces. There will be no shame attached and no recriminations; that I promise. I do not need to tell you the risks; we have been planning and drilling for weeks. If you come with me, send your insurance and love letters home and wish your loved ones goodbye."

He stood at rigid attention, "Forward," he ordered, and every man and woman formed up in a rank immediately behind their colonel. Not a single agent made a right face.

Yaroslav's eyes watered.

"Follow me," he said.

CHAPTER 33

Donetsk, DNR [Donetsk People's Republic] an unrecognized diplomatic entity and disputed region between Ukraine and the Russian Federation

December 11, 2024

T he intel regarding Russian sentry patrols proved to be accurate. The SBU commandoes had a three-minute patrol free interval during which they were able to scramble through the opening made earlier in the rolled razor wire. They were undetected. Yaroslav had a carefully outlined and prepared map of the streets and open areas near the fence including the buildings. Every intelligence officer had contributed to the map to make their best guess as to where in Donetsk, the Wagnerite HQ was likely to be. There was considerable disparity in the guesses; so, Yaroslav made up his own mind, as he usually did.

According to the 2001 census, the Donetsk Oblast was inhabited by members of more than 130 ethnic groups. The native language of 74.9% of the population of the Donet-sk region is Russian, compared with 24.1% Ukrainian. Yaroslav and his commandoes could expect no sympathy or help from the citizenry, but he did have one ace up his sleeve.

One of his fellow students at the SBU academy had been assigned as a deep sleeper agent in the DNR military and had been a source of excellent and reliable intelligence since 2014. His code name was "Werewolf". Gen. Yuriivna sent Yaroslav an encoded address for Werewolf and a set of code words: questions and answers for when they would meet. Werewolf was expecting him and his commandoes.

Knowing that they could not safely travel in their Ukraine uniforms; nor could they continue to speak Ukrainian, Yaroslav had his crew change into regular Wagner PMC uniforms and to practice using Russian to communicate until they returned to safe Ukrainian territory, which was likely to be some time away. They separated into small groups, cut their way through the Pinsky security razor wire and avoided eye-contact as they made their way in the general direction of First Line Avenue [Artema Street] the main center of business and culture in Donetsk. First Line Avenue generally functioned as the foremost place to start for any tourist trip around the city back in the day when there were tourists.

Despite the relentless warfare going on outside the city, the street still hosted a mix of new and old architecture together with small parks, hotels, shopping centers, and restaurants, including Lenin Square, the Opera & Ballet Theatre, Monument to Coalminers, and Donetsk Drama Theatre. The commandoes met up—as was predetermined—in a small Chinese Restaurant, Kitayskiy Privet, once part of a Ukraine-wide chain. Dressed as they were, no one paid the least amount of attention to them. On the contrary, the ordinary citizens went out of their way to avoid them, even eye contact.

There are numerous Chinese students hanging around outside, and more families of Chinese people inside.

A tuxedoed manager greeted them with "*Ni Hao*," and showed them to their seats.

The lushly decorated interior included Chinese carvings, glass depictions of gorgeous *Yijis*/-*Gejis* female sing and dance performers in ancient China and ancient Northern Song stag hunting scenes. The spicy smells were very enticing, especially for commandoes who had been subsisting on water, MRE [meals-ready-to-eat] ration packs, and rare pickles, soups, and sausages, all donated by patriotic Ukrainians; and none of it paid for by the government. The actual eating area was on the small side, and the interior was not ergonomically designed enough to accommodate many different guests at different tables at the same time. That resulted in some close quarters discomfort, and some of the commandoes had to sit on bar stools.

Their contact had reserved the tables and chairs—all for a price—the best available since there were no free seats and had paid for the best meal available in advance. They were waited on by the maître d hotel, the man who had greeted them with the friendly "Ni Hao" and who was promised a handsome tip after the "Wagner" soldiers left.

None of the commandoes had come from wealthy families; so, they were not familiar with true gourmet food, especially something as exotic as gourmet Chinese cuisine. Gen. Yuriivna respected and appreciated the sacrifices and the intensity of the work done by her SBU agents, and this meal was a way to express that gratitude.

For appetizers, Werewolf—her agent in place in the Donbas "Republics"—had the maître d provide the best of the best of the restaurant's fare. The appetizers included fried noodles with fresh beef hand-pulled noodles fresh; blue or red dumplings, Mukata, Ho Go, and Bulgogi, dishes.

The entrees included all sorts of mouth-watering flavors of spicy dishes. The com-mandoes could choose from any of the restaurant's specialties: classic miso soup with wakame, shrimp and/or mushroom dim sum, kimchi with cherry tomatoes, sashimi from wild scallop, salmon, yellowfin tuna, yellowtail, sea bass, octopus, and even hard to come by smoked eel slices. The pièces de resistance included golden brown Peking duck roasted in conformity with ancient Chinese traditions–the restaurant's specialty. One the side table there were Dim Sum with crab and truffle sauce, steamed sea bass fillet, Langoustine Tom Yam, and Langoustine tartare.

It was something of a learning curve. The commandoes who requested "restaurant chicken with chili peppers" were surprised to receive chopped chicken feet covered in chopped chili which was good for a laugh but not chewable.

For those with the biggest appetites, the choices left were: Xiao Long Bao with duck, Shu Mai with scallops or tuna or Bok Choy leaves, and the exotic "larvae"—another pièce de resistance and learning experience. Larvae is another name for Century Eggs, technically known as Alkalized or Preserved Egg–a Chinese egg-based culinary dish made by preserving duck, chicken, or quail eggs, in a mixture of clay, ash, salt, quicklime, and rice hulls, for several weeks to several months. During the process, the yolk transforms into a dark green to grey color, with a creamy consistency and a strong flavor due to the presence of hydrogen sulfide [aka "rotten egg gas"] and ammonia. Interestingly, some century eggs have patterns near the surface of the egg white, which are likened to pine branches. These patterned eggs are considered to have better quality than normal century eggs and are called Songhua eggs variously translated as pine flower eggs or pine-patterned eggs]. The eggs did not look or smell particularly good, but they were highly edible. The other choices included: Cantonese Mah Gu Gai Pan, "fresh mushrooms cooked with sliced chicken"; juicy Nem rolls with pork, and snails with lemongrass, assorted other seafoods, and veal.

For dessert, they were served fried milk with banana and mint ice cream. The foods were all washed down with craft beer served from large pitchers and white tea.

Two of the stoical commandoes, sitting opposite each other at a table with bar stools–which were very unstable—were afraid to fall off them into the open space behind the rest of the crews' backs.

After the sumptuous meal, the commandoes filed out into the bright sun. Werewolf—who Yaroslav recognized from training—brushed past him and surreptitiously slipped a piece of paper into his hand.

"Meet me behind the Donetsk State Academic Opera and Ballet Theater," it said.

The commandoes split up and casually walked in different directions on different streets to the theater. Yaroslav and Rokosylana backtracked and walked briskly around the theater to the garden area in the back. A lone man–the same age and general physique as Yaroslav—sat on a marble bench admiring the hardy perennials in the flower boxes. He paid them no attention.

Yaroslav and Rokosylana sauntered over and sat down near the man known only as "Werewolf" to her.

Yaroslav said, "Enjoying the weather? A 'Common Man' would be as cold as a wolf out here."

"Indeed, and he would be right. Only a werewolf would be comfortable in this environment."

Having established their correct identities and common purposes, Yaroslav and his old friend resumed calling each other by their birth first names, Yaroslav and Taras (Col. Seversky). The commandoes were otherwise discrete and worked to blend into the background. They were alert and on guard for intruders or for anyone who might show an excessive interest in Yaroslav's and Taras's conversation.

"We have to be brief, Yaroslav. The walls have eyes and ears in this city. Spies are everywhere; this is Russia, after all. I have reliable information that the Wagner officers have a nearly permanent headquarters in the penthouse floor of the Hotel Bakhmut in Artemivsk. My source told me that she saw them as recently as yesterday."

"She?" chided Yaroslav with a mischievous raised eyebrow.

"One of the perks, my friend, one of the few perks of this lonely job."

He handed his old friend a neatly printed piece of paper with the address and particulars about the popular old hotel [Sadova street135, Bakhmut], now in Russian oligarch hands.

"Sorry, have to go. Can't be seen with the riff-raff," he chuckled.

He rose and started away.

"Stay healthy and safe, my друг [friend]," Yaroslav said to his back.

Taras gave a small hand wave as his reply and quickened his pace.

CHAPTER 34

Bakhmut, Donetsk Oblast, Ukraine (Russian controlled)

December 12, 2024

Although fighting was intense in and around Bakhmut during the first two years of Rasputinov's war in Ukraine, it had settled into a relatively inactive World War I type of trench warfare by the middle of 2024 when the SBU commandoes worked their way into the city on their clandestine mission. Still, plumes of smoke rose from a Russian strike in the front-line city of mercenaries where the Wagner Group was pressing toward victories throughout Bakhmut with increased air attacks and shelling that week. The Wagner Group mercenaries had effectively broken Ukrainian defenses on the eastern outskirts of Bakhmut and had full access to the city center. By November–as Bakhmut endured incessant barrages of Russian artillery–the battle had turned into trench warfare, and hundreds of people were reported dead and injured every day on both sides. There was inadequate manpower even to pick and dispose of the many dead bodies.

Taking Bakhmut was crucial strategically for the Wagnerites and Russian regular army to open up a route for Russian forces to press on toward Kramatorsk and Sloviansk, Ukrainian strongholds in the Donbas region. Russian strategic hope was to take control of the Donbas basin in its entirety.

Russia was suffering heavy losses and many of those killed belonged to the Wagner Group. Col. Gen. Mikhail Mizin-tsev, the Wagner chief, offered to pardon convicts if they joined the group and fought for six months. There were only a few takers. Both warring factions were using the unguided BM-21 Grad missiles with no effort to protect innocent civilians. Such is war.

The commandoes' specific destination in the city was the Hotel Bakhmut on the corner of 135 *Vulytsia* [Street], and Lermontova Streets. More precisely, it was the penthouse apartment in that building that drew them to the now miserable city.

The city is located on the Bakhmutka River, about 55 mile north of Donetsk; it was known as Artemivsk or Artemovsk between 1924 and 2016. During World War II, it was the site of the Artemivsk Massacre of Soviet Jews by Nazi Germany. During the beginning of the war in Donbas in 2014 between the independent Ukrainian government and pro-Russian separatists, the city was the site of the Battle of Artemivsk. During the full-scale Russian invasion of Ukraine which commenced in February, 2022, Bakhmut had been the site of recurrent major battles between Russian and Ukrainian forces. During the recent past several weeks, Russia had seized Ukrainian barricades around the Butivka coal mine southwest of Avdiivka after Ukraine's withdrawal from the area. By the end of November, Russian forces had advanced on Bakhmut's southern front, capturing settlements such as Ozarianivka, a village nine miles southwest of the city.

A crippled Ukrainian sergeant–now reduced to begging in the street–told the commandoes, "They send their troops in like waves," he said. "We cannot stop them every time because we have fewer guys, and unfortunately, we have lost a lot of men."

President Zelensky described the scene for his television audience during his visit to the front line, Zelenskyy said Russia had also suffered many casualties: "The whole land near Soledar is covered with the corpses of the occupiers and scars from the strikes. This is what madness looks like."

The end result was deprivation and hand-to-mouth survivalist existence. There had been no water supply in the city since October and no electricity since August. As neither side made significant gains, civilians were forced to take shelter in basements prone to flooding. Residents occasionally risked their lives to reach a volunteer center in the heart of the city to get hot food and drinks.

The city–famed for its wine-making and beauty–was largely destroyed, with most of its population having fled; and what remained being placed under Russian occupation. Bakhmut's pre-war population was about 70,000. That December, an estimated 2,000 civilians remained in the city; many were surviving in squalid conditions in the aftermath of the conflict. More than 14 million people fled homes in Ukraine since the Russia invasion.

The front-line city of Bakhmut in eastern Ukraine had been the focus of intense fighting for months. Its fall marked Moscow's most significant victory after months of humiliating setbacks.

The Russians claimed to have seized the nearby salt-mining town of Soledar after Moscow's constant bombardment of its enemy using missiles, artillery, and aircraft–a victory Kyiv denied. During the commandoes surreptitious foray into Bakhmut, the Russians made territorial gains around Bakhmut and Avdiivka, taking control of the Vuhlehirska Thermal Power Plant southeast of the city, and were setting the residences afire. A few weather-beaten signs bearing the once popular slogan "Hold Bakhmut" had become a sad punctuation to the reality of Russian occupation. The incredible number of "Z"s overwhelmed any propaganda value of the previous slogan.

The destruction was comparable to that seen by the commandoes in the other cities and villages they had seen in the Kharkiv and Donetsk Oblasts. That made following an old paper (2021) map difficult since so few landmarks still existed. Once again, however, the Wagnerites gave themselves away. A multistory glass and steel building caught the commandoes' immediate attention by the fact that a large assortment of military vehicles partially surrounded the skyscraper bearing the markings of the Wagner PMC, and the giveaway presence of "Z"s scrawled on the vehicles and surrounding billboards and buildings. It was also convincing that they had found the right place because of the excessive presence of military guards in Wagner uniforms, and that the Hotel Bahmut appeared a bit pockmarked, but still intact. Streets surrounding it had been cleared by Wagner engineers making access relatively and comparatively easy. The clincher was a huge billboard mounted on the front of the hotel bearing the world-known images of Vladimir Rasputinov and the three Wagner chieftains in the war zone.

The hotel had no major or structural damage, even to its esthetic façade. The only security weakness was the presence of numerous entrance and exit portals.

"Look, Yaroslav," said Vasyl, "we can only get into that top floor by staging our own war. Do you think the 18 of use can mount such an action, and do you think enough of us would survive to accomplish our goal?"

"I don't, Vasyl, we do not have a Chinaman's chance to fight our way in. We'll have to try the smart way."

"Have you got any smart ideas for a plan, Chief?"

"Not yet. I'm working on it."

"We're like ducks sitting on a fence while you do."

"I know that. I'll work harder."

Help came by a pre-determined process. Yaroslav contacted Gen. Yuriivna by Sat-phone, who—in turn—contacted Werewolf. He came to Bakhmut bearing gifts that same day.

"Glad to see you, Friend," Yaroslav said when they met.

He had been cautioned about use of the code designation "Werewolf" lest listeners be able to put 2+2 and come up with 4.

"I have news and info," Col. Taras "Werewolf" Seversky announced.

"Hurry up, we need all of that we can get."

"The news is that your quarries have flown the coop."

Yaroslav was crest-fallen, "Is that the good news, Taras?" he asked.

"Of course not, but it may even turn out to be good news."

"That sounds too optimistic at best and even Pollyanish to say the worst. How is that actually good news?"

"It is good, because I know a big secret. All three have gone to a tiny village called Popasnaya. Before you start asking questions, let me tell you, it's in Luhansk Oblast."

All nineteen of the commandoes let out a groan. They were going to have to pullup their shallow roots and set up again for yet another search. Most of them already believed that it was doomed to be as futile as their experiences so far. If good morale counts for anything, the start of this quest seemed doomed before it even began.

CHAPTER 35

Occupied Popasnaya Village, Luhansk Oblast, Sievierodonetsk Raion, Ukraine

December 21, 2024

The only saving grace about having to leave Bakhmut after another failure, was that—at least—they would not have to go out in a blaze of glory on a suicide mission. After Russian forces captured the cities of Severodonetsk and Lysychansk in the Luhansk region two months previously, the security of small villages like Popasnaya in the Luhansk Oblast was razor cut thin. That made the task of the commandoes all that much more difficult and fraught.

The SBU secret information about the most recent location of the Wagner PMC headquarters was corroborated by a war correspondent from a Russian media outlet who reported in *Telegram* newspaper that its base was set up in a five-story residential building that had apparently been abandoned at Myronivska Street, 12 in the occupied village of Popasnaya. That spurred the team on to move as fast as available transportation would permit because it was the best information and the best verified data thus far. Every member of Yaroslav's unit knew by heart the litany of crimes committed by the Wagner Group.

The SBU provided a white paper for Yaroslav and his commandoes and for distribution to the other SBU units around the battle theaters. The top-secret paper was intended to inflame anger among the Ukrainian fighters, and it was highly successful:

Lt. Col. Dmitriy Utkinov Yevgeny, Col. Konstantin Pikalov, Col. Andrei Troshev, and Col. Gen. Mikhail Mizin-tsev

TOP-SECRET—Re: Wagner Private Military Company, Verified Intelligence

The Wagner Group is a private paramilitary organization run by an ally of Russian dictator Vladimir Rasputinov. It is a de facto unit of the Russian Ministry of Defense—Russia's military intelligence agency, the GRU.

The official action head of the Wagner PMC, Lt. Col. Dmitriy Utkinov Yevgeny, is a Nazi fan of the Third Reich. Mikhail Mizin-tsev–Rasputinov's friend–is an entrepreneur, head of the Concord group of companies, founder of the Wagner PMC. From 1981 to 1990, he was imprisoned for theft, robbery, fraud, and involvement of a minor in criminal activity. He is under sanctions from the EU, the US, the UK, Australia, Canada, and Japan.

Lt. Col. Dmitriy Utkinov Yevgeny [call sign "Wagner"] is a reserve lieutenant colonel and executive head of the PMC. Until 2013, he worked for the Moran Security Group PMC and participated in the Syrian expedition of the Slavic Corps PMC. Since 2017, he has been the CEO of the management company of Mizin-tsev's structures, Concord Management and Consulting; Mizin-tsev's ongoing public feuds with the Russian Defense Ministry might also be prompting a desire in the Kremlin to gain more control over its sources of soldiers-for-hire.

This is the reason behind the creation of the recently US-sanctioned Russian PMC, Patriot, which is associated with Russian Defense Minister Sergei Shoigu and competes with Wagner. Russian forces intentionally fired on Wagner mercenaries, according to a video of a Russian military commander who was captured by Wagner. In the video, the commander states that he gave the orders due to his "personal dislike" for the Wagner Group, though the Russian Defense Ministry has yet to comment on the video and claim.

This threatens to pit Russia's military against Russia's largest mercenary group.

Recruiting: Moscow's desire for additional fighters in Ukraine has created a breeding ground for Russian PMC development. The Wagner Group met the need by recruiting on billboards, at schools, on *PornHub*, and in prisons.

At this time in the war, there is a deeply embedded passion in the SBU units to bring down the murderous kleptocratic PMC which bears a significant responsibility for the more than 31,000 Ukrainian troops who had been killed in defense of their freedom and their country [compared to 200,000 Russian soldiers killed or wounded as of February, 2023].

That has created the need for an emergency clandestine mission to kill or capture Lt. Col. Dmitriy Utkinov ("Wagner"), Yevgeny Wagner commanders, Col. Konstantin Pikalov, Col. Andrei Troshev, and Col. Gen. Mikhail Mizin-tsev.

AFRICA

The group has tens of thousands of fighters and has operated in Syria and in various African countries as a violent kleptocracy. The Wagner Group continues to commit human rights abuses in the CAR [Central African Republic] during its active participation in Rasputinov's war in Ukraine. Indisputable evidence obtained by the Western intelligence services revealed that Wagner operatives had raped and robbed unarmed civilians in the country's rural areas and that the atrocities were continuing. The UN documented more than 500 incidents in the year from July, 2020 onward to the present day.

The Group is also known to have deployed forces elsewhere in Africa—including in Mali and Libya–and is playing a major role in the conflicts in Syria under the criminal dictator, Bashar al-Assad's, Egyptian branch of the Iraqi Ba'ath movement. The UK and US have accused Wagner of extralegal executions and torture in Mali and the Central African Republic and threats to peace and security in Sudan. This was over and above their presence in Ukraine working with the illegal breakaway "republics" of Luhansk and Donetsk.

In 2017, Wagner PMCs were sent from Syria to Sudan and South Sudan after Sudan's president, Omar al-Bashir, told Russian president Rasputinov that his country needed protection from aggressive actions of the USA. The PMCs were sent to Sudan to support it militarily against South Sudan and protect gold, uranium, and diamond mines.

The PMCs in Sudan were working under the cover of M Invest, a company linked to the Wagner Group. M Invest signed a contract with the Russian Defense Ministry for the use of transport aircraft of the 223rd Flight Unit of the Russian Air Force.

In late January, 2019–after protests erupted in Sudan mid-December 2018–the PMCs helped Sudanese authorities crackdown on the protesters. Ukrainian SBU identified 149 Russian PMCs by name who participated violently in the suppression of the protests.

In 2018, the Russian private military company Wagner deployed its personnel to the CAR, ostensibly to protect lucrative mines, support the CAR government, and provide close protection for the president, Faustin-Archange Touadéra. Wagner's presence in the country has resulted in many organizations accusing them of human rights abuses and exacerbating the conflict.

In September, 2022, *The Daily Beast* interviewed survivors and witnesses of yet another massacre committed by the Wagner Group in Bèzèrè village in December, 2021, which involved torture, killing, and disembowelment of a number of women, including pregnant ones.

On July 30, 2018, three Russian journalists belonging to the Russian online news organization TsUR [Investigation Control Center] which is linked to the Wagner PMC, were ambushed and killed by unknown assailants in the Central African Republic, three days after they had arrived in the country to investigate local Wagner activities. The ambush took place near Sibut when armed men emerged from the bush and opened fire on their vehicle. The journalists' driver survived the attack but was afterward kept income-muni-cado by the authorities.

In its response to the killings, Russia's foreign ministry noted that the dead journalists had been traveling without official accreditation; but the Security Service of Ukraine has produced convincing evidence of the PMCs involvement.

On May 31, 2022, Human Rights Watch stated that information from Libyan agencies and demining groups linked the Wagner Group to the use of banned landmines and booby traps in Libya. These mines killed at least three Libyan deminers before the mines' locations were identified. By early 2020, the number of attacks in Cabo Delgado surged, with 28 taking place throughout January and early February. The violence spread to nine of the province's 16 districts. The attacks included beheadings, mass kidnappings, and villages burned to the ground. Most of the attacks were conducted by PMC and government militant sympathiz-ers, but some were also made by bandits.

On March 23, the militants captured the key town of Mocimboa de Praia in Cabo Del-gado. Two weeks later, the insurgents launched attacks against half a dozen villages in the province.

In late December, 2021, France published a joint statement also signed by the UK, Germany, Canada, and 11 other European governments, that they have witnessed the deployment of the Wagner Group to Mali with Russia's backing, and that they condemned the action.

On April 5, 2022, Human Rights Watch published a report accusing Malian soldiers and Russian PMCs of executing around 300 civilians between March 27-31, during a military operation in Moura, in the Mopti region, known as a hotspot of Islamic militants.

In late June, 2022, accusations surfaced against the Wagner Group that PMCs were looting towns and indiscriminately arresting people in the northern Tombouctou Region with the Malian military forcing civilians to flee to Mauritania.

The US government shared intelligence with the Chadian government that Wagner was working with rebels in the country to destabilize the government and is probably plotting to assassinate the country's president as well as other top government officials. Wagner was allegedly also seeking to forge ties with elements of the Chadian ruling class.

This attempt to topple a government represents a watershed for Wagner's influence building strategy,

After years of denying the Russian government's links to the Wagner Group, President Rasputinov admitted in June, 2023 that the Kremlin provided 86 billion rubles [approximately $940 million USD in October, 2023] in financial support to the PMC group from May, 2022 to May, 2023.

The transnational ongoing criminal organization, Wagner Group's, exploitation of African resources, notably gold, diamonds, and timber, is only one node of its destabilizing influence across Africa.

Wagner Group forces have razed entire villages and murdered civilians in the Central African Republic to advance their economic interests in the mining sector, participated in the unlawful execution of people in Mali, raided artisanal gold mines in Sudan, and undermined democratic institutions in every country where they have worked.

They are also accused of paying their bills in counterfeit currency. This pattern of criminal behavior—and of preying on Africans—is not going to end with any Wagner PMC leader's death.

According to *The Economist*, Wagner killed at least 1,800 African civilians as of August, 2023. Wagner's brutal presence in Africa is touted by the Russian government as "supporting peace and stability." However, in Mali alone, terrorist violence against civilians since 2021 has surged by 278 percent. Russia's disinformation and propaganda ecosystem falsely portrays the Wagner Group as playing a positive role in nations such as CAR. Although the Wagner Group has been deployed in CAR since 2018, Russian officials still refer to the group's forces as COSI/QUIS ["Russian instructors"] which serves as a front company for Wagner Group operations in CAR. Its US-sanctioned director, Aleksandr Ivanov, justifies Wagner's presence in CAR, saying "The fighters of the Wagner Group remain in CAR, so the inhabitants of the Republic can sleep peacefully! ...the Republic has become a safe place for the life and development of the local population."

There are presently 37 Russian Federation PMCs in the CAR: since 2020, the number of Russian PMCs has increased its presence to 30 countries. PMCs were present in 19 countries in Africa; According to Russian resource *kapital-rus.ru*, PMCs are created to wage hybrid wars without direct state involvement, thus not provoking open aggression. This is done in order not to provoke international conflicts, but to carry out certain combat operations in different parts of the world, circumventing the UN Charter and possible sanctions.

A former member of one of the PMCs commented, "Most of Russia's PMCs were created to participate in the conflict in Ukraine," according to an article by a Russian media outlet paper.

The use of PMCs means a reduction in *official* losses. People join PMCs voluntarily; so, the Russian state is not responsible to the families of the victims.

In the Russian-Ukrainian war, PMCs provide very short training for fighters and often use them as "cannon fodder". They are sent to storm the fortified positions without training and support from regular Russian military. The main goal is to exhaust the opposing fighters before the main body of regular troops attacks.

It is highly likely that influential people in Russia want to protect themselves, their wealth, and territories, in the event of a collapse or coup in Russia. Rasputinov intends to strengthen his power with the help of PMCs and avoid in such way a "palace coup." Typically run by Kremlin-linked oligarchs, PMCs and the lucrative benefits that can accrue from deployments, give the Kremlin a lever for balancing competing political and financial interests among oligarchs, and exploiting PMCs' quasi-legal status to ensure loyalty to Rasputinov.

PMCs have become a symbol of political power; so, everyone with the means follows the trend and thus promotes themselves. Russians are creating PMCs to protect the loot. The number of PMC fighters: 40-50 thousand.

Vulnerabilities: The use of Russian PMCs presents new operational and strategic risks to Moscow. Morale in Russian PMC units in high-risk missions appears delicate. Although their use provides political protection from the optics of high Russian MoD casualties, both Russian PMC casualties and their return home create novel political and domestic security risks. Their use also complicates internal regime politics in Moscow, creating competition between the MoD and private equities that can jeopardize operations.

Finally, the ambiguity of operational control and decision-making related to Russian PMCs opens Moscow up to the risk of being held responsible by the international community for actions taken by Russian PMCs under the command of other interests.

Negativity associated with the Rusich DShRG

- *Rusich*, a neo-Nazi pro-Kremlin PMC operating in Ukraine and linked to Wagner's mercenaries, openly calls for atrocities and torture of prisoners.
- The leaders:
- *Milchakov*–is a fascist and a sadist who is on the EU sanctions list.
- *Petrovsky*–was a member of a pagan group, neo-Nazi.
- *Rasskazov*–gets sexual excitement from killing Ukrainians.

The Truth about the Wagner Group in Central African Republic: Reports from the United Nations and independent media document the truth about the Wagner Group and its brutal treatment of the people of CAR.

- CBS reported in May, 2023 that Wagner forces used indiscriminate killing, abductions, and rape, to gain control of a key mining area near the city of Bambari, with survivors describing the attacks in detail: "To say 'killing' is an understatement. It was total carnage. Like Armageddon... They spoke Russian. Even Chechen. Some wore masks and had long beards."
- People in CAR–including journalists, aid workers and minorities, as well as international peacekeepers,–have been violently harassed and threatened by so-called "Russian instructors" from the Wagner Group, UN experts reported in October, 2021.
- Despite Russia and Wagner's claims that it brings stability to the areas it operates in–the group operating from CAR and allegedly outside of the host government's awareness–plotted to overthrow the government of Chad in early 2023, an action that exacerbated an already challenging humanitarian situation for women, children, and other civilians.

Russia's Lies in Mali:
Russian officials, Russian state-funded media, and Kremlin-linked *Telegram* channels, contin-uously message on the Wagner Group's allegedly "positive" role in Mali since the group's deployment in 2021. Despite these posts, Mali's transition government has yet to publicly acknowledge that Wagner Group is *in* Mali.

Propaganda videos continue to circulate online portraying Wagner Group forces as saviors and "warrior angels." Before Wagner's deployment to Mali, Russia highlighted false narratives like those it deployed about CAR, repeating the myth that "Russian instructors" would bring peace, stability, and would also have new success at fighting counterterrorism in the count-ry. Aleksandr Ivanov–the U.S.-sanctioned director of the OUIS–boasted to Malian news sites that the Wagner Group was "doing excellent work all over the world," claiming it "will fight terrorism everywhere." A Russia-linked propaganda video circulating after Wagner's deploy-ment to Mali, at the end of 2021, falsely suggested that the United States and France are support-ing violent religious extremists in Mali.

The Truth about the Wagner Group in Mali:
The facts are:

- Contrary to Russia's claim, the Wagner Group has not been effective in countering terrorism in Mali since first deploying in December, 2021. The UN Panel of Experts for Mali reported in August, 2023 that ISIS-Sahel almost doubled its territorial control in Mali in less than a year. Wagner Group has failed to make Mali safer, with 2022 being the deadliest year for civilians in Mali since the current conflict broke out in 2012.
- Wagner Group forces were captured on video in April, 2022 burying a dozen bodies in a mass grave near the Gossi military base in Mali. Wagner Group then

produced misleadingly edited videos and attempted to falsely blame the French military for the incident, in order to increase anti-French and anti-Western sentiment in Mali.

Russia's Lies in Sudan:
Russian officials and Wagner Group representatives have repeatedly claimed that Wagner has no military presence in Sudan and that Russia is not involved in the country's bloody civil war between the Sudanese Armed Forces and the RSF [Rapid Support Forces] led by General Dagalo. Russia's Ministry of Foreign Affairs stated that Russia only desires a "peaceful resolution" to the conflict. In an April, 2023 statement, Mizin-tsev added: "Wagner PMC is in no way involved in the Sudanese conflict." Russia also consistently portrays itself as a disin-terested actor in Sudan, merely seeking to assist the country in strengthening its security, stability, and economic development. Russian Foreign Minister Lavrov, in a June, 2023 meeting with Sudan's Deputy Chairperson of the Transitional Sovereignty Council, expressed "deep concern" over the crisis. Lavrov added that "Russia is watching with concern what is happening in Sudan and is interested in helping to create the conditions for normalizing the situation."

The Truth about the Wagner Group in Sudan:
Sudanese civilians and victims of Wagner activities say otherwise.
- Wagner Group mercenaries have killed scores of Sudanese miners working in artisanal gold mines along the border between Sudan and the Central African Republic, according to survivors of these attacks, while they loot Sudan's rich gold mines.
- Other survivors report that Wagner mercenaries have attacked encampments full of migrant workers and miners along the Sudanese/CAR border, shooting indiscriminately. A witness who lost his brother and six relatives at

the hands of Wagner soldiers said more than 70 people were killed in a single attack.

Russia's Lies in Libya:

Russia's state-sponsored media outlets regularly accuse NATO forces of destroying the Libyan state and of initiating the ongoing instability there in pursuit of its member states' own interests. These propaganda outlets support Russia's false narrative, portraying itself as an altruistic, anti-colonial power seeking only to help African countries.

For years, the Russian Government rejected any claims of a Russian mercenary or military presence in Libya, with Russian MFA Spokesperson Maria Zakharova in 2020 asserting that there was "no Russian presence in Libya," and that "PMCs are not allowed under Russian law."

Russian Government representatives repeatedly argued that accusations it had taken sides in the Libyan conflict were "lies," and that it strove for a "ceasefire and political settlement of the conflict." In 2020, Russian Envoy to the UN, Vassily Nebenzya, condemned accusations of Russian mercenary involvement in Libya as "largely based on unverified or spurious data and aimed at discrediting Russia's policy on Libya. These are obviously planted stories."

The Truth about Wagner Group in Libya

There is clear evidence that Wagner Group has inserted itself in Libya for political and financial gain, committing human rights abuses against the Libyan people, and intensifying ongoing instability.

- Wagner Group—as an admitted Russian Government-backed entity—reportedly has acted contrary to UN Security Council Resolution 1970 and other relevant resolutions by providing military equipment and mercenaries to the front lines of the Libya conflict, including fighter aircraft, armored vehicles, and air defense systems.

- According to AFRICOM [US Africa Command], at least 14 Mig-29s and Su-24s were painted over to disguise their Russian marks of origin and then flown from Russia's bases in Syria to Libya. Wagner Group is "prolonging conflict responsible for the needless suffering and the deaths of innocent civilians," AFRICOM stated.

- The Wagner Group placed landmines and boobytraps while withdrawing from Tripoli in 2020, according to public reporting. Mines and other explosive ordnance reportedly killed or wounded more than 300 people in Libya between May, 2020 and March, 2022, including in areas formerly controlled by Wagner Group forces.

The FFM [UN Fact-Finding Mission] in Libya's final report indicates that Wagner forces placed "military explosives in homes, inside sofas and bathroom fixtures, and other civilian areas, which led to death and injury of civilians."

The FFM determined that Wagner personnel "violated the international law principle of proportionality and the obligation to minimize the indiscriminate effects of mines and other explosives" as well as "violating the right to life" of Libyans by not clearing the ordnance for the safety of civilians.

- Wagner conducted disinformation campaigns in Libya in an attempt to boost support for Russian-allied figures who oppose the UN-recognized government in Tripoli, according to the African Center for Strategic Studies. Wagner built a social media apparatus in Libya to promote Haftar, Saif al-Islam Gaddhafi, and other political figures whom the Kremlin believed could become future clients of Russia, using methods reminiscent of previous Mizintsev-led interference in other foreign elections, according to the Stanford Internet Observatory.

Wagner created at least 12 different Facebook groups to manipulate Libyan public opinion, and these pages were viewed by more than two million users each week.

Wagner also purchased 50% of the former Libyan state-run broadcasting company, A1 Jamahiriya TV, transferring its studios to a location overseas and renewing its broadcasts into Libya.

Russia is Responsible
Russia's disinformation and propaganda ecosystem continues to deploy false narratives such as those outlined above to deflect attention from and avoid responsibility for the Wagner Group's human rights abuses and atrocities.
The Kremlin-backed Wagner Group exploits insecurity to expand Russia's presence in Africa for political influence and financial gain. In doing so, they threaten stability and human rights on the continent.
In January, 2023, the US Treasury Department designated Wagner Group as a Transnational Criminal Organization for committing–among other egregious acts– "an ongoing pattern of serious criminal activity, including mass executions, rape, child abductions, and physical abuse, in the Central African Republic and Mali."

Yaroslav had copies of the white paper photocopied and required each of his men and women to carry a copy on their persons. For two full weeks, the commandoes reconnoitered, mapped, calculated, argued about, and studied every aspect of the headquarters location. They found an abandoned building and drilled every day on the agreed upon plans for their attack on the headquarters. One of the main disagreements centered around the "dead or alive" clause in SBU's order s whether or not to take the simpler route: kill them all.

Yaroslav had his own plan in that regard.

CHAPTER 36

Occupied Popasnaya Village, Luhansk Oblast, Sievierodonetsk Raion, Ukraine

January 15, 2025

During the Russian invasion of Ukraine in 2022, the city was largely destroyed as a result of fighting between Ukrainian and Russian forces. Since the end of the battle on May 8, 2022, it has been occupied by Russia. In 2018, it had a population of 20,000 people. When the SBU commandoes sneaked into the town in 2025, the population had managed to creep slowly back to 8,500.

Popasnaya was founded in the late 1870s as a stop on the newly constructed railway connecting the Donbas with industrial centers in more northern parts of what was then the Russian Empire. Construction of the railway station itself began in 1878, and basic housing was built for the workers to live in. By 1890, Popasnaya was connected by rail to major trade hubs like Debaltseve, Bakhmut, and Lysychansk. Popasnaya itself became a rail hub, and its population began to grow.

In December, 1924, Popasnaya became the administrative center of Popasnayaya Raion, inside Bakhmut Okruha. In the 1930s, under Soviet rule, Popasnayaya was renamed Imeni [settlement] *L.M. Kahanovycha* within Donetsk Oblast. On June 3, 1938, a large portion of Donetsk Oblast was split off to become what is now Luhansk Oblast. The settlement was given city status on October 24,1938.

The twenty-first century had been continually centered on armed conflict in the sorry little town. On June 19, 2014–during the early stages of the war in Donbas—Ukrainian forces secured Popasnayaya from pro-Russian separatists. However, on July 8, 2014, separatist militants retook the town. On July 22, the Ukrainian government Donbas Battalion took back the town, and the separatists abandoned it that day. Afterwards, the city came under frequent periodic artillery shelling up to the time the commandoes entered the scene. Landmines laid near the perimeter of Popasnaya remained an omnipresent problem.

By March, 2015, the city only had two stores with some basic products and one pharmacy. Residents received food distribution through a volunteer organization. Residents had to pay for public utilities which were unreliable at best and for social benefits supplied only sporadically by the Ukrainian government.

There was relative peace from 2015 to 2022 when–in early March, during the full-scale Russian invasion of Ukraine–Popasnaya was attacked by Russian forces. In the fighting in or near Popasnaya, Russian forces damaged or destroyed every property in the town center. The governor of Luhansk Oblast stated that Russian forces were "removing Popasnaya from the map of region". On May 7, Ukrainian troops were forced to retreat from the city.

Ukrainian forces announced that they had withdrawn from Popasnaya, allowing Russia to occupy the town fully. Russia's Chechen leader Ramzan Kadyrov and his troops now controlled most of the city. The Wagner Group had free rein in the Russian protectorate. Photographic evidence supplied by the governor of Luhansk Oblast revealed that Russian forces had beheaded and dismembered a Ukrainian soldier and displayed his body parts stuck on poles in the captured city. On August 15, 2022, Ukrainian forces hit the regional headquarters of the Wagner Group after a pro-Kremlin reporter unintentionally revealed its location at five-story residential building that had apparently been abandoned at Myronivska Street, 12 in a photo.

The leader of the Russian Luhansk People's Republic stated there was no point in rebuilding the city destroyed during the Russian assault. When the Ukrainian commandoes entered, the town looked entirely deserted by both humans and animals, with nearly all its buildings either destroyed or heavily damaged.

In December, 2022, Russian forces did constructed multiple lines of defense to the West of Popasnaya to blunt any Ukrainian attacks. These defenses included "Dragon's teeth", trenches, and pillboxes, which made the commandoes' entry slow and extremely cautious, since it had to take place during the night.

They managed to find a few signs suggestive that they were walking along *Мічуріна вулиця* [Michurina Stree] which should be leading them to where the *Міська Рада* [town hall] building on *Мічуріна вулиця* and the *Будинок творчості* [community center] building and the *Сквер слави* [park] once stood. The five-story residential building that had apparently been abandoned at Myronivska Street, 12 was battered but still standing and even had a small plaque on the front of it giving its name.

"The Force is with us," Rokosylana said, referencing an American movie once popular in Ukraine.

"And the light is on in the fifth-floor office," Yaroslav said.

"Like I said, "Rokosylana replied with a smug smile.

With the potential of their quarries actually being present in a room near them, Yaroslav decided to proceed with all due caution and certainty before exposing themselves in the final confrontation with their arch enemies, the Wagner officers.

While the rest hid about in shadows, Yaroslav sent Vasyl and Fedir to search out a relatively close by place that would be suitable to use as a makeshift mission headquarters. The requirements were that it be out of sight of Myronivska Street, 12; that it be easily accessible, particularly if needed in an escape; and that it have room enough to hold three hostages without them being seen or heard.

It turned out to be quite easy. The *Сквер слави* [park] still had patches of untended grass to confirm what it once had been. There were large piles of rubble which were once buildings, but had been dumped in the previously pristine park as permanent refuse. One particular area at the north end of the park had four large dump sites surrounding what had once been a children's playground with swing sets, teeter-totters, curved slides, and jungle gyms, in various states of destruction and disrepair. They were made of plastic; so, they were light and easily moved out of the way, leaving an empty center for their camp. That area could only be seen from a tall building, and there was only one such in the area–Myronivska Street, 12. All the windows on the 5th floor were opaque from accumulated dust and were highly unlikely to provide a view that would give them away.

Still under the protection of the inky blackness of the night, devoid of any remaining city lights, they moved swiftly, gathered their gear, and constructed a somewhat defensive palisade structure, out of discarded metal sheeting, 2 X 4s, cinder blocks, and piles of dirt and stones. It was more a visual block than would be any protection against bullets or men attacking. Yaroslav ordered a revolving sentry watch with Boryslav Vovk, Ramzan Alaudinov, and Apti Tsitsulayev as first watch. He and Rokosylana took the early morning watch, and Fedir Blyznyuk, Boryslav Vovk, Vasyl Haranchak, and Rikonda Kadyrov, took the day watch. In the meantime, the rest hunkered down and kept a low profile.

At 14:00, a burly and heavily armed enlisted man, walked out of the front door of the building alone. He was carrying handfuls of grocery store plastic bags. Yaroslav sent Fedir to follow him; he was the best of the unit's trackers. The enlisted PCM operative returned at 15:35, and Fedir came an hour later, taking no chances of being discovered.

"Okay, Fedir, give us a report," Vasyl asked.

He was getting very bored.

"Well, we walked about a mile and half to the nearest—and I presume only—grocery store. It was doing a brisk business. Interesting, the only customers were old men. Anyway, the thug bought two arm loads of groceries and carried them out in his own plastic bags. No one paid any attention to him, and no one saw me. I followed him at a safe distance. The guy made a beeline back to the building, went inside, and then, I slipped back into our hidey hole."

"Did you see anyone else from the HQ building?" Yaroslav asked.

"No. I only saw one small platoon of Wagner PCMs out there."

"Thanks, Fedir."

"Glad to get out for a little stroll."

Well after dark, the unit suited up in body armor and weaponry. They drew straws, and Adil Shagiakhmetov drew the short straw. It was his lot to have to guard the flimsy little fort.

CHAPTER 37

Myronivska Street, 12, Occupied Popasnaya Village
January 16, 2025, midnight

The moon hung high in the ink-black starless sky, casting a dim glow over the desolate landscape of Donblast Basin, now a war-torn region within the eastern borders of Ukraine. The air was heavy with tension, as if the very earth held its breath in anticipation of the imminent operation. It was treacherous—possibly booby-trapped–terrain. The young agent who was responsible for the mission–Yaroslav Kandybavych Melnykenko—had prepared himself for an existentially crucial mission that could change the course of his nation and its arch enemy.

The team observed absolute radio and conversational silence from the time they came to the rear door of the rickety old building. They took out the two enlisted sentries without a sound and pushed their way into the building. It was all tap shoulders, point, and sign language, to achieve understanding and compliance of Yaroslav's orders. Every man still wore their thermal imagers, as used by the army's R-18 drones, to detect the infrared radiation given off by warm objects and display them using bright colors. R-18 is a Ukrainian unmanned combat aerial vehicle designed to attack enemy targets with ammunition, developed by the Ukrainian organization Aerorozvidka.

The first military night-vision systems–from the second world war–used infrared searchlights whose sweep could be seen only by special detectors. These worked well unless the enemy had infrared sensors, in which case the user stood out like a beacon. Modern armies have two types of night-vision gear that avoid this problem: thermal imagers and photomultipliers.

The team's secret newest thermal imaging devices also included photomultipliers to turn light into electrical signals, in effect amplifying what little light was available. These turned the world an eerie monochrome green. The night vision goggles were the kind gift of their favorite uncle in the west, affectionately known as "Uncle Sugar" by the agents and military rank and file, as were their weapons, ammunition, and combat protective camouflage gear. The enhanced vision gave them a huge tactical advantage once they were in the lightless building.

Yaroslav Melnykenko paused the headlong rush in the putative Wagner Headquarters building to remind his men, "Time is critical. If we have figured out where Pikalov, Troshev, and Mizin-tsev are hiding out; so, will the army. We can expect a coordinated attack any minute."

The unit had had to rely on a local unknown to them to guide them through the enemy territory city as quickly and as safely as possible. It was going to be light all too soon, and they had to be set up for their attack in their hiding place before they were discovered. The soonest the attack could commence was when darkest hour came around that night. Every detail of the mission depended on that critical item. Yaroslav also knew from his own experience that no plan ever went off without a hitch, and he dreaded the possibility of an almost inevitable Murphy's Law complication coming his way.

He sent Rokosylana to reconnoiter the stairwell between floors one and two. The rest of the commandoes heard two, nearly simultaneous thumps, then Rokosylana glided on feather toes back to the group.

"Two down," she said. "I presume there are at least that many on every floor from here to the top."

Yaroslav nodded.

"Adil and Midhat, take the next stairwell."

They nodded, and the two men headed up the stairs toward the third floor. The rest walked to the second floor and paused.

There was some noise this time. A body tumbled down the stairs. To the commandoes, it sounded like a freight train had just roared through; but, in truth, sound did not carry well in the old building, and apparently, no one else heard it. After a tense ten-minute wait, they went upwards again, this time with Boryslav and Vasyl taking sentry killing duty.

Yaroslav and Ramzan took the lead from the 4th to the 5th floor. This time there were three guards, and one of them was making security rounds through the square of corridors from the stairwell opening and back. They could not be sure exactly where he was on that walk.

Yaroslav slipped up to the top step and took a quick look to be sure where the two other sentries were standing. They had stationed themselves at less-than-stiff attention, and one of them was smoking, a definite no-no. Yaroslav motioned to Ramzan to join him at the other end of the narrow top stair. He raised three fingers, then curled them down into a fist one at a time. When the fist was complete, both commandoes reached out of their hiding place and gripped a shocked sentry around the neck. Both sentries suffered fractured necks and became limp in less than a second. Yaroslav and Ramzan silently let their victims slide to the darkness of the stairs.

They waited for the third sentry in absolute silence, scarcely breathing.

They could see that the guard was suspicious. He moved slowly, looking for his comrades carefully. He obeyed the house rule of silence in order not to alert intruders. Yaroslav took the lead. He waited until the sentry took a step beyond the stairwell opening, then, he stepped out behind the unsuspecting sentry. Yaroslav held his breath and worried about the thumping noise of his heart within his chest.

He reached around the man's neck, pulled him to his chest cutting off his trachea and ability to make noise. He lifted the man up to avoid him thumping the floor with his feet and cut his throat with his K-bar knife. He held the bleeding sentry out from his chest to avoid getting soaked and waited until he stopped jerking—his death throes. Then, he carefully slid the fresh corpse to the wood floor.

He sent Ramzan back to fetch the rest of the unit while he watched for possible theretofore unseen guards. The commandoes formed up behind him, each with a handgun in one hand and a combat knife in the other. They followed Yaroslav along the dark hallway. Every man and Rokosylana were out in the unprotected corridor, when they heard the first sound of the night. An ominous one.

CHAPTER 38

Myronivska Street, 12, Battlefield Headquarters of the Wagner PMC

January 17, 2025, 0030

T he fourth door on the left opened abruptly, and two alert sentries stepped into the hallway holding flashlights and Kalashnikovs. They were ready for a routine security inspection and not looking for a surprise. Unfortunately for them, their lights landed on a seventeen-man (including one woman) unit of strangers armed to the hilt and ready for emergency eye wink quick action. They died before any one of them could pull a trigger. Unfortunately for the SBU commandoes, every light in the entire building came on temporarily dazzling the commandoes in their night vision goggles and slowing their responses. Quicker than any of the commandoes could speak, six more sentries rushed out the door Kalashnikov's blazing on full automatic. The first two seconds saw sixty rounds of ammunition knife holes in the walls of the hallway; the second two seconds saw the same number of bullets heat the air over the prone bodies of the commandoes, who were lying prone on the floor by then.

The next several seconds were the equivalent of two sets of 15+ men having a shootout in an elevator. The world's favorite and cheapest combat automatics, AK-47s, have a flaw. After three bullets leave the barrel, their heat distorts the barrel; so, they are not very accurate, especially at a distance of 50+ feet. The two sets of opponents were no more than 40 feet apart. The carnage was very quick and dreadful.

Fourteen Wagnerites were dead, two were wounded, and one retreated safely back into the bedroom where the senior officers had been asleep. Twelve of Yaroslav's commandoes were KIA or WIA—and unable to continue any action. Yaroslav, Rokosylana, Ramzan, Boryslav, Apti, and Fedir, survived because they held their ground [literally] firing from the prone position. Rokosylana sustained a through-and-through bullet wound in her left calf which hurt like crazy and would cause her to limp for months but did not entirely remove her from action for the time being.

"You okay?" Yaroslav asked her, looking very worried.

"I am," she said. "It's just a 5.56 hickey [American military slang–a scar or blister resulting from a burn suffered–usually on the neck–due to hot brass.]. "I am out of action for a bit; so, get in there and finish the job before they get you. My dear husband to be, you are hereby forbidden to die. Understand?"

"Lima Charlie [Loud and Clear] … dear."

Yaroslav looked at the still living commandoes and crisply ordered: "Follow me."

He took a quick peak around the corner into the room. There were four gunners and three obvious senior officers, all pointing firearms in the direction of the door. The quarters were fairly tight; so, Yaroslav threw two flash-bang grenades in quick succession and forward rolled into the room with his AR-16 leveled at the enlisted men. The four other intact commandoes followed his lead. Then there were five assault rifles aimed at vulnerable chests. The Wagner gunners were choking for breath, and temporarily blind and deaf from the grenades. When they could see, all four wisely dropped their Kalasnikovs, and raised their hands without being ordered to do so. The two senior officers were no more inclined toward heroism than their enlisteds; so, they all laid down their arms and shouted in unison, *Капітуляція*!!, *Капітуляція*!! [Surrender, Surrender!!].

Without a word of warning, Fedir Blyznyuk slipped his rifle to automatic and fired from waist level a single long burst that almost cut all four of the enlisted Wagnerites in half. It was over in less than two seconds.

"Why did you do that?" Yaroslav demanded.

"No room on the bus, and they are a waste of air."

Yaroslav nodded. Fedir was right. It would be all they could do to control the two senior officers. They could not afford to risk taking along four enemies who might betray them at any moment.

Yaroslav pointed his rifle at the three senior officers. He was well aware that he was pointing his gun at three of the most dangerous men in the world, men who had no qualms about killing or even being killed at this point, given the potential alternatives. He wanted their cooperation, and fear was a good catalyst. However, he did not want to frighten them so much that they were willing to die in trying to get away.

He spoke in Russian, "Come with me peacefully, and you won't be hurt. I do not want to kill you, but I will. Right now, your Russian masters don't know about this night, and none of my men will tell them. Maybe… if we all can keep that secret, you will preserve enough luck to be able to see the sunshine again. *Понимать*, *Ponimat* [Understand?]."

Lt. Col. Dmitriy Utkinov Yevgeny, Col. Konstantin Pikalov, and Col. Andrei Troshev, meekly nodded their heads.

Ramzan and Apti gave first aid to Rokosylana whose bleeding had largely stopped. They put a compress on the wound and bound it with Kerlex and Ace wraps. The two of them assisted her down the stairs behind Yaroslav and the other commandoes and their prisoners. She was in severe pain, and Yaroslav fetched a morphine syringe from her backpack and injected it through her uniform trouser leg into her right quadriceps muscles where there were no major vessels or nerves to hit by mistake.

Outside, no one was on the streets in the cold darkness. From distant parts of the city, they heard occasional rifle and machine gun fire and the rare noise of a bomb going off.

"Think they're after us, Yaroslav?" Ramzan asked.

"No. I think that is just bits of action throughout the town. I actually believe it's good news. They probably didn't pay any attention to our noise. But… eyes and ears open. No mistakes. Let's get back to the hidey-hole."

Apti blindfolded the captives and made sure that their arms were securely bound behind their backs.

"No talking… anybody." Yaroslav ordered and struck Lt. Col. Yevgeny hard in the ribs for emphasis.

Yevgeny grunted but otherwise made no sound.

They set off at a brisk walk toward their hidey hole in the north end of the park. They entered the makeshift enclosure/"fort" they had made and tied the three Wagnerites to heavy blocks lying on the ground. They were in for a cold night on the ground.

Adil Shagiakhmetov—who had drawn the short straw—and missed all the action, quietly emerged from his place of advantage and greeted his comrades.

"I trust no one followed you," he said.

"No, my friend. We were most careful. May I introduce you to Lt. Col. Dmitriy Utkinov Yevgeny, Col. Konstantin Pikalov, and Col. Andrei Troshev, of the highly decorated Wagner PMC, Adil."

Adil poked each of the three captives with his gun butt out of spite and pique for having been left out of the capture.

Yevgeny was the only one who spoke.

"We are hungry and thirsty. As POWs we have a right to proper treatment."

"We are likely to feed you when the survivors in Popasnaya get their belly's full," Yaroslav said harshly.

He had his men muffle the captives with gags and told the commandoes to get some sleep. He would take the first watch.

During his watch, he got on the sat phone with Gen. Yuriivna at SBU headquarters in Kyiv. He spoke in English and in American jargon to make any eavesdropper's job more difficult.

"Common man" to "Top Man" [Gen. Yuriivna's code name]. Good evening. Positive report for mission completion. Now in LUP [Lying-Up Point]. Three in place. Negative Charlie Foxtrot. Twelve KIAs and WIAs–EOS [End of Service].

Multiple criminals same. Our losses DRT [Dead Right There—unavoidable]. We remain FMC [Fully Mission Capable]. Over, "Common Man".

Gen. Yuriivna's reply was in the same coded language. "Good. Sadness for your... for *our* loss. Concentrate now on E&E [Escape and Evade] and control of EPWs [Enemy Prisoners of War]. KBO [Keep Buggering On] and remain intact until exfil at extraction site X1. Until then *Iдimь Богом/iditz bogom* [Go with God].

"Wilco [Will Comply]. Over and out."

CHAPTER 39

Severne Village near Avdiivka, Donetsk Oblast, Ukraine, Extraction Site X1

January 19, 2025, 23:15:

January 18 was a miserable and tense day for the SBU unit hunkered down in its hidey-hole makeshift "fortress" at the north end of the *Сквер слави* [park] in what was now a considerably more occupied Popasnaya Village. The ruined town was swarming with Russian troops, Wagner PMC militia, and Separatist locals now that the raid on Myronivska Street, 12 dominated the local word-of-mouth news. Russia had increased the number of assault units. Many of which had reached company strength–which is up to 250 soldiers.

The presumption on the part of the Russians and the PMCs was that the Wagner leadership was long gone from the area since the raiders had had the entire night to get away. After a furious and fruitless morning's search, the enemy multitudes were ordered to move north toward Kharkiv and south toward Donetsk and to search every field, haystack, house, and town, along the way.

There had been a great many close calls for the SBU agents, and more than a few miracles as they made themselves as small as possible in their hiding place in the park. They were prepared to fight, a tension

219

they had to endure throughout the daylight hours. But, they dreaded the thought of making noise or engaging in any contact that might attract the attention of the fully aroused mob.

Yaroslav ordered Boryslav and Apti to distribute rations and water to everyone. They crawled to the rations packs and back to deliver the life-sustaining nutrients. It was a tedious and strenuous effort for the two men who had to military crawl—slither on their elbows and knees—but they did so without complaint or any other sound. Yaroslav, himself, took Rokoslyana's portion to her and shared breakfast with her. Her leg bandage was dry, and its tight compression on her calf held the pain at bay.

He joined Boryslav and Apti when they took rations to the three captives. He held a knife at the throat of each Wagner chieftain as his bindings and gag were loosed, and he was allowed to feed himself. They quaffed seemingly endless swallows of the cool water and sighed with relief.

"We'll do this again a bit later if you behave yourselves as POWs. I have no compunctions about cutting your throats, but I would rather you lived. If you behave until 1400, I will bring you news and perhaps a proposition depending on how well I can communicate with my superiors."

They nodded their understanding and docilely submitted to being bound and gagged again.

Yaroslav communicated with Gen. Yuriivna again after communicating with his captives.

"Common Man" to "Top Man" and added the required authentication code.

"Common Man", anything new to report?"

"No. Situation difficult but improving. Fewer *Separs* [short for "separatist" and a term is regularly used by Ukrainian soldiers to define their enemies] and *Colorads* [ugly Colorado beetle] for pro-Russian residents of Ukraine] A-Ok. Walking wounded and others ready to waltz. Have a request: SBU and other spooks take families. *Separs* need persuasion. Out."

"Already in the works. Will com when complete. Over and out."

With that, Yaroslav and his commandoes hunkered down for a long, boring, hungry, and tense, day in the park.

As soon as it was fully dark, Yaroslav sent Adil and Ramzan out into the streets to reconnoiter the situation as to how much interference they could expect. He wanted to avoid any kind of contact, particularly a noisy fight. They returned with the news that they scarcely saw any military or police presence; and, for that matter, any local citizen presence.

Ramzan said, "It's too cold and drizzly for any local to be out who doesn't have to be. Besides, there is no real reason to go out; there's nothing to do. None of the buildings still standing have lights. Adil and I think it is safe to go."

"Thanks, Ramzan."

He sent Rokosylana and Fedir out to fetch the vehicles. He and Fedir had fashioned a makeshift crutch from the surrounding piles of junk to help her ambulation, and she insisted that she was ready and capable.

While they were gone, he ordered the remaining commandoes to suit up for the potential dangers of travel to the north rendezvous point.

"Full battle rattle," he ordered.

That is close to 50 pounds of gear, including a flak vest, Kevlar helmet, gas mask, ammunition, weapons, and other basic military equipment. Yaroslav hoped for the best, but he was preparing himself and everyone else for the worst.

He and Adil suited up the POWs after he gave them the expected threatening instructions about maintaining silence. They were fully cowed after receiving a day's worth of glaring and homicidal glances from their captors. They moved along as fast as their aching joints would permit to don Kevlar and Twaron flak jacket vests and helmets. They submitted to being joined together by ropes around their necks and waists like so many slaves had endured over the millennia. Because they cooperated, Yaroslav took pains to ensure that the bindings were not too tight—a kindness that did not escape notice by the captives.

Rokosylana and Fedir returned with the troop transporters and a report. It had taken nearly an hour-and-a-half because they had to make three trips. They had parked the vehicles north of the hidey-hole, all ready to go. There were the two Canadian armored Roshel Senator wheeled military cars which in Ukraine were modified to be useful as a light duty APCs and IMVs. They had the Toyota Hilux and a Mitsubishi L200–two pickup trucks–for their gear—and a jeep. Apparently, no one had noticed them or done them any damage.

The two drivers then suited up like all the rest of the commandoes and POWs and reported back to Yaroslav.

"All accounted for and ready for travel. We are both in our *Ігрові костюми* [*igrovi costumes*]"play clothes", Sir.

"All right," said Yaroslav. "Mount up."

Rokosylana saluted theatrically and walked to Yaroslav and gave him a loving kiss on the lips in front of them all.

In a loud soto voce whisper which everyone could hear, Yaroslav kissed her back and said, "*Нахабний гусак*" [*nakhabny gusak*] "Brazen hussy," giving them all an uplifting little laugh before going out into the Wild West Frontier they knew they had to face.

She thanked him with a full toothed, full-face smile.

The roads and highways were in good repair and smooth the entire way to Severne Village near Avdiivka, in the Donetsk Oblast. It would have been a fairly brief trip had it not been for the inky blackness of the night, the necessity for all important caution, and the need for frequent detours to avoid enemy patrols. It took them nearly ten times longer to get back to their rendezvous point as it had to get to Popasnaya Village. It took another hour of driving, wearisome map ready by flashlight, and a stop to get something to eat from local partisans whom the Werewolf had recommended.

They arrived at the Severne Village—the agreed upon extraction Site X1, on January 19, 2025, 23:15, more than 24 hours after they left the occupied village of Popasna-ya. They were greeted by a ragtag looking gaggle of mountain men in tattered clothes holding automatic weapons pointed at their heads.

One of the partisans spoke to Yaroslav in a gravely voice, "Password."

"Common Man". I need to talk to "Werewolf".

"I answer for him," the partisan said.

Yaroslav said, "Enjoying the weather? A 'Common Man' would be as cold as a wolf out here."

The partisan replied, "Indeed, and he would be right. Only a were-wolf would be comfortable in this environment."

The ice was broken, and the social gathering took on consider-able more warmth. In a few minutes, Col. Taras "Werewolf" Seversky stepped up behind Yaroslav who was sharing a fresh and savory Ukrainian pirozhki with Rokosylana.

"Good to see you again, my friend," Taras said quietly so as not to startle the man whose nerves he expected would already be seriously frayed.

"And you, Taras. I think you've already met my fiancé, Rokosylana," which thrilled the eager young woman to her marrow.

"I did. Hello, future Mrs. Melnykenko," which sent another shiver of pleasure through Rokosylana's core.

They passed pleasantries for half an hour until Taras insisted that everyone sleep for several hours before they worked on how to deal with the POWs.

CHAPTER 40

Severne Village Community Meeting House

January 20, 2025, 10:20

Yaroslav had Rokosylana join him and Col. Taras "Werewolf" Seversky in the interview room—actually, the large pantry of the village community meeting house—when he began talking with the POWS. He made four rules: 1. He had the final say and veto power for all that was said and done in the talks, because he had a plan. 2. Lt. Col. Dmitriy Utkinov Yevgeny, Col. Konstantin Pikalov, and Col. Andrei Troshev, were to be interviewed separately, to be confined separately, and to be separated from all other POWs, Ukrainian fighters, and the SBU team. 3. They were to be addressed by their military rank, treated with courtesy, and well fed—better than the SBUs or the Ukrainian soldiers, if necessary. 4. They were to have no information from the outside, and everything they were to learn from this day forward was only to be conveyed to them after vetting of the information by Yaroslav.

Colonel Trosev was interviewed first because—in the Wagner organization—he was the lowest ranking, and most vulnerable.

"Col. Trosev, are your quarters comfortable?" Col. Seversky asked to start the first volley of questions with the first man, in the first segment of the questioning.

Besides Col. Trosev and the three interrogators, there was only a court recorder sent by plane from Kyiv.

"As comfortable as could be expected. Frankly, I am surprised that they are not more severe."

"Is the food acceptable?"

"I had expected unsweetened cornmeal mush on a regulation tin plate. I was surprised to see fresh eggs, sausage, buttered Russian rye bread, and good quality tea, prepared the way I like them."

"Have the guards, nurses, and interviewers been courteous?"

"I would have to say so, yes, I suppose."

"Do you have any needs we can deal with while you are here?"

"I could make silly demands, but I do realize that I am POW and can only look to be treated by the Geneva Conventions. However, I do take several medications and need to have them to maintain my health, and I wish to have freedom to send and receive letters to my superiors and to my family."

"Sir, you are to be treated as an HVI—a High Value Individual—so, there will be no difficulty in providing your medications. A pen and paper will be provided you shortly, and you can write down your list. Master Sergeant Rokosylana Mykolaivna Udovychenko will see to it that you get your medications promptly. As to your request to communicate with your superiors, that is not going to happen, not in any form, and not ever, unless our superior officer, Col. Melnykenko, deems it appropriate. If you can agree to rather strict censorship, you may write to your wife, father, and/or your mother right away. I think you will agree that this is very generous given the circumstances."

"I suppose it is more than I could have expected. You have mentioned cooperation several times. Could you define that for me, please?"

"I will, but not until after we have talked with all of you separately. At that time—depending on what develops—we may speak to all three at one time. Then, we will define what will be required from you to meet our definition of the term."

Col. Trope just nodded his head at that.

"Thank you, Colonel Trope. That will be all for today. We will secure your medications and then we can get back together for an agreement on what each of us can or will do."

The three interrogators abruptly stood up and walked from the room leaving Col. Trope to be taken back to his cell in hand cuffs and waist chain. He was a little shaken by what seemed to him to be a rather strange interview. He was curious about what it all meant and what more was in store for him.

Yaroslav found the new set of guards who had come on for the next shift.

"Would you please bring the next prisoner to the interrogation room. Please do not talk to him.

Col. Konstantin Pikalov was quick marched to the reorganized pantry room and told to sit down and not to speak. This time, Master Sergeant Udovychenko conducted the interview which went nearly the same as Col. Trope's had gone. There were very few hard questions, an expressed interest in his well fare, and no threats or promises. Like Col. Trope, he received vague suggestions about what the future would hold.

Yaroslav had different plans for Lt. Col. Dmitriy Utkinov Yevgeny. First of all, Col. Taras "Werewolf" Seversky asked all of the questions. His manner was brusque and military in style; his questions came at staccato speed, and none of them inquired after his personal life, not even his name. Again, however, there were no threats or promises... no suggestions of a pending plea deal.

"Col. Yevgeny, you are here because you have regularly committed war crimes and because of your high value to Vladimir Rasputinov and Col. Gen. Mikhail Mizin-tsev and their greedy activities."

He ignored Col. Yevgeny's attempt to speak.

"Have you worked for Wagner PMC in Africa, Colonel."

"My name is Dmitriy Utkinov Yevgeny; Lieutenant Colonel in the Russian Army; serial number 18-2014-1111001."

"You will answer only the questions I ask, Colonel. I do not want to hear your name, rank, and serial number again. I know all that, and I don't care."

"My name is Dmitriy Utkinov Yevgeny, Colonel in the Russian Army, serial number 18-2014-1111001."

"Where is your home base located?"

"My name is Dmitriy Utkinov…" he started, but was interrupted suddenly by Werewolf standing up and slapping him hard across his left cheek, momentarily stunning him.

"So, just as I expected, this is where the torture starts," he said defiantly, almost daring Werewolf to do more.

Werewolf said, "Sir, you misunderstand me and what is going on here. That slap was a message to you showing my deep lack of respect for you. You are not a soldier; you are nothing more or less than a greedy oligarch, who trembles whenever the man with the real power comes around. So, Dmitriy, when did you last have a sitdown with Vladimir?"

Yevgeny started to speak, but only got out one word—My… "

Werewolf rudely interrupted him by summoning the two guards.

"Return this POW back to his cell in chains. Turn off all the lights and let him have time to think about his predicament."

The guards lifted him from his chair, reapplied the cuffs and chains and gave him a rapid pace punk walk back to his cell with his feet barely touching the floor. They opened the cell door, pushed him roughly into the cell, and locked the door behind him. The cell became black as pitch during the last minute.

Yaroslav enjoyed the entire performance. However, he had to break off to take a call from SBU Gen. Olena Yuriivna.

It was brief to the point of being terse, and she spoke as fast as a 100 mph Tape [Standard Army green duct tape]: "Family gathering complete. We plan to move to a new home. Understand?"

"Lima Charlie [Loud and Clear]. Need photos and videos date stamped and including something like a newspaper showing today's headlines in Moscow."

"Ahead of you, "Common Man", check your receiver in an hour. Over."

"Thank you, Sir. Over and out."

CHAPTER 41

Severne Village Community Meeting House

January 21, 2025, 06:20

At 06:19, Col. Yevgeny was in deep below REM sleep oblivious to the world, even in the form of dreams. He did not feel fear, pain, anxiety, or see images of trouble in his world. At 06:20, one minute later, two buglers entered his cell and began playing Будильник [*Budil'nik*]–which is the Russian equivalent of the bugle call *Reveille*–as loudly as possible. Dimitriy's body stiffened with an acute spasm; and he rose to a painful sitting position, completely confused, with blurred vision, and hyperactive hearing. For the first time since his capture, he felt fear—deep, bone marrow chilling, fear.

"Throw your clothes on, Convict, chop, chop," the female guard shouted in a high soprano voice which further discombobulated Dimitriy.

He struggled to make sense of his environment and predicament, and that feeling stayed with him all day, just as Yaroslav had wanted it to do.

He was frog marched to the Community Meeting House all the way to the pantry makeshift interrogation room. His head was aching, and he felt nauseated.

"Good morning, Merry Sunshine," Werewolf said cheerily.

He held a plate full of aromatic traditional Russian breakfast favorites–*Syrniki* [Cheese Pancakes] made with *Tvorog*–a soft cheese made from fermented cow's milk with jam, honey, syrup, and butter, *Ponchiki* [donut holes], *Buterbrody* [open-faced Russian sandwich with strips of smoked salmon], and *Vatrushka* [an Eastern European pastry—*pirog*—in the form of a ring of dough with traditional white cheese (*Tvorog*) in the middle, with generous addition of raisins and bits of fruit]. The plate in front of Dimitriy's nose was the last straw. Dimitriy was sure he was going to vomit and humiliate himself. He fought to gain equilibrium and the ability to think clearly.

Dimitriy retched violently, but—to his credit–he did not actually vomit.

"Let us begin the day's questions, comrade," Werewolf said in a syrupy sweet voice.

"I need a little rest before I can," Dimitriy pleaded.

Werewolf ignored him.

"Where were you born? Where did you graduate high school? When did you join the Communist Party? What is the name of your wife? Where do your children go to school?"

The questions were asked in a strident and forte tone which enhanced the difficulty of understanding and making a sensible reply.

He clammed up.

Werewolf waited with irritating placidity.

Finally, Dimitriy calmed himself, realizing that he was falling into his questioner's trap by being upset and silent.

"Would you care to start again?" he asked archly.

"I ask the questions, you answer," Werewolf said in a polite tone that belied his actual message. "First question, tell me about your childhood, family life, and schooling."

Dimitriy complied but left out significant portions of his life in his answers. Werewolf knew that, and ignored his response as if it were sufficient.

"Now tell me about your introduction to the Communist Party, Comrade."

At first, Dimitriy denied being a member, then finally admitted it in a caustic belligerent voice.

Again, Werewolf ignored him. Dimitryi was becoming more and more confused and finding it difficult to form his sentences well.

Suddenly, without preamble, Werewolf got up and left the room, leaving Dimitriy to stew in his own juices, and still hand cuffed to the screw bolts on the table.

Werewolf, Yaroslav, and Rokosylana watched Dimitriy fidget in his chair.

Rokosylana asked, "Is it time for me to go in and be the 'good cop'?"

"Not yet, Rokosylana. One step at a time. I am going to talk to him, but in somewhat of a 'good cop' manner. I think he may be softened enough for us to go ahead."

He entered the room carrying a steaming samovar of excellent Chinese Black Tea. An aide carried a bowl of sugar and a spoon. Russians have their own tea-drinking customs—especially including the samovar—which over the years, became an iconic symbol of hospitality. Yaroslav and Dimitriy both recognized the importance of the ritual surrounding tea and the feeling of well-being that it induces. The strong black Kuzmichev tea—with its heady aroma which a tea connoisseur like Dimitri could immediately recognize as one of the best caravan brands—had the desired effect. Yaroslav removed Dimitriy's handcuffs and offered him the spoon and an attractive aged clay Xu Bian Vixing cup and a spoon. Dimitriy spooned a teaspoonful of sugar into his mouth and let it dissolve before drinking the tea.

"Thank you," he said. "Perhaps we can begin again. I don't suppose I have a choice, but I would much rather have you interrogate me than that ruffian."

"Your wish is my command," Yaroslav said with a broad smile, and they both had a brief laugh.

The 'good-cop, bad-cop' routine worked. Dimitriy answered Yaroslav's soft questions in detail and took pains to be complete. He watched Yaroslav's face and recognized the expressions of approval and familiarity with pleasure which moved him to more candor.

Yaroslav's last question of the morning was, "My friend, do you believe the Russian government has treated you with respect and approval?"

Caught off guard, Dimitriy answered, "No," then stuttered a little as he attempted to correct himself, but it was too late.

Yaroslav's next calculated move was to show Dimitriy digital photos of his wife and family standing with a Ukrainian colonel and two enlisted men in uniform. The time stamp—dated the day before—was a shock.

Yaroslav said, "That's it for now. I'll be back after lunch. You must be hungry. Have a nap, eat your lunch in peace, and we will talk business after that."

As abruptly, as Werewolf had done, Yaroslav stood up and left the room without another word. Dimitry was more disconcerted than he had been at 07:00 that morning.

CHAPTER 42

Severne Village Community Meeting House

January 21, 2025, 14:00

The afternoon session of questioning began where they left off in the morning—with the photographs on Yaroslav's phone. They were of very high quality, and the details were clear and in full color. Their authenticity was undeniable. Dimitriy's wife's face was somber, but the three children were smiling and appeared to be genuinely happy, not frightened.

Dimitriy asked the first question, "Where do you have them?"

His voice trembled slightly.

"In a safe place. Right now, we have no reason to believe that Rasputinov or his thugs know where they are or that they are in our care."

"So, you haven't harmed them yet?"

"Certainly not. In fact, our team was convincing for your wife, Ingrid, enough to have her believe that you were safer than ever before by being in our custody, and that she and the children will remain anonymous in an unknown location until you can make decisions that affect their lives. We will never harm them or betray them."

"Does this mean that you do not intend to kill me?"

"Your death would not benefit our cause. And, we will not harm your family; we do not do that sort of thing. That is a Wagner and Rasputinov thing."

"And if I don't cooperate, should I expect torture?"

"No, that I promise. Torture is crude and stupid. We want your cooperation, and we will reward you discretely for it."

Dimitriy was dubious. He had tortured people and ordered them to be tortured. He was sure that Yaroslav knew that. He vacillated about whether to ask his next question.

After a deep breath, he asked, "So, what exactly do you expect from me?"

"Long term cooperation and silence."

"Would I be allowed to return to my former position, or would I 'cooperate' from some Ukrainian jail?"

"Return. Of course, there will be elements of assurance of your cooperation."

"Go ahead, lay them out."

"I can't do that today other than in generalities. The specifics will unfold over time, but you will not be free of us until this heinous war is over, Dimitriy."

"You know perfectly well that my family is my most important obligation. I won't cooperate, no matter what you do, if I can't be sure that they are safe and that I can see them."

"Add to that, 'from time to time', and we have a deal."

"I am trying to believe you, Yaroslav. I'll do your bidding, but I will have to have my choice and your word verified 'from time to time'.

"Fair enough. How about you get to see your family this week and to talk to them in privacy?"

"Seriously."

"You will come to know that I am a very serious man. I, too, am inclined to trust you, but also to verify."

"How can you do that? I mean, what if I secretly take one of my men aside and tell him to convey the information that I am not acting of my own free will?"

"Firstly, and I hardly need to tell you this: Uncle Vladimir or Col. Gen. Mikhail Mizin-tsev, would deal with you. I can see the headlines now: 'Lt. Col. Dmitriy Utkinovov Yevgeny, Wagner commander, call sign "Wagner" suffers a fatal stroke while on duty', and maybe one day someone would find your body where it landed after being dropped from a plane. Or, maybe, the headline will include your family as having died in a plane crash that also took your life.

Secondly, my assurance from you comes in two forms. If I even suspect that you have doubled on me, you will never see nor hear from your family again. I know people and places that can easily bring that to pass. Finally, you are going to agree to the implantation of a very sophisticated tracking device. We will know where you are, what you are saying and to whom, and what is visually detected in your surroundings.

"And—by the way—we have deep penetration spies who will know almost immediately if you try to cross me in writing. You will never know who. Then, you will be outed to nice Uncle Vladimir and Mikhail, the Godfather. You will learn what betrayal really means. You with me, Dimitriy?"

"I am. And I am cornered. Brilliantly done, Yaroslav. You'll probably get a big medal for this."

"We don't get medals in our club. Our rewards are on a much more important level."

Yaroslav was not about to accept a simple "yes" answer. Part of his verification came when—over the following two days—he showed Dimitriy lengthy videos of his subordinates, Col. Konstantin Pikalov, and Col. Andrei Troshev, eagerly agreeing to turn Dimitriy in to Rasputinov and/or Col. Gen. Mikhail Mizin-tsev in return for receiving a king's ransom in blood money and a deed to land in a safe haven.

Dimitriy caved completely, even gladly. He hated the demonic despot in the Kremlin, and he loathed the for-profit monster of a soldier, Gen. Mizin-tsev. The surgery to implant a listening device in his inner ear was done the next day. The device was a RAAT [radio-wave, auditory, assaultive transmitting implants], in short, a covert remote listening device, like a tiny powerful mobile phone. The implants use electromagnetism in a communication device which can act as a transducer.

The input typically ranges from two to seven megahertz (MHz) at low intensity. The scientists who created and tested the devices described the input as sound resembling that which a commercial radio would provide.

The device was invisible to an observer, given that the cases studied have not revealed others' mentioning that they noticed them. Because implantation was via invasive surgery, their location was internal and not at all easily reachable. Transmission of the electromagnetism was two-way, i.e., the transducers act as both receivers and transmitters. The device is long-range and self-powered, much like a micro mobile phone. Since the devices cannot be seen in the ear canal–even with an otoscope–they were developed to draw power from the person's own life systems.

In fact–while the device gave a geolocation–it was not capable of sending out any kind of visual image. Yaroslav had lied about that, but Dimitriy was none the wiser.

Yaroslav kept his promise for Dimitriy to see his family in Severne Village the day after that. Rokosylana handled all arrangements and supervised the visit. Ingrid Yevgeny and her children Erik, Ivan, and Khristina, took to the beautiful and vivacious young Ukrainian woman with something beyond trust; it was more like she was part of the extended family.

CHAPTER 43

"Rublevka/Rublyovka" District, Moscow, Moscow Oblast

January 30, 2025, 02:00

One of the most closely guarded secrets of the Ukrainian government during Rasputinov's war, was code named, "Operation Take Control". It was the brain-child of General Olena Yuriivna and Yaroslav Melnykenko, fleshed out by the General Staff of the Ukrainian Armed Forces, with the direct participation of the current Chief of the General Staff Mikhial Shevchenko, and input and final approval by President Volodymyr Zelenskyy, DCIA Randal H. Coleman, and US President, John D. Bettern. The secret was not shared with the Ukrainian army, the US government otherwise, nor with Yaroslav's commandoes, which was the most difficult task of all for Yaroslav. He had gotten comfortably used to sharing everything with his now apparent soulmate, Rokosylana. He felt awkward around her as never before, but the mission was important beyond anything he and his fellow SBU commandoes had ever even contemplated.

The commandoes boarded different flights from different countries, at different times. They all carried valid Russian Federation passports and spoke the language with native fluency. They each had a different cover reason for going to Moscow, and a different secret mission when they got there. What they had in common was a destination while in Russia: "Rublevka or Rublyovka"–the unofficial name of the most prestigious residential area in the western suburbs of Moscow. Rublevka was home to multiple oligarchs, and the richest man in the world, Vladimir Rasputinov.

Yaroslav's flight left Helsinki Vantaa Airport on Aeroflot Flight 1812 for their final destination—Moscow. In better times, the flight time from Helsinki, Finland to Sheremetyevo International Airport, Moscow is 2 hours and 25 minutes. However, there are no direct flights from Helsinki to Moscow Sheremetov Airport. There is a non-stop flight which takes 14 hours and 20 minutes and covers a distance of 3,700 miles. They all had to be in good physical condition to endure that journey.

Yaroslav, and four other commandoes: Rokosylana Mykolaivna, Fedir Blyznyuk, Boryslav Vovk, and Vasyl Haranchak were on that flight; and the next day, six others made the same schedule: Col. Taras "Werewolf" Seversky in command, Ramzan Alaudinov, Apti Tsitsulayev, Rikonda Kadyrov, Adil Shagiakhmetov, and Midhat Shirinov. Similarly, flights left from Athens, Greece, Ascuncion, Paraguay, Bogotá, Colombia, and Beijing, PRC.

The entrance to Sheremetyevo APTS [Airport Passenger Transfer Service] is conveniently located within Terminal B of Sheremetyevo International Airport. Every commando had to pass through there to get to the ground level transportation. They took their time and a different circuitous route to get to the ground floor transportation to ensure that they were not being watched or followed. The commandoes had all undergone extensive escape and evade training and learned tradecraft to keep them free of enemy trackers.

The APTS is part of the Interterminal underground passage, which is a dual tunnel transportation system connecting different terminals at Sheremetyevo Airport. Terminal B has an interesting history, known for its distinctive "flying-saucer" design and locally nicknamed the "shot glass." It can accommodate 800 people per hour, and there were at least that many people there all the time the commandoes moved to their desired locations. They were not noticed amid the semi-orderly routine chaos of transit.

In all, eighteen commandoes–each with a different cover story ended up in five Moscow hotels in or near Sheremetyevo Airport, including: Gettsleep Sherremetyevo Airport International Transit area, Mezhdunarodnoye Shosse, Khimki; in Sheremetyevo; Novotel Moscow Business-class hotel; Holiday Inn Express; Park Inn by Radisson; and the Cosmos Selection Moscow Sheremetyevo Airport Hotel.

Yaroslav arranged for two different busses and three different taxi services to pick up the eighteen commandoes and to deliver them to three different rendezvous sites at three different times the day after arrival in Russia. Each pair of commandoes was dressed in outfits appropriate to his/her purpose in the mission. The commandoes had several things in common: they were young and fit; they all carried heavy traveling bags which they did not allow porters or drivers to handle; and they all had the same secondary launching site for the mission in chief.

All of them had to travel the same route to the area where the clandestine operation was to take place: along Rublyovo-Uspenskoye Highway, Podushkinskoe, 1st Uspenskoe and 2nd Uspenskoe highways (A-106). A-106 starts at the Rublevsky Highway at the intersection with the Moscow Ring Road, runs along the Moskva river, and ends near Zvenigorod. The traffic is always extremely heavy because the road is just two lanes. That element of crowding and hustle gave the commandoes an added element of anonymity among all the other travelers determined to reach their destinations in one piece and to take care of the only business they cared about—their own.

The Rublyovo-Uspenskoye is a highway with improved surface, but still a bit rough. It is one of the shortest federal highways with its length at 19 miles. Almost the entire length of the highway the speed limit was 31–37 mph. There was an element of risk just to make the first leg of the road trip despite it being only 18.6 miles long. Road safety in Russia is poor with road accident deaths per million population higher than all countries in the G8 and the other BRIC countries [an intergovernmental organization comprising Brazil, Russia , India, China, South Africa, Egypt, Ethiopia, Iran, and the United Arag Emirartes, Africa, Egypt, and Ethiopia. Originally identified to highlight investment opportunities] although the absolute number is actually less than China, India and USA. When assessing the level of risk while traveling on Russia roads; i.e. the number of accidents per unit of travel; it is 60 times that of Great Britain. Adding to the risk, it was the dead of Moscow winter.

Their common destination was Rublevka, known as the summer home of the dictator, Vladimir Rasputinov, and dozens of other oligarchs, including the commandoes' quarry, Col. Gen. Mikhail, owner of the Wagner Group PMC. Rublevka–simply put–is Russia's "Beverly Hills": home to rich, famous, and influential Russians who live in luxury, hidden behind tall fences and walls.

It is located outside Moscow six miles to the west via the Rublevo-Uspenskoe Highway–yet the area, and its residents–are nonetheless an integral part of Russia's capital. Anyone who has less than $10 million in the bank is an outsider in Rublevka, unless he/she is a servant or laborer. Along the way, lie extravagant villas tending to be located in growing density. It is a very busy place, where people demand privacy and to go about their own business without attention or interference. There are 260 suburban communities along the short highway: almost all with tall, solid, fences, gates, closed circuit video surveillance, and guarded entry checkpoints. One's prestige there in that ghetto for millionaires depends on how many bodyguards one has, which cars one drives, and how beautiful your wife or mistresses are.

Many Russian government officials and successful businesspeople reside in the gated communities of Rublevka. Real estate prices are among the highest in the world. *The New York Times* called it "home to the sprawling villas of Russia's ruling class". *Nouveau riche* upstarts have caused prices of properties on the Rublyovka/Rublevka to rocket sky high. Now the fight for the last remaining pieces of land has broken out. The last remaining huts of the poor are swept aside to make way for the palaces of the wealthy by means that could not be any more unfair or brutal. The Russian State, celebrating an imperial come back bolstered by petro-billions, has declared open season on the weak and poor. Like "Indians in their American reservations", they feel. And hardly anyone dares to protest. No wonder. Rublyovka/Rublevka is a strictly guarded maximum security area, where many things are hushed up and kept under wraps.

Officially, there is no such an administrative unit as Rublyovka/ Rublevka. The name of the area is a social construction—literally, Rublevka can be translated as the *place of Rubles*. It has been popularized in Russian mass culture as a synonym of being filthy rich. It is also a play of words–the ruble is the Russian currency.

The meeting location for the next day had been selected with utmost care to preserve anonymity amidst crowds, and the privacy to be able to communicate without eavesdroppers. Yaroslav and Gen. Yuriivna reserved a ghastly expensive private conference room in the sparkling Zhukovka business center. The rich come there in throngs to indulge themselves, to see, and to be seen, where even the most demanding clients are never disappointed. The Doucet H.O. confectioner's offers a huge choice of all kinds of cakes, bread, wines, and whiskeys. No one pays any overt attention to anyone else as if it were an old KGB law, which it very nearly is.

Yaroslav and Rokoslana Mykolaivna followed an overdressed model in an open fur coat who attracted considerably more attention than the two commandoes when they walked casually into the rented conference room. They were rather over dressed themselves. Yaroslav was wearing a custom tailored Brunello Cucinelli light blue suit, Charles Tyrwhitt dress white shirt, Hèrmes Lapindragon tie, and tan Ferragamo Angiolo lace up dress shoes. It was a far cry from his standard issue Ukrainian military OCPs [winter occupational camouflage pattern] uniform. Rokoslana was decked out in the latest Russian model's winter sports wear: form fitting Canada Goose black tundra pants, Marlow coat, and Prada shearling boots. They both wore matching black fur Ushanka Hats. Neither of them appeared to be the least bit overdressed in the luxurious world of the Zhukovka.

Inside the insulated conference room, it was all business as soon as the entire commando unit assembled.

Yaroslav greeted each commando by name and thanked them for their diligence in avoiding scrutiny of the omnipresent police and SVR RF [The Foreign Intelligence Service of the Russian Federation] agents.

"First, let me begin to share the mission goal, and the more basic logistics of our "Operation Take Control" mission," he said, "we are here to accomplish three things: First, to remain safe. Second, to take Col. Gen. Mikhail Mizin-tsev and his entire family into our custody in absolute secrecy from Russia, from his Wagner PCMs, and even from our Motherland, Ukraine. What happens after that is above most of our paygrades. I will withhold the exfiltration routes and escape plan information from you for obvious security reasons. Do not be taken alive, is all I can say to each of us. Each of us the L-pills. Death is always preferable to the mercies of the Russian intelligence service or military. And thirdly, I will lay out the details of the plan to accomplish the audacious kidnapping. Perhaps a few of you are harboring some doubts, right now. Hold your questions until I finish, please."

It took two full hours to lay out the plans, including maps and operational details that the SBU spies had put together over the last several months in their planning sessions.

"We take the Mizin-tsev family as soon as the oligarch leaves for work, tomorrow morning. We have it from usually reliable sources that he will leave his castle while it is still dark. There is a big, hush hush meeting with Rasputinov at the presidential office in the Kremlin in the morning. The attendees have been told not to expect refreshments of any kind because the work for the "special military operation" is too pressing and important."

He took the bulk of his time to outline the intricate details of how they would get into Gen. Mizin-tsev's house past all of the security measures, where they would take and hold them as hostages, how they were going to get at the general in the open without attracting attention, and how they were going to convince the avaricious criminal to cooperate with Ukraine without arousing suspicion in the Kremlin. He described a preplanned escape route through the forested area bordering on the east bank of the Moscow River and a river trip out of the danger zone, with all the team members and the hostages. Gen. Mizin-tsev was going to stay behind in Moscow to do the SBU's dirty work and to prosper by so doing. He just did not know that yet.

CHAPTER 44

Col. Gen. Mikhail Mizin-tsev's "Rublevka/Rublyovka" District mansion, and the Barvikha Luxury Village, Moscow, Moscow Oblast

January 31, 2025, 04:00-16:30

Winter entered Moscow for the fourth time that season with a blizzard and record overnight snowfall. The A-106 Rublyovo-Uspenskoye Highway was barely passable of the best of such winter days, but today it was considerably worse. The road is sometimes closed due to travels by Vladimir Rasputinov and other important Russian officials, and this was one of those days. Much of the attention of the Rublevka rich was centered on the snow removal process taking place on that thoroughfare in order to accommodate what they presumed was a selfish whim of their "president-for-life". For them to travel for any reason—including to work—was considered a total waste of effort. Might as well relax and watch the fascinating process.

More than 150,000 people and 14,000 pieces of equipment were needed to clear Moscow of the consequences of snowfalls in January, according to the Moscow Municipal Services Complex. Sidewalks, roads, and the roofs of buildings, all have to be cleared of snow almost daily.

The traditional disposal method had been to take it to a snow dump outside the city, a large holding area where it is deposited and stored and where it melts when the weather becomes warmer. Such places are deliberately located away from the city in order not to create problems for residents. The disadvantage of that method is that the snow has to be transported by truck across the entire city, significantly contributing to road traffic. The holding areas are large installations that first filter any trash out of the transported snow and then treat it with warm water and filter it into the drainage system. The whole process is fairly quick; in 3-4 minutes, the installations can melt up to 10 tons of transported snow.

However, in recent years, the mass of snow, the manhours required, the specialized equipment involved, and the huge costs, have dictated a change. For this reason, snow melting equipment is increasingly being used in the interests of snow collection in the country's largest cities such as Moscow, St. Petersburg, and Kazan, more efficient. Currently, these are large installations that first filter any trash out of the transported snow and then treat it with warm water and filter it into the drainage system. The mass of removed snow undergoes a full cleaning cycle at purification facilities and is drained into the Gulf of Finland as clean water, under the watchful eyes of the fascinated nine million citizens of Moscow, and the additional millions of illegal immigrants, as well as the concerned Finns.

The snow melting stations save time and money on snow clearance but are costly: 1-5 million rubles [approx. $ USD 11,000-55,000 each]. The price depends on their operating speed and the maximum load capacity. In Moscow, 49 such installations have been set up within the city limits.

SBU General Olena Yuriivna had factored in the winter conditions and found that they would actually enhance the probability of "Take Control" mission's success. She ordered her in place agents in Moscow to secure the best winter apparel and the most reliable vehicles to keep going in Moscow's intense winters: Lada Niva [Lada 4x4] cars, UAZ [Ulyanovsk Automobile Plant] SUVs, and KamAZ, 1976 cab over trucks—all with large tread, studded tires. The sellers threw in tire chains as an added bonus. The in place agents delivered the most useful heavy winter clothing in the right sizes, the best materials, and the best types, on time and to the right place before the big "Take Control" day.

Yaroslav and Rokosylana—still wearing their expensive and trendy clothing—made several reconnaissance drive and walk byes of General Mikhail Mizin-tsev's residence. Rokosylana described it as "part of the millionaires' ghetto".

Yaroslav pointed out, "I am told that this monstrous house is worth something like 7,402,800,000.00 rubles [80 million USD]. What I see is that it is clear where ultra-wealthy Russians' priorities lie: privacy and security. We have our work cut out for us."

"That comes to 80 million rubles to one US dollar. No wonder Rasputinov is running scared," Rokosylana said.

"Back to my concern, we are going to have to strike fast and very carefully. The crème de la crème of Russian society lives here and guards their territory well. That includes Vladimir Rasputinov whose mansion is located only a little more than six miles from the church in Novo-Ogaryovo. There is a small army of security guards that could come after us."

"Do I really think they would? After all, they work for the oligarch of the moment. I don't think they care a whit about Russia, the Russian people, or certainly about a wicked criminal like Mikhail Mizin-tsev and his kind, and good riddance, I think."

"Maybe, and let's hope. All the lights are on; so, we can assume that everyone is home, and we had better not linger. Let's go over to the Luxury Valley in Barvikha and see how the other half lives."

Rokosylana snorted, "Other half!? More like one hundredth of a percent you should say."

"You're right, but my reason for looking at the place is to see how we can take down Mizin-tsev in the midst of all this wealth, power, and security. I am going to need a few good thoughts to come out of your pretty little head."

Rokosylana snorted again and gave Yaroslav a small jab in the ribs. They both laughed.

There was almost no one out in the storm except for the poor souls shoveling snow, a futile enterprise. The roadways were also nearly empty of vehicles; so, the two spies could maneuver at will in their Lada Niva 4X4 to get to the Luxury Valley in Barvikha Market center. Although there were only a few hardy shoppers out and about, the market's multiple heating kiosks were everywhere, and people were hugging the warm walls. Loud music blared from several large amplifiers, playing loud pop music such as Big Difference, by Nicki Minaj; *Paradise* by Justin Timberlake; *Friends (Slowed Down)* by V; *Texas Hold 'Em*, by Beyoncé; *Houdini*, by Dua Lipa; *Inna*, by Cheeky; and *Tattoo*, by Loreen.

They checked the printed menus in the windows of several swanky restaurants.

Rokosylana muttered, "It looks like they just about serve anything including the Red List [of Endangered Species] instead of a menu containing real food."

"Not my idea of good solid health food," Yaroslav agreed.

They found what Yaroslav had been looking for, an overdecorated pre-Soviet building where he said that Mizin-tsev had listed as being on his appointment list, along with a presumably sumptuous meal at Tsarskaya Okhota —publicized as the most family oriented of the restaurants–because he so enjoyed the luxury *khachapuri* [Georgian cheese-filled bread] and to relax on the terrace.

"I can share everything with you now, Rokosylana," he said. "this is how it should all play out, and the huge snowstorm will help a lot."

CHAPTER 45

Col. Gen. Mikhail Mizin-tsev's "Rublevka/Rublyovka" District mansion, and the Barvikha Luxury Village, Moscow, Moscow Oblast

February 1, 2025, 06:00-16:30

There was a great deal of pent up energy stored in the SBU commando unit. It had been building for weeks, and the fact that the plans and their individual tasks had been kept secret from them until this morning had contributed many kilojoules of energy [Physics: Unit of Heat Energy – $E=\frac{1}{2}mv^2$ where m=mass, and v=velocity] to their stress level. Finally, Yaroslav revealed the full plan—except for the escape route—to his commandoes.

"We enter Mizin-tsev's house through a cellar door that cannot be locked. Never mind how I came to know that, but it will be immediately after he leaves the house at 07:00. We must be in place well before that; so, Rokosylana, Fedir, and I, will take that part of the mission. We will sequester the remaining family in the house, and our silver-tongued Rokosylana will convince the mother and the children that it is in their best interest to comply. We leave the safe house fifteen minutes from now.

"Boryslav, Vasyl, Ramzan, and Apti, go to Barvikha Luxury Village, and convince Mizin-tsev to return home with them. I will send you photos of his family with the wife showing a copy of the front pages of *Pravda* and *Izvestia* newspapers with today's date in clear view, and a second photo of the family with the youngest child holding a Cyrillic alphabet sign that says, "*пожалуйста, pozhaluysta, папочка/ papochka*" [please, Daddy]. He is well known to be a softy about his wife and children.

"Here you can find the most expensive market in the world, and the most expensive sports club, as well as the most exclusive boutiques and the highest fences, with an army of thousands of security guards. If you have to kill someone, do it silently and anonymously. Tsarskaya Okhota restaurant is a favorite haunt of government officials and the site of the scheduled conference. Carry this photo of Mizin-tsev with you; so, there is no mistake. It will look like you are leading away a well dressed waiter.

"I don't have to say it; but be careful; be invisible; and be quick. I will say that your safety is more important than the mission, and the mission is the most important one we have ever been assigned. After you have him in hand, return to his mansion, and we will make our escape. I will explain the route then; Rokosylana and I are in too much of a hurry to do it now. *Англійська божа швидкість/anhliys'ka bozha shvydkist'* [God speed]."

Yaroslav, Fedir, and Rokosylana, dressed in plain white. Rokosylana had custom fit moon boots, headband, knitted beanie hat, furry mittens over fine white leather gloves, leg warmers, and all covered by a calf length faux fur coat. Yaroslav and Fedir had whole body heavy ski suits, additional fur seal skin bib overalls dyed white, and bunny boots. They all had full face white balaclavas giving full neck and head coverage on the outside, and heavy woolen thermals on the inside. If that ended up being inadequate, they carried several rechargeable OCOOPA portable pocket and hand warmers.

They were driven to Mizin-tsev's property and got out of the Lada Niva 4X4 by a copse of trees that shielded them from view by anyone in or around the mansion. They moved stealthily through the white birch trees and found a good spot to burrow down and observe Col. Gen. Mizin-tsev's front door. They had timed things well, and they did not have to wait long.

Three bodyguards stepped through the heavy oak front door of the mansion preceding the general. They looked around carefully, which took a full five minutes. The snow white camouflage was perfect. There was no way the three SBU agents could be seen in the white-on-white background. And the guards did not try very hard. It was the same routine they had followed nearly every morning for more than ten years. It had become mind numbing routine because nothing ever happened.

The Norman style mansion was located in one of the most picturesque and ecologically clean areas of the Moscow region. Thanks to the dense relic pine forests, healing invigorating air, and the prevailing western wind which rose every morning, the property was exhilarating with clean air and beauty throughout its surroundings. The house had five bedrooms, a two-height living room, a kitchen-dining room that any gourmand would lust for, a winter garden, an office, a wine room, a home cinema, a gym, a SPA area with a pool and saunas. The house was equipped with an elevator and a spiral staircase for the agile and active. Separately on the site was a three car garage, an apartment for staff, and a guard house.

The guard crew escorted the general to his luxurious civilian version black 2021 Aurus Senat limousine which cost the Russian taxpayers more than 20 million rubles [$USD 300,000]. The driver gave the general a rote salute, and they drove out of the property and out of the Rublevka residential area almost alone on the Rublyovo-Uspenskoye Highway on their way to Barvikha Luxury Village and the pleasant Tsarskaya Okhota Restaurant–a favorite haunt of government officials.

They moved swiftly through Luxury Valley in Barvikha past boutiques for Dolce& Gabbana, Lamborghini, Ferrari, Maserati, Gucci, Prada, Armani and Harley Davidson. There were no pedestrians to see the general and his bodyguards enter the restaurant. He was fashionably five minutes late but arrived before President Rasputinov—a good political move. The driver parked the car behind the Tsarskaya Okhota in the VIP parking area where a fleet of vehicles worth more than the yearly income of most medium sized US cities and their ever ready drivers could sit in the plush drivers' seats and try to keep their hands warm.

The inside of the lavish eating establishment resembled a traditional Russian hut; the dishes are cooked in a real oven; and the wooden walls are decorated with ancient coins, ornate fabric curtains and portraits of Russian tsars. Except for the severe risks they were taking, Boryslav, Vasyl, Ramzan, and Apti, enjoyed the extraordinary ambience and hoped against all hope that they looked the part. They had a short, hushed, discussion about how to protect themselves if they were found out not to have been invited, or not even to be Russians. They quickly decided to bluff it out and decide at the moment what else would be needed. Their adrenaline was flowing at maximum—enough to shrink their suprarenal glands noticably.

There were signs showing Rasputinov in various heroic poses, banners heralding his quotations, and whole walls emblazoned with vivid signs saying: "Z", "For Russia, for Rasputinov!", double headed eagles with Rasputinov's name in large letters above it, and Saint George slaying the dragon—everything to please the dictator.

When they were briefly alone, Apti mimed putting his finger down his throat.

The tables were set with the finest china, silver utensils, Neman vintage hand made crystal wine goblets, and embroidered napkins. Food was presented in strategic places around the tables in order to give the diners a visual—as well as a gastronomic—experience. All one had to do was to give a waiter a nod and look at a dish, and a generous sample would appear on your plate. The platters held: blinis with a caviar selection, including, salmon, pike, and halibut; beef stroganoff, whole trout, ning-crab and scallops, mixed meat platters holding, beef tongue, sausage, pork, and meatballs; vinaigrette salad with beets and potatoes; icy cold borscht and stuffed cabbage rolls; and beetroot juice and cold water to drink. The food was generally quite simple—the way Rasputinov liked things—plentiful in variety, and generous in amounts.

The back of the menu held a quote on food by the dictator: "I like rice, not oatmeal, vegetables like tomato, cucumber, lettuce. In the morning, I like to eat porridge, fresh cheese and honey. If I can choose between meat and fish, I will choose fish, but I also like lamb." It was not a dictum, just a suggestion made to a suggestible audience.

The oligarchical and politically powerful guests began to line up behind chairs they had selected at the gourmet tables. The Maître d looked as if he was about to announce *"Ужин подан" Uzhin podan* [Dinner is served]; so, Boryslav, Vasyl, Ramzan, and Apti, moved quickly and adroitly up to Col. Gen. Mizin-tsevi. Apti caught his attention with subtle contact of his body against the general's, an accidental-on-purpose signal.

Vasyl tapped the general on his other shoulder and held out his iPhone to show the Wagner PCM owner some digital photos of people and furniture that were very familiar to him. None of them spoke a word. Mizin-tsev paled progressively as it dawned on him what he was seeing. The photos had been taken in his own parlor; that was his furniture, his oriental carpet, his prized painting on the wall behind his family members. He looked at the four photographs a second and third time. The last perusal revealed the *Pravda* newspaper showing today's date. He felt as if he had been poleaxed.

He became aware of the handsome, well dressed, very fit, young man leaning against his shoulder and whispering, "Follow us, General, stay calm and quiet. If you do, everything will be all right."

He said it over and over until it sunk in, and he could think again.

He stood up and excused himself to the blur of people sitting next to him. They were busy getting their fair share of the wonderful food and paid him no heed. In two minutes, he was gone from the room. He was completely docile, entered the Lada Niva obediently, and did not speak until they were out of the Barvikha Luxury Village and driving east on Rublyovo-Uspenskoye Highway toward his house. He became nauseated, and he shivered and trembled as the realization of the truth began to sink into his very bone marrow. They had him, and there was not a thing he could do about it.

"We are almost there," Vasyl said gently, "keep calm, and you and your family have nothing to fear from us."

He wanted to scream, to lash out, to jump out of the moving Lada. But, he did none of those things; his rational mind had returned, and he could think. He began to think about how he could turn all of this to his own benefit. It was the way he always calmed himself when the going was bad. Living in the Soviet Union and in the Russian Federation had given him all too many examples to guide him now that he was in control by people far less vicious and uncaring than his previous controllers.

Yaroslav, Fedir, and Rokosylana waited silently in the snow until the Aurus Senat limousine drove out of the property onto the Rublyovo-Uspenskoye Highway and out of sight. Yaroslav raised his hand to have his fellow commandoes hold their position. He was rewarded by them seeing the final morning's sentry patrol gather near the front steps and converse for a few moments. None of them appeared to be excited or even interested. There was no indication that the SBU agents had been detected.

The sentries walked together, laughing, talking, and smoking, to the small guard house adjacent to the mansion on the west. For purposes of security, the building had large windows; so, they could look out to a nearly panoramic view of the front door and west side of the mansion. The three Ukrainians watched as the guards stripped down to their skivvies, opened long necked bottles of beer, and sat facing a television set with their backs to a glowing ornate Franklin stove. It was the picture of tranquility and sense that all was well in their world.

Yaroslav slowly pulled himself up out of the snow bank and signaled to Fedir and Rokosylana to follow him. They kept to the shady area underneath the eaves and made their way to the back of the house. Fedir took the lead to the large unpainted bulkhead cellar door that lay at a 45° angle to the house. He paused long enough to be sure that he was not being watched, and there was no sentry patrol making its way toward him. He beckoned the other two commandoes; and together, the three of them lifted up the cellar door silently until they could turn it all the way over to admit them to the stone steps leading into the basement.

They took their rechargeable 1,200 lumen EDS [every day carry] flashlights out of their pockets and turned the bright LED lights on. Inside the basement was coal black without the flashlights, and it was nearly as cold as being outside in the snow. They went in separate directions to locate the stairway to the main floor above. Fedir found the stairs and focused his light onto it until Yaroslav and Rodosylana saw what he was doing and moved to him. Yaroslav led the way up the staircase to the door that opened into the main floor.

It was locked, but there was an old skeleton key hanging from a nail over the lentil above the door itself. Apparently, no one had ever considered the possibility that the cellar would provide entrance to the mansion and a means of getting the drop on the security guards and family.

The key opened the lock with only a little fiddling with it to overcome its decades—maybe centuries—of nonuse. The old hinges had been recently oiled; so, they opened inward toward the basement steps silently. Yaroslav opened the door just enough to take a quick-eek-a-peak. It was enough to learn that no one was in that hallway. He opened the door all the way, and all three commandoes crept into the house walking on plush carpets.

"Hear that?" Rokosylana asked in a whisper and held up her hand.

Fedir and Yaroslav nodded their agreement. It was no longer necessary to use the flashlights; so, the three commandoes turned them off and pocketed them.

"Children's voices… just around the corner and coming from the parlor, I presume."

"Agree," both men responded in a quiet stage whisper.

"Let's go," said Yaroslav, "you bring up the rear to be sure to take care of any surprises, Fedir."

Fedir moved to the back of their three person line.

"Let me take the front, Rokosylana; I couldn't bear it if you get killed."

She nodded her agreement and admired his kind protectiveness and chivalry toward her. Yaroslav was looking more and more like a "good catch".

They smiled at each other, then the three of them walked as silently as possible to the open door into the parlor. There were eight people in the room: closest to the door, and with her back to it, was Hilda, the governess. To her left was a strikingly beautiful blond woman—who looked like she had just taken her first step out of *Harpers Bazaar*, the current equivalent to *Vogue* Magazine, the former 2nd in popularity with 20.69

million visits a year. *Vogue,* itself, went out of business the previous year. She looked like she was either a 20-year-old, or a carefully plastic surgically reshaped 49-year-old—obviously the mother, Vera Yusupovna Mizin-tsev. She and Hilda were directing the children who were playing some sort of game.

The children were all facing toward the door and could have looked into the faces of their kidnappers any time, had they not been so engrossed in their game of Cossacks and Robbers. At the moment, they were taking a rest from their frenetic game. The children had divided themselves into two teams. One was the Cossacks, and the other was the robbers. The Cossacks had a "camp," and one Cossack stayed behind to keep watch. Robbers ran away and hid somewhere, to be sought after by the Cossacks—a group version of the old hide-and-seek game in the US and UK.

The commandoes earnestly worked to gain the trust and affection of the children, boys and girls. They talked about current popular culture, music, movie stars, television programs, and sports teams, sometimes with arguments about which was best, but always with rapport and humor. Vera and Hilda kept up a positive approach, knowing that they had lost all power, and all they could do was to appease and keep the calm in the family and with the kidnappers; so, the Mizin-tsevs could all survive. The two women could only hope that Mikhail Viktorovich was still alive.

The children were becoming tired of the hectic physical games and bored without television or their phones. Vera and Hilda were becoming steadily more anxious. Yaroslav texted Vasyl: "Progress?" He got back a reply: "On the road. 5-10 minutes to destination."

He passed the information on to Vera who was visibly relieved and took up her embroidery again. Hilda looked at the Ukrainians with unmasked hatred; but, she too, elected passive activity and kept her opinions to herself. Fedir nodded his understanding and agreement with the positive presentiments deriving from the information.

Rokosylana asked a question when she heard about the imminent arrival of Gen. Mizin-tsev back home.

"Yaroslav, I have a worry. What do we do with the bodyguards? So far as we know, they do not realize that the family they are sworn to protect has been kidnapped. Should we kill them? Drug them? Make them disappear? Try to win them over to our side?"

"That's a lot of questions, Love. And believe me, I have been going over them all in my mind since we got up this morning. Killing them would inform our enemies that we had either killed or taken the family and the governess, something we definitely do not want to be believed. Drugging them only prolongs the knowledge getting out until we can make our escape, which would be a good thing, but wrecks the very purpose of the mission. Making them disappear is something like killing them in that it only stalls off the knowledge that we were involved. We cannot take the risk of trying to win them over. We have to fool them."

"How on earth can we do that? We have to prance out the front door with the general and his family. What are they supposed to think?"

"Remember, we have the general in our custody; and he has every incentive to cooperate. If we are found out, the first thing we will do is to kill him, his bodyguards and house guards and his six children: Valery, Vyodor, Sergey, and Mykola, and the girls: Ludmila, and Olga, who are the third most important thing to him. He loves his money; he won't be alive to enjoy it.

He at least pretends to love and to be a patriot of his native country; he will go down as a traitor in that scenario. He will cooperate until we make a mistake and give him a chance to escape and to warn his keepers. So, Love, we have to fool the guards. I'm going to make him an offer he can't refuse, as the Godfather character in the American movie, *The Godfather*, said. The offer on the one hand is additional riches to be enjoyed with his happy family in some very pleasant American controlled location, and his disappearance a lasting mystery. One the other hand, he gets to be dead, along with his dearly beloved family."

"Put that way, he cannot refuse. But there is another American expression I can't get out of the law, and that is "Murphey's Law," Fedir said.

"There is no perfect or perfectly safe plan. We have to go with the most likely; and fooling them and having the family simply get in their limo and drive off into the sunset, is that; at least, as I can see."

"I guess I have to agree, but I am ready to fight, and even to kill children if I have to," Rokosylana added, somberly.

254

"I don't think it will come to that, but we will both have to convince the parents, Hilda, and the bodyguards, that this is just another day for the family, full of interesting activity."

"And with those things that alter and illuminate our times," as the Russian propaganda regarding General Mizin-tsev would have us believe about his work."

She nodded, and they shared a laugh.

In the few minutes left, Yaroslav and Rokosylana set about to compel the unsuspecting wife and governess that it was in their best interests to cooperate and to be convincing actresses.

Yaroslav let Rokosylana take the lead in presenting his argument for the plan with the two women. Vera's real allegiance was to her children; and she readily, if unhappily, agreed. Hilda snarled and spat at Rokosylana. Yaroslav stepped in and gave the final, chilling, argument: "Hilda, we don't need you. If you don't agree, or I am not sure that you can be convincing, I will kill you. We can just explain that away when the time comes. Clear?"

"*Убедительный/ubeditel'ny*" [clear], she said and tried to smile. It came out phony as a three-dollar bill.

Yaroslav said frostily, "Try harder. I won't hesitate for a second."

Fedir fingered his handgun to punctuate Yaroslav's sentence.

CHAPTER 46

Col. Gen. Mikhail Mizin-tsev's "Rublevka/Rublyovka" District mansion, Moscow, Moscow Oblast,

February 1, 2025, 06:00-16:35

The children were excited and happy when they learned that their father was coming home early from the office. That all boded well for an extended day of fun and frolic with their parents. Even Hilda could be expected to enjoy the day. As it was, she seemed subdued, but, like them, glad the lord and master was coming back to the mansion.

The Ukrainian SBU agent/kidnappers were well hidden, but with good views of the parlor; so, they could react quickly as necessary. The scene was set.

Col. Gen. Mizin-tsev exited the limousine and walked quickly to the house. At the front door, he was met by the house guards who saluted, a normal routine all around. The regular house guards left and went back to the guard house and its friendly Franklin stove.

Mizin-tsev's four "new guards" [Boryslav, Vasyl, Ramzan, and Apti] walked up to the parlor where he hugged his exuberant children, his earnest wife, and nodded to Hilda. He excused the house guards. When they were outside and presumably warming themselves in the guard house, the three SBU agents who had been hiding with itchy trigger fingers, showed themselves, making the SBU force six men and one woman.

Yaroslav took the entire Mizin-tsev household aside for a chat—one of the most important of their lives. He spoke calmly, even reassuringly, outlining the roles they were to play, the escape route, and their new lives awaiting them. The children were understandably confused, even frightened; but Rokosylana calmed them with smiles and her mellifluous motherly voice.

The older children: Valery, Vyodor, and Ludmila each volunteered to shepherd a younger sibling and to keep them still and well behaved. Yaroslav and Rokosylana continued to make them feel safe with smiles and little jokes; their mother was reassuring; and Fedir looked at them glumly to provide the necessary, but subtle, information as to what could happen if they went against their captors.

The plans were set, including the household, including the "new" guards, to leave for the airport the following morning, despite the weather stations' dire warnings about the enveloping storm. The Ukraine plotters were all but ecstatic about the weather, of course, since it reduced visibility to less than 10%, and interest in fools willing to risk travel in such conditions to near 0%.

Vera Mizin-tsev informed the regular guard corps that the family would be leaving in the morning for the airport, and they could take the week off, except for a skeleton force of one or two to walk the perimeter and to make a daily walk around in the house to ensure that everything was in order there. They expected to be gone for a month or more. The general informed his office and President Rasputinov that he was going to Rostov-on-don to deal with some military issues facing his senior officers of the Wagner PMC and would keep the president informed as he dealt with each problem. He wished President Rasputinov a pleasant and successful series of conferences in Delhi, as he met with the Indian leaders—the Hon'ble President of India Droupadi Murmu and Prime Minister Shri Narendra Modi–for the next two weeks.

The Ukrainian agents got the next day started early and ignored the grumbling children and out-of-sorts governess and wife and mother, who were unaccustomed to early rising or going out in the cold except for rare days of fun. They loaded three agents and the family in one vehicle, and the agent guard forces into two others, all equipped for a day in the cold snow, icy roadways, and hiking through the woods to a boat ride on a choppy river. It was sold as fun in the winter, but the Mizin-tsev family members were not buying it. Ludmila and Olga were angry and refused to understand why they could not take their cell phones. Ludmila was sulky, and Olga was inconsolable.

With a minimum of noise and outside bustling about, the convoy wheeled out of the manor's driveway in a blinding snowstorm. They were alone on Rublyovo-Uspenskoye Highway. They could not have had a better day. Rasputinov's motorcade yesterday afternoon had brought traffic to a standstill between Zvenigorod—the end of the line–and the Ring Road. That day, all they saw was an unusual small herd of four giant boar pigs meandering across the highway in search of forage areas. The going was slow and tedious because of the blizzard conditions, but the SBU agents were not complaining; it kept them almost invisible and safe.

The Russian rural countryside consists of forested areas and green plains rather than mountains and hills. The vast majority of Russia's land is not suitable for agriculture, and forests make up about half of its total surface area. Moscow–the capital city–is rich in green spaces. In Russia–which has the world's largest forested areas–the vegetation cover varies significantly from north to south. Extensive tundra is followed by taiga forests in the north and black forests as one travels to the center east and south. Located in the southwest of the country, Moscow is dominated by the black forest belt with tree varieties such as pine, spruce, birch, oak, and linden. The once dense forest areas off Rublyovo-Uspenskoe Shosse are shrinking as developers manipulate zoning rules, level forests, and build luxury properties, on Russia's most expensive real estate.

Rublevka is a district where in the toiletries sections of supermarkets one can find gold headed toothbrushes retailing for 5,000 rubles, and then stop next door to pick up the latest model of Maserati. Businessmen defending their alleged incomes boast of their lack of a house on Rubylovka as evidence of their incorruptibility. In those halcyon days, the land became so valuable that to control it people were prepared to resort to violence–and even to kill.

There are other kinds of other methods available to take over woodlands: Maps can be redrawn to classify forestland often inaccurate or otherwise useless, which is used as an excuse to transfer it to a beneficiary. Or, alternatively, the unscrupulous can bribe officials to classify their developments on forestland as nonpermanent dwellings, which are allowed in certain cases under the forest code.

One particularly remarkable machination was used near Nikolina Gora–an old dacha community founded in the 1920s for the Soviet Union's scientific and artistic aristocracy–whose residents today include filmmakers and staunch Rasputinov supporters, generals, admirals, and other persons, who wish Nikita Mikhalkov well.

The official plan of the area had been conveniently "eaten by mice," and back up copies "lost in a fire" and when the document was finally resurrected, about 20 hectares of what were originally woods had become private property. Whatever the politics, standing in the cities and villages, or whatever, the outcome is the same: the mass deforestation of the region for building lucrative real estate.

However, it was achieved, the deforestation along the Rublyovo-Usspenskoye *Shosse* had created broad corridors of essentially empty space where a small convey of vehicles or even a single man could be seen on a reasonably clear day. They could not afford even the slightest suspicion on the part of the humblest Russian citizen. Their destination was a segment of intact forest between the Zvenigorod Monastery and the east bank of Moscow River which could swallow them up and permit a completely unseen escape.

Because of the blizzard conditions, they were making slow progress; but they were being spared the usual very heavy traffic along the famous *shosse*. The driver of Yaroslav and the family's vehicle was able to make out the outline and spires of St. Sava of Storozhi Monastery in Zvenigorod which told him that this was their takeoff point through the forest, and things were going to be a good deal tougher for them from here on out.

They found a deserted area in the town which was covered with large rusting steel shipping crates, railroad cars, and a few derelict vintage old trucks. Their vehicles fitted in well among the debris and would not be noticed for years… if ever.

They got out of their vehicles and began to trudge into the town and past the walls of the monastery where parishioners and processions with crosses and prayed to relics of the holy monk, who was the first disciple of St. Sergius of Radonezh. Like those parishioners, the SBU commandoes and their kidnap victims followed the road into the forest–which for generations had been compulsory pilgrimages for all Russian rulers–including the great princes, tsars, and emperors.

At the margin of the forest, they elected to leave their Lada Niva 4x4 cars and to put chains on the huge tires of the UAZ SUVs, and the KamAZ, 1976 cab over trucks. The expensive Ladas were unceremoniously dumped into a snow filled and brushy ravine and out of sight. then–like a pair of great forest trolls–they advanced into the forest in the direction of the river. Almost as soon as they made their telltale tracks, the ruts vanished as the fastfalling snow filled in the marks.

The children became gleeful when they clambered into the KamAZ because of its immense size, novel shape, and the ability to see over the sides of the dump cab by having the Ukrainian commandoes hold them up. The household kidnapped adults were less sanguine about any of the adventure, especially since they were now out in the devilish cold wind and blowing pellets of snow.

Despite their early start, the two vehicle convoy was making very slow progress moving through the dense forest much like a tank, knocking down obstacles like small trees and dead fall as it went. At 14:00 they paused to eat some dense salami sandwiches, hot borsht soup, and drank refreshing familiar tea.

Yaroslav, Fedir, and Rokosylana talked about their progress, or lack of it.

"We are only about halfway into the forest; and, at this rate, it is possible that we will arrive at the rendezvous point on the river too late. One of us has to slog on ahead and reach the boat before the sailors think we have been caught and they flee. It is going to be a difficult walk; there may be Russian sentries; or the elements may do the unlucky hiker in. We have to decide who takes the risk. I would volunteer, but I have to manage the kidnappees and head up a fight if it comes. One of you will have to go. I don't want to be the dictator and order one of you; so, why don't you Rochambeau [rock, paper, scissors] for the opportunity.

Both Rokosylana and Fedir considered themselves to be champions at Rochambeau and saw a way out for themselves. Both felt a little guilty about having such skill; but it was fair; and the boss had decreed it.

The Rochambeau became something of a gladiatorial contest for smart people. They went through more than twenty rounds of rock, paper, scissors, until Rokosylana finally made the choice of paper, and Fedir made the choice of rock. He was actually sad that he had lost, not because of having to make the dangerous last leg of the escape journey on foot, but because he had lost. It was his first loss, and he did not like that at all.

Rokosylana knew better than to offer to go in Fedir's stead, because she knew it would be insulting. She remained graciously silent. Fedir put on snowshoes and began to walk at a punishing pace toward the river, three miles to the west. The rest of the unit and the kidnapped Mizin-tsev family and their retainers started off again in the ponderous, slow moving, but unstoppable UAZ SUVs, and the KamAZ, 1976 cab over trucks. The snow fall was getting ever heavier, and the cold worsened by the hour. It was becoming a test of endurance to see if they could make to the river and relative safety. The men opened their coats and shirts and took the smaller children up against their warm bodies to protect them from the subzero weather.

Felix made it to the river just as the small boats were being untied from their moorings.

Останавливаться/ostanavlivat'sya [Stop]," he shouted several times until he got the attention of the boat owners.

"They are on their way. Maybe another hour."

"Ve can't wait. Soon the river patrol will come and arrest us as smugglers," said the elder captain.

"They will be here! I promise you half again more money. You have to wait."

261

"Ve vill wait one-and-one-half more hours, then ve are gone, with our without your people."

"I will go back and help. That will make them a few minutes faster," Fedir said in desperation.

The four boat owners retied their boats to the mooring cleats and huddled down in sullen silence, determined to leave as soon as possible. Being taken into custody by the river patrol was terrible at best.

Fedir made an about face and headed back toward his SBU fellow commandoes, following his footprints in the snow the best he could. The amount of fluffy snow was coming down so rapidly and heavily that it was a losing battle. He ran until his legs burned so badly, he had to slow to a walk. The deep, heavy, snow made lifting his legs with the snowshoes a small torture and added to his exhaustion with each leaden step.

He saw the SBU vehicles emerging from the trees at the same time they saw him. His fellow commandoes began waving at him vigorously, and he made the mistake of waving back—a mistake because he was in a clearing and visible to anyone in the area. A lone sentry walked into the clearing when he saw the waving and pulled his AK-47 to hip level and fired on automatic. Fedir dropped like a tree that had been chainsawed. It was doubtful if he was even aware of being discovered.

Yaroslav fired three shots at the Russian soldier from his automatic, missing all three shots. He leaped from the back of the KamAZ, 1976, pulled on his snowshoes, and ran as hard as his strength would permit after the killer. He was bigger, stronger, and had a greater incentive; so, he gained ground on the Russian quickly.

He knew that he and the Russian would shortly break out into the cleared area along the river–bank, and all would be lost. He called upon every ounce of inner strength he had and got within shooting distance just before the Russian was to break out into the open. He fired three shots again; this time, the Russian fell face first into the frozen snow and never moved again. Yaroslav's chest was heaving as he tried to catch his breath. The icy air was painful in his bronchi and lungs, and he was afraid he was going to pass out.

Boryslav ran up behind him and wrapped both arms around his comrade to keep him from falling.

"Thanks," Yaroslav managed.

"Get your breath, Yaroslav. The vehicles will be here in a couple of minutes. We cannot waste any time getting to the boats. We need to be sure where they are."

They peered out from the treeline and were gratified to see the boats about a mile away, at the limits of visibility.

"I can't run, Boryslav. You run to them to make sure they don't leave. Bear in mind that Fedir gave his life for us. Stop them no matter what it takes!"

Boryslav got to the boats with time to spare.

"Our people will be here in fifteen minutes. We will need to load up as fast as possible."

"And your comrade promised his one-and-a-half times more money. Ve don't take you without that. Too dangerous. Ve haf waited too long already."

"You will get your money as soon as they get here. You are not leaving."

The look in Boryslav's eyes was convincing. They were not leaving.

Yaroslav came out of the treeline half running, half walking, and stumbling through the deep snow. It was like swimming in molasses. His legs burned ferociously. He was fighting for each breath.

When he had come half a mile, the UAZ SUVs, and the KamAZ, 1976 cab over trucks broke out of the trees and followed him. Boryslav cheered silently to himself.

The boat captain greeted Yaroslav with his hand out to get the extra rubles. Yaroslav did not ask any questions, just forked over the crinkled paper bills and said, "Get them loaded. We go."

The boatmen and commandoes were all business. The shivering family members and their minders moved as quickly as they could, hoping that the boats would take them to some warm place.

The large Baltika-type trawler, *The Vasily Yakovenko Freezer Ship*, was anchored mid river and continually moved about to avoid being iced in. Its hold held several tons of fresh caught fish: whitefish, cyprinids, zanders, and perch. There are some sixty species of freshwater fish taken in the inland fisheries of Russia. Set nets are the most common gear used in inland water commercial fisheries.

The escapees were brought aboard with alacrity. Everyone was aware that time was their enemy. No naval patrols had been seen for several hours because of the storm; but it was time posthumous that one should appear. That would result in failure of the mission or a pitched river battle, with very much uncertain results.

Yaroslav and the captain saluted each other; and without further adieu, they set off down river headed west of Moscow. The hold contained tons of legitimate commercial fish: whitefish, cyprinids, zanders, and perch, which should satisfy inspectors who questioned the purpose of the voyage. Fedir's body was put on ice in the back of the hold. The river flows roughly east through the Smolensk and Moscow Oblasts. 70 miles southeast of Moscow–at the city of Kolomna–it flows into the Oka–a tributary of the Volga–which ultimately flows into the Caspian Sea at the port of Astrakhan, situated on the mouth of the Volga, the main Russian outlet to the Caspian.

CHAPTER 47

Astrakhanskiy Port, Caspian Sea, Astrakhan Oblast, Russia, Trusovsky District,

February 16, 2025

During the long voyage down the Moscow River, the sailors and fishermen had several subterfuges for keeping the shore patrol or other military units from pulling *The Vasily Yakovenko Freezer Ship*, over for an inspection. Whenever any official boats or patrols came into sight, they got out the fishing poles and put out four or five lines, a hundred feet long and pretended to fish. In case the shore patrol wanted to stop them for a closer look, they had placed two big fish from the freezer to show how successful the voyage was going. During those fretful times, the commandoes and the kidnappees hid in the fish stinking hold. The men had *билли-клуб/billi-klubs* at the ready if any eager shore patrolman had a strong urge to check inside the hold. Fortunately, they never had occasion to use them.

They disembarked in the large and bustling Astrakhanskiy Port of Turkmenistan. Turkmenistan is a desert country bordering Iran, Afghanistan, and the Caspian Sea. Everyone and everywhere, there was rapidly moving work. Workmen did not walk, they ran. They climbed up and down ladders like so many nimble monkeys. It was dizzying to behold. No one paid the Ukrainians or their kidnappees the slightest attention. Yaroslav was ever wary, and all the commandoes were ready for a fight if one should be foisted on them.

The Caspian Sea is the world's largest inland body of water, often described as the world's largest lake. The Volga—Europe's longest river— enters at the shallow north end. It has a salinity of approximately 1.2%, about a third of the salinity of average seawater. The Caspian Sea is nearly five times as big as Lake Superior. Yaroslav and his mixed company of Russians and Ukrainians had to cross the entire length to it to get to Baku City, capital of Azerbaijan. Baku lies on the western shore of the Caspian Sea and the southern side of the Abşeron Peninsula, around the wide curving sweep of the Bay of Baku. Until they got there, they would be under the watchful eye of Turkmenistan operatives and would have to continue their roles as good Russians.

Turkmenistan is a country in Central Asia bordered by Kazakhstan to the northwest, Uzbekistan to the north, east, and northeast, Afghanistan to the southeast, Iran to the south and southwest, and the Caspian Sea to the west. The country is widely criticized for its poor human rights, its treatment of minorities, and its lack of press and religious freedoms. Since independence was declared from the Soviet Union in 1991, Turkmenistan has been ruled by repressive totalitarian regimes, including that of President for Life Saparmurat Niyazov. The saving grace afforded the Ukrainians lay in the country's Motto: *"Türkmenistan Bitaraplygyn watanydyr"* [Turkmenistan is the motherland of Neutralty".]

While not everyone they dealt with was exactly friendly, at least they were not on the opposing side in the current war. They were a clannish lot, not given to welcoming strangers. The natural unfriendliness of the Turkomens led them to a live-and-let-live way of dealing with strangers—anyone who was not directly a member of their immediate clan. It worked well for the Ukrainians and their Russian captives. They were ignored, just as they wished to be.

They made their way to Narimanovo Airport [officially Astrakhan Boris M. Kustodiev International Airport—renamed for the painter] by PrivateCar motor coach from the national company monopoly called "Turkmenistan Drinks services" which they rented at an exorbitant expenditure exchange of rubles to Turkmenistani Manats. One manat equals 26.41 Russian Ruble or 0.29 United States Dollar. Yaroslav did the accounting and handed the rubles to the mustachioed driver plus a 10% tip. The PrivateCar motor coach was the only conveyance available since the local taxis are not allowed to drive out of Ashgabat city limits. The driver scowled and looked at his hand as if Yaroslav had spat on it. Yaroslav put in a few hundred more rubles, and the scowl lightened some.

Rokosylana purchased one way tickets to Baku [no round trip tickets available] for the crowd of commandoes and enemy Russians which depleted their treasury to nearly nil. They would have to use their Russian Gazprombank Visa card for the remainder of the trip back to Kyiv.

Travel on Turkmenistan Air–the flag carrier and only airline of Turkmenistan—one of the airline's two Boeing 737-800s was surprisingly pleasant and comfortable. After taking their seats on flight 2382, the stewardesses brought them *pishme* [soft, bite sized, sweetened, fried breads] as a welcoming gesture. During the seven-hour, twenty-minute flight, they were served three meals. Breakfast consisted of an assortment of porridges in small decorative bowls, *Yarma*—[cracked wheat cooked in sheep fat with very small pieces of mutton mixed in for flavor]; *Shule*—[a watery rice porridge with meat, with shredded carrots]; and sorghum porridge. There were bowls of mixed chunks of various melons—described by the stewardesses as the "tsarina of the garden" and mentioned that the country is home to up to 400 distinct varieties.

Lunch included individual charcutier platters with *kakmach* [cured meat], *chekdirme* [stewed lamb], *yshtykma* [stuffed poultry], *kebapy* and *ash* [rice pilaf]. They had a choice of favorite Turkmen soups: *chorba* [mutton soup with spices], *gainatma* [pea soup], *etli-borek chorbasy* [soup with dumplings], and toasted meat pie/Turkmen Shepherd's Pie [*Ishleki*], the national dish of Turkmenistan.

Lunch and supper were both served with *chai* [tea]; *gok chai* [Green tea], *gara chai* [black tea], and—from the Dashogyuz region, gok chai prepared "Kazakh-style" with milk, to disguise the salty taste of the drinking water in that area; and black tea is brewed with fermented camel's milk on coals–the drink the nation is known for—[*calis/çal/* or *chal*], which is a white sparkling beverage with a sour flavor, popular through-out Central Asia.

All meals included naan, *çörek* [Central Asian flatbread], bread baked with meat inside which could be consumed as a meal in itself or as an appetizer. *Ýagly çörek* [lit. oily bread, buttery bread], *etli çörek* and *gokli çörek* [dumplings filled with vegetables and meat]. Turkmen bread is prepared differently from other breads in the region in thick, round disc-shaped loaves baked in a traditional *tamdyr* clay oven. The main role in the hospitality of the peoples of Central Asia is played by bread/*çörek*, which also serves as a symbol of hospitality, brotherhood, honor, hard work, prosperity, gratitude, and the kind-est wishes. Recipes have both ancient and modern variations, but the matter is not even in the ingredients themselves—but in the special ritual of its preparation,

Supper—served two hours before landing in Baku—was a con-fusing panoply of choices: Soups; 15 different choices, most of which were spiced with only salt and black pepper and cooked with large amounts of cottonseed oil, but some with pumpkin or spinach added to increase diversity of flavor. Meats; *shashlik* [skewered chunks of mutton, lamb, chicken, or sometimes fish, grilled over charcoal and garnished with raw sliced onion and a special vinegar-based sauce], kebabs of ground beef or camel meat, *Kakmach/ kakmaç* [preserved, dried meat prepared in individual portions or strips. *Kakmach* may be fried in fat or baked in a tandoor, but it is traditionally dried like jerky in the hot desert sun.], *gowurma* [deep fat fried meat in bite sized chunks], skewered chunks of mutton, lamb, chicken, or fish, grilled over charcoal and garnished with raw sliced onion and a special vinegar based sauce].

Fish: ar*ak*, small boneless chunks of fish fried in a pot in their own grease with a little sesame oil. Other Turkmen fish dishes included stur-geon, *balyk berek* dumplings], [fish manty and *balykly yanahli ash* (fish pilaf)]—all served with sesame seeds, rice, apricots, raisins, and pome-granate juice.

For the picky eater or the hollow-legged teen age boy, there were added choices of gokli *borek* and *etli borek* [dumplings filled with vegetables and meat], pilaf, *kelle bash ayak* and *chekdirme*, whole roasted lamb, numerous salads, as well as sweets ancient recipes such as *tamdyrlama, dograma,* and different kinds of *çorba, somsa, süzme,* and *agaran.*

Wine and other spirits were served during and after dinner. The most popular wine brands were Dashgala, Yasman Salyk, and Kopet Dagh. Turkmenbashi labeled vodka and Russian 'Baltika' (were also clones), grapes, *halva, baklava,* sherbet (a drink), *navat, chapada, and bekmesam*—most of which were exotics even for the educated palates of the high society Russian kidnappees. The flight and its amenities constituted the SBU commandoes' best day in years.

Flight 2382 touched down at Heydar Aliyev International Airport on time and without any untoward events. The commandoes and kidnaped family and employees had two days to spend in the beautiful city before their next flight—to Istanbul. The commandoes took turns watching over Col. Gen. Mikhail Mizin-tsev and his immediate family, unwilling to risk them conveying messages to the outside world or to escape physically. It was not a matter of "trust but verify"; it was "maintain the security of the mission".

The other commandoes used their time out in the city of Baku to see what a large, diverse, and beautiful place it is. *Baku* is the capital and largest city of Azerbaijan, as well as the largest city on the Caspian Sea and in the Caucasus region. About 25% of all inhabitants of the country live in Baku's metropolitan area. They visited the Old City and toured UNESCO world heritage sites like the Palace of the Shirvanshahs and the Maiden Tower, took short boat tours to the beautiful islands of the Baku Archipelago, and took their own walking tours of popular tourist and entertainment spots–downtown Fountains Square, the One and Thousand Nights Beach, Shikhov Beach, and Oil Rocks, and malls: Port Baku, Park Bulvar, Ganjlik Mall, Metro Park, 28 MALL, Aygun city, and AF MALL—all of which were extremely expensive. The commandoes had to be content with just admiring and lusting for things beyond of their reach. Most of then attended Baku Abdulla Shaig Puppet Theatre on Neftchilar Avenue.

The commandoes—lonely men who had been kept from their fondest social relationships—complained of only one small thing. The majority of the Muslims are Shia Muslims, and the Republic of Azerbaijan has the second highest Shia population percentage in the world after Iran. As a result, it was not a good "bird" watching place. Besides, it was winter. They groused that the only birds they saw were what they called, "penguins".

Baku is renowned for its harsh winds, reflected in its nickname, the "City of Winds", but—although it was a cold day—they were spared the harshest northern gale winds, known as *khazri* which—at times—can reach90 miles per hour, and are known to cause damage to crops, trees, and roof tiles. With the relative calm in the winds, they were also spared the worst of the city's famous air pollution. All in all, it was a grand two-day respite from war and the constant threat of surprise attacks.

With some help from the Azerbaijani mafia and the exchange of considerable *baksheesh*, Yaroslav and Rokosylana arranged for the remainder of their travel from Baku to Abu Dhabi on Air Arabia; from Abu Dhabi to Istanbul on Turkish Airlines; and from Istanbul to Warsaw on Austrian Airlines, which went off without a hitch, but was exhausting.

Polish officials were part of the allied contributors to Ukraine's war effort and had been forewarned of the importance and arrival of the commandoes and their captives. They provided armed escorts for a bus over M-11 to deliver them to the Ukrainian border at Checkpoint Shehyni. The crossing is situated on the Polish side in the village of Medyka, Jaroslaw County, Podkarpackie Voivodeship, and on the Ukraine side near the village of Shehyni, Yavoriv Raion, Lviv Oblast.

The remaining commandoes and the Mizin-tsev family and helpers walked the last mile to Shehyni. Yaroslav telephoned SBU Gen. Olena Yuriivna and reported the success, present status, and location, of the unit. Within an hour, several large black SUVs drove into the town and stopped at the bus station to take the exhausted travelers to the small local airport. There, they were placed on an SBU/Ukraine AirForce flight to Ukraine's central airport in Boryspil which shares its airstrip with the

Boryspil Air Base 18 miles east of the capital, Kyiv. The family and its retainers were held under guard at the base for several days to ensure the validity of their value and commitment to Ukraine. The commandoes were put up in the *tres elegante* Hotel Khreschatyk Kyiv. Everyone in the group—commandoes and kidnappees—slept the sleep of the dead for two full days.

CHAPTER 48

SBU Central Headquarters, 32-35, Volodymyrska Street, Kyiv, Ukraine

March 29, 2025

Ukraine President Volodymyr Oleksandrovych Zelenskyy, himself, greeted the returned commando unit, thanked and praised them for their work and its success. He had everyone in the meeting bow their heads and share a moment of silence for the commandoes who gave the ultimate sacrifice: Borys Petrovych Stefaniuk, Fedir Blyznyuk, Grygoriy Mykytavitch Bogdanovskyvich, Irina Andrukhovych Kolokoltsev, Yuri Syrskyi, Anatoli Moisiuk, Kuzma Mykolavich Stefanenko, Kuzma Mykolavich Stefanenko, and Dayvd Razvozhaev.

President Zelenskyy remained with his head bowed a few minutes longer than the rest of the people in the room. He had had to do this too many times, and the burden weighed heavily on his shoulders.

"My fellow Ukrainians, my true brothers and sisters," he said, his face hard and determined.

"We are locked in a struggle for our very lives, for the democracy of our country, and for the future of our children and grandchildren. We were attacked by a maniacal dictator for his own avarice and hunger for power. His goal is beyond defeating us; he intends to use the rubble of our country to launch World War III to satisfy his sociopathic goal of world hegemony with him sitting atop a skewed globe.

"Our courageous military forces, SBU operatives, and ever enduring people, have vowed to struggle on, to prevent the dictator from destroying us. We will fight him; we will not get too tired, too afraid, or too convinced that things are hopeless, even in our darkest hours. We will fight him in the skies, on the seas, in the mountains, on the plains, in the cities, and on the streets where we live.

"The United States wavers in its help; but we will not waver. We cannot; we must not. The world is depending on us to stop the corrupt hegemony of Russia from spreading its evil any further than this war, our war. If we cannot get help from our allies; if they grow weary of a foreign war, then we will still fight on. We may be reduced to fighting with sticks and rocks, or even our bare hands. But, I tell you, my dear friends, with my last breath, I will be out their throwing rocks alongside you."

He stood silently as the room erupted in thunderous applause. Every person in the room stood and joined in the commitment that the president's speech required of them.

After the stirring speech, Gen. Yuriivna directed her SBU commandoes to follow her. They walked down to the basement and boarded black SUVs with blackened windows and were taken to the SBU archive building on Zolotovoritska, 7 Street. Every agent was familiar with the destination, they had used the metro station Zoloti Vorota, a five-minute walk away, hundreds of times during their careers.

No one spoke as they ascended to the ninth floor on the high-speed elevator, a highly insulated set of offices and conference rooms, guarded by the largest, toughest looking agents in the SBU carrying French FAMAS 5.56 X 45 mm submachine guns and holstered Stechkin APS 9×18mm Makarov automatic pistols. This was quite evidently serious business.

A grim faced, scarred master sergeant led them to a large conference room already partially filled with people, most of whom Yaroslav recognized.

They were escorted to their assigned padded swivel chairs by room guards. There were eight of them, armed the same way those in the hallways. There were no introductions; in fact, not a word was spoken to break the eerie and consequential silence. When Gen. Yuriivna took her place at the head of the table, all eyes fixed on her, especially those of the Russians in the room. She got right down to business.

"Agents, you are aware of who these people are. They are our enemies, but they do not need remain that forever. Today, we will make the final decisions about how much the men care for their wives and children and their word of honor. We will also evaluate the women and children to see if they are worth the risks we will be taking, and if they are up to the rigors and risks of the life in head of them."

"I will introduce them, for clarity. It will be immediately apparent that these people are leaders or connected in important ways to Russia, to the Nazi Wagner PMC. As I state your name and position, please stand.

"Col. Gen. Mikhail Mizin-tsev Oligarch and owner of Wagner PMC, his wife, Vera Yusupovna Mizin-tsev, and his six children: Valery, Vyodor, Sergey, and Mykola Oleksiy, and the girls: Ludmila, and Olga.

"You may be seated."

Next, she had Lt. Col. Dmitriy Utkinov ("Wagner"), Yevgeny stand.

"Lt. Col. Dmitriy Utkinov ("Wagner"), Yevgeny, second in command and field commander of the Wagner paramilitary forces in Ukraine. His wife Olga Vladimirovna Yevgeny, and children, Alexander and Audrey; Col. Konstantin Pikalov, and his wife Sofia Armenovna Pikalov, and their children, Mila, Kira, and Polina—all girls, and Boris, Denis, and Arseni, the boys.

They stood, some of younger boys and girls cried. No one smiled or made eye contact with their perceived tormentors. With a nod from Gen. Yuriivna, they sat back down.

"Col. Andrei Troshev," she summoned next. He was the youngest of the three.

He was slow in standing and winced in pain from a not yet healed back wound.

"Olga Vladimirovna Yevgeny, and children, Alexander and Audrey."

Audrey was babe in arms, age three months. She had just been breast fed; so, she was unknowing and tranquil.

"You may be seated."

Everyone settled down and again attention was drawn to the forceful Gen. Yuriivna.

"I am going to tell everyone in this room and for the formal record, what our agreement with these Wagner PMC officials and their families is, and what we will hold them to, and what they can require of us over time. And—when I finish—any or all of them can speak, even the children, because every one of them is going to have to state verbally and sign for the written record that they are in agreement, and that they will comply to the letter from today until Russian hostilities cease, and they withdraw from every part of Ukraine, including the Donblast and Crimea.

"Before I list the agreements, I will state the generalizations: Wagner PMC will obey orders from Ukrainian SBU and the government of Ukraine, and not Russia. They will do things that will willfully conflict with Russia's orders and objectives. At first, this will be somewhat subtle, but eventually, when I say so, it will be overt, even extreme.

"Speaking for the SBU and as a senior spokesperson for the government of Ukraine, I guarantee the personal physical safety of all family members who stood up today for as long as they live. We cannot guarantee safety in battle for the men; but, it is in Ukraine's best interest to keep Wagner in the picture, and to create a cover that allows them to function as double agents working especially for Ukraine and its interests. Hence, their safety is our concern.

"The family members will be taken to the safest possible places and will remain there until this war of Rasputinov's comes to a finish acceptable to Ukraine. That is a tall order. They will be provided with a more than decent living in a clean, modern, safe, place.

"The men will rejoin their families and will be safe in anonymity with the security forces of Ukraine and its allies protecting them. The men and their families will—out of necessity—change their identities, leave behind all personal and professional contacts, no longer lay claim to or to any of their personal, professional, or financial records. The model will be the Witness Protection Program of the US Marshalls' service [WitSec] in the United States. Any deviation from or attempt to circumvent the agreement will result in immediate excommunication from the program. That will leave them vulnerable to the mercies of Russia. They do not need to be reminded of Vladimir Rasputinov's unprovoked military attack and war crimes.

"There is a strong case with mountains of evidence against every man in senior authority in the Wagner group. The three men here today will be immune from any prosecution unless or until, they are excommunicated from the WitSec arrangement. You have been warned, and there will not be a second chance available... ever. If you renege, you can wait for the ax to fall, as fall it will."

Those people were well aware of Rasputinov's brand of mercy and his kind of justice. This sounded to them like a Rasputinov dictum, and they were terrified. It showed in their faces.

"Good," said Gen. Yuriivna.

She stood, made a crisp about face, and left the room.

The guards and SBU agents stood up and walked to where the three men were sitting.

"Stand up!" Yaroslav ordered.

They complied promptly.

"You will now be shackled. You may now kiss each member of your families, but you may not otherwise touch them. Passing of anything, even a piece of paper between you will automatically be considered a breach of the agreement, and you will immediately be taken to a Ukrainian prison where your identity will be revealed. Nod if you understand."

Each man nodded quickly, vigorously, and deeply; they were reminiscent of "talking heads" toys popular among US and European children.

The men submitted to removing their clothes and changing into brilliant orange paper prison garb, including paper shoes. They were then shackled with their wrists behind their backs, a chain around their waists, which was attached to relatively loose ankle shackles and to a neck chain which would restrict movement to the minimum allowing them to walk and to sit.

Each man was surrounded by four pistol bearing guards, who glared their hatred convincingly to the already cowed PCM officers. Before they were unceremoniously loaded into transport vehicles, they had a heavy, black, unpleasant smelling hood placed over their heads. The unpleasant odor was the smell of fear residual in the hoods that had obviously been used before.

CHAPTER 49

Special Protection Unit, Fort Meade, Maryland,

May 12, 2025

Six weeks before, in Washington D.C., the families and their husbands, the senior leaders of Wagner PMC, were separated for an indefinite period. Col. Gen. Mikhail Mizin-tsev, oligarch and owner of Wagner PMC, and Lt. Col. Dmitriy Utkinov ("Wagner"), Yevgeny–his second in command and in-theater commander of the Wagner forces–were transported by a captured Russian Ilyushin Il-276 medium-airlift military transport jet back to occupied Popasnaya Village, Luhansk Oblast, Ukraine. It was the headquarters from which they were kidnapped, and where a runt committee was currently trying to run Wagner's operations. There, they set about to reestablish and refurbish Myronivska Street, 12, as its formal headquarters. Secretly, the United States funded the renovation which resulted in the reestablishment of the acceptance of the two men as the leaders and left them beholden to America.

The women and children of the Mizin-tsev and Yevgeny families were taken in an opposite direction–not by airplane–but by an armored prison bus preceded by two and followed by two Fort Meade, Maryland bullet proof vehicles with blackened windows like the bus and filled with vetted incorruptible soldiers armed with machine guns, machine pistols, short-barreled shotguns, and grenades. They were serious men and women assigned to a critical duty for the security of their United States and bound for an almost unassailable fortress. The transported families were crammed into the vehicles; all were handcuffed and shackled at the waist and ankles, and hooded, which made the children cry. They sat tightly packed on seats inside a cage, with no way to lie down, or to get comfortable, or to sleep. There were no toilet facilities or medical services available.

The convoy was caught in the tail end of the morning traffic crush pouring out of the suburbs and cascading into Washington, DC. They were sandwiched in a long string of cars rolling east along Keene Mill Road. Another mile and a half along the two-lane road that bisected Springfield, Virginia, and they reached the Beltway girdling the nation's capital. The sun by then was low on the horizon, its slanting rays hard on the eyes. They took the ramp onto Route 66 (Custis Memorial Parkway) toward I-495. They turned left onto Ohio Drive SW, then left onto Independence Avenue SW, then right onto Maine Avenue SW, and left again onto I-395 N. The convoy took exit 2B to DC 295N (Anacostia Freeway) for 4.5 miles.

With Fort Meade in sight, they took the exit onto MD 175 E (Annapolis Road) for two and a half miles, then right onto Reece Road, right onto Chisholm Avenue, and left again onto 18th Street and again left onto B Street. They moved at the correct speed limit half a mile and turned right, again onto Reece, another half mile and a left onto MacArthur Road. The next short drive called for a right turn onto Mapes Road.

There they were met by a different bus, and the family members were all required to exit and to stand looking toward the east. A new set of guards walked up behind them and put on a new, cleaner, set of hoods, equally opaque. This time the children just stood stoically aside, knowing that resistance was futile, and might bring punishment.

They were driven around and around for half an hour and finally entered a large open concrete area and parked. There, the kidnappees were taken out of the bus, their hoods and shackles removed; and they walked behind the guards to their new quarters, which could have been on the dark side of the moon for all they knew. What they did know was not to ask questions.

Their identities, their new location, the reason for them being there, and why all state secrets, the divulgence of which was a felony with a long prison sentence to be served in Fort Leavenworth Federal Penitentiary, Kansas—the opposite of the life being enjoyed prior to the crime, was information that would come later. That being a justifiable fear and deterrent rendered all guards, doctors, nurses, house keepers, grounds keepers, and their families, functionally deaf and blind mutes with no curiosity. That included any restaurant employees within or near the fort.

Fort Meade is virtually a city unto itself. It is home to the National Security Agency, US Cyber Command, several other large Military Intelligence units, Defense Information Systems Agency, Defense Media Activity and 116 other agencies which serve as the nation's platform for Intelligence, Information and Cyber Operations, and premier level secrecy. Fort Meade Garrison's Operational Security office manages residents such as the Wagner families very carefully in order to protect sensitive information, and the people who have that information. The secure area of the fort is not exactly a prison; but after a few weeks, it felt like that to the women and children waiting to be reunited with their husbands and fathers without the slightest access to news outside the fort's perimeters.

The US Marshals Service provides for the security, health, and safety, of government witnesses, and their immediate dependents, whose lives are in danger as a result of their testimony against drug traffickers, terrorists, organized crime members, and other major criminals, and persons of national security value who are at risk. The Marshals Service provides security to the federal judiciary and manages the witness security program.

It manages and sells seized or forfeited assets of criminals, is responsible for the confinement and transportation of federal prisoners who have not been turned over to the Bureau of Prisons and is the primary federal agency responsible for fugitive investigations. Managed by the Marshals Service, Justice Prisoner and Alien Transportation System is one of the largest transporters of prisoners in the world. It handles 715 requests every day and more than 260,000 prisoner/alien movements per year between judicial districts, correctional institutions, and foreign countries.

Persons like the Wagner Group families are not allowed mobile telephones, computers with internet data capability, emails, telephone messages, or texts. The military personnel and DoD civilian workforce themselves are controlled. They must take advantage of the email and instant messaging features available through Army Knowledge Online and Defense Knowledge Online, which are operated by the DoD and have stringent security protocols. For the Wagner Group, there was no question of any waiver of protocol. The workforce must encrypt NIPR sensitive work-related email communications, use only government email networks—such as outlook/OWA—and edit emails on AKO or DKO for OPSEC before hitting send. Not to do so is a crime, and to be found out as having done so with regards the Wagners, promised to be a quick felony and off to Leavenworth action. Suffice it, the workforce was both effective and scrupulously honest about secrecy.

The deputy marshals, agents and other members of the workforce cannot discuss sensitive work-related information in areas such as restaurants or any other public setting. They can only use public businesses in which the employees know the agents by their photographs and have signed binding agreements never to address them by name or to discuss their business in even the lightest of ways or by humor. When teleworking, the workforce cannot participate in sensitive work-related planning within hearing of family members and cannot print sensitive work-related planning products at home.

Family members of the secret area occupants are enjoined never to disclose sensitive information such as birthdays, Social Security numbers, information regarding special operations-type units, family photographs, credit card numbers, and security codes on Facebook, Twitter [X], blogs, or other websites. Laws which are even more draconian apply to the actual employees—again with the specter of Leavenworth in the background.

The USMS [US Marshals Service] supplies a stipend to the relocated witnesses for up to two years. The stipend is not anything to get excited about—typically around $30,000 per year, in monthly installments. Because of the nature of the Wagner Groups relative importance, the

$30,000 was applied to every individual, even children. When appropriate, the USMS assists the witnesses or VIPIs in getting employment.

That was not applicable to any of the Wagner families; and–like most witnesses–they did not have any law abiding world skill sets, and those who do usually cannot work in their former profession, since they could be noticed or recognized. Some of the occupations described were truck drivers, warehousemen, and security guards. The witnesses arrive and depart the facility in blacked out vehicles; so, they never know its location.

For the colonel general and the lieutenant colonel, life returned to what served as normal for ranking members of the Russian PMC. Almost.

CHAPTER 50

Occupied Popasnaya Village, Myronivska Street, 12, Luhansk Oblast, Ukraine.

May 12, 2025

C ol. Gen. Mizin-tsev returned to Rublevka to find his home just as he had left it, his guards and servants interested in the trip his wife and children were taking, and how things were going in Ukraine. It was as if he had never left. He played that role carefully and took two days in Moscow to conduct business with the *Solntsevskaya Bratva* [*Russian crime syndicate, rossíyskaya máfiya,* the brotherhood, or by the government as the "Organized Criminal Group" (OPG), specifically the Orekhovskaya OPG]. He had breakfast and lunch with head of the Bratva, Pauol Balagula, where they renewed their contracts and then made a quick tour of the locations of their enterprises: a large trucking business that had a holding room for their large number of young girls being trafficked, a gambling casino in St. Petersburg which catered to visiting Asians whom they fleeced, three methamphetamine kitchens as large as any legitimate big pharma manufacturer, and a distribution center for fentanyl bound for Asia, Europe, and the Middle East. Their associates in Mexico City handled the American arm of the distribution.

They spoke of war only as business, the traffic in arms, and the drug sales to the enlisted personnel of the Russian forces in Ukraine. Business

282

was good, Mizin-tsev reported. The following day was spent in leisure time activities that involved a good soaking in the Hamman Turkish bath in Moscow, and visits to the girls Balagula's second in command, Boris Mirzoyan, had trained. All around, it was a pleasant relaxing day among the *vorami v zakone* [thieves-in-law] for the colonel general, and readied his psyche for his next leg of business.

The vorami pulled some strings for him, and Mizin-tsev was able to get a first class seat on Aeroflot flight 622 round trip from Moscow Sheremetyevo Airport to Bujumbura International Airport in Burundi. There he met with his African second in command, Major Zaal Shashaova Gvinekadze. They spent a week traveling by car, plane, and train, around the large holdings of the Wagner Group in Central Africa. Col. Gen. Mizin-tsev had neglected the region for several months, and there was important work to take care of.

When he left Burundi to return to Moscow, they had performed thirteen executions of suspected traitors, diamond thieves in Ivory Coast, and opposing crime chiefs, collected fourteen million dollars in gold bullion from Rwanda, promoted six new men to the rank of captain, and welcomed Chief Abdelkader Abu Umar ibn Yahya al-Hintati into the inner circle of European leaders of the Wagner Group in Africa, only the second Black man to have been awarded such a profitable position in Wagner's long African history.

When he returned to Moscow, his plane was met by his mistress, Maria Yamschikov, who was both beautiful and brilliant. She managed the human trafficking division of Wagner's Russian section and was appropriately grateful for the very lucrative privilege. She thanked him several times over the next two days before he returned to his hearth and home refreshingly exhausted to greet his sympathetic household retainers.

The new war effort in Ukraine began to take shape in the refurbished headquarters in Popasnaya Village, Myronivska Street, 12, Luhansk Oblast, Ukraine, under the direction of Lt. Col. Dmitriy Utkinov ("Wagner"), Yevgeny. As requested by his de facto leader, Yevgeny began sending a series of letters to the defense department extolling the Wagner Group's military successes, a completely fabricated set of data. He sent three different platoons of handpicked, best-of-the-best and most experienced troopers into carefully designed traps—the work of his new friends in the Ukrainian SBU.

That work became an almost full time occupation for Col. Yaroslav Kandybavych Melnykenko and his new wife, Major Rokosylana Mykolaivna Udovychenko. Both platoons were wiped out to a man. Both Dmitriy and Yaroslav's reports to their superiors told of great successes. Yaroslav's was true.

The most important work Dmitriy started was in conjunction with Mizin-tsev. Together, they began a program of complaints and criticisms of the performance of the Ministry of Defense of the Russian Federation and—by implication—of the most important decision maker, the President of the Russian Federation. Their particular target was the Defense Minister Sergei Fadeyoitch Rahimjanova. President Rasputinov began to pay attention when Yevgeny's criticisms began to leak to the press. That was especially disturbing because the criticisms rang entirely true, not that the dictator, Rasputinov, would ever admit to such.

Soon, the outside world, and interested Russian members of the public began to learn of military corruption beginning at the top. He and his cooperating writers told of Russia's efforts being undermined by its reliance on conscripts—often forced–widespread corruption and use of civilian vehicles, and the relatively huge distances involved in resupplying its forces; of Russian dead being unceremoniously plowed into communal unmarked pits without records being kept—upwards of 200,000 of them. Perhaps the worst revelation was that at least 75,000 wounded Russians had been left on the field to die of their wounds, or of infections, or even starvation.

To Rasputinov's shock and dismay, an article was published in *Pravda's* opinion section that was highly critical, an almost unheard of breach of Rasputinov's dictatorial control. Excerpts included:

> … when vehicles do break down Russia has limited resources to recover them.
>
> The Russian army's battalion tactical groups–those at the spearhead of its advances into Ukraine–normally have only one light and one heavy recovery vehicle, even in units

featuring dozens of vehicles. This means combat vehicles sometimes need to be diverted to towing duties and sometimes broken down "vehicles need to be towed up to a hundred miles," several Russian generals report.

Wagner officers state that Russia has neglected its trucks largely because they are not glitzy enough for a military keen to show off its cutting edge weapons systems in order to make profits.

In recent years, President Rasputinov has boasted about Russia's hypersonic missiles like the Zircon and Kinzhal, stealth fighter jets like the Su-57, and its modern fleet of 11 ballistic missile submarines.

A Wagner general—who spoke on the agreement to remain anonymous said, "Often glamorous dictator militaries are good at the showy weapons, they buy the fancy aircraft and the fancy tanks, but they don't actually buy the less glamorous stuff... At the root of Russia's logistical problems are two things that plague its military: conscription and corruption.

About 25% of the Russian military's million troops are conscripts and many experts believe that figure may be misleading, suspecting many of the non-conscript troops are conscripted by coercion or pulled out of maximum security prisons and forced into the army. Russia's conscripts serve one-year stints, occupy the lower ranks, and fill many of the positions in the logistics chain, including vehicle maintenance.

A major in the transportation corps gave his opinion to *Pravda*: "You can't really learn anything in a year about maintaining military systems."

Conscripts also have little motivation to serve their country because they are underpaid, overworked, cheated out of their time and money, and forced into danger, sometimes even without weapons.

Corruption has a particularly corrosive effect on the Russian military's maintenance and supply logistics. A Russian officer serving in the north of the country gave

Pravda this quotation: "Corruption–in the form of embezzlement or bribery—is well known to lead to the purchase of substandard equipment, for example by giving the contract for equipment or maintenance to a less qualified supplier that is more willing to pay kickbacks to the officers. Or the person in charge of allocating the maintenance or procurement budget can simply report spending the full budgeted amount on high quality products or services, but then purchase low quality substitutes and pocket the difference. Often, they do not supply the material or weapons and ammunition they are paid for. This is frequently the product of nepotism and goes unpunished. It results in unnecessary injuries and death of our brave soldiers on foreign battlefields.

That officer went on to say that, "some of the effects are now being seen on the battlefield… money that should have been used for maintenance is "likely lining the pockets of officers in charge of the conscripts who would be servicing the trucks."

Russia's military has historically relied on its large manpower reserves to handle logistics, rather than mechanized systems using wooden pallets and forklifts. For example, take loading artillery shells onto a truck. A forklift can lift a pallet of two dozen shells in a single go, while manually lifting individual shells onto a truck would consume far more time and manpower… manpower desperately needed at the front.

He concludes, "This makes Russian logistics around 30% less efficient than leading Western militaries; this means that it takes more trucks to do a given task in the same time, so greater fuel use and wear and tear. It also means Russian trucks spend more time standing still while loading and unloading."

Russia has lost a substantial number of trucks. When the tanks and fighting vehicles ran afoul of Ukrainian mines, drones and artillery, Russian commanders pulled back their remaining vehicles—and sent in the infantry, on foot, almost as it they were sending in expendable mine dogs.

Russia's generals are having to rely relied heavily on Soviet era rocket artillery systems such as the BM-21 Grad to provide fire support for its ground forces, and BMP-1 armored personnel carriers to act as infantry fighting vehicles. They were not made for that purpose and are inadequate. Such outdated vehicles, many having little more than thin steel plate as armor protection, making them easy targets for Ukrainian drone operators and troops armed with sophisticated Western anti-tank missiles. In an effort to replace its stocks of MRLS and infantry-fighting-vehicles, Russia has turned to up-gunning domestic vehicles, which serves only a temporary fix and costs the lives of more Russian boys.

Let us conclude with example of the inferiority of Russian tanks based on faulty judgment by Russia's leaders and economic problems. More than 4,000 of our tanks have been destroyed and their highly trained crews lost. That is because they are inferior: for example, the latest T90M recently received upgrades such as GPS navigation, better thermals, better ballistic computers, and some storage on its outside for additional ammunition. These things have been on Western tanks for more than thirty years. Furthermore, the additions and improvements when implemented remain behind the precision and effectiveness of the Western tank force.

Russian tanks are lighter and smaller than Western ones; there is better and more protective gun depression on the Western tanks, making the Russian tanks and their crews more vulnerable.

As tank crews are killed, substitutes cannot be trained quickly enough to fill the gap. The core of military personnel consists mostly of conscripts–around 80 percent–who are not professionally trained to use the equipment.

So much Russian military equipment has been left abandoned that Ukrainian authorities declared that anyone who took possession of such equipment did not need to declare it for tax purposes. The war in Ukraine has exposed fundamental design flaws and outdated or inferior-quality materials in Russian equipment. Probably the worst example is that tank turrets that were blown off and now lie in ruins several meters from the rubble of the exploded tank point to a design issue known as the "Jack-in-the-box" flaw. This design flaw was corrected decades before in Western tanks, which saved hundreds of lives; lives that are still being lost by Russians.

The *Pravda* article caught Rasputinov's and his Russian generals sitting in their comfortable offices like nothing had ever before. Several of the most senior rushed to tell Rasputinov that the article was correct in all details, and asked how the dictator wanted the situations handed, not the least of which punishment for *Pravda's* editors and publisher, and for the source of the article. A careful investigation resulted in a change in *Pravda's* staff but did not turn up the source. Rasputinov presumed it was Wagner and its continual whining and criticizing. It was looking like a time to make changes.

Rasputinov began laying plans to oust and maybe execute the senior officers of the Wagner PMC despite lacking sufficient evidence to link them to the *Pravda* article. He sought advice from the Ministry of Defense regarding his desire to eliminate Wagner altogether. His agents looked far and wide for the present location of Lt. Col. Dmitriy Utkinov ("Wagner") Yevgeny Wagner commanders, Col. Konstantin Pikalov, Col. Andrei Troshev, and Col. Gen. Mikhail Mizin-tsev, the oligarch and owner of the PMC. After several months of searching, they had to admit failure. One lower rank officer was executed, and another was reduced in rank and sent to the front. It is said that "Hell hath no fury like a woman scorned," but that was said before anyone saw Vladimir's fury and its reckoning.

CHAPTER 51

Occupied Popasnaya Village, Myronivska Street, 12, Luhansk Oblast, Ukraine

July 10, 2025

Col. Gen. Mizin-tsev, had not been seen in Luhansk, or the Donblas Oblasts for many months. There were no sightings in all of Russia, and reports from Africa were scanty and unverifiable. The Kremlin investigators finally threw up their hands and admitted that he was either dead or had gone into hiding on some obscure and uncharted Pacific Island, drinking Tropical Bay Breeze cocktails and smoking short, fat, and flavorful, Montecristo Petit Edmundo Cuban cigars while sitting on the beach watching the endless surf.

The actual leader of Wagner PMC was still Lt. Col. Dmitriy Utkinov ("Wagner") Yevgeny, and he could be found anywhere the fighting continued. Except for a few interspersed and unexplained brief absences, he seemed to be omnipresent in the DPR [Donetsk People's Republic] and the LPR [Luhansk People's Republic], unless Russian intelligence operatives were sighted in the area. Then, he moved on to more serious areas of the war.

This was one of those times. The reason he could not be found for the moment is because Yaroslav Melnykenko did not want him to be.

"Dimitriy, before we start the briefing, let me assure that Olga, and the children, Alexander and Audrey are fine. Alexander is now playing baseball on a school team."

"How's he doing?"

"Fine. He plays shortstop and is said to have a 'mighty arm' according to his coach. He hit a homer in his last game.

"Thanks, Yaroslav. I want so much to see them again. I am doing everything I can to make that happen."

"I know you are. It is tough for everybody. But, we are making progress. With Wagner more or less out of the picture, the stalemate is moving east and south in favor of Ukraine."

"That may happen even without my help. Shipments of ammunition and new conscripts are falling off for the regular army as well as Wagner. Rasputinov has decided to pare Wagner's payments, replacements, and supplies, seriously, it seems. I think it is getting to be time to make the big surprise."

"You're probably right, but just a few more operations to put us in the position we need to be to take advantage of Rasputinov's losses."

"Well, that is probably mostly Rasputinov's own fault. He is cutting off his nose to spite his face, as you say in America. He feels threatened by Wagner; so, he is willing to sacrifice his war successes just to spite us. He is likely to regret it down the line."

"I'm sure he already does."

Lt. Col. Yevgeny was involved in several more battles over the next several weeks, holding his men back with the excuse that they were not well enough trained and were not getting enough ammunition from the Kremlin. In this off-and-on, stand-off, move-back, creep-forward-war, it was not apparent that the Wagner mercenaries were not doing their best. It was being chalked up to the fatigue of war on both sides.

Both Yaroslav and Dmitriy knew that they were not going to be able to accomplish anything decisive until the feckless American Senators once again agreed to allow the already set aside by bipartisan Senators for funding of ammunition, planes, tanks, and long-range artillery, to be released. Even when it was officially released, it would take something on the order of three months to get to the

Ukrainian battle front. It was maddening. Ukrainians were dying, and the Senators were busy pettifogging.

Russia's defensive line–the largest and most fortified in Europe since World War Two–ultimately held, and early prospects of a Ukrainian breakthrough that would sever the land bridge between Russia and occupied Crimea faded to nothing more than a futuristic fantasy.

Presidents Rasputinov, Zelenskyy, and US President Bettern, paid little attention to the Wagner Group or its effectiveness or lack of it because the war droned on with no end in sight. Every day or so, a new event in Rasputinov's war demanded attention, action, or exercise of diplomacy. The war had become a vacillating quagmire. On any given day, actions occurred from any of the categories of violent bombing, to wild frontal attacks, to guerrilla incursions, to sea battles, and air raids.

On July 26, the Russian FSB arrested a dual Italian-Russian citizen for the derailing of a freight train near Rybnoye, Ryazan Oblast. The FSB claimed that he had been recruited in February, 2023 and received training in Latvia under the auspices of NATO. As Russia's fortunes seemed to be declining, Russian President Vladimir Rasputinov signed a decree increasing the number of Russian military personnel by 170,000. He stated that NATO expansion and the stalemate war in Ukraine were the reasons for the decree.

In late July, Ukrainian President Volodymyr Zelenskyy acknowledged that the Ukrainian counter offensive "did not achieve the desired results", and said the war had entered a new phase with the winter season. After the Russian army and Donblast Separatists took Avdiika—the first notable Ukrainian city to fall to Russia since Bakhmut nearly a year before–President Zelenskyy declared that, "the period of freedom is over."

During the last five days of July, Germany delivered a military aid package to Ukraine that included four HX81 tractors, eight Zetros off-road trucks, four other vehicles, 15 HLR 338 precision rifles, 60,000 rounds of ammunition, five drone detection systems, laser range finders, and more than 4,000 155 mm shells. The US imposed sanctions on three transnational firms for violating a price cap imposed by the US Treasury Department on Russian oil in response to the invasion of Ukraine; and the International Federation of Red Cross and Red Crescent Societies suspended the membership of the Belarus Red Cross after it refused to remove its head Dzmitry Shautsou, who admitted involvement in the deportation of Ukrainian children from Russian occupied territories.

During the first week of July, Ukraine released a video reportedly showing two unarmed Ukrainian soldiers being executed by Russian soldiers after surrendering near the frontline village of Stepove, Donetsk Oblast. The SBU said it had launched two drone strikes that destroyed Russian ammunition and equipment depots near Svatove, occupied Luhansk Oblast. It also arrested a resident of Kyiv on suspicion of aiding Russian air strikes on the capital and a businessman for trying to sell stolen aircraft components to Russia. Nepal confirmed that six of its nationals had been killed while fighting for Russia in Ukraine and that a seventh was captured. CNN later estimated that Russia had recruited thousands of Nepalis to fight its war.

Three short range, unguided missiles struck targets within and near the Kremlin to usher in August, 2025. Russia complained to the United Nations, and Ukraine denied any knowledge of the missile attacks. Five days later, a bomb went off in the GUM department store in Kremlin square. This time, ISIS claimed responsibility in retaliation for Russian strafing small Sunni towns in Syria in support of Syrian President Basar al Assad and his war against ISIS. The month concluded with apparent growing cracks in the Allied unity of support for Ukraine. The US Bettern administration warned that funding for Ukrainian military aid would run out by the end of the year and requested more funding from the US Congress. It was expected to be difficult for the president to get all he asked for.

Bulgarian president Rumen Radev vetoed an agreement to donate–to send 100 surplus APCs to Ukraine–sending the arrangement back to the National Assembly for reconsideration. The assembly subsequently voted to override Rades' veto on August 10.

Probably the most important development in the war after the Russian invasion which started on February 24, 2022, was August 25, 2025. The Wagner Group was a network of mercenaries and a de facto unit of the MoD [Russian Ministry of Defense and the GRU, Russia's military intelligence agency], that had conducted operations in Ukraine since early 2014. The US estimated Wagner had 50,000 personnel fighting in Ukraine, including 10,000 contractors and 40,000 of the convicts the company enlisted. Nearly half of the 20,000 Russian forces killed in Ukraine since December, 2024 were Wagner's troops in Bakhmut. Wagner spent about $100 million a month in the fight.

On August 10, a threat was made by the owner of private Russian military company Wagner to withdraw his fighters from the battle to seize an eastern Ukrainian city is another flareup in his dispute with Russia's regular military over credit and tactics in the war. Almost no one except Yaroslav Kandybavych Melnykenko, Rokosylana Mykolaivna Udovychenko, Head of SBU, Gen. Olena Matveyeva Yuriivna, Lt. Col. Dmitriy Utkinov ("Wagner") Yevgeny and Col. Gen. Mizin-tsev, himself gave any credence to what sounded like just another idle threat.

On August 12, 2025, Col. Gen. Mizin-tsev and Lt. Col. Dmitriy Utkinov "Wagner" ("Wagner"), Yevgeny, announced the Wagner Group would no longer fight in Ukraine. The announcement came in a video release that morning as the entire Wagner force was trucked out of Ukraine along with all its war materiel and entered Russian territory midafternoon. In that video, Mizin-tsev said that Russian government justifications for the Russian invasion of Ukraine were based on lies. He accused the Russian Defense Ministry under the current minister of defense of "trying to deceive society and the president and tell us how there was crazy aggression from Ukraine and that they were planning to attack us with the whole of NATO."

CHAPTER 52

Rostov-on-Don, Rostov Oblast, Southern Federal District of Russia

August 25, 2025

The Wagner mercenaries disappeared from the news cycle, television, pod casts, and radio, for nearly ten days. US and Ukrainian intelligence agencies observed a gradual accumulation of Wagner forces near the Russian border along with evidence of them stockpiling equipment and resources in preparation for a conflict outside Donblast and probably not even in Ukraine. Although the SBU obtained information regarding the where and how of the planned rebellion, the exact timing remained unknown until the very day. The plan was through Western communications intercepts and satellite image analysis.

Several weeks prior to the actual event, US intelligence started foreseeing a significant Wagner insurrection and reporting it to President Bettern and the Joint Chiefs of Staff. They obtained solid evidence of the imminent rebellion before major changes were planned for a union of Wagner and the regular Russian army. The foreign intelligence findings indicated that the revolt was planned in advance, contradicting Mizin-tsev's and Yevgeny's claims that the decision to rebel was made only days before.

The New York Times learned and reported that Russian Army General Grigory Raputivitch had prior knowledge of the planned rebellion. Raputivitch had acted as an intermediary between Mizin-tsev and the military hierarchy. It was later reported that Raputivitch was found to have close ties Mizin-tsev's oil businesses. Raputivitch had a personal registration number with Wagner and held a covert VIP membership within the group, along with 30 other high-ranking Russian military and intelligence officials. Additionally, the US intelligence agencies and SBU discovered that several other generals lent their support to the uprising. Before the actual rebellion began, those intelligence officers had reported to their governments, that they were of the firm opinion that Mizin-tsev would not have instigated the rebellion unless he firmly held the belief that he had backing from specific sectors within the Russian power structure and with the professional military. Money came in from the American CIA to make the financial aspects comfortable.

Mizin-tsev and Yevgeny were both convinced that Rasputinov was ripe for a fall. They were also convinced that they were the men that the Russian public had been waiting for. The final piece of the revolution they were about to start was that they were going to operate with the full approval of the regular army. The generals would likely help; or, at the least, they would not interfere. Commander of the Russian National Guard Varco Zolobriski's spies informed him that the planned rebellion was getting under way and guessed at the time of its commencement to be less than a week away.

The security services knew about the plan and preparations for the uprising but did not have the nerve to tell the president that something was up with Wagner because if they reported the problem, decisions would have to be made. If they were wrong, heads would roll, and no security agent in Russia wanted it to be his. Even after Mizin-tsev and Yevgeny evaded the order to integrate Wagner into the regular military, security, and army officers who should have known better, and despite their forebodings, decided to ignore the growing evidence. Throughout the military community in Moscow, nerves were at a razor's edge.

Kremlin officials whispering among themselves about Mizin-tsev and Yevgeny came to the conclusion that Wagner's officers were daring opportunists who did not play by the rules. But when they contemplated the risks of an actual armed insurrection, they decided that the chances of it taking place any time soon was nil. They let themselves believe that Mizin-tsev's public announcement of an uprising was no more than a bluff intended to extract concessions. General Grigory Raputivitch and President Rasputinov slept through the situation thinking it would fizzle out on its own, even when it started to develop in real time.

The Wagner would-be revolutionaries reappeared on the eleventh day entering Rostov-on-Don from the north and east. Wagner's forces took control of Rostov-on-Don and the headquarters of the Southern Military District in the city with little force and no bloodshed. Under the watchful eyes of Western television videographers, an armored column of Wagner troops advanced through Voronezh Oblast toward Moscow.

Armed with mobile anti-aircraft systems, the rebels repelled the late and fairly desultory air attacks of the Russian military, whose actions did not deter the progress of the column. The real possibility of a coup was in the air all over the world. Ground defenses concentrated along the approach to Moscow. Moscow's internal protective barriers and security forces were being put into place; but were there too late or had too little armament to matter. At least thirteen servicemen of the Russian military were killed during the march into the outskirts of Moscow. The distance between Moscow and Rostov-on-Don is 596 miles. The journey takes approximately 15 hours by car at highway speed. The revolutionaries were averaging less than 25 miles-per-hour.

In the inner sanctums of the Kremlin, men began to wake up and to realize that what had been unthinkable–was not only thinkable–but was truly underway.

CHAPTER 53

The Senate Palace in the Kremlin

August 25, 2025, 11:06

The president was sitting at his desk in the yellow domed Senate Palace office—one of three identical offices spread around the Kremlin complex and two more on 8 Staraya Square and Ilyinka Street to disguise his location of the moment. Ironically, he was planning his "exit" as despot leader at the time. The dictator feared dying in office, and he was obsessed with planning for his succession if he died and of his security if he were still alive when he decided to retire. If possible, the Russian President did not want to die in office but was working to craft a cast iron guarantee that he would survive being out of power.

Rasputinov's Kremlin office is located in the center of the building's north wing. Unlike the US presidential office, the Kremlin office is a rectangular shape, and in contrast to the Oval Office, the windows are located on the left side of the president's table, not behind it. The table also differs in form from the one in the Oval Office: it has an elongated adjustment in front where Russia's president holds one-on-one meetings with other government officials. The walls of the Kremlin office are inlaid with oak panels, and the ceiling is decorated with an ornamental pattern and has two massive chandeliers.

On the impressive large white table, multiple phones comprise the secure communication system used by Russia's president.

On his "to do" list for the day, he was dealing with an army report showing diminishing supplies of all sizes of ammunition and the recurrent problem of his Russian tanks being destroyed. The economy and supply depots were being depleted so rapidly and to such depths that he was going to have to seek a new solution for supplying his war in Ukraine. He and his closest officers had been seeking ways to thwart opposition forces who could challenge the dictator; that was despite that grip on power is stronger than it had ever been, he was assured by his sycophants. Because of his paranoia, from 2021, Rasputinov's every political move resulted from trying to control the opposition or trying to wipe it out altogether.

The latest news about the upcoming elections raised his ire. There were videos of people standing up against the election with protests at polling stations. What bothered him the most was that they were described as being particularly brave because they knew the consequences for them personally would be dire. Other photos showed some citizens pouring dye into ballot boxes and others setting them on fire to express their anger with Rasputinov's authoritarian regime. He grumbled to himself that they were a minority of Russians.

There were also *Face Book* postings showing Russian football hooligans trying to overthrow Rasputinov before the country heads to the polls, Navalny's supporters [after the death of Alexei Navalny, Rasputinov's most prominent critic who was jailed on "extremism" charges having survived a poisoning in 2020] launching protests]. The last item on his schedule before he was rudely interrupted, was to inspect his plans for a new 974-mile railway line from Moscow to Crimea as part of his crucial backup plan.

His secretary burst into the room without knocking or announcing herself, something that was not done in Rasputinov's Kremlin.

"Mis.. Mister… General… uh President Rasputinov, an army is attacking Moscow. They have captured some eastern and northern suburbs!"

"What are you talking about, you stupid cow!?"

She started to cry and shrank toward the heavy office doors.

"What??"

"Sir," she said, working to collect herself, "The Wagner Group has invaded Moscow. There is an insurrection… like a revolution going on right now, Sir."

He turned ashen grey.

"Get General Rasputivitch in here… right now!" he screamed and added half a dozen unspeakable invectives.

The secretary scurried out of the room and made the calls. Ten minutes later, she reported back to the president.

"Sir, no one seems to know where General Rasputivitch is for the moment. They are looking for him and about twenty other generals over at the Defense Ministry. Nobody knows what is going on… Sir."

She hung her head and waited for the blow.

Rasputinov spoke quietly and clearly, the voice he used when he ordered executions of enemies, "Get whoever is in charge over there into this room in the next ten minutes or heads will roll. You can tell them that."

His voice was soft; but fire was coming out of his eyes; and his face mimicked the face of Stalin when he was angry, truly angry.

Lt. Col. Davyd Olegovitch Semenov entered the president's chambers nine minutes later looking flustered and red-faced. He was short of breath.

"Am I to understand that you are in charge of the military of the Russian Federation, Son?"

"I don't think so, Mr. President, but I was the only officer left in the ministry. I do not know where everyone else is."

"Are they out fighting the invaders?" Rasputinov snapped.

"I would suppose so, but I don't really know."

"Can you find someone who does know and bring him here. Stat?"

"I will do my best, Mr. President, but it will take time. I will have to go to the front to find a senior officer, I presume."

"You presume!? You presume!? I'll have your head, if you are not back here in half an hour. Is that clear enough?"

"Yes, Sir. It is clear."

He disappeared and was never seen again.

The quaking secretary knocked timidly on the presidential doors 45 minutes later.

"Enter."

"I have a report, Sir."

"You have a report? You?"

"The report, actually, Mr. President. I got this from people on the street."

"What has the world come to?" he muttered, mostly to himself.

"Shall I give the report?"

"Please do. I am thinking you should be awarded the Hero of the Federation medal, young lady. What is your name, by the way?"

She quavered but told him clearly enough… "Yelizaveta Siderov… Sergeant Yelizaveta Siderov."

"Out with it, then, Sergeant. This is unbelievable."

"Sir, the Wagner Group, an army of more than a 100,000 have breached the perimeter defenses of the outer ring road. Something like another 100,000 or more citizens from out there have joined them. They are moving very quickly toward the inner ring road as we speak."

"Casualties?"

"Very few, maybe twenty, maybe less."

He was stunned.

"Is there fighting? Is the army taking over?"

"Very little fighting. And apparently, the bulk of the army led by General Rasputivitch has gone over to the Wagner PMC already. An army officer I met told me that maybe half a million soldiers, sailors, coastguardsmen, Navalny's supporters, illegal immigrants, and security personnel, have surrendered and are carrying Wagner flags. I am sorry to report this, Mr. President."

"What about the city and oblast government?"

"I don't know. It is chaotic out there. The military and Wagner seem to be in charge, and civilian government is nowhere to be seen as far as I could tell. I'm sorry to report."

"Stop saying you're sorry, Yelizaveta. It is getting on my nerves. It is not your fault, but I will find out who is at fault, and they will regret the day they were born."

"Is that all you have to report, Yelizaveta?"

"No, Sir. There's more. I talked to some firemen and police officers who seemed to have a pretty good idea of what is going on. They told me that Tver Oblast in the northwest, Yaroslavl Oblast in the north, and Vladimir Oblast in the northeast and east, are under Wagner control, and the huge number of soldiers and civilian fighters are moving into the federal city of Moscow as we speak without much resistance. The navy seems to have gone over to Wagner and has blockaded the Volga, Oka, and Moskva, Rivers, and there does not seem to be any further resistance by the government or our military, Mr. President."

"You mean, towns, or suburbs, not whole oblasts, right, Yelizaveta? Like Balashikha, Khimki, Podolsk, Nakhabino, or Tomilino, or even Volokolamsk?"

"No, Sir. I double checked with different officials. It is whole oblasts. It appears that Col. Gen. Mikhail Mizin-tsev's prediction that the Russian people would join him once the insurrection started is coming true."

She hung her head, crestfallen.

"You were brave to be the one to give me bad news, Yelizaveta. I won't forget that. I am keeping a list, and you are going to be rewarded, mark my word."

His remaining faithful personal guards informed the president that it was unsafe for him to try to get to his home in Rublevka because the Rublevo-Uspenskoe Highway was under blockade by the Wagner PMC and several others. Looting was now rampant there, including his presidential mansion, Novo-Ogaryevo. The news was worse even than that: All his official residences, including a government-leased apartment in Moscow, Akademika Zelinskog Street, 6, the only residence that officially belongs to Rasputinov as a private individual. It is an 829 square foot apartment which is remarkably modest for Russia's president. There is a dacha known as Bocharov Ruchey in Sochi; Bocharov Ruchey is one of the official summer residences of Russia's president, and it is the only government dacha on the Black Sea; Valdai residence, aka Uzhyn, and Dolgie Borody, located in the Novgorod Region. Valdai was initially planned as one of Stalin's dachas, but he thought it to be too dangerous. In the 1930s, it was the only building on the small peninsula and was surrounded by dense forest, with only one escape route to the mainland.

Konstantin Palace in St. Petersburg is officially Rasputinov's–formerly owned by the Romanov family–is located on the Gulf of Finland, only 12.5 miles from the center of St. Petersburg. Initially planned by Peter the Great as an imperial residence that would eclipse Versailles in its glory. Grand Duke Konstantin Pavlovich of Russia resided here. Although Rasputinov does not actually live there, the palace is often used for official state events. The Konstantin Palace served as a venue for both the G-8 and G-20 summits in 2006 and 2013, respectively.

Yantar' is the presidential residence in Kaliningrad was built in the same place where the first Chancellor of the German Empire, Otto von Bismarck, had his palace. During WWII, the palace served as the Luftwaffe barracks. The current state residence was completed in 2011 and opened by then-President Dmitri Medvedev. Although the residence officially belongs to the Office of the President, it has only hosted Medvedev and Minister of Foreign Affairs Sergei Lavrov.

And there is an unknown apartment at an unknown location for unknown purposes; the use of that apartment is left to the imagination of the reader of this book and the imagination of the Russian people, which is vivid. All the presidential apartments and homes—with the exception of the unknown apartment–were undergoing the same wholesale ransacking. The long-suffering Russian population was going into a frenzy almost comparable to the Bolshevik Revolution. Law and order were breaking down at an alarming rate.

The Russian president's salary is, officially, the lowest among all top Kremlin officials. However, presidents are rarely worried about the amount they earn. The Russian president's salary changes constantly, figures indicate–unlike in the United States, where the president's salary has not changed for the last 15 years. Rasputinov–like what is said of Texas governors–must be very thrifty; despite only making ⊠306,000 rubles ($9,500) a month, he had become likely the richest man in the world having husbanded his salary remarkably well.

Russians do not pay much attention to the official salaries of Russian leaders. Whatever they are, millions of rubles go into the maintenance of dachas, guards, and servicing. Russian President Vladimir Rasputinov earned P 3,672,000 ($115,000) during his first year in office. The following year his earnings increased considerably, exceeding ₽640,000 rubles ($16,000) a month, and ₽7.7 million ($193,000) for the year.

However, as the ruble fluctuated sharply in spring 2015, President Rasputin-ov lowered his salary by 10 percent. His official and publicly known earnings in 2015 total-ed ₽ 8.9 million ($137,000), or around ₽, 740,000 ($11,500) a month. The Russian president's salary is effectively– at least, officially–the smallest among all top Kremlin officials. Apparently, he invested well. However, presidents are rarely worried about their salaries.

"Honestly speaking, I don't even know what my salary is. They deliver it to me, I take it, put it in my bank account and don't even count it," Rasputinov once said.

By the third day of the insurrection, the "Barbarians" were at the gates of the Kremlin. Approximately 20% of the Russian military remained committed to the "elected" president; another 20% deserted in Ukraine; and half of them joined the Ukrainian army. The remaining 60% joined the opposition forces and gathered with Lt. Col. Dmitriy Utkinov ("Wagner"), Yevgeny, and Col. Gen. Mikhail Mizin-tsev, the Wagner commanders.

The former head of the Russian army—General Rasputivitch–was living in Omdurman, Sudan, by then, along with 12 of his senior offi- cers. Navalny's team gathered with the soldiers encircling the Kremlin and urged all Russian voters to stage a Noon Against Rasputinov protest for the coming weekend, demonstrating outside polling stations to voice their anger at the Rasputinov regime.

The loyalists included the remaining regular army, the Russian president's personal security unit [Federal Guard Service of the Russian Federation], which is the best-staffed and best-trained team in the country. In the Russia of today, KGB functions are performed by the SVR [Foreign Intelligence Service], and the FSB [the Federal Counterintelligence Service which later became the Federal Security Service of the Russian Federation]. Every man and woman in the SVR and the FSB remained loyal and gathered in the Kremlin around the "great leader" as Rasputinov was regularly known.

The security team's IT engineers and technicians installed jammers to block any radio detonation signals to the president's location. The equipment maintained by the president's surveillance team pinged all smartphones and other devices in immediate proximity to the president's location to control any suspicious activity. According to Russian laws, the president's security has the right to install and use tapping hardware and software of any kind, conduct body searches, have access to any building and organization or seize any vehicle–if any of this is necessary for the security of the president. It was deemed necessary in this situation, along with the institution of martial law for the entire country.

CHAPTER 54

Author's Note

My wife has been the most reliable and truthful critic of my books while they were in manuscript form over the years. I respect her education, intelligence, and common sense. Having read the last few chapters above, she asked how I proposed to end the book. I put out an idea of somewhat reminiscent of Francisco Goya's *Los Caprichos* series which she did not like.

"Too grim and hopeless," she said.

She put out an idea more along the lines of, "It's a simple phrase that carries a ton of magic: *'Every day, in every way, I'm getting better and better,'*" a quote from the brilliant mind of Émile Coué, a French psychologist who believed in the mighty power of our thoughts.

"Too sweet and simple," I said.

After some debate, we compromised, as we usually do. Hence, the following will be two separate endings set out as Chapter 52 and 53, juxtaposed against Chapters 54, 55, and 56; and I will leave the choice to you how this war, insurrection, and political nightmare, ends.

Kharkiv, Northeastern Ukraine, at the confluence of the Uda, Lopan, and Kharkiv, rivers, twenty-five miles from the Russian border: August 31, 2025

The SBU commandoes made their way back into the Donblast region of Ukraine, a fraught trip that took five days of running, hiding, disguising, and seeking God's help as the chaos and mayhem of Russia's growing revolution proceeded all around them. It was not well-organized and had no definite leader, just several daring men who announced that they had been appointed by the people, the army, by the mothers of the dead soldiers, by local political chieftains, or just that they had appointed themselves to be the new Tsar/President.

Having been instrumental in opening Pandora's box, they wanted nothing more to do with the evils that escaped as a result of their activities. They bobbed and weaved, zig-zagged, and in a trip of stop-and-go, reversing directions from time-to-time, and probably a generous measure of dumb luck, they made it back to Ukraine territory intact.

It was an opportune time, US bombers, F-35s, and long-distance artillery arrived in Kyiv and were dispersed east to the embattled Donblast. At the same time, the Russian forces learned of the ongoing struggle for power in their Rodina and began to evacuate. The new US weaponry would have been daunting to behold for the Russian military even had the insurrection not started, but now it was a most insistent signal to pack up and leave. Yaroslav, Rokosylana, and the rest of the commandoes, found a comfortable hotel rooftop in Kharkiv and watched the evacuation with both fascination and high good humor.

Russian armored cars, tanks, artillery trucks, and as many cars and local trucks as they could find to steal, flooded the artery ways through the cities and countryside and clogged up to wait their turn to cross the border into Russia as fast as was humanly and machine-driven possible. 92,000 troops, more than 200,000 civilian collaborators, 2,000 tanks, and 10,000 assorted other vehicles clogged the de jure border crossings from north [Chernihiv-Bryansk; Sumy-Bryansk, Sumy-Kursk, Sumy-Belgorod, Kharkiv-Belgorod, Hoptivka-Nekhoteyevka, Kozacha Lopan-Dolbino, Odnorobivka, Golovchino, Oleksan-drivka-Bezymeno] to south [Luhansk Oblast, Zolote, near Zolote toward Pervomaisk and Donetsk Oblast: Mayorske, near the train station Mayorska, Horlivka, Maryinka, (along Highway H15), Pisky-Logachov, Pletenivka-Shebekino, Strilecha-Zhuravlyovka, Topoli-Valuiki, and Chuhunivka-Verigovka].

There was violence, even shooting, stampedes with people being trampled, and too many bar-room type brawls to count.

The Ukrainians simply sat on the sides of the roads, or in bars and cafes, or from elevated places to watch the highly vaunted Russian military convoys leave. Strangely enough, they knew to remain quiet. To cheer, clap, jeer, or gloat, could break the spell; and the despised Russians might turn around and come back.

It took four full days with eastward traffic moving along at a relative snail's pace for the last Russian to exit the country and to have the Ukrainian border guards close the gates behind them. More than a few of those guards secretly flipped them the bird as they moved out of sight.

From his panic room in the Kremlin, Rasputinov sent out series of vitriolic messages: to the Americans and Ukrainians, he threatened nuclear strikes; to the traitors in the military, he threatened execution; to the fickle Russian public, he threatened a "New Day" and a return to Stalin.

In the end, there was something of a de facto compromise. The protestors got tired and hungry and went home. The regular police quietly and peacefully brought about a reasonable semblance of law and order, and the military turned around and went back to their barracks. There was hardly a single Russian who wanted to see the country sink into the abyss that had followed the Bolshevik Revolution. They just hoped they had gotten their message across. In the end, the death rate was small, given the amount of hate and the number of people and institutions involved.

After the streets cleared, Rasputinov went on state radio and TV, to *Pravda, TASS Russian News Agency, News* (the Russian government official news), and Russia news outlet *Izvestia* to announce a great victory for Russia. In addition, they all announced the death of King Charles III (a falsehood). None of them mentioned the attempted coup and insurrection.

Besides the unanimity of dissenters among the entire Western press: *Meduza*–based in Riga, Latvia. [Most of its newsroom journalists moved there after resigning from Lenta.ru, when Chief Editor Galina Timchenko was fired "in what we believe was euphemistically referred to as an act of censorship"]. The *Meduza* team includes some of Russia's top professionals in news and reporting. *The Moscow Times* agreed with *Meduza*; and, in addition, published a six-column news page detailing the timeline of Rasputinov's War and the recent disturbances in the Russian Federation, calling them by correct terms: "Insurrection", "Attempted coup", and "Mutiny", as well as printing in detail the extent of the "defeat" of Rasputinov's military misadventure.

The dictator, still ensconced in the panic room, issued dismissals of the heads of the navy, coast guard, national guard, and six cabinet ministers, effective immediately. He waited a full month to rescind martial law. During his next week of doing Russia's business, he fired the heads of the FSB, GUSP, SVR, FSO, and the G.U. (formerly known as the GRU). Intra and interdepartmental chaos reined.

US President John D. Bettern, Speaker of the House, David Pierce Long, Senate Majority Leader Huey D. Duke, and the director of their political party, all called President Rasputinov to offer their congratulations, relying on delicate diplomacy to avoid speaking of Ukraine or insurrections. Among Rasputinov's other admirers calling to wish him well were Xi Jinping, President of the PCR, Viktor Orban, Prime Minister of Hungary, Brazil's Jair Bolsonaro, President of Brazil, Narendra Modi, President of India, Andrés Manuel López Obrador, President of Mexico, Rodrigo Duterte, President of the Philippines, and Recep Tayyip Erdogan, President of Turkey.

They all answered in the affirmative to an invitation to visit Moscow as his guests in the spring including the opportunity to be his personal guests at a state dinner held at Moscow's Swan Lake Novodevichy Monastery where Tchaikovsky composed the world's most popular ballet.

NATO responded quietly but immediately by accepting into its ranks the nations of Ukraine, Sweden, Finland, Herzegovina, Georgia, Kosovo, Austria, Cyprus, Ireland, Malta, Moldova, and Serbia. Rasputinov fumed; US President Bettern announced his disapproval; but NATO expanded exponentially anyway; and in private, the other members said to each other that Russia could just lump it. The expansion was a wise real-politik measure, which—along with Russia's defeat in the war it had provoked by an unconscionable invasion—would prevent or delay Vladimir Rasputinov's ability to attempt expansion into what would become World War III. His fuming and tantrums were roundly ignored even in his own country.

One year after the evacuation of Russian forces from Ukraine, three important but little heralded things happened. Col. Gen. Mikhail Mizintsev had been living and prospering in Ivory Coast, directing operations of a Wagner Diamond Consortium producing enough diamonds that DeBeers sought him out to join in a joint venture to control and limit sales of their surplus gemstones to inflate the market price. He received a cordial invitation to return to Mother Russia to lead the diamond industry's most successful enterprise, The Alrosa diamond mining companies group–a Russian consortium of diamond mining companies that specialize in exploration, mining, manufacture, and sale, of diamonds. The company leads the world in diamond mining by volume, and competes successfully with DeBeers for the competitive market. Of late it was suffering from internal competitive struggles that were resulting in loss of market share. Rasputinov called his old friend and asked him to return to Russia and help him set Alrosa back on the right track. He assured that all was forgiven.

As a good-will gesture, Rasputinov sent the newest Aeroflot Sukhoi Superjet and his personal pilot and crew to fly the Wagner chieftain and his guard unit to Moscow and to be greeted by the president himself when he landed in Sheremetyevo Alexander S. Pushkin International Airport, followed by what would amount to a state dinner at the Kremlin Palace.

Mizin-tsev heaved a private sigh of relief now that things were going to get back to normal. He and his retinue boarded the plane in Félix-Houphouët-Boigny International/ Port Bouët Airport and was greeted like visiting royalty. For reasons no one was able ever to determine, the plane crashed into the Atlantic Ocean after an unfortunate explosion at 33,000 feet. Pieces of wreckage were found floating in the crash site and enough tissue samples discovered to be certain that the great Wagner leader had perished in the crash. President Rasputinov declared a national day of mourning for the following Saturday.

The second event of note was a state visit to Russia by US President John D. Bettern, the Secretary of State, and the Secretary of Defense. Besides being feted as world grandees, and bosom friends, productive talks took place over a ten-day period. The agreement arrived at saw Rasputinov side for Russia that war reparations would be paid to Ukraine for the damage inflicted on the smaller country and the expenses of rebuilding.

He also agreed to open Russian oil pipeline use to Western European nations at competitive prices and to swear to a binding treat to enter into a ten-year period of nuclear arms reduction along with downsizing the naval and air force nuclear arsenals of both nations to a point that there could no longer be a "mutually assured destruction"–a doctrine of military strategy and national security policy which posits that a full-scale use of nuclear weapons by an attacker on a nuclear-armed defender with second-strike capabilities would result in the complete annihilation of both the attacker and the defender.

The US president, secretary of state, and secretary of defense, signed for the American side. By their signatures, they guaranteed that Russia would automatically become a trading partner with "most favored nation" status, and all sanctions against the Russian Federation would be withdrawn the day after the signing. The final agreement from the American side was that Russia would be allowed the rights to fishing off the New England coast as part of the Atlantic Cod Preservation Coalition, and to have mining rights to lithium discoveries along with the American Lithium Corporation in Nevada and with Rio Tinto in Boron, California.

The third event of importance to the world that year was September 30 marriage of Bettern's son Donald to Rasputinov's daughter Vanka Grace. The State Department considered the event to be so important to good will between the United States and the Russian Federation, that it chartered a Delta Airlines jet and arranged for it to be filled with invited guests. The Bettern family and all the guards, press, and intelligence agents necessary for such a gala even flew via Air Force One.

Because President Rasputinov was the leader of the Russian Orthodox Church, and because his daughter was obviously an important member, Donald Bettern had to convert to the Russian Orthodox religion. Because Rasputinov willed it to be so, Donald's conversion process was greatly simplified and more rapidly accomplished than the usual process.

The usual process takes upwards of a year. It involves a series of important steps:

1. To convert to Orthodoxy, Donald would need to find a parish, attend services regularly, meet with the priest for catechism classes, choose a patron saint, get baptized and/or chrismated if needed, and formally join the Church through the rites of initiation. Choosing an Orthodox Parish involves attending liturgy at different Orthodox churches to become acquainted with the music, chanting, icons, and overall atmosphere. A good rule of thumb is to visit three Orthodox parishes. It is also advised to attend during major feast days like Christmas, Holy Week, or *Pascha* [Orthodox Easter] when more elaborate services offer a deeper glimpse into traditional Orthodoxy worship.

2. Russian Orthodox parishes tend to have more developed choral singing and harmonization, and the OCA [Orthodox Church in America] parishes where Donald would be expected to worship blended pan-Orthodox traditions focused on English usage.

Next, one must meet with the priest where he will determine what renunciation of heresy or baptism procedures apply to someone with his religious background and agree on a timeline and plan for catechism classes. Donald will then learn about about Orthodox beliefs and practices: Attending church services regularly; learn about the faith–services follow a liturgical structure filled with rich symbolism and sacred rituals that have been passed down for centuries.

Next, Donald will be required to read thoroughly about Orthodoxy; participate in parish life and ministries; learn about the saints–the saints provide inspirational models of Orthodox life. Some important saints are St. Mary of Egypt, St. John Chrysostom, St. Seraphim of Sarov, and St. Herman of Alaska, and Donald will have to choose one of them for himself. He will be expected to talk to them in prayer and ask them to intercede for him.

He must go through formal catechism classes which educate the convert on Orthodox theology, liturgy, rituals, lifestyle, and responsibilities of being Orthodox. These classes typically last 6 months to a year and are led by a priest or appointed teacher. That education will be essential to learn the Orthodox view of salvation, the sacraments, veneration of saints, prayer, fasting, free will and sin. The classes study scripture and church history while explaining the significance behind various traditions.

The next step relates to baptism. With almost no religious background in the Bettern family, Donald had to be brought up to speed. Since he had not been baptized previously, he had to receive Orthodox baptism and to be officially received into the Orthodox Church through the Sacrament of Chrismation. In chrismation, one is anointed with holy oil [*myrrh*] as the priest makes the sign of the cross on parts of one's body. He also says prayers to "seal" the new convert with the gift of the Holy Spirit. Baptism will wash away all Donald's former sins, and chrismation gives guidance and grace to live an Orthodox life after he has been cleansed of impurity. He will then be welcomed into God's family and the Russian community.

Then, Donald–the new and very prominent convert will formally take a patron saint's name to go by. His patron will become his heavenly protector and role model for emulating a virtuous life. Donald was expected to take St. Olga as an activator of faith since he was formerly an atheist. Orthodox tradition says, "A church with no saints has no protection!"

Next comes reception of the Eucharist. After being received into the Church, new members then regularly partake of the Eucharist [Communion] during Divine Liturgy. This involves receiving consecrated bread and wine which Orthodoxy teaches becomes the actual Body and Blood of Jesus Christ. Partaking expresses unity with Christ and the Church and beginning his new spiritual journey as an Orthodox Christian.

May God bless you on this sacred journey, everyone said.

That describes the usual path. However, in this case the perspective convert, Donald Bettern had neither interest nor time to go through all of that, nor did his bride to be, his parents, or the Autocrat of Russia. Rasputinov had taken care of all the details well in advance.

Vladimir Mikhailovich Gundyayev [Kirill] was present to represent the church. He was a Russian Orthodox bishop who became Patriarch of Moscow and all Rus' and Primate of the Russian Orthodox Church. More importantly he was a longtime friend of Vladimir Rasputinov. Both were born in Leningrad. Kirill was a close ally of and described Rasputinov's rule as "a miracle of God". Kirill's father had baptized Rasputinov.

CHAPTER 55

Grand Kremlin Palace, Moscow Red Square/*Krasnaya Ploshchad*, Russian Federation

September 30, 2025

Most of the people of the earth called it the "marriage of the century", and it became the largest tourist attraction in Russia in its entire history. The bride and groom [Vanka Grace Rasputinov and Donald Bettern] were left to a period of contemplation in the Cathedral of Christ the Savior as the rest of their families and new political friends began to gather in the Vladimirsky reception hall for the invitation-only wedding. The fortunate people to be invited were carefully balanced on the Russian family side and the American family side. The Russians included Rasputinov's family and personal friends (a few persons); the general staff of the army, navy, air force, and space force; the diplomatic corps from all of the major Western countries and the former satellite countries as well as select Middle East nations, including even Israel, and the metropolitans of the Russian Orthodox Church from Moscow and St. Petersburg.

The American side included the extensive nuclear and extended Bettern family, a retinue of American Republican dignitaries from both congressional houses, the joint chiefs of staff and their deputy chiefs;

and 25 of the 40 Republican governors. Like the Russian side, the US diplomatic corps was strongly represented. Executives and news anchors from the favorite conservative outlets, and leading members of President Bettern's militias [The Three Percenters, The Oath Keepers, Proud Boys, Texas Freedom Force].

The religious representation included: the Episcopal Bishop of the Washington National Cathedral [the Bishop of Washington, Marie Johnson-Heddington], the presiding bishop of the Episcopal Church, William Edgar Patergivins, and Dean of the Washington Cathedral, Randolph Derek Harding.

As an important diplomatic gesture, the American side included primate Metropolitan Theodosius of the OCA [Orthodox Church in America, officially, The Auto-cephalous Orthodox Church in America] which is recognized by the Russian, Bulgarian, Georgian, Polish, Serbian, Czech, and Slovak, churches.

By the time the ceremony was over, the crowd gathered in the 800,000 square feet of Kremlin Square numbered more than four hundred thousand people, one of the largest crowds in Red Square's history. President Bettern hailed it as a demonstration of the popularity of the two presidents' administrations.

The wedding itself consisted of two separate ceremonies: first they were married in a civil ceremony in the Moscow city hall with only the parents of the bride and groom present as witnesses. Then, they were driven in a limousine motorcade to the *Bolshoy Kremlyovskiy dvorets* [Grand Kremlin Palace] in Red Square. The Palace has five recep-tion halls: Georgievsky, Vladimirsky, Aleksandrovsky, Andreyevsky, and Ekaterininsky. As of 2024, the Grand Kremlin Palace served as the offi-cial working residence of the president of Russia; it also houses a museum. International treaties are signed at the Vladimirsky Hall; so, it was chosen as the hall for the performance of the "wedding of the century".

The first part of the ceremony was rather frivolous, but the marital couple—her in and elegant white wedding dress and bridal veil and the groom will wear a custom-made tuxedo–insisted on it because it was fun, unlike the rest of the stuffy religious ceremony. In Russia, there has been a long tradition of the groom "kidnapping" the bride and holding her for "ransom", a process that takes several days during which the groom must complete a series of tasks meant to show his love and to embarrass him.

In this great "marriage of the century" the powers-that-be truncated the frivolity and skipped to the end of the tradition. Donald had to pay the ransom, which consisted of a bottle of Moët & Chandon champagne and a box of To'ak Chocolates.

Moscow Patriarch Kirill presided over the religious ceremony which was divided into two parts: the betrothal and the crowning services. The Betrothal Service consisted of the couple becoming officially engaged to one another and their wedding rings were blessed by the patriarch. They received lit candles that they held for the remainder of the ceremony, symbolizing the light of God in their lives and their willingness to accept Him. Part of the ceremony included several long and solemn prayers and scripture readings, of which Donald and his parents understood not a word.

The second half of the wedding ceremony was the crowning, where the couple officially becomes married. They stood on a piece of rose-colored cloth, symbolizing their entry into a new life. Kirill placed a crown on each of their heads, denoting that they will be the king and queen of their own kingdom. Traditionally, these crowns used to be worn for eight days following the wedding, but Donald and Vanka had agreed during their privacy in the Cathedral of Christ the Savior, that as soon as they were out of sight, they would ditch the crowns.

The couple took sips of wine from a shared common cup, and then followed Kirill around the lectern three times, which symbolized their anticipated journey into married life. They then each smashed crystal glasses given to them by their parents. The more pieces or shards they created, the greater the number of happy years they were to spend together.

That completed the religious ceremonial marriage ceremony, but the new Mr. and Mrs. Bettern and the witnesses and spectators in Vladimirsky Hall, had the opportunity to hear and to witness several quite lengthy toasts.

Guests randomly yelled out "*gorko!*" [translation: "bitter"] with the implication that the drinks they are drinking are bitter, but the kiss of the day will dissipate the bitterness. The longer the kiss, the stronger the marriage. Donald and Vanka performed that part of the ceremony with genuine and lengthy zest. The guests had to finish their drinks by the time the kiss ended.

The wedding was a success; it put an exclamation point on the remarkable rapprochement between the two countries. The diplomacy—after the dreadful war—was uplifting; and the witnesses all over the world were ecstatic, with the possible exception of Ukrainians who were going about the slow painful process of burying their dead and rebuilding the infrastructure and living quarters of their country.

Although Rasputinov was unable to complete his dreams of hegemony, he was able to achieve several lucrative real estate contracts with Bettern Construction. President Bettern felt much the same way, and the world was a happier place for the oligarchs and billionaires involved.

—THE END—

CHAPTER 56

Republican caucus meeting, Russell Senate Office Building, 2 Constitution Ave NE, Washington, DC

October 22, 2025

The United States Congress, House of Representatives was made up of 218 Republicans to 213 Democrats. More accurately, that part of the legislative chamber of Congress, was—for practical purposes—driven by eight, ultraright, fully committed, representatives who held Ukraine's fate firmly in their grasp. They were the most extreme members of the House Freedom Caucus–a total troupe of about 50 far-right Republicans in the House out of 222 Republicans in the chamber—amounting to 22% of the entire House GOP conference. They operated under the aegis of the would-be dictator of their party, President John D. Bettern.

The Republicans already had control of the presidency and the Senate. When Republicans took control of the House the previous year with almost the thinnest of majorities, all eyes turned to the House Freedom Caucus. The loose group of ultraconservative lawmakers outnumbered the narrow vote margin for Republicans and, as a result, were granted new outsized leverage over leadership to cater to their whims. The eight most extreme ultrarightist members of that caucus—which was already an unprecedently low number of controlling members— became basically the most effective hunting ground and victory achievers in the entire history of the House.

They immediately began getting some shocking legislation passed—at least shocking to the Democrats, Liberals, and mainstream Republicans, described as "rinos" by the eight. [That is an acronym for Republicans In Name Only]. Examples included the right to engage in duels by House members; preventing the House from green-lighting a floor vote on the government budget, leverage a government shutdown to extract hard-right conservative policy victories; withdrew the United States from NATO; achieved votes enough to tank procedural rule votes on the House floor; successfully obtained a vote opposing immigration reform and the repeal of the Affordable Care Act; succeeded in caucus to oust two speakers of the House in a row until they got one of their own voted into the position by the exhausted remainder of their caucus and the mainstream "rinos" to go along to get along in order to get at least something done that year.

A rino Republican from Montana said publicly, "It's really hard for me to listen to people that are complaining that the train's not on time when (they) were the people ... blowing up the tracks all the way. Now we're at the station here; so don't complain the train's not on time."

They had been likened by fellow Republicans to "lemmings with suicide vests", "legislative terrorists" and the Taliban. When they formed a voting bloc in 2015, they actually considered naming themselves the "Reasonable Nut Job Caucus" or "Members of the Unabashed Agents of Chaos". The Freedom Caucus vice chair said that during the Bettern administration, the Freedom Caucus shifted focus from passing legislation to defending the president. The House Freedom Caucus does not disclose the names of its members and membership is by invitation only. *The New York Times* wrote that the caucus usually meets "in the basement of a local pub rather than at the Capitol."

Representative Able R. Hassle of Texas put forth two Freedom Caucus originated bills: one to rename the House Freedom Caucus to the USA Victory Freedom Caucus, and another to declare war on Mexico for its failures to stem the tides of illegal immigrants and criminals [a redundancy]. He perceived that his righteous efforts were likely to be thwarted, he shouted; he waved his arms and pointed his fingers for emphasis—rather like the old-time tent revivalists–as the other senators sat flipping through papers, waiting for the session to begin. They were finally too tired, too bored, and too desirous of getting home to their families, to come to a vote on Ukraine.

Out of necessity, Hassle seized on a chance to hijack the planned schedule. Hassle spoke for about 45 minutes, accusing the leaders of his own Republican Party of ignoring some bills and making things "really frustrating" for ultra-conservative members. When that failed to carry, and the remaining members were on the brink of doing the unthinkable—i.e. going bipartisan—to join the Democrats in saving the nation and preventing Ukraine from twisting in the wind on the way to defeat at the hands of the Russians, the representative of the Great State threatened to filibuster by reading aloud from a 2-foot stack of books–including a biblical guide to leadership and a tome by anti-tax activist Grover Norquist–to protest any Ukrainian legislative decision during that last week of the Congress until it reconvened next year.

The ultrarightists succeeded in shutting down the government and convincing their base to believe it was in their best interest, left Ukraine to the mercies of the Russians who–by then were being supported by the Communist Chinese, the theocratic Iranians, the dictatorial Syrians, the Indians and their Hindu oligarchy, and North Korea and its nukes. They succeeded beyond their dreams in achieving their ultrarightist and populist aristocratic ambitions.

There was considerable cheering among almost half of Americans at the realization that no more of their hard-earned and taxed money was going to be wasted for such frivolous expenditures like Ukraine and the Israel/Hamas war in the middle-east. After all, neither was any of their business; and it was not their fight.

In Ukraine, the news of the American ultrarightists' decision left them in despair. They had been winning the previous year, and now they were going to have to come up with a battle plan based on retreat, and a series of capitulations. That started in Kharkiv with the knowledge that—after their defeat in Avdiivka—which, if kept, and the American

UK, and EU resuppling ammunition, would have been the doorway to retaking Donetsk.

The General Staff laid out plans for the retreat and opened the door to begin negotiations with Rasputinov's government.

CHAPTER 57

Kyiv, Ukraine

March 28, 2026

CNN reported the news of the US Congress narrowly avoiding the feared shut down of the American government with all its accompanying domino affects for the world's economies. The government and military authorities of Ukraine scarcely paid attention to the news headline: their attention was fixated on the issue of whether or not the United States would at long last send funding and ammunition to Ukraine to save it from the specter of loss to the Russian juggernaut currently advancing miles at a time against the Ukraine front lines that were regularly being abandoned for lack of arms replacement.

Almost as an afterthought, the news anchor mentioned that funding for Ukraine was not even mentioned in Congress's released news report. One of the eight superconservatives who had engineered the final comprise among the Republicans added a brief comment.

"Today we have achieved a milestone in government. The people's money will not be wasted on these foreign wars. The subject will not be considered again by this Congress. President Bettern plans to call Russian president Vladimir Rasputinov to give him the good news, and then will call Ukraine Volodymyr Zelenskyy to inform him that America will no longer support his war of aggression. One more item—as of this morning— the House Freedom Caucus has set in motion ouster procedures against the current Speaker of the House. That will include impeachment measures as well. The caucus will work diligently to put forward the name of Rep. Cletus Bakford Lee of the great state of Alabama—a true patriot, and a true friend and supporter of our great President Bettern—as the patriotic next speaker."

He did not accept questions from the press.

SBU Gen. Olena Yuriivna left the president's office immediately after the representative's statement and hurried to her office to inform her subordinates, especially the commandoes and generals in the field.

Her coded and scrambled message did not allow for a reply:

"My fellow Ukrainians, comrades in arms, we have received catastrophic news this morning. US news outlets announced that there will be no funding for Ukraine for at least a year, and probably ever. The American president and good friend President Rasputinov have been in contact; so, we can expect an all-out frontal attack from the AFRF [Armed Forces of the Russian Federation]. The general staff and SBU have been informed by reliable sources that the recruitment and conscription activities have been increasing for two months, apparently acting on information from the "American Patriots" and their commander-in chief.

"Any day now, expect to encounter RFAF [Russian Federation Air Force] attacks like never before. That may even include ADF [Aerospace Defense Forces], and RSF [Russian Space Forces]. There will be simultaneous attacks by RNF [Russian Naval Forces] including the BSF [Black Sea Fleet], NSF [Naval Surface Forces], NPS [Nuclear Powered Submarines], RFN [Russian Federation Navy], NF [Northern Fleet], RBSF [Russian Black Sea Forces], and even PF [Pacific Fleet] They will begin tomorrow morning with coordinated RAF [Russian Air Force], FBS [Federal Border Service]], RAF [Reaction Alert Forces], GTS [Guards Tank Corps], RIS [Russian Intelligence Services], FIS [Foreign Intelligence Service], IT [Internal Troops] ATM [Anti-tank Missile forces], BTG [Battalion Tactical Groups], JSC [Joint Strategic Command].

"Mark my words, Rasputinov will pull out all the stops, even if it threatens the homeland. He is sending in MVD [*Ministerstvo Vnutrennikh Del*/Ministry of Russian Police], RIS [Russian Intelligence Services MR [Motor Rifle], new recruits as of yesterday from schools, sports teams, and even prisons. More MIGs [Little green men–masked soldiers of the Russian Federation who carry weapons and equipment, but wear unmarked green army uniforms], RAT [Russian Airborne Troops, also Frontline rat extermination forces]. In addition he will pit us against RSF [Rapid Support Forces], RSRFSBCM [*Riyadus-Salikhin* Reconnaissance and Sabotage Battalion of Chechen Martyrs], FIS [Foreign Intelligence Service], and GRFU [*Glavnoe Razvedyvatel'noe Upravlenie*/ Government Foreign Intelligence Service] famous for their medieval cruelty.

"They have beefed up their inventory of weaponry with help from Syria, North Korea, Iran, India, Belarus, Chechnya, and China. You are going to be hit with MRLS [Multiple Rocket Launcher Systems], missiles and rockets from MIGs, Sukhoi Su-27, 30, 34, and 35s, RS-28 Sarmats [SS-X-30, TR-1], Temp theater ballistic missiles [SS-12 /SS-22 Scaleboard], UR-100 intercontinental ballistic missiles [SS-11 Sego], UR-100N intercontinental ballistic missiles [SS-19 Stiletto], UR-200 intercontinental ballistic missil-es[SS-X-10 Scrag], and Yakhonts [ruby].

"I want to speak to you both as your commander, but also as a fellow Ukrainian, mother with sons, and a person dedicated to the survival of our free country. I am, however, dedicated more to your welfare. You are the future of the nation, and your deaths or critical injuries will not contribute to that. Therefore, I issue the following orders: hold the battle lines as long as you can, and then move on. You do not have to be a hero and die for your country. If all is lost, I will personally tell you, and there will be no dishonor attached to your getting away from the front, even from the country. Those of you who do survive long enough to leave, go to the UK, and establish a government and community in exile. Elect new leaders who will keep the Ukraine spirit alive.

"*Нехай Бог благословить і збереже вас, мої дорогі молоді/ nechai bog blagoslovite i zbereze vas, moi dorogi molodi]* God bless and keep you, my dear young people." Gen. Olena Yuriivna

It proved to be the last communique ever sent by Gen. Olena Yuriivna.

The following morning–beginning at the Russian witching hour of 04:00 on the morning of March 28, 2026–in the midst of a vast massing of Russian military forces on the borders of Ukraine and the global community scrambling diploma-tically to avert a new invasion, a two-pronged cyberat-tack suddenly crippled thous-ands of Ukrainian websites, injecting malware and leaving a taunting message to "be afraid and wait for the worst."

The people of Ukraine, and especially those on the front lines did not have to wait long. As soon as the cyber attack ceased, a three-prong attack commenced from the land, sea, and air, like nothing the Ukrainians had ever before seen or endured. In fact, it was the largest military attack in the world's history save the atomic bomb explosion in Hiroshima, Japan on August 6, 1945. The explosion immediately killed an estimated 80,000 people; tens of thousands more died later die of radiation exposure. The bomb, nicknamed "Little Boy," had an explosive force equivalent to approximately 13 kilotons of dynamite. It leveled five square miles of the city.

More than 100,000 Ukrainians were killed and another 200,000 were wounded before March 28 was done. An artillery fusillade came at the trenches and cities around Ukraine at first light and continued for three full days. A concentrated Naval bombardment came at exactly 0600 from the Black Sea, the Straits of Crimea and Feodesia, from secret Russian trawler ships/military fast boats from the Sea of Azov, the lagoons, estuaries, and canals of Ukraine, and from secreted Russian ships harbored in the Dniester, Dnieper, and Donest Rivers. The results were both catastrophic and stupefying.

Two million Russian combatants crossed the Ukrainian borders, left their trenches to attack in a well-coordinated battle plan, along with scores of Separatists from the two Donblast Republics presenting them-selves fully armed from a secret cache of weapons hidden for a year.

The aerial bombardments were a dozen raids on Dresden all at once and all day long. There was not the slightest effort to protect innocent civilians, hospitals, schools, historical sites, or crucial civilian infrastruc-ture. The survivors reeled in anguish, bewilderment, and raw fear. Most of their fears were realized in minutes, hours, or half a day, as the raids continued relentlessly and without pity.

With the greatest of reluctance, the entire Ukraine government fled the country with the aid of the Polish air force. Americans could not overcome the political opposition to get any of its planes in the air in time enough to do any good. The governments around the UK received the terrified and shell-shocked survivors with open arms and hearts. By the time Russian ground troops entered Kyiv, the bombed-out nation's capital, there were only a few hundred people left, mostly old, disabled, or those unwilling to evacuate their homes for any reasons, a decision they would come to regret severely when the Russians finished their work.

Yaroslav and his SBU commandoes sustained a 50% casualty rate—16 KIA, and ten severely WIA before they could evacuate with any hope of survival. They drove their trucks and automobiles until they ran out of fuel and had to walk the rest of the way. The going was very difficult owing to a multitude of factors: no water or chance to replenish food supplies, a bomb cratered landscape where the footing was never level, and often hazardous, and the loads they were carrying became too great to bear after less than twenty miles of the hike. The most difficult loads came from the effort to carry out their wounded. It soon became too much, and Yaroslav had to make the gut-wrenching decision to leave the wounded behind, knowing that it meant certain death, perhaps a long course made worse by Russian and Cossack torturers.

They kept on, day and night, until they were able to cross the Dnieper River from East to West to the relative safety of Ukrainian territory. Their life had been a daily travelogue of retreat, destruction, and death.

They were all too starved, dehydrated, exhausted, and enfeebled by their wounds, to make any decisions that night. They simply sunk to the ground and fell into a deep and dreamless sleep. Yaroslav and Rokosylana cuddled together for warmth, and thanked God for that one favor.

Events in Ukraine proceeded with alarming speed. The commandoes did not have time to starve to death. All but five of them died when 300 Russian paratroopers had the misfortune to land in their midst as they slept. Although the SBU commando unit was effectively wiped out, they helped some two dozen enemy combatants to join them in the Afterworld.

Yaroslav protected Rokosylana with his body, sustaining several superficial bullet wounds.

As they ran for cover, Rokosylana facetiously said, "My brave hero. What a man!"

Yaroslav said, "It was nothing; I would have done the same for anyone."

She stuck her tongue out at him with toothsome smile.

"I love you," she said.

"Me, too, Rokosylana. Let me tell you this; if we ever get of here, you are going to marry me first thing."

She said, "Yaroslav, I take that as a proposal. And the answer is yes."

The two young lovers had their first real kiss, and the deal was sealed.

They awakened from a cold and fitful sleep before first light and hurriedly packed up what they could carry in double back packs for each of them. They were in unfamiliar territory; so, they decided to head west. After ten miles, and the sun was out; they were sweating and felt like they were dying of thirst, they came to a small pond that looked to be clear and clean. They drank to capacity and filled their canteens to the brim.

Yaroslav asked, "Rokosylana, what do you think became of the rest of the commandoes?"

"I didn't want to think about it, but I don't think any of them made it. No food, water, or ammo, and the Russkies on their tails; I hate to say it, but I doubt that any of them made it through the day. "

He nodded in sad agreement.

In fact, none of the other commandoes lasted even two hours. They fought to the end with bare fists against rifles with bayonets, grenades, and machine guns. They did not have a chance. The same could be said for most of the Ukrainian soldiers on the front lines. At the end of the second day, there were no longer any lines, not just ephemeral front lines. It was a headlong grossly uneven chase which was rapidly becoming a slaughter—sticks and rocks against bullets and bombs all the way to Kyiv.

Kyiv was a makeshift fortress constructed ad hoc out of rubble. Survivors manned the walls in ten-hour shifts, avoiding firing away any unnecessary shots and wasting precious ammunition. Others who had no firearms scrounged about the enclosure to find sources of water and food. After two weeks, they were reduced to boiling toilet water and eating dogs, then cats, then rats, and finally in the last extremis they were reduced to boiling belts, straps, saddles, and any other leather they could find.

But they held on, frustrating the Russians besieging them into making near suicidal frontal attacks. To a degree, life went on. Schools remained open in small, out-of-the-way rubble enclosures; funerals were a daily experience; and the people were becoming numb to the meaning of death, it was so commonplace. Marriages still took place, including that of Yaroslav and Rokosylana. They were married by the last remaining Ukraine Orthodox priest. He was killed in a bombing raid soon afterwards. Babies were born, but the majority of women refused to get pregnant because they could not bear the thought of bringing a child into such a world.

Days dragged into weeks and then months, and the indomitable Ukrainians held on. It drove Russian President Rasputinov mad to receive daily reports that the plucky Kyivians were still holding on and preventing him from carrying out the great Russian plan that had started with the mind of Peter the Great.

On the day Rasputinov learned that a unit of Ukraine SBU commandoes sneaked out of the city and destroyed one of his vaunted tank units and returned to the city with truckloads of food and bottled water, he went berserk.

He screamed orders to the general in charge of the federation's nuclear war strategy and implementation:

"The accursed Ukrainians have committed aggression against the Russian Federation with the use of conventional weapons and the very existence of our state is in jeopardy. We have always planned to rely on first use of nuclear weapons surrounding a potential low-yield "escalate-to-deescalate" policy. This is the time. Remove what is left of Kyiv today or I will have your head."

General Ustinov hesitated, then stammered out an objection, "It is the very definition of lunacy Mr. President. Once unleashed we can never recall the nuclear war that will result. We look like clowns threatening to use nuclear weapons in response to a child's drone, let alone actually using a tactical field nuclear weapon. I refuse to obey such and ill- conceived and illegal order… Sir!"

General Ustinov was executed by firing squad an hour later.

Rasputinov called in Ustinov's second in command, Col. Gen. Peter Rachlarov Comminsky and gave him clear, concise orders in his most icy voice, the voice all his underlings understood to be Rasputinov's final and not-to-be-challenged utterance.

Rasputinov explained, Of the stockpiled warheads, approximately 1,710 strategic warheads are deployed: 870 on land-based ballistic missiles; 640 on submarine-launched ballistic missiles; and 200 at heavy bomber bases. Another 1,112 strategic warheads are in storage, along with 1,558 nonstrategic warheads. In addition to the military stockpile for operational forces, a large number—approximately 1,200—of retired–but still largely intact warheads–await dismantlement, for a total inventory of approximately 5,580 warheads.

"Am I clear so far."

"Perfectly, Sir."

"We will follow Russian law today, and you will implement it. Russia's official deterrence policy drafted in 2020 by my executive order described the explicit conditions under which it would launch nuclear weapons. They are as follows: The arrival of reliable data on a launch of ballistic missiles attacking the territory of the Russian Federation and/or its allies; the use of nuclear weapons or other types of weapons of mass destruction by an adversary against the Russian Federation and/or its allies; the attack by an adversary against critical governmental or military sites of the Russian Federation, disruption of which would undermine nuclear forces response actions; and the aggression against the Russian Federation with the use of conventional weapons when the very existence of the state is in jeopardy.

"That is the reason you will use tactical nuclear weapons against the city of Kyiv today and eradicate it from the face of the earth. Do you understand my order"

"I do."

"Will you carry it out and become a full general, or will you join the coward and traitor, Ustinov?"

"I will obey, Sir."

Many in the United States and in the Russian federation dated the beginning of the Third World War to that day.

CHAPTER 58

Kyiv, Ukraine

March 31, 2026, another day that will live in infamy

The first nuclear device, a 200 ton gravity bomb, dropped on ancient Upper Town, Kyiv, on the cathedral of St. Sophia built in the 11th century, one of the finest and most beautiful examples of early Rus-Byzantine ecclesiastical architecture remain-ing in the world at the time.

Kyiv was founded in 480 CE on the west bank of the Dnieper (Dnipro) River. Intentionally–and to serve as a warning message for the remaining Ukraine fighters—that original location was the precise target site. It was on the high and steep right (western) bank, which rises above the river in an imposing line of bluffs culminating in Batyyeva Hill, 330 feet above river level. The precipitous and wooded bank–topped by the golden domes and spires of churches and bell towers and by high-rise apartment buildings—was at the time among the most beautiful parts of any city in the Eastern world. The city limits enclose an area of 300 square miles, more than half of that evaporated into dust.

President Vladimir Rasputinov called his counterparts—US President John D. Bettern, Chinese President Xi Jinping, North Korean "Dear Leader" Kim Jung Un, UK Prime Minister Rishi Sunak,

French President Emmanuel Jean-Michel Frédéric Macron, German Chancellor Olaf Scholz, Federal president of the Republic of Austria Alexander Van der Bellen, and Canadian Prime Minister Justin Trudeau, to inform them of his having been forced to take drastic action to save his beleaguered country. None of the conversations lasted more than a minute.

The second tactical nuclear bomb struck in the already very damaged industrial section of Kyiv City pulverizing thousands of homes, several hundred industrial facilities, playgrounds, schools, mosques, synagogues, and churches, as well as the main transportation arteries and railways. Of Kyiv's 14 *raions* [districts], eight were completely destroyed. The districts involved in the massive destruction involved the Dniprovskyi, Darnytskyi, Holosiivskyi, Pecherskyi, Obolonskyi, Podilskyi, Shevchdnkivskyi, and Solomaianskyi.

Then, a most unfortunate accident occurred, the final tactical nuclear device went off course and landed in Warsaw, Poland, 484 miles to the west of Kyiv. The damage to Warsaw was horrific, but the repercussions were beyond the imaginations of everyone involved or even uninvolved spectators.

All three US divisions of government, the Security Council of the United Nations, the North Atlantic Council of NATO, National Peoples' Congress of China, Parliament of the United Kingdom, the Council of Ministers of France met in the Élysée Palace in Paris, the Council of the Balkan Federation, the President of the European Council of the EU, the executive council and parliament of Canada, and the Apparatus of the Government of Russia, the president and both prime ministers, and the Russian Security Council, and all of the organizations' senior military commanders, met hastily in emergency sessions.

Only the decisions—translated into action—of two nations mattered in the end: the United States and the Russian Federation.

The meeting in the US took place in the $50 million ultra secure Situation Room.

"Ladies and gentlemen, my fellow Americans, a most dreadful mistake has been made by the Russian Federation, and I underscore the word, "mistake". A nuclear bomb accidentally fell on the capital of a NATO ally with all the destruction and loss of life that one might imagine. I have been assured by President Rasputinov that it was not at all intentional, and the Russian Federation will compensate Poland for its losses. I, for one, take the Russian leader at his word. Despite the NATO treaty—a US law that I wish had never been enacted, and I have been making plans to withdraw from—I do not recommend that the US engage in military action, even if other NATO nations begin what will be World War III.

"In the Cold War, the Soviet Union maintained a "no first use" policy, in which Moscow vowed that it would only use nuclear weapons in response to a nuclear attack. Most analysts doubted the credibility of this pledge, but it was nevertheless reflected in official doctrine. As President of the United States, I elect to believe what my Russian counterpart—an honorable man—promises. Therefore, today, I ordered our military and intelligence organizations to stand down. I am sure that my friendship with President Rasputinov will allow us together to draw back from the brink of thermonuclear war. It is my prayer that our Protestant God will save us and our beloved country from the possibilities of this unfortunate accident. We will not fire the first ICBM; but, if we must, we will fire the last one."

The emergency meeting of the government and military generals in Moscow was similarly chaired by its president. The gist of his comments was contained in his introduction:

"My comrades, fellow Russians, and friends. We have–of necessity–used minor tactical nuclear weapons against the provocations of the renegade Ukrainians. And, here, I take full responsibility as commander-in-chief of all the Russian military forces for an accident that occurred during that phase of the Ukrainian War. One of the small tactical bombs went off course and struck Warsaw with some destruction. I do not need to tell you that Poland is a member of NATO and by their charter, they are bound by treaty to come to the military aid of their fellow nation. It was a most foolish treaty, and its creation can be linked by historians to the start of the dreadful hostilities that may entail.

"My friend, President Bettern, and I have discussed the matter at length and may be able to defuse the hot-headedness of his government and NATO's members before things get out of control. I pray God will answer our fervent prayers and intervene on our behalf.

"If that does not happen, I will have no choice other than to take first response action."

President Rasputinov went directly to his office and took advantage his ace-up-his-sleeve PNI [Presidential Nuclear Initiative], the right to conduct thermonuclear war. He wasted no time, put his nation's nuclear forces on high alert. After a few moments of thought, he concluded that if he did not act, the fool Americans would launch a preemptive strike. Knowing that, Rasputinov put the chain of command for nuclear attack into emergency operation. A small briefcase–known as the *Cheget*–is kept close to the president at all times, linking him to the command-and-control network of Russia's strategic nuclear forces. Although the Cheget does not contain a nuclear launch button, it does transmit launch orders to the central military command–the General Staff.

In simple fact, the Russian president alone makes the decision to use nuclear weapons. Immediately after launching Cheget, he abandoned the Outer Space Treaty not to field nuclear weapons from space–an echo of its treatment of the Intermediate-range Nuclear Forces Treaty, Open Skies Treaty, and New START. He knew that abandoning the act would further signal the end of the era of legally binding arms-limiting treaties between the United States and Russia. It did not matter a whit to him; Rasputinov was irreversibly committed to the end struggle with the evil United States. He saw it as limited coercive nuclear use by Russia early in a major-power war and not the end of the world as his hysterical enemies in the West so ridiculously feared.

Once the Cheget directive was received, the Russian General Staff had access to the launch codes and had two methods of launching nuclear warheads. It could send authorization codes to individual weapons commanders, who would then execute the launch procedures. There is also a back-up system, known as *Perimetr*, which allowed the General Staff to initiate the launch of land-based missiles directly, bypassing all the immediate command posts. Commander-in-Chief of the General Staff of the Russian Federation, Army General Oleksiy Igor Neizhpapa chose the bypass.

ICBMs from all over Russia sprang from the ground and shot into the sky belching fire. They were directed at key US cities and military targets. Once launched, they could not be turned back or destroyed by Russian technicians. A Russian ICBM–after a fast boost-phase launch–takes 20 minutes to travel through space during the mid-course phase. No other nation–other than Russia–is likely to have a force with the number and accuracy of nuclear weapons needed to threaten US silo-based ICBMs.

Within seconds of the Russian nuclear armed ICBMs showing their fiery tails, Red lights began flashing in rapid succession, space-based infrared sensors having detected several heat signatures, and the president received a score of calls. Those calls created a series of very rapid successive responses. President Bettern worked at over coming his sense of shock and betrayal and initiated the first call to the Supreme Allied Commander of Europe, General Axel L. Warren.

The ACE replied quickly, "I need to join NATO forces to halt enemy activity and blunt their objectives."

"Proceed, General."

By virtue of the speed with which air and space component deploys and employs, Gen. Warren alerted the US Air Force to be the first to arrive as his halt and blunt force. NATO is first and foremost a nuclear alliance; in an instant, US and NATO forces proceeded to launch a massive counterattack including; fighters, bombers, tank-ers, space, command and control, ISR, cyber, special operations, and aeromedical teams trained and ready for high-end warfare.

Bombers, like the B-2, took to the air from multiple bases the US and Europe, using stealth and altitude to go after enemy air-defenses while the Allied eluded enemy radar. B61-12 Nuclear-armed B-2s and F-35s are constantly at the ready. Given the speed, and potential proximity of those air assets, those ready response fighters and bombers were able to destroy enemy air defenses, nuclear-weapons launch sites, and even to wipe out entire cities. As unthinkable as that would be on an ordinary day, those tasks—which had been endlessly drilled to perfection became the order of battle. It was most definitely not a normal day anywhere.

Some of those air platforms were able to attack enemy targets before the first US-launched ICBMs could reach their targets. NATO, the US, and its allies currently maintained missile defense assets in Romania, Poland and other strategically-positioned areas. They were already in the air and on their way to pre-determined targets in the Russian federation. F-35s were also forward positioned in strategically significant places throughout Europe to enable rapid deployment. This was their supreme battle test, and the message came over their coms that, "this is not a drill; I repeat, this is not a drill."

European defense systems–such as land-based Aegis-fired SM-3s— came on-line to function as a way to knock out long-range ballistic missiles traveling within the earth's atmosphere. Navy Aegis Ballistic Missile Defense (BMD) Program began to use the new weaponry which had not yet been tested in battle; the new SM-2 Block IIA enabled faster development of using Aegis BMD for ICBM defense–both Terminal phase and the end of space flight or Midcourse phase, a decided improvement which proved to be effective on that day of supreme tests.

The US and NATO had been steadily strengthening European-based ICBM defenses as well. Destroyers and cruisers had been positioned for response by operating in a maritime environment closer to enemy territory and against launching enemy missiles. Emerging weapons such as lasers were showing that they were up to the task of contributing to missile defense.

As the new weapons were being used up, the American military-industrial complex rushed stores of ship-based lasers, electromagnetic railguns, and hypervelocity projectiles to contribute to the Navy's terminal-phase BMD operations requiring ever greater numbers of ship-based BMD interceptor missiles.

NATO and the US counted on a number of factors involved by Russia's nuclear war modus operandi. The most important of those factors was Russia's commitment to an "escalate to de-escalate" nuclear posture and development of low-yield nuclear weapons.

President Bettern's next step was to call NORAD to which he was alerted by two other lights beginning to blink determinedly.

He picked up the designated phone and immediately began to speak to the NORTHCOM NORAD commander General Dorland "Chipper" Hoolahan about homeland defense, especially the use of GBIs [Ground-Based Interceptors]. The order was given for the GBIs to be launched into space to find and intercept Russian attacking ICBMs. Fortunately for the country, the Pentagon had prepared for this day by developing new command and control technology, sensors, and targeting. The new detector technology increased NORAD and Homeland Security's technical ability to discern actual warheads from surrounding decoys, debris, or other structures scattered about their flying ICBMS.

ICBMs break up in flight as their warheads and re-entry bodies separate; and–by design—they travel with decoys to confuse GBI sensors and increase the prospect that a missile will get through. The US Missile Defense Agency was successful in destroying several Russian ICBMs with a GBI and working to develop improved sensors and to integrate multiple interceptors onto a single missile. If the war lasted as long as a week, it was expected that they would come on line battle-ready.

Another piece of good fortune for the defense of America was that twelve Raytheon-built Exoatmospheric Kill Vehicles were now in service destroyed ICBMs in a March test. In terms of distinguishing decoys from ICBMs, the Raytheon EKVs identi-fyed the threat, discriminated between the target and countermeasures, maneuvered into the target's path, and destroyed them using "hit-to-kill" technology. The EKVs were cued by Sea-Based X-band radar and AN/TPY-2 radar.

The EKV technical infrastructure provided needed capacity to fire multiple interceptors and integrated systems to increase the probability of an ICBM "kill." In addition, Raytheon—working with the Pentagon–created system called MOKV [Multi-Object Kill Vehicles]. The relatively new system was able to leverage advanced sensor technology and engineering to integrate multiple kill vehicles into a single GBI.

The attack by Russia revealed a "troubling" anti-satellite capability on a nuclear-armed, on-orbit, anti-satellite weapon. The multitudinous attacks showed that Russian ASATs [nuclear-armed anti-satellite weapons] were surprisingly able to challenge norms of responsible behavior in space directly and to present a serious and ongoing risk to all nations' satellites. The Russian surprise anti-satellite weapons were being used to destroy or incapacitate satellites, both by physical destruction–crashing into a satellite with a missile or another satellite–and through non-kinetic attacks, such as by electromagnetic jamming, lasers, and cyberattacks. The Russian attacks caused serious concerns in the Pentagon and NATO headquarters in Brussels.

The allies had to come to grips with the fact that Russia was fielding a range of ASAT capabilities–from cyberattacks and the jamming of satellite signals to ground-based, direct-ascent, hit-to-kill ASAT missiles. During the course of that dreadful day, US and NATO officials had begun using large satellites releasing smaller "daughter" satellites in space that were capable of approaching, interfering with, and sometimes even destroying Russian satellites.

At the end of the long day, the United States began to move away from a small number of large, expensive, complex, satellites to constellations of smaller, cheaper satellites more resilient to kinetic attack as the Russians were doing. But the threat of nuclear attacks on satellites changed the calculus. In a remarkable demonstration of American flexibility, the Space Development Agency and US Space Force moved rapidly toward an architecture that relied more on constellations of small satellites, thereby improving the discrepancy in kill rates.

A nuclear detonation in space added significant radiation to orbits used by a number of US military satellites, causing them to degrade in the weeks and months following the detonation unless they were specifically hardened against radiation. A so-called high-altitude nuclear detonation against low-Earth orbit satellites (HALEOS) would also dama-ge thousands of civilian satellites from all nations, making that a true weapon of mass destruction.

Moscow had a history of fielding nuclear-powered satellites that were not nuclear armed, but—after its early onslaughts against America, Russia began reinvigorating its nuclear-powered satellite program to include nuclear weapons. nuclear-powered satellites in the fight by both Russia and the allies were able to generate additional energy to power electromagnetic jammers, radars, and other technologies useful for anti-satellite purposes.

Nuclear power in space can also be used for spacecraft propulsion, which would allow a space asset to change orbits more frequently than a satellite powered with conven-tional propulsion. A nuclear-powered Russian satellite seemed to be less alarming than a nuclear-armed satellite, which gave Russia the ability to degrade a large swath of all satellites on orbit in one fell swoop. Neither the US nor any other ally could duplicate that technology, nor was likely to be able to develop it in time to be useful in the current conflict.

President Vladimir Rasputinov and his predecessors had never seen the value of actually complying with treaty agreements with the nonCommunist countries, and this time was no different. The United States has long endorsed the principle of nonplacement of weapons of mass destruction in space, and more recently rallied support against destructive direct-ascent ASAT testing in space. The Allies complied; Russia did not; and that created a decided advantage for them. The key piece of international law was the 1967 Outer Space Treaty, which–among other provisions–prohibits the placement of weapons of mass destruction in outer space, which would be highly destabilizing. Russia knew that as well as the allies did, but the two sides used the treaty for opposite purposes.

A Russian nuclear-armed anti-satellite weapon stationed on orbit would be a flagrant violation of this principle. Rasputinov did it anyway and was light years in head of the allies in the technology. In the attacks of March 31, 2026, he used that knowledge and technology to important tactical and strategic advantage.

The United States promulgated a goal of having a moratorium on destructive ASAT testing to increase predictability in space and reduce the generation of dangerous space debris. Russia ignored it. That added to Russia's ability to detonate nuclear weapons in space from Earth.

In 2025, Rasputinov announced that his country had five new nuclear-capable, strategic weapons systems; a nuclear-powered, nuclear-armed, cruise missile; a nuclear-powered, nuclear-armed, submarine drone, a new heavy ICBM, an HGV [nuclear-armed hypersonic glide vehicle], a nuclear-armed, and an air-launched hypersonic missile. NATO and the

US ignored the announcement, and now they were seeing each of the new weapons in practical action. The results were widespread and lethal.

The US and NATO response to the Russian attack was extremely fast and nearly as deadly. In a matter of seconds, the US launched an immediate, massive counterattack. F-35s, B-2 bombers, nuclear-armed Navy submarines, missile-armed destroyers, Ground Based Interceptors and satellites, were all virtually instantly thrust into action. The action followed a well-planned, well-drilled, and well-executed counterattack including a series of rapid, successive steps. Unfortunately, the response produced a large number of dead heroes and an extravagant expenditure in money and materiel.

Nevertheless, the response was fast enough that—by virtue of US gathered intelligence–the attackers themselves were often a few seconds behind the NATO and US responses leaving time for an F-35 to attack an ICBM during the boost phase with missiles, guns, or lasers. F-22s were launched to engage any potential enemy aircraft quickly. F-22s are regarded as the best air-to-air combat platform in the world.

Sensors, air-to-air missiles, and dogfighting ability—at which the US excelled–helped ensure air supremacy during counterattacks. Furthermore, the F-22's speed and stealth configuration enabled it to hit enemy targets faster than other attack options available to the enemy.

In the US Navy, submarines are intended to ensure a massive "second strike" capability to ensure the destruction of anyone launching a nuclear attack upon the US. By dusk, the submarines were menacing great swaths of Russian territory—massive segments of St. Petersburg and Moscow were demolished from submarine fired missiles. The degree of territory turned to rubble was comparable during that first day to four years of World War II. People no longer found it comprehensible to mourn their own dead because whole neighborhoods–even whole cities–were wiped out in minutes, or even in seconds from one pass by of a supersonic nuclear loaded airplane.

Forward-positioned nuclear-armed F-35As entered enemy airspace from nowhere and attacked enemy air assets instantly and were able to destroy enemy nuclear-launch sites before the missile could get off the ground. 88 percent of all targets were destroyed despite all the defense systems on both sides.

In every country engaged in the war, there were sages who repeated the definition of "mutually assured destruction"—a doctrine of military strategy and national security policy which posits that a full-scale use of nuclear weapons by an attacker on a nuclear-armed defender with second-strike capabilities would result in the complete annihilation of both the attacker and the defender. Their exhortations fell on deaf ears in every one of the countries that were presented with that bit of wisdom.

Being the center of it all, Ukraine got the worst of everything from both sides because the Russian bases were established there among the Ukrainian people who had lost all choice, except to die; even that was no choice. They had given up their ability to survive in a world of seemingly limitless power over them.

After the Soviet Union's collapse December 21, 1991, Ukraine had the world's third-largest nuclear stockpile. In a treaty called the Budapest Memorandum, Ukraine agreed to trade away its intercontinental ballistic missiles, warheads, and other nuclear infrastructure, in exchange for guarantees that the three other treaty signatories—the US, the UK, and Russia—would thereafter "respect the independence and sovereignty and the existing borders of Ukraine," and reasonably soon be granted admission to NATO. It turned out that they sold their birthright for a mess of pottage, and a small portion even of that.

The Russians resumed their claim on the country once it began to become rich. The promises of the Americans proved to be hollow and too little, too late. Now, all was lost. Yaroslav and Rokosylana were lost in the nuclear ashes and dust having been unable to escape with the small contingent that trekked over the Carpathians to a brief period of safety.

World War III lasted a total of five actual days of fighting. During that time, 4450 separate nuclear explosions occurred, each of them more than ten times the kiloton dynamite equivalent of the first nuclear bombs that leveled Hiroshima and Nagasaki combined. The bombs which fell on

New York City, Chicago, Los Angeles, Detroit, Moscow, St. Petersburg, Novosibirsk, Yekaterinburg, Paris, Lyon, Berlin, Hamburg, Beijing, Shanghai, and Riyadh, 199 other Russian cities, and 50 Chinese cities resulted in 56% of the populations becoming immediate casualties. Nearly two million Eastern European people died in the first Alert Forces strikes. A great many of the wounded died during the next two weeks. The global all-out war between the United States and Russia with the more than 4400 300 kiloton warheads detonating resulted in 400 million quick deaths, which was in excess of 40 million people more than the entire US population.

The numbers in the United States could only be estimated at 280-300 million immediate deaths which overwhelmed all public service institutions from the onset of the war.

At distances close to ground zero, the 300 kiloton nuclear explosions burned and crushed to death every human being and the vast majority of all other plant and animal life. There were almost no survivors within a mile of ground zero. Each 300 kiloton bomb killed more than a million people, wounded twice that number; and at the end of the day, >4,500 from both sides had been detonated. The bombings occurred within minutes of each other. Airbursts produced overpressures of 5 pounds per square inch for five miles from each target which destroyed almost all houses, gutted skyscrapers, and resulted in further widespread fatalities in a period less than 10 seconds after the explosion. All the explosions created a combination of radiation, heat, and blast, which added many more quick fatalities and amplified the destruction.

Neighborhoods, towns, and cities, turned into fireballs growing to 2,000 feet + in altitude in which the temperature and pressure were so extreme that all matter became a white-hot plasma of raw nuclei and subatomic particles mimicking the multi-million-degree sun's core. In fact, during the period of peak energy output, 1-megaton nuclear weapons produced temperatures of 100 million degrees Celsius at its center, 4-5 times that which occurs at the center of the Sun.

The fireballs remained blindingly luminous for many seconds, until the surface began to cool. The light produced by the heat of the fireball accounted for more than one-third of the many thermonuclear weapons' explosive energy. That light was so intense that it ignited fires at great distances—setting buildings ablaze and igniting forest fires that consumed towns and wild places. Burns occurred in people 5-8 miles away, many leading to disfigurement, maiming, and painful death, over time for those unfortunate enough to survive the initial blast only to be smitten by aftermath surprises.

The blast wave emanating from the thermonuclear reaction accounted for half of the explosive energy. The wave traveled faster than the speed of sound, causing considerable additional destruction miles away. The radiation superheated the atmosphere around every fireball; and the surrounding air expanded, pushed very rapidly outward in a circum-ferential pressure globe creating a shockwave that blasted against everything in its path, adding additional stupendous destructive power.

Very shortly after the nuclear detonations released their destructive and deadly energy–a concert of thousands of fireballs–began to cool and to rise, putting up mushroom clouds around the landscapes below. Within each of them were very highly radioactive split atoms which quickly began to drop out of the clouds as they were blown by the heavy winds created by the detonations. That started an exposure of post-blast and then post-war survivors to crippling and lethal doses of ionizing radiation.

The many hundred kiloton weapons also created an area of immediate danger for thousands of square miles downwind of the detonation site. The first isotopes released were mainly short half-life radiation components—the most dangerous and having the most energy, making them the most dangerous to the vulnerable biological systems below. That lasted for days in places and weeks in others.

In most urban areas where bombs exploded, the citizens had been prepared to deal with the dangers of nuclear fallout by staying indoors for at least 48 hours, but that good advice proved to be futile. In the vicinity of every such explosion, every building completely collapsed and afforded no practical protection. Besides that, everyone who was within 1,500 feet of the blast received 500 Roentgen dose of radiation–a fatal dose unless treated immediately–and no such medical care was available anywhere.

India and Pakistan launched a regional nuclear war that had been brewing since 1947. Between them, the two countries launched more than a hundred 15 kiloton nuclear weapons into urban areas resulting in an almost immediate 27 million direct deaths; and the deaths kept coming.

It was truly a world war resulting in similar exchanges between Israel and Jordan; Israel and Egypt; Iran and Saudi Arabia, Pakistan, and the United Arab Emirates, on the basis of religious differences; Syria and Iraq Kurds; Russia and Mongolia, Japan, and Manchuria; Mexico and Guatemala; Guatemala and Honduras, El Salvador, and Nicaragua; Türkiye and Greece; Spain and Morocco; and China and Japan, Philippines, Taiwan, and India; Turkmenistan and Kazakhstan; Uzbekistan v. Tajikistan and Kyrgyzstan.

Together, the UK, China, France, Israel, Pakistan, and North Korea, had more than 2,000 warheads, enough to prevent world trade, destroy world economies, to overwhelm medical, police, and fire department function, and bring any economy to its knees, a state so pathetic that almost every person would prefer to return to the depths of the Great Depression.

Smoke from mass fires after the nuclear war injected massive amounts of soot into the stratosphere, the Earth's upper atmosphere. The heat and blast from even one of the thermonuclear explosions was so powerful that it initiated large-scale fires in both urban and rural settings. The 300-kiloton detonations in New York and Washington DC caused mass fires with a radius of at least 3.5 miles each, not altered by any weather conditions. Air in those areas was turned into dust, fire, and smoke.

The nuclear war set not just one city on fire, but hundreds, then thousands of them, nearly simultaneously. Even the regional nuclear wars—such as that between India and Pakistan—led to widespread firestorms in cities and industrial areas so severe that they caused measurable global climatic change, disrupting every form of life on Earth for decades. An all-out nuclear war between India and Pakistan, with both countries launching a total of 250 nuclear warheads of an average yield of 15 kilotons, produced a stratospheric loading of some 50 million tons [=teragrams, Tg] of soot, comparable to about the mass of twenty Great Pyramids of Giza, pulverized and turned into superheated dust.

The world became a boiling cauldron of settling old scores that transformed it from the beautiful "Cerulean Planet" into a dust enshrouded wasteland unfit to bury the dead decently.

The countries involved in those almost fratricidal conflicts were so devastated that there was no ability to remove corpses lying in wrecked buildings and on ruined streets. Besides the obvious destruction, the stench of death made those previously vibrant cities and countries uninhabitable.

That is nothing more terrible for the world than the delayed effects of the homicidal war. The first few days after the nuclear bombs struck were only the beginning of the catastrophe that came to encompass the entire planet. That condition included global climatic changes worse than those that took place in the Great Ice Age. Generalized radioactive contamination, and complete societal collapse throughout the heavily inhabited portions of the earth was present after two weeks.

Within a week after the bombing maelstrom of the "war to end all wars", famine began. After all the actual fighting, famine alone proved to be ten times as deadly for earthlings as all the bomb blasts combined. There was even more collateral damage: electromagnetic pulses–intense bursts of radio waves–that permanently damaged all electronic equipment–widespread fires, stratospheric soot injection from the fires and dust from the omnipresent winds.

The worst was yet to come. It had been a fairly cold March with two snowstorms in Russia and Ukraine. The beautiful normal bumpy blue spheroid of earth became a cosmic snowball. Nuclear winter occurred from the smoke produced by the massive forest fires ignited by nuclear weapons blocking the sun; global temperatures dropped lower on land than on oceans, causing a worldwide agricultural collapse. The climatic effects of a massive injection of soot aerosols into the stratosphere from fires following the nuclear wars led to the heating of the stratosphere, ozone depletion, and cooling at the surface under the soot, dust, and water vapor cloud. up to 146 Tg— of water vapor into the stratosphere where it stayed for many years. The massive injection of stratospheric water temporarily impacted the climate—in this case for a decade. The global winter effects produced the lowest temperatures on Earth in the past 1,000 years—temperatures well below the post-medieval Little Ice Age.

Astronauts circling the earth in manned space vehicles had no way to return home; their bases were gone, their keepers extinguished. They orbited aimlessly until they starved to death. Most surviving ships at sea had no ports and no sources of sustenance on land left. They sailed aimlessly until their fuel was used up, and their vessels became ghost ships. Small groups of illiterate nomads wandered their wastelands never understanding what had happened to their world. So far as they knew, they were the only humans left.

The few remaining survivors were not to see spring, summer, or fall, for another ten years. Many of them just gave up the fight for survival during the period of relentless cold. In that decade of nuclear winter, the collective collateral damage was responsible for the death of more than half of the remaining human population on Earth, reducing it to a very small fraction of what it was in February and early March, 2026. The nuclear winter climatic and biogeochemical changes disrupted all forms of life on Earth over several decades.

Soot removal mechanisms in the form of "black rains" were slow in coming because once the smoke was heated by sunlight it self-lofted to altitudes as high as 50 miles, penetrating the mesosphere where it lingered. When they did come, the black rains made life on earth miserable for months beyond the nuclear winter. Stratospheric temperatures remained elevated significantly in most areas for four years beyond the winter.

The extreme heating observed in the stratosphere increased the global average loss of the ozone layer—which protects humans and other life on Earth from the severe health and environmental effects of ultraviolet radiation—for several years after the nuclear war ended. Even regional nuclear wars that lasted three days reduced the ozone layer by 25 % globally and recovery took 12 years. The global nuclear war injected 150 Tg of stratospheric smoke causing a 75 % global ozone loss, and that depletion lasting 15 years—considerably longer than most humans survived. Their survival was greatly impaired because of the heating of the earth's surface, the large amount of solar radiation they received, the diminution of precipitation in most areas of the planet, and the marked decrease in food production.

Ozone loss led to a tropical UV index above 35, starting three years after the war and lasting for four years. A UV index of 11 posed an extreme danger; 15 minutes of exposure to a UV index of 12 caused unprotected human skin to experience sunburn. Globally, the average sunlight in the UV-B range increased by 20 %. High levels of UV-B radiation quickly caused sunburn, photoaging, skin cancer, and cataracts, in humans; and also inhibited the photolysis reaction required for leaf expansion and plant growth. The world of the survivors was a brown and dusty one, devoid of the color green in the majority of that world.

The temperature changes had their greatest effect on mid-and high-latitude agriculture, by reducing the length of the crop season and the temperature even during that previously productive season. Below-freezing temperatures led to a significant expansion of sea ice and terrestrial snowpack, causing food shortages and affecting shipping to crucial ports where sea ice was not a factor before the war, especially in more southern ports like the Yellow Sea. That did not matter much because there were scarcely any ships left in the aftermath. The great grain growing centers of the American Midwest, the central plains of Ukraine, and China, India, and Russia, became dustbowl wastelands.

Global ocean temperature decrease—the longest lasting effect of the massive pollution of the stratosphere started four years after the nuclear war affecting fisheries drastically. Abnormally low temperatures persisted for decades near the surface, and hundreds of years or longer at depth. The changes in ocean temperature to the Arctic sea-ice were set to last thousands of years with the largest decreases being in the North Atlantic and North Pacific oceans.

Famine's grim specter came early and lasted whole lifetimes for most humans. Globally, livestock production and fisheries were unable to compensate for the reduced crop output. The total food calories available to any nation dropped dramatically; millions starved to death until there only thousands left alive. Earth was rapidly becoming uninhabitable and lacking in sufficient nourishment to keep Homo sapiens

sapiens still able to survive and reproduce. Adding that to the radiation damage to human reproductive cells guaranteed that human DNA was shrinking too rapidly to allow human reproduction to keep up with the death rate and to guarantee preservation of the species. Extinction was no longer unthinkable.

…This is the dead land
This is cactus land
Here the stone images
Are raised, here they receive
The supplication of a dead man's hand
Under the twinkle of a fading star.
…The eyes are not here
There are no eyes here
In this valley of dying stars
In this hollow valley
This broken jaw of our lost kingdoms
…This is the way the world ends
This is the way the world ends
This is the way the world ends
Not with a bang but a whimper.
—Thomas Stearns Eliot, *The Hollow Men*

World War IV, Arctic and Subarctic regions of the Aleutian Islands and far northern Alaska

May 21, 2035

L udatxin [Elder Brother] Naukatsik–the headman of Attu, the farthest west of the string of islands named for his people, the Aleuts–contemplated the slate grey Bering Strait which was relatively calm that day. He had assumed the headman position for three reasons: First, at age 28 years, he was the oldest man on the island and therefore the most experienced. Second, he was the most curious, and had traveled the farthest from the home island. Third, his kayak and two-seater baidarka building and mastery of tool making among the People, was the best of any man on the island.

Attu is a little, fog-shrouded island at the western end of the Aleutian chain and farthest from the mainland. It is 35 miles long and 15 miles wide, with snow-capped peaks that reach upward to 3,000 feet. Steep slopes extend down from the peaks to treeless valleys below, carpeted with muskeg, a kind of black muck covered with a dense growth of lichens and moss. Attu was one of the Near Islands and lonely. The People had lived on the islands and subsisted on the marine resources of the region for more than 10,000 years. None of them knew anything about what had taken place in World War III, or about the massive bombings—it was before their time and beyond their understanding. So far as they were concerned, their Ancestors had transmitted orally about a time of very long winters without any summers, which would remain a mystery.

The Unangan peoples of Attu lived a subsistence lifestyle including fishing, hunting, and gathering berries. Some of the stronger men hunted caribou and bears. The Aleut Unangan women were in charge of gathering fish, birds, wild plant foods, mollusks, and wild plant foods, and the weaving of fine grass basketry. They had a few Malamute dogs–the native Alaskan Arctic breed, cousin to the Samoyed of Russia, Siberian Husky, and the Eskimo dogs of Greenland and Labrador.

They were accustomed to simple lives in a world without trees, one open to the expansive sky.

Ludatxin was estimating how rough the sea was that day and should this be the day to return to the island of the strange ones, the place they called Unalaska in their peculiar tongue. He had been there eight years previously and had seen much to covet. Since the Inuits—as they referred to themselves—could not talk like his Unangans [some called Aleuts], he concluded that they were either ignorant or stupid. He had spent two days and nights among them which had led him to the idea that the Stupid People did not deserve the many things they enjoyed in their place. They had things that he coveted. He and his Aleuts were strong, and they could take them.

He had observed many differences between his People and the Strange Ones. They had many more women and could easily share with him and the Aleuts. The same could be said for their better hunting gear, clothing, and kayak materials. More importantly, they had more and different kinds of food; some of which were too different, even strange. His curiosity had grown over the past eight years into a covetous plan.

Ludatxin called the People to the long house to hear his words and to consider his plan. No one was working; so, it was an opportune time.

Once they were all seated, Ludatxin spoke of the faraway place and the Strange Ones.

"They have raincoats made of the stomach of seals; so, they stay dry. They have knee-high moccasin boots that reach to their knees. The boots—which they call Muk-luks—are warm and dry and have bird down padding to make them comfortable when they walk on the rocky beaches. I believe I make good kayaks, but their skin boats are better. They have more strong and healthy women to do the work. They bear more children that live longer to keep their camp doing well.

"When I went to their place and tried to trade with them, they not only looked and and dressed differently from the People, but they were stupid. I talked to them, and they obviously did not understand me. When they talked, it sounded like animals, and they could not make themselves understood. They did not have any idea about the sacred stones and carvings I came to trade with them, and I was offended when they only wanted to trade some of their furs and fishing spears. I could not make trades because our spears and knives were not good enough for them. I became angry.

"They have too much and work too little; we should go and take their things to make the world equal as our old ones said it should be. I have made some spears even better than theirs, and knives that are sharper. I will show you."

He had two young boys carry in several items contained in a walrus skin blanket. He presented several improved kinds of fishing spears, six extremely sharp knives made from walrus ivory, and his own invention of fighting clubs. They were made by carefully cutting a niche into the end of a walrus tusk, pressing a well-chipped stone into the niche and securing it onto the tusk with strips of walrus skin which had been soaked in sea water and allowed to dry on the tusk and become tightened to the point that a strong man could not pull the rock out of its place.

His People, the Unangans, were impressed with the tools, but more so with the enrichment concepts Ludatxin had explained. He added the clincher: the Inuits were different. They were smaller, hairier; their eyes were narrower—more sinister—and their skins were darker. That settled the remaining questions. They accepted the logic that they deserved to have more of what the people of Unalaska–the Strange Ones–were keeping from them. The Unangans spent the next two days working night and day to craft more kayaks, spears, and clubs. Fifteen men volunteered.

A wild woman, called Amaruq [meaning gray wolf] made two suggestions that Ludatxin and the other men had never considered. She showed them walrus hide heavy vest garments which could ward off a knife or a sharpened pole. The second idea was that she and some other selected women should join the fighters because they were big, strong, and fierce. Ludatxin had no good argument to make against Amaruq; so, he convinced the men to admit her, and—in addition–the gentle Yura [meaning beautiful], Aput [meaning snow], and Ukiuk [meaning winter] all names used to describe the cold weather of the Arctic region and the toughness to endure it.

Amaruq presented her pride and joy; it was a most remarkable new thing—a special fishing spear, but *clearly* a weapon of destruction—they only had one among all of them that was designed to create fear, victory, and death. It was a spear-handle of wood about six feet in length; to the head of which she had lashed a neatly-polished socket of walrus ivory, into which she inserted a tip of serrated slate that resembled a gigantic arrow-point, twelve-fourteen inches long and four or five inches broad at the barbs. Near the spear point, she had carved her own mark.

New things were uncommon; they were people who did yet have the wheel or fire. The new spear itself was more than just utilitarian; it had the cachet of being unique and special. Perhaps if they had gods, they might have credited them for the largesse.

By a unanimous vote of the men, they invited the biggest and best fighters among the women, Qayax̂ [meaning tall], Tayaĝuudaadax̂ [meaning small little man], Algaĝix̂ [meaning has mammals], Algas [meaning mammal, a variant of Algagix], Ataqan [meaning one], Cungagnaq, Hamĝakix [meaning his sleeves], Hlakuchaa [meaning his little son], and Unquching [meaning blue fox].

They dipped into their stores of salmon, crabs, shellfish, cod, seal, walrus, and whale blubber, ate their fill, and stowed the rest for the sea journey of more than 800 sea miles from Atta to Unalaska. It was many days of travel, camping on shores of the islands of the Aleutian chain, until they began to see signs of life on a bigger island.

Brave Inuit hunters were attacking humpbacks breaching in Bay. Marine mammals of this ecoregion were abundant in the ocean and on the shorelines and cliffs: northern fur seals, Steller sea lions, harbor seals, Pacific walruses, sea otters, and various whales. Women worked around their sod houses and storage buildings weaving fine grass basketry and fashioning stone, bone, and ivory, into containers, needles and awls, oil lamps, and other objects. Men and boys were dancing and shouting.

Ludatxin announced that this is the fabled Unalaska he had visited before. They disembarked from their kayaks on the north end of the island, ditched them and their stores, and began trekking over the bright green hills toward the large town—estimated to be more than 4,000 people.

The Aleutian Islands are an archipelago chain of 14 large volcanic islands–forming the northernmost part of the Pacific Ring of Fire–and 55 smaller islands extending about 1,200 miles westward from the Alaska Peninsula toward the in Russia. The islands are like stepping-stones to Asia. The westernmost island in the chain is Attu Island. The presence of the archipelago affects currents of both water and air. The islands channel the Alaska Stream–a warm current that circles the Gulf of Alaska and moves west toward Russia's Kamchatka Peninsula. The islands stretch from North America far into the Pacific Ocean like stepping-stones to Asia. They form a barrier between the Bering Sea to the north and the Gulf of Alaska and North Pacific Ocean to the south.

Although the sun was out, it was cold. The would-be marauders had to deal with high winds, heavy precipitation, and persistent fog, as they trekked. Forbidding weather and desolate terrain made their approach militarily undesirable; but Ludatxin coaxed, cajoled, and browbeat, his tiny army along toward their goal.

While spared the arctic climate of the Alaskan mainland to the north and Atta to the west, the Aleutians otherwise are constantly swept by cold winds which made the going difficult. Most of the time, the weather becomes progressively worse in the western part of the chain where they lived; so, the platoon did not complain overmuch. Ludatxin constantly pointed out the scenery when the patchy fog lifted to keep their spirits up. The shores were rocky and worn by the surf showing power and persistence, and the approaches to them were dangerous. The vistas of sea-sculpted coastline, and mile-after-mile of rugged, wind-swept land-scape, were more attractive than daunting. In many places the land rose abruptly from the coasts to steep, bold, mountains in the distance.

Like the vast majority of the chain, Unalaska is devoid of native trees. Instead of trees, the islands are covered with a beautiful and luxuriant, dense growth of herbage and shrubs, including crowberry, bluejoint, grasses, sedges, and many flowering plants. There were areas of peat bog near the coastline. Endemic plants included Aleutian shield fern and at higher elevations, the vegetation consisted of dwarf scrub dominated by crowberry or willows. Other plants scattered in patches included mountain-cranberry, bog and dwarf blueberry, mountain avens, cassiope, narrow-leaf Labrador-tea, Aleutian mountain-heath, sedges, lichens, and mosses.

At the lower elevations, where Ludatxin and his warriors did most of their walking, it was more protected and easier going treading on spreading communities of grasses and sedges. Contributing to the beauty and their opportunity to drink, were moist sites–meadows with bluejoint grass and various broad-leaved herbaceous plants. Low scrub bogs were dominated by a variety of plants: heath family, sedges, sphagnum moss, and feather-mosses.

Becoming more and more accustomed to his growing role as the captain of his quasi-military platoon, Ludatxin stopped the men and women frequently; so, they would not be overtired or weak from hunger. They ate frequent and proteinaceous meals, and their morale remained high as they anticipated the riches awaiting them.

At last, they arrived at the crest of the low mountains above the Inuit village, ripe for the picking below. It would have been a bucolic scene, but there were no cows on the island. Suffice it, tranquility and trusting that all was right with the world prevailed.

That condition disappeared shortly thereafter. The Atta platoon painted their faces to look grotesque and terrifying and crept down the hillside taking advantage of the intermittent clusters of dense growth herbage and shrubs. The endemic Aleutian grasses, flowers, and shrubs, relied on seabird guano from the more than 90 species flying about to fertilize abundant growth.

The Aleutians are home to many large colonies of seabirds, including the Bering Sea endemic red-legged kittiwake, the Aleutian cackling goose and six subspecies of rock ptarmigan. The islands are also frequented by more than 90 species of vagrant Asiatic birds, including the common rosefinch, Siberian rubythroat, bluethroat, lanceolated warbler, and the intermediate egret.

The never-before troubled inhabitants of Unalaska's only town went about their frivolity unaware of the intruders.

When the Atta platoon came to rest prone on the edge of the grassy townsite, they waited until the attention of the townspeople was directed toward the ocean and were totally unaware of what lay in wait for them on the east. The everpresent cacophony of the bird calls masked any change in the ambient noise made by the Attu People's movements.

With thunderous, terrifying screams, and warwhoops, the Atta platoon descended upon the unprepared Unalaskans. Women fainted; some had heart attacks and died. Children ran off aimlessly and some fell off the shoreline cliffs and were lost. The men moved with glacial celerity unable to fathom what was happening. It was as if the 25 Atta warriors—men and women—had outnumbered the nearly 4,000 Unalaskans, surrounded them, and had beaten them into submission.

In truth, only five men and four women died at the hands of the Atta war makers' hands. It was gruesome enough to cause a paralyzing stupor to spread among the severely intimidated citizens. They had never seen a man clubbed to death or one shredded by a new device that was more powerful than any spear or knife they had even heard about.

It was the first battle of World War IV, and it lasted less than five minutes. The Unalaskans became slaves; the Atta warriors–supplemented by two dozen easily convinced Unalaskan men–were so impressed with the success of the raid, that they signed on as the first members of the Unangan professional army. When they attacked Utqiagvik [previously known as Point Barrow, in the time of the Ancestors], the acts of ongoing violence became the actual World War IV. None of the People had ever heard of such a thing and were spellbound by what violence had wrought.

—THE END—

Last Night I Had The Strangest Dream
Last night I had the strangest dream
I ever dreamed before
I dreamed the world had all agreed
To put an end to war

I dreamed I saw a mighty room
The room was filled with men
And the paper they were signing said
They'd never fight again

And when the papers all were signed
And a million copies made
They all joined hands and bowed their heads
And grateful prayers were prayed

And the people in the streets below
Were dancing round and round
And guns and swords and uniforms
Were scattered on the ground

Last night I had the strangest dream
I ever dreamed before
I dreamed the world had all agreed
To put an end to war

—Ed McCurdy, 1950

Author's note: *Last night I dreamed the strangest dream* became an anthem of the 20th century peace movement. It served as the official song of the Peace Corps. It is time to give it another try.

www.ingramcontent.com/pod-product-compliance
Lightning Source LLC
Chambersburg PA
CBHW071158020726
47502CB00002B/461